the Jungle Law

a novel by

VICTORIA VINTON

The Jungle Law

a novel by

VICTORIA VINTON

MacAdam/Cage

MacAdam/Cage
155 Sansome, Suite 550
San Francisco, CA 94104

Library of Congress Cataloging-in-Publication Data

Vinton, Victoria, 1954-
  The jungle law / Victoria Vinton.
      p. cm.
  ISBN 1-59692-149-8 (hardcover : alk. paper)
  1. Kipling, Rudyard, 1865-1936–Fiction. 2. Fiction–Authorship–Fiction.
3. British–Vermont–Fiction. 4. Brattleboro (Vt.)–Fiction. 5.
Authors–Fiction. I. Title.
  PS3622.I58J86 2005
  813'.6–dc22

                                                        2005013939

Printed in the United States of America
10 9 8 7 6 5 4 3 2 1

Book and jacket design by Dorothy Carico Smith

FOR MICHELA

The Curse of all Art is that the devotee or disciple is always more certain than the Priest.

—Rudyard Kipling

BRATTLEBORO, VERMONT

AUGUST 1892

REMEMBER THE NIGHT IS FOR HUNTING

Three o'clock and all is not well. Sleep has abandoned him again. He sits bolt upright in his bed, panic rising from his stomach like bile. In the past eight months he has crossed two oceans and whole continents—from Bombay to London, New York, Vancouver, Yokohama, and halfway back—and now, dislocated by the darkness and the hour and the jumbled swirl of distances he's come, he does not know where he is.

He looks around but can make out nothing, not even the hump of a bedpost. This is not surprising since he's been all but blind since the age of twelve. That was when his eyes went wrong, as he likes to say, and his aunt, the Good Aunt, the Beloved Aunt Georgiana, found him pummeling a mulberry tree, thinking it was a monster.

"There, there," she'd said soothingly, guiding him back to the Grange with her hands on his shoulders. Then she set him up in the nursery with a pot of chamomile tea and proceeded to write two letters: one to a specialist she knew about in London who fitted him with glasses, the first of the wire-framed spectacles that he has worn ever since; and the second to his mother in India, urging her to return, thereby restoring to him both his vision and what had seemed the lost heart of his family.

He reaches for his spectacles now, his fingers routing over the bedclothes like the blunt snout of a mole. They sit on a nightstand next to the bed, where he fails to recall setting them. And as his fingers inch and grope and finally find and clutch them, he feels a grateful wave of relief, though the spectacles themselves have often been a source of shame. The Bad Aunt, Auntie Rosa, not really an aunt at all, saw them as an affectation, one more pretension of a spoiled, deceitful boy who was mocked and bullied and called Giglamps at school and made to sit in corners. And recently, with a pang of chagrin that he couldn't quite dispel, he has seen himself in the pages of newspapers portrayed by cartoonists and their lampooning pens with eyes as big as saucers, as mill wheels, like the dogs in the old fairy tale.

He shoos these thoughts and images away as he sets his spectacles over his nose, blinks, and blinks again. Now out of the darkness he identifies shapes. A pine commode with a chipped china basin. A maple rocking chair. The other bed, twin to the one where he sits, where his new bride, Carrie, lies sleeping. And as the room contracts into this dim but manageable focus, he is able at last to give it a name: Home. This is his home.

Of course, he sees the irony here. The whole notion of home is as exotic to him as the ports of call in his travels. And this home, in particular, is not much to speak of. A hired man's cottage rented out for the season with money borrowed from his wife's family, with skunks in the cellar and no water save that from a half-inch lead pipe connected to a spring. It is an uninspiring backdrop for a man with his ambitions, though the sparseness and simplicity appeal to part of him. And besides, as soon as his fortunes change, as he knows they will, he plans to build a great ark of a house on the crest of a neighboring hill. Naulakha, he will call it. Jewel beyond price. A home to call his own.

He thinks of the building plans for that house rolled up in a drawer of his desk, the pencil-thin arrows that mark elevations, the arcs denoting doorways, the breaks in the lines that indicate windows that will open onto grand vistas. All comforting thoughts, though unfortunately not ones that will lead him back to sleep. From experience he knows that even though he has now located himself, pinpointed his exact position, here, in a corner of southeastern Vermont, that knowledge will not buy him safe passage back to the realm of rest. No, now the true torment of wakefulness begins. He lies there deep in the summer night listening to the sounds around him. There are crickets in the woodshed, frogs in the old cedar swamp, a parlor clock on the mantle shelf, chipping away at the hour. To his wife, he imagines, these sounds are lulling, the familiar backdrop of her childhood. It is not her curse to hear things as he does, to imagine that every croak and chirp, each tick and chime of the clock, mocks him for some failure—to fall asleep, to make a home, to see with his own two eyes—and deeper still, for some more basic lack of character or worth, that he does not wish to pursue.

So he says to himself what he has said before: the night has gotten into his head. And the phrase takes some of the edge away, transforming the night from a nemesis into something more foolish, but finally benign, a schoolboy on a prank. That sly, devil night up to its old tricks. How well and long he has known them! He thinks of

Lahore, when he worked for the papers and his parents went up to the Hills, when the heat had the grip of a stranglehold and the night seemed to last forever. He would carry a pallet from room to room in a futile search for fresh air, setting it finally up on the roof where he'd make the waterboy douse his parched skin with water from a cistern, willing to risk the threat of disease for a few brief moments of rest. Or he'd give up on sleep entirely and just walk his way to dawn, wandering through the narrow alleys beyond the Delhi Gate, the moon above him a scorch in the sky, as white as the shrouds of the dead by the river and the marble of the Wazir Khan Mosque.

And earlier still, on the Brompton Road: was that the first time sleep failed him? In the thick of the night, with the clock inching forward and even the crickets wearying, the question seems suddenly urgent to him, as if, should he settle the matter of onset, he might decree an end.

So the Brompton Road: he is twelve years old, an owl of a boy in his new spectacles with a pet toad in his pocket. He has just been liberated from the House of Desolation, though he hasn't yet dubbed it that. That will be later when he gains more mastery, when he knows how words can be a revenge, how a phrase can sum up and dismiss— in this case six years of scoldings and cuffs and banishments to basements under the tyranny of Auntie Rosa and her lout of a son, fiendish Harry. For now he is too deliriously happy and grateful to think of phrase-making. His mother has finally returned from Bombay, appearing out of nowhere on Auntie Rosa's doorstep in a broad-brimmed hat tied under her chin with a skein of white chiffon, looking for all the world like an angel or a fairy godmother in a tale. She has taken him and his sister, Trix, away from that horrid place and installed them here, in this rooming house on the Brompton Road, right across from the old South Kensington Museum. Here he should sleep in blissful peace, rescued at last from Auntie Rosa, reunited with his mother. But instead he finds himself wide awake, eyes open and ears alert.

At first it is thrilling to be up at this hour, the dark electrifying. He hears a stray cat caterwauling from a rooftop, the last omnibus bound for Knightsbridge, the deep and mysterious groaning of pipes from the walls of the water closet. He feels no fear, only a strange, exhilarating sense of power. He is a sahib, a sultan, a raja, and this is his domain, a world of flickering shadows and moonlight and at least one minion, the toad. It sits by his bedside in a specimen dish, as wide awake as he is: the wart-riddled back in dulled jewel colors—emerald, topaz, gold—the barreled chest with its palpitations; the filmy, bulbous eyes. He stares at it, in a contest of wills, to see who will blink first. Boy or toad, master or lackey, each hunkered down and glaring. But when a breeze blows in the window, he turns away, distracted, and watches as the bedroom curtain first lifts then undulates, seeming to him like the arm of a wraith that beckons him outside.

So he grabs the toad and stuffs it into the pocket of his nightshirt, sets his new specs on the bridge of his nose, wriggles his feet into slippers. And then he is off, on an adventure, past the room where his mother sleeps, past the door to the landlady's quarters, down the back stairs, through the kitchen, the scullery, past the black heap of the coal box, to the door that leads out to a small walled-in garden, magical in the moonlight.

Immediately he claims the place as his own, a part of his empire: from the ancient horse chestnut that stands in one corner to the ginkgo tree in the other, an old stone birdbath, the thick ivy vines, and—now what's this?—an invader. Climbing onto the lip of a toppled urn he sees a marmalade cat on the rooftop, the one he must have heard from his room with its miserable rutting cry. Spying him too, the cat arches its back, then sits and lashes its tail as he scrambles to the horse chestnut tree and gathers an armful of seeds. These are hard, spiked balls, like the spheres of maces he imagines crusaders once must have swung outside Jerusalem, and he chucks them up at the cat who attempts to hide in the gutter. But it is no use: the cat is doomed. He throws another barrage of seeds, this time hitting his mark, and the old Tom slinks away over the slates, quickly conceding defeat, as he throws his arms up victoriously—and almost dislodges the toad. But when the cat has finally vanished among the chimney pots, instead of feeling a swell of triumph at a battle well fought and won, he is seized by a sudden, lonely ache and an emptiness in his bones.

In the sky the moon still shines but its light seems cold and barren. He smells for the first time the seeds from the ginkgo, fetid as rancid butter. And when he wanders to the birdbath, thinking that his toad might like a swim, he finds the scalloped basin choked by a scrim of algae scum. So he goes inside, retracing his steps, back through the kitchen and scullery, back up the winding stairs. Though when he comes to his mother's room, he pauses before slipping in.

She lies in the bed, her hair strewn across the pillows, thick strands of twisted gold, her skin as white as alabaster and still as stone as well, except for a thin blue vein in her temple that quivers as he comes closer. He stands by the bedside, watching her sleep, studying her face. Her eyes betray no signs of dreams, her nose doesn't flare with breath, though her lips seem to curve round the edge of a secret that he cannot begin to guess.

Then he feels the toad squirm in his pocket and takes it out for air, holding it in his two cupped hands where its shape and weight and beating thump make him feel like he holds a live heart. He knows, of course, what happened when a princess kissed a frog, but what if a frog kissed a princess instead? Would she wake from her slumbers, startled or grateful? Sprout warts and turn into a hag? Then kneeling down by his mother's bed as if to say his prayers, he lifts his cupped hands to her face, makes a small opening at his thumbs, so that the toad pokes out its head, straining its thin reptilian lips toward his mother's smile. And he notes with a curious detachment, an almost clinical calm, how the pulsing cords in the toad's throat seem to keep time with the fluttering vein in his mother's forehead just before she opens her eyes and lets out a piercing scream.

But no, that is not the way it happened. Or so he thinks now from his vantage of years and several thousand miles. He had simply thought the toad was thirsty and had wanted to give it a drink. What happened next was a comedy of errors, not some woeful tale. The toad leaped away, too slippery to catch, and landed on the nightstand where it toppled over a water jug, which crashed and broke on the floor. The sound was what woke his mother and Trix, who appeared in the doorway in a rumpled nightgown, rubbing sleep from her eyes, and their landlady too, bundled up in her wrapper, fretting about prowlers and Peeping Toms and all things combustible, as he got on all fours and crawled under the bed to catch the errant toad, feeling in truth more pride than shame at all the commotion he'd caused.

No, the only damaged thing in that room was the water jug, which wasn't worth much anyway. As worthless, he thinks, still wide awake, as this whole train of thought. He is no closer to sleep than he was when he first stirred up the memory, and from the thick pitch of black at the window he seems no closer to dawn. What he needs now is a new strategy, something else to focus upon, so he moves in his mind from those lodging rooms to the museum across the street, thinking, perhaps, he will catalog wonders, conjure up marvels like counting sheep to lull himself back to sleep.

Then he sees again the boy he was with a season pass in his hand, trembling as he enters the hall and stands beneath the dome. Thin light pours through the clerestory windows filled with whole galaxies of motes, and the guard gives him a nod and salute and, if he is lucky, a toffee. Then he is in the galleries, chock-full of amazing things. Gilt-wood boxes, altarpieces, coffers, ewers, globes. Helmets, gameboards, ivory combs, daggers, goblets, lutes. There is a mountain of a clock, all weights and dials and wheels, that shows not just the time of day but the Zodiac signs and the phase of the moon and the tides at London Bridge. And a candlestick made of molten gold whose base is a column of goblins, scrambling up from the pit of hell, each climbing on top of another. He loves the grand, heroic sculptures— *Samson Slaying a Philistine, Neptune Taming a Seahorse*—along with the small, more intimate objects: the pendant made from a narwhal's tusk (could it be a unicorn's horn?), the salt cellar in the shape of a ship whose hull is a nautilus shell.

Such a stirring of tenderness he suddenly feels for his young, impressionable self! If only he could stay in those rooms, the air thick with dust and the piety of art, where everything was labeled and ordered with dates and provenance and he, himself, was in a state of pure and simple awe. But already his mind has wandered to another Wonder House: the Grange, the home of Aunt Georgiana and his Uncle Ned. He spent his Christmas holidays there, on leave from Auntie Rosa, playing charades and rounds of snapdragon—snatching plums from bowls of flaming brandy—dawdling, drawing, watching magic lantern shows: all rich, heady stuff for a boy whose usual diet was Proverbs and canings. And best of all there was Aunt Georgiana, reading the tales of Scheherazade in the nursery late at night, and Uncle Ned with his practical jokes and ventriloquist voices and paintings. He would hang his works-in-progress along the house's passageways, large canvases with figures sketched in charcoal and only the eyes painted in. There was Merlin and Nimue with her books of spells, Circe with her potions, knights and damsels, undines, gorgons, Briar Rose, and Galatea. He would pass them on his way to bed, each set of eyes marking his progress. Wistful, vacant, they haunt him still, staring out of the white void of canvas with their yearnings and their needs. He would scare himself by imagining that he was subject to the fates depicted in the paintings. He might be turned into a swine or a laurel tree, be drawn by a siren into dark, murky depths where he would flail and drown. And so he'd creep down the hallway cautiously, bolting the last stretch to the nursery door where Aunt Georgiana stood patiently waiting with Sinbad and Ali Baba in hand.

Now, as if there's no safety in distance and years, he feels those eyes upon him again, those baleful, longing glances. And amid that perilous sea of stares, he sees his great friend Wolcott, his wife's younger brother who died eight months ago in Dresden, felled by typhoid. There he is, miraculously risen from the dead and reinstalled in his old digs across from Westminster Abbey. The same old Wolcott, in his Inverness cape, poised on his balcony, waiting for him with the sherry decanter and a box of Indian cheroots, while beyond him a tottering gander of a bishop leads a gaggle of altar boys across the abbey yard.

Could it be, he thinks, his mind all a-swim, that those telegrams were wrong, all those dire cables he received in Lahore, charting his dear friend's demise? In this nebulous hour, unmoored by the dark, such a thing seems not quite impossible. And if it were true, oh, if it were true! He would leave right now, this very moment, pack up his bags and go. Hire whatever conveyance was needed, book immediate passage. And once ashore, he would go to Dean's Yard and rush to that balcony, clap his friend firmly on the crest of his shoulders, light a cheroot, and raise a hale toast, saluting him for so bravely escaping and outwitting the clutches of death.

But something stops him from embarking, even in his mind. A shudder rises up from his bowels and unfurls down the length of his spine, as he sees what he's never really quite seen before: how much his friend resembles the figures in Uncle Ned's drawings and paintings. There's the same ashen skin, the same low sloping shoulders, the same pouting, tremulous lips. And the eyes—he sees those same sunken eyes, bewitching and imploring. Not a captive's, trapped, as he feared he would be, but one of the ambushing legion, just lying in wait to catch him off guard, to hook him and then reel him in.

Quickly he turns and looks at his wife, hoping to banish the ghost of the brother with the sight of the real, living sister. And in this, at last, he is rewarded. She is Carrie, solid, dependable Carrie, good with the reins of a carriage horse and his business correspondence, without a drop of wispiness or hauntedness about her. What dreams he imagines float in her head are practical and concrete: new table linens for the dining room, a christening gown for the baby who lies curled up, inside her womb, a sweet mound under the bedding. He watches as she grinds her teeth atop her pillow sham, applying herself to the task of sleep as diligently and methodically as she keeps the household ledgers. And noting the movement of her jaw, the slopes and swells of her shape, he realizes something else as well: there is light in the room, the first hint of day that signals his release.

He rises from his raft of a bed and walks toward the window. Beyond the mesh of the rusting flyscreen he can see the silhouettes of pines jutting against the mountains and the first of the swallows darting out from the eaves, parabolas of flight. He sees the hill he will crown with his house and the hayfields all around it, the last of the summer's chicory a dark blue in the pale light. He is tired, yes, but has no thoughts of sleep. They are gone along with his night's companions and their parcels of doubts and old wounds, and he feels now only an eagerness to make his mark on the day and an almost dizzying sense of elation, as if he's outwitted a wily opponent, sailed through an obstacle course. He's beyond the reach now of Auntie Rosa with her walking cane raised to cast blows; he's outsmarted at last old Devil-Boy Harry and his schemes to get him in trouble. His mother is back where she belongs too, writing him witty letters from Simla, where she waits out the long, stagnant hot months, informing him of the polo matches and the doings of the Viceroy and the role she will play in the upcoming amateur theatricals at the Club. At the Grange, Uncle Ned stands at his easel, painting the death of King Arthur. Aunt Georgiana plays with her grandchild and devotes herself to good works. Even Wolcott is still, his eyes shut in his grave, deep in the cold, German earth. And he is here in this new world, coming to life all around him, with a child and a house both on the horizon, and scores and scores of plans. He will learn the names of birds and plants, the habits of the wildlife. He will study the local vernacular of his neighbors, the townsfolk and farmers. But before he can launch himself into these studies, he must host one more visitation, for with a preternatural knowledge, he knows that his Daemon has arrived. He can feel it like a change in the wind or a quickening of his pulse, the presence of the numinous spirit he believes inspires his work. For this he's been accused of false modesty, of denying his own toil and gifts, but he knows better than his critics. He knows he is only a vessel. And all he must do now is what his Daemon asks: he must drift and wait and obey.

He does this willingly enough, trusting that unlike the night, his Daemon will not force him to stalk dimly lit passageways, poking his head into musty old rooms that are best left forgotten. He stares out the window and lets his mind drift and wait among the pine trees, watching the swallows swoop and dive, feasting on the dawn's insects. And as he does, the landscape before him seems to give way to another. The swallows turn into fork-tailed kites wheeling above the treetops. A grove of birches is a bamboo thicket, the brook a wide, muddy river. Twisted creepers hang from the branches, camouflaging pythons. There are palms and vines and sweet tall grass where tigers prowl at night. Then he cuts through the brush, his mind sharp as a scythe, as the prince in one of Uncle Ned's paintings cuts through a thick briarwood. And coming to a clearing he finds, not a castle brooding under a spell of sleep, but a cave with an animal's den. There are wolf cubs there and a pile of gnawed bones, and deep in the shadows, a boy. He sits on his haunches with a stick in his hand, playing with a handful of pebbles, as he once played with a coconut shell, pretending to be Robinson Crusoe. The boy's hair is black and matted to his forehead, his body caked with dirt, and when he opens his mouth to speak, what comes out is an animal cry, a mournful, feral moan. And following his Daemon again, he reaches back into his mind, pulling on a thin thread of remembrance that leads to his ayah in Bombay, long before he was shipped off to England and paradise was lost, telling him the Hindi names of the jungle beasts: Baloo, the bear; Bagheera, the panther; Tabaqui, the jackal. But what of the boy? What is his name? Again he drifts and waits, contemplating the boy's hunched back and his long, squatting legs, until finally it comes and he obeys: He is Mowgli, the Little Frog.

Then he hears his wife stir in her bed and turns to meet her gaze. She props herself up on one elbow, cradling her cheek in her palm, her other hand raised to shade her eyes from the first full stream of morning light that now pours into the room.

"Ruddy? Have you been up all night?"

"Yes, but it doesn't matter now."

He plants a chaste kiss on her brow and then hurries to his desk. Outside the sun rises over the mountains. Inside the jungle awakens.

THE STRENGTH OF THE WOLF IS THE PACK

*A*nd so another day begins, with the cows in the barn already lowing and a layer of mist in the fields. Joe Connolly feels a nudge at his arm and opens his eyes to see his father hovering next to his bed. He stands backlit by the morning light, the planes of his face in the shadows, one thumb hooked around the strap of his suspenders, the other hand still prodding Joe's arm. He has come, as he does each and every day, to wake Joe for his morning chores. And Joe, in turn, does what he always does: He startles then scrambles to waken, kicking the bedding away with his feet and pushing himself up with his elbows, rousing himself with a shake of his head to shed the last remnants of sleep. Then he blinks to adjust his eyes to the light and quickly scans the room, grounding himself in the sight of the dresser, the window, the washstand, his father.

With him, Joe steals a brief, hasty glance under cover of rubbing his eyes, for he knows that his father won't brook any hint of inspection or surveillance. Jack Connolly doesn't like to be questioned or doubted, to be challenged in any sort of way, particularly not after a night like the last, when he sat by the hearth with a jug at his feet, working himself up to a grand, self-pitying pitch of drunkenness. Joe had watched him then too, from the corner of the room, where he sat by his mother, who was busy with the wash she'd taken in from up the road, hoping, as Joe did, to stay out of his father's way as much as she could. For they both knew the risks of engaging him then, the danger in interaction: how a passing look might be deemed insolent, a stray remark considered disrespectful, the chance brush of an arm or the tap of a foot a provocation that wouldn't be ignored. Then Joe and his mother would be added to the list of vexations that have plagued his father's life, the ordeals and afflictions, the burdens and woes he recounts whenever he drinks.

Joe has heard of these trials ever since he was old enough to sit up at the table—nearly eleven years now, he reckons, give or take a month or two. And from them, he has managed to piece together a rough sketch of his father's past, unraveling the tangled heap of his stories to form a clearer chronology. He knows of his father's poor childhood in Ireland, in a tumbled-down cottage near Doolin. The doomed voyage that took him from Tralee to Boston. The rail work that landed him here. And he knows how that rail work almost literally killed him, though his father is vague in the details; how he met Joe's mother one fine spring day; how they tried, but failed, to raise sheep. As his father portrayed it, each step of his life began with hope and promise, though through some cruel twist of fortune or fate, hope led to despair, promise to disappointment again and again and again—which, depending on how much he drank, left him feeling either bitter or bewildered. His family had survived the Great Famine only to be evicted afterward, setting sail on a ship that promised deliverance but instead was a vessel of grief. And while a generation before him Vermont men had made fortunes selling wool to the Union Army for blankets and uniforms, as soon as Jack Connolly invested in sheep, the market precipitously dropped as farmers moved their herds out West to graze on the flat, sprawling grass of the prairie instead of these rocky slopes.

That's where he should have had the foresight to go, Joe's father repeatedly says. West, like John Deere, a Rutland man, who knew unfarmable land when he saw it and opportunity too, forging steel to make a plow that could turn up the prairie's rich earth. But instead he stayed; he forged on here, believing in perseverance. Though this is what embittered him most, the reversal he found the most galling: the fact that after all these years of hardship and struggle and loss, he'd managed to get no further than this, to these dozen-odd acres of soil-covered rock that called itself a farm. It was under snow nearly half the year and then awash in mud, and when the mud dried, there was little use in plowing, even if you could, since the snow would start back up again before most crops grew full.

For Joe, though, this life his father despises is the only one he knows; this place with its harshness and its meager rewards, the very nexus and definition of home. Joe knows it and loves it, in spite of himself, just as he loves his father—even now as he furtively peers at his face trying to determine his mood. And even last night, as he sat in the corner, fearful of being observed, Joe felt the pull of attachment. Certainly he couldn't bring himself to leave, not even when his father was too drunk to notice if he carefully crept up the stairs. Joe couldn't stop listening to him, though he'd heard it all before, couldn't manage to dismiss or discount or ignore him, couldn't plug up his ears and just go. No, he felt compelled to stay seated there, taking in his father's tirade—in good part, Joe thinks, because during the day his father is so closed-lipped, wrapped in a steeliness that seems to preclude the asking of questions and talk. Yet at night, with his tongue unleashed by the jug, he suddenly becomes loquacious, a fountain of words spilling out from his mouth, a great torrent of grievances and gripes.

And the stories, themselves, always draw him in, filled as they are with swindles and tricks, conniving and exploitation—with his father appearing as the unwitting victim of forces beyond his control, a role so at odds with the way Joe perceives him, as the ultimate wielder of power. And there's something about the telling itself that Joe cannot resist. When his father speaks of the railway, for instance, he invariably recalls the diggers and drillers who were crushed by falling embankments that hadn't been properly braced, who were trapped under cave-ins, maimed, even killed by charges that went off too soon. "There's an Irishman buried beneath every tie," he'll lament, his voice choked with resentment. And hearing him, Joe will picture the tracks that extend from Brattleboro, and imagine, beneath them, a line of men entombed and encrusted with dirt, lying shoulder to shoulder and hip to hip, one man to every tie, their arms crossed over their sunken chests, hapless martyrs to the crushing cause of progress. Or his father will allude to what happened to him, to the accident that nearly killed him, referring to it darkly as his "brush with death," which always prompts Joe to picture a great, swooping black bird with deadly, razor-sharp talons, brushing his father's cheek with its wing before wheeling and flying away.

And sometimes amid all the usual woes that his father will pick at like scabs, there will be some new complaint. Just last night he lit into the couple that rented the house up the road, the very people whose laundry his mother was then pressing on the ironing board. Joe knew them, of course, or at least he knew of them, as everyone did in these parts. It was not, after all, a common occurrence to have people like the Kiplings living here, though from his mother, Joe has heard many stories about other notables in town. Before she married Joe's father, she had worked at the Brattleboro Water-Cure, the hydrotherapy spa that sat on the banks of the Whetstone Brook. There she'd had the privilege of ironing the crinolines of Harriet Beecher Stowe's sister and had seen the grand names in the registry books—Henry Wadsworth Longfellow, President Martin Van Buren—their signatures centered and scored on the page with much looping and swirling of letters. She had even encountered Mrs. Kipling's family, the Balestiers of Newstone, who regularly spent a month at the spa to take in the waters and cures. And she'd come across others of certain repute whose names she no longer remembered, like the man from Schenectady who was carried aloft on a chair set with poles like a palanquin and the old crippled woman who rose to her feet, clutching a silver-tipped cane, so overcome with astonishment and thanks for the healing powers of the local springs that she pressed a handkerchief filled with gold coins into Joe's mother's poor hands.

He'd heard other stories as well through the years about other residents who, by deeds or skill or just serendipity, had managed to intersect history. There was Larkin Mead, a hardware store clerk, not all that much older than Joe at the time when a patient from the Water-Cure noticed him carving small, intricate figures of marble and paid for him to go to New York and study the art of sculpture. For two years he lived there, learning technique and craft, visiting sites and museums; until arriving home one New Year's Eve, he found the town buried in snow, and feeling the need of a prodigal son to commemorate his return, he built an angel out of the snow, working all night to form a maiden, eight feet of packed snow and carved ice, a beacon with wings that caused newspapermen from Boston and Springfield and Troy to rush to the scene and file front-page stories before her great wingspan could melt.

Stranger still, there was T. P. James, an itinerant printer who rented a room in a downtown boardinghouse. He attended a local séance one night and went into a trance in which he claimed he was summoned by Mr. Charles Dickens, recently deceased, who asked him to take up his "Spirit Pen" and complete his last, unfinished novel. He returned to his room and went back into a trance, emerging to find his floor strewn with papers on which he—a man who had never written more than a paragraph or two in his life—had actually scripted whole chapters, creating a mystery as difficult to solve as the one about Edwin Drood.

But, for Joe, these stories all pale beside the area's most recent distinction, if for no other reason than they happened in town, not here, at the edge of the county, where the road peters into a steep, narrow track overgrown by laurel and nettles and the only conveniences and comforts to be had must be earned through one's own sweat and blood. And, besides, all those others took place in the past, not now, with Joe here to witness, as he's witnessed Rudyard Kipling with his very own eyes, wading through the tall grass of the meadow that stretches between his house and the Kiplings', pausing to collect things he found underfoot—a few pinecones, the globe of a thistle.

In truth, though, he wasn't quite the dashing, worldly figure that Joe at first had imagined from the few stray facts he had managed to glean from his mother and the local newspaper. In fact, the few times Joe actually spied him, he seemed rather odd: not all that much taller than Joe himself, with a broom of a mustache and round spectacles that made his eyes seem to bulge, dressed in a pair of old knicker-bockers and a broad hat like a sombrero. But then just yesterday after-noon, as Joe and his father were leading the cows from the pasture back to the barn, he had passed with his wife in a canopied surrey driven by a groom in full livery, with doeskin breeches tucked into high boots, a blue coat, and a cockaded top hat. The carriage descended so suddenly on them that Joe and his father were both forced to scramble up to the side of the road, hugging the flank of the nearest cow in order to maintain some balance and swatting the air in front of their faces to clear the cloud of churned dust. Yet Kipling seemed undisturbed by it all. He sat in the carriage nursing a pipe with his arm threaded around his wife's shoulder. And driving by, he nodded to them, tipping his hat and raising his arm to toss off a lordly wave as if to acknowledge a whole crowd of onlookers, not a man, a boy, and some cows.

"Acts like we're nothing but a bunch of damn coolies," his father had said under his breath, catching Joe's arm as he started to raise it to prevent him from waving back.

And it's this Joe remembers as he looks at his father, still trying to read his face—the pinch of his fingers pressing into his shoulder, the disgust he had heard in his voice. It was there last night too, as his father rehashed the incident by the hearth, his disdain swelling into full-fledged indignation as he found himself reminded of the gentry he would see as a poor child in Ireland. They'd parade about their holdings and parks in their fancy coach and four, stopping to collect samples of lichen and moss for their precious curio cabinets, while his mother, his own mother, was reduced to serving broth she had made from grass and kelp, and his sister was out somewhere shitting in the fields, her stools loose as mud from the bloody flux that had twisted her gut into knots.

Joe's father recalled it all last night: the thin soup, the loose stools, his own hungering gut, his poor downtrodden mother, and the pomp of the carriage like a slap or obscenity that dismissed their very existence.

"And that's what they were like," he said of the Kiplings. "That's what they were bloody well like."

Then he spun around and looked at Joe's mother, who stood heating irons on the stove, glaring at her as if to say that this was all her fault—as if their neighbors wouldn't be here now were it not for her laundering skills, as if she had somehow betrayed or deceived him, been caught collaborating with an enemy force as his own mother never had; though, in fact, Joe had heard his father agree to his mother taking in the Kiplings' wash, at least until they found a proper servant. And so from his corner of the room, Joe watched with a knot of apprehension to see what his mother would do, defend herself or try to appease him, smoothing over his father's outrage and wounds as she'd smooth wrinkles out of a sheet. But instead she kept her sights on the stove where the flatirons hissed and spat, poking and stirring the embers up with the handle of a spoon. Then she grabbed an iron with a towel-wrapped hand and took it to the ironing board, where she pushed it over a handkerchief, back and forth and back and forth, with her mouth grimly set and her arm bearing down, her eyes pinned to the square of white cloth, until Joe's father finally turned back around and reached out again for the jug.

But where is all that anger now, all that blame and indignation? Joe cannot find a trace of it as he scans his father's face. It's as if it's all been purged or erased, or had never existed at all, a figment of Joe's imagination, or a dream that vanished at dawn. For now here is his father at the side of his bed, looking sober, somber, almost kind, filling up with misgivings as the sky fills with light, ready to set to work, with his mind churning around nothing more than the chores that await them both in the barn.

"I'll not have those cows pestering me now," he says with a grunt and a shrug, and Joe flings the quilted counterpane back and casts himself from the bed, relieved at what seems like his father's transformation, though he's not fully sure that he trusts it.

So Joe watches his father as he turns around and lumbers to the doorway, for this is what Joe *has* learned to trust: his own vigilance, his own eyes. He knows, for instance, the way his father looks—the particular grimacing pinch of his lips; the tensed, pulsing cords of his neck—when some of the blackness of the night before still hovers and weighs upon him and he is liable to lash out with words or belt or fist. And he knows that certain looseness in his father's limbs that signals a reprieve, a jauntiness in his step and voice that says the cloud has lifted. On those days he will have Joe come with him to take the cows to the high meadow, and they'll sit on the granite outcrop of rock that hangs above the river, watching as the mail train barrels down from Bellows Falls, trailing a thin ribbon of smoke. And if he is lucky, his father will even offer a morsel from his past. He will talk to Joe of his railroading days and those Irishmen under the ties, even share with him some of the songs the crews sang as they hammered spikes into ties—"Drill, Ye Tarriers, Drill," perhaps, or "Paddy Who Works on the Railway," with its *Pat, do this / And Pat, do that* and its

Yankee clerk with pen and ink / Who cheated poor Pat on the railroad.
Or he'll recall the sheep he attempted to raise after leaving the railway
behind, the flock of merinos he claimed were as fine as any Irish Shet-
land. And his voice will fill with such pride and regret that Joe will
flush with pride too, though, in fact, the whole enterprise was
doomed from the start, with half of the ewes infected with foot rot
and their fleeces too matted to card.

But will today be a lucky day? Will they head up to the high
meadow? Probably not, Joe thinks as he adds up his father's grunt and
shrug, the beleaguered tone in his voice, and decides that his father is
probably too weary, not stoked enough for true flashes of anger nor
heartened enough for the meadow — in a middling mood to which
Joe can respond with only a mild bit of caution.

So he slips on his shirt and pulls up his trousers, quickly stuffs his
feet into boots, for his father, Joe knows, hates being kept waiting as
much as he hates being pushed. Then Joe follows him down the stairs
to the kitchen where his mother has already heated up the stove and
started back in on the laundry, standing in the same place she stood
last night, beside the ironing board, so she seems like a fixture as per-
manent and sturdy as the pie safe or the stove. But she looks up the
moment Joe enters the room and tries to catch his eye, hoping to
trade a quick, reckoning glance behind Joe's father's back. It is what
they do most every morning, let each other know by a look or a nod
what they think the day might hold. For years, Joe has done this willingly enough, happy to trade his take on his father for a dose of his
mother's steady eyes; but recently he has felt an urge not to meet her
gaze, to just keep walking across the room, matching his father, stride
to stride. And he feels it now, that sense there's something shameful
in seeking his mother out, a need that he should avoid giving in to,

that brands him as a child. But as if his mother has sensed his reluctance, she lifts up the shawl she's been ironing and lets the jet beads that trim the fringe clatter and catch the light. And Joe instantly turns, lured by the sound and the sight of the glistening beads and the knowledge that it belongs to their neighbors, the Kiplings from up the road.

"So?" his mother seems to ask with her eyes once she has caught Joe's attention, and Joe lifts up his shoulders and screws his lips to one side, all to say that he thinks things are well enough now though the forecast remains in question. Then she tilts her head toward the table where, between a tower of shirtfronts and tea towels, she's set a hunk of buttered bread. Joe grabs the bread and stuffs it into his mouth, spilling crumbs from his lips, as his mother tells him to hurry. And he gulps and dashes after his father who has pushed the screen door open with his hand, without breaking his pace or his silence, and is now nearly halfway across the dusty yard, heading toward the barn.

Joe slips through the door before it slams shut and runs to catch up with his father. Already the mist is rising from the hollows; soon it will burn off completely, though soon, as well, in a few weeks or so, the mist will give way to frost, leaving the thinnest sheath of ice over each blade of grass. Six weeks till frost from the first cricket's voice, Joe thinks with a quick computation. Six weeks or less to get the hay in, six weeks till he goes back to school. Six weeks to deal with the crops and the threshing, to repair the fences and roofs, all the chores that must somehow get done before the winter sets in.

As always, it is a monumental task, this preparation for winter, though it doesn't yet feel so pressing to Joe that it stops him from dawdling. He slows as he makes his way to the barn and peers down the length of drive to the road, half hoping to see the carriage again.

The coachman with his cockaded hat, the whip poised in his white kid-gloved hand. In fact, it seems not entirely impossible that he'd see the coach that his father had spoke of, transporting a lord in a waistcoat and top hat, a lady gaily twirling a parasol, perhaps even see his father himself, standing barefoot at the side of the road, his thin arms hugging his chest. But there is nothing to be seen past the drive except for a few wisps of mist. No sound to be heard but the rustle of leaves and the warbling trill of a finch. Until, that is, Joe hears his father calling out from the barn.

"Get a move on, now. They won't wait all day," he says, gesturing to the cows. And Joe jerks around and scrambles again, following his father inside where the cows stand restlessly shifting in their stalls to relieve the weight of their udders while their tails flick and slap at the cloud of black flies that hovers and lands on their hides.

Then Joe and his father take up stools and pails and settle down to milking, each planting a stool at the rear of a cow with the pail placed beneath the cow's udder. They each grab two teats, one in each fist, and begin to squeeze and pull until a thin stream of milk spurts into the pail and Joe's father's face twists in a scowl. Joe knows that he hates this whole intimate business: the rhythmic pumping of the slick, drooping teats to yield a meager trickle, this twice daily wooing and bowing to beast, a constant humiliation. Yet Joe has come to love this time, especially on days like today, when his father is absorbed enough in his thoughts to let Joe lose himself in his own. Now he leans his head against the cow's flank and takes a deep comforting breath, smelling hay, cow, dung, milk, and beneath that, the sharp scent of lye. Then he sits back again and stares at the markings on the cow's wide barrel, as he'd stare at the sky to see something fanciful in the shifting shapes of the clouds. And what he imagines he sees is a map, an elongated, swaybacked globe: the edge where black meets white a coastline, each patch a continent, with the white in between the landmass of patches corresponding to the span of the seas. And the map makes him think of voyages, as he's done before on those days when his father's preoccupation has allowed his mind to drift, leaving him free to daydream of places: Byzantium, Atlantis, Cathay.

He has sat here often and thought of his father, setting sail from the harbor at Tralee. He has even imagined Charles Dickens's ghost, rising up from his deathbed in London to head down the Thames and then cross the Atlantic in order to settle here, in this small, provincial Yankee town hemmed in by pines and hardwoods, so a traveling man in a boardinghouse room could channel his last book's final chapters. Joe has even traced the course of these journeys across the flank of the cow, moving his finger from back haunch to foreleg, as if from the Old World to the New. But as the pail at Joe's feet fills with milk, he finds himself thinking of another voyage he heard about recently, the one Rudyard Kipling took that began, many years ago, in Bombay. It is a place so foreign, so distant, that Joe wouldn't know precisely where to find it, even if he had a proper map; though the fact that Rudyard Kipling was once there and now is here makes Joe feel as if he's connected, linked to the place through a fluke of geography, a strange overlapping of fates. And so he conjures the word in his mind—*Bombay, Bombay, Bombay*—squeezing the teats to the rhythm it makes, the steady alliterative beat. He even whispers it to himself, feeling a need to let the word pass, with a punch of his lips, out his mouth; though he suddenly fears that he's said it loud enough for his father to overhear him—his father who will likely want to curb his tongue as he curbed his arm yesterday.

With a quick, guilty glance, Joe looks down the aisle to check if his father's been listening, only to see, with a rush of relief, that he's moved on to the next cow. He has set his pail beneath her udder, placed his stool at the base of her hooves, and now is firmly rubbing her flank, not to reassure or comfort, but to hasten the letdown of milk. Then all Joe thinks he must worry about is a charge of idleness, an accusation that he's being lazy or too inattentive and slow. So he moves on too, first lugging his pail to the back of the barn where the storage cans sit and bob in the water trough in order to keep the milk cool, and he pours his take through the mesh of the strainer until his pail is empty again. And all the while, as he lifts and pours, careful not to spill a drop or to let any chaffs of hay in, his mind returns to the newspaper story that he read with his mother last week, and a new set of names rises up to his lips: Rawalpindi and Mandalay. Again Joe mouths the words to himself, summoning each with his lips and his tongue. And as he does, he feels the guilt lift, replaced by revelation: how easy it is to lead this double life, how thrilling the deception, his body going about its business, his mind a million miles off, while his father sits near, unaware and unsuspecting of what he would surely deem treason.

But perhaps Joe has been a bit too hasty and not camouflaged his dreaming enough, for his father turns and studies him, setting his eyes on Joe with such force that they seem to bore right through the plate of his skull and latch onto those clandestine thoughts.

"I'll finish the cows. You start cleaning up, then get inside to your ma. She needs you to take that wash up the road. It'll break her back to do it. But you listen to me: You take it, you leave it, and you come right back after that. You're not to be hanging around down there. There's work to be done back here."

"Yes, sir," Joe says, rising slowly from his stool, not wanting to betray any eagerness, though his mind has already sped back up the road, transported by curiosity.

But before his body can follow his mind, Joe must finish his chores, cleaning the stalls with a pitchfork and shovel, carrying dung to the compost. He brings their old Morgan a pail of oats and some timothy, tosses fresh sawdust under the cows, hangs the stools back up on their pegs. Then he gathers up the pails to scrub and heads outside again, where the mist has now burned off completely and the sky is a bright August blue. He sees two blackbirds quarreling by the pigpen, their old sow lolling in the mud. The clump of petunias his mother has planted, bright candy-striped pink and white bugles. And as he spies a hawk gliding high in the sky, riding the crest of an updraft, it's all he can do not to spread his arms out, tilt and veer them like the bird's great wings, twirl 'round and 'round until he is dizzy, a whirligig set free. But then he hears the barn door creak, and he turns to see his father heading out to pasture the cows. He has claimed a piece of straw to chew on and a hickory switch, which he flicks at the rumps of the cows, urging them first across the yard then through the gap in the old stone wall that marks the near edge of the meadow. Joe watches their slow, stately procession, the cows lifting their cloven hooves gingerly to avoid the bramble of blackberry canes that grows along the wall, his father behind them, ambling along, with the thin slip of straw at his lips. And just before they head up the hill ablaze with loosestrife and milkweed, Joe thinks he hears something that stops him from flight. It might simply be the drone of bees among the black-eyed Susans, or some mixture of breeze and the swishing of tails trying to shoo away flies. But Joe is convinced that what he hears is his father singing. And thinking that, he grows confused, suddenly unsure as he stands in the barnyard between the road and the meadow, watching his father's figure recede along with the lumbering cows, if he has really been released or, in fact, been exiled.

AND THE STRENGTH OF THE PACK
IS THE WOLF

There is much that can be learned from laundry, Addie Connolly thinks. Such a curious, intimate window it offers—and she doesn't just mean underthings. Take the stain she worked at the other day: a dark ruby splotch the size of a half-dollar, dead center in a fringed table runner that she set in a tub with some salt and cream of tartar and a healthy chunk of borax for good measure. Claret was what she assumed it to be, though Addie Connolly has never in her life had personal experience with wine—not even at the Water-Cure, where the beverage of choice was iced water from the springs, occasionally mixed with squeezed lemons. But she's heard the rumors going around and now has seen the proof—that the Kiplings drink wine each night with dinner, that they dress in full evening wear, while beyond the pool of light from the candles whose wax she has had to scrape from the runner with her thumbnail and a blunt knife, moths beat at the fly screens, bats dart from the eaves, the trees lean close and shudder.

She has heard, as well, what her neighbors have to say about the Balestier girl, how she's come back from London not just with a husband but with fancy Mayfair ways. It is she, they say, who insists on formality—at the table, for the coachman—and on the observance of the new London custom of serving high afternoon tea. For this she has not endeared herself to her fellow Vermonters; they deem her behavior pompous and haughty, though Addie Connolly is trying her best to abstain from judgment. This is a point of policy for her: to try to understand what she can and forgive what lies beyond that, an approach that is frequently pushed to its limits by her life here at the farm. Now, though, as she folds the last of the laundry for Joe to deliver this morning, she thinks it might be only natural for such attire to cause the wearer to adopt certain attitudes and airs. Why, who knew what changes might happen to her—in accent and bearing and outlook—if she were to don such fancy things and stroll through Hyde Park or the Battersea with a jet bead chatelaine bag at her waist, filled with scent and a small stash of calling cards.

Certainly she hadn't seen clothes like these since she married Jack Connolly: brocaded waistcoats lined with silk, flared dresses with panniers and sashes, all in the deepest and richest of colors—cerise and heliotrope. Truth told, she had been a little afraid of taking on such delicate work. She has none of the specialized equipment she had at the Water-Cure, no washing dolly or crimping iron to finish the ruffles and frills. And while, fortunately for her, Mrs. Kipling is stylish enough to have abandoned her bustle, the new puffed-up sleeves—gigot or leg-of-mutton—put her ironing skills to the test.

Still Addie has her store of tricks, her secrets of the trade. She managed the rust marks from the hook and eye fasteners that run down the backs of dresses by applying a spoonful or two of stewed rhubarb (the acid eats at the rust) and removed the spots of town street tar on the hems of Mrs. Kipling's skirts by rubbing them with a bit of lard before she set them to soak. And she used a thin shaving of paraffin to bring out the favored, prized look of gloss on Mr. Kipling's shirtfronts, proving, she hoped, that he needn't forego fashion because he had come to Vermont.

Now she looks at the clothes all piled up around her and feels a deep satisfaction. The linens, as well, from bed, table, and bath: she has soaked them, boiled them, wrung them, rinsed them, with bluing and with starch, set them to air and dry in the sun, pressed them with iron and mangle, so that they sit on her table and chairs as downy and white as new snow. She cannot quite resist touching them, pressing the palm of her hand into their sun-warmed, flattened surface. Nor is she able to stop herself from fingering the rows of pearl and horn buttons, the cascading lace jabots.

What would it be like to wear such clothes? Truly she cannot imagine. Not even the nightdress she starts to fold, a simple sweep of finespun muslin with a high-ribboned neck and lace yoke. Surely such a garment would not be subjected to the kind of tussling that goes on in her house when her husband is not too drunk to stumble into their bed. Then he grabs at her, at her buttocks and breasts, with an almost punishing fierceness, pushing away her own graying gown, a bothersome bit of rag. Would it be different in different attire? Maybe, or maybe not; for every time, Addie has come to learn, there comes a moment when all her husband's brutishness melts away. Then he cleaves to her and clings to her, clutching the folds of her gown in his fist like a string of rosary beads, and pressing his lips to the thin, tattered fabric in a way that lets Addie understand how desperately she is needed.

Needed as opposed to loved, which she imagines just for a moment might be enkindled by the snowy white muslin and the high, chaste collar of lace. A foolish thought, and presumptuous as well, which she dismisses by setting the nightdress, now folded, at the bottom of the heap. Then she looks out the window and sees her son, standing in the yard. That's what inspires her stirrings of love, not a piece of cloth and tatting, her own flesh and blood with its flaws and perfections—from the smattering of freckles on the bridge of Joe's nose to his thatch of straw-colored hair, from the knobs of his knees always crosshatched with scratches to the thin crust of dirt between his toes.

For years after her marriage Addie had feared that she was doomed to be childless, afflicted for some reason she could not comprehend with the curse of a barren womb. She tried to accept this fate with forbearance, giving herself to the work of the house with diligence if not true joy. But then Joe arrived, changing her fortune and filling her heart near to bursting, transforming—from the moment he slipped out of her—whatever sorrow she had felt before. And her work, what had sometimes seemed the drudgery of it, he changed all that as well. She would set him on the floor in a basket that she'd tied with a length of cord to the rockers of a broken chair. And the look on his face, his coos of contentment, as she rocked him and started the wash, made the swish of the linens and the sloshing of water sweet sounds, like babbling; made the sheets hung to dry from the crossbeams and rafters when it rained or snow kept them inside seem part of a dreamy, celestial landscape, great steaming swags of white cloud.

She sang to him then, to the thunk of the mangle and the rhythm

of brushes on scrubboards. *Rock-a-bye, baby, thy cradle is green /
Father's a nobleman, mother's a queen.* Then when he was older, she
told him things, about her days at the Water-Cure, about the preem-
inence of town. And older still, he joined in the telling, sharing with
her odd facts from his lessons as she heated up the irons, listening as
she told him bits of gossip and news they collected together like coins.
Why, just the other day they had sat here together, pouring over a
clipping from the local newspaper of Mr. Kipling's poems, a long,
rambling story she could barely make sense of that took place in the
Far East. It had none of the flowery or salutary language she associ-
ated with verse, none of the fancy *thees* or *thous* of the Psalms or the
Book of Isaiah. In fact, it seemed a bit coarse to her, with "wot" for
"what" and "git" for "get" and "'arf" instead of "half"—though Joe
said he reckoned that that was the current fashion and she supposed
he was right.

And now she imagines that he'll marvel at the sight of all these
clothes and linens, that he'll eagerly head up the road on his task and
return with news to share. But the way she sees him, there in the yard,
gives her a momentary pause, reminding her that the trouble with
love is the potential for heartbreak. He will leave one day, that much
is for certain—Addie already knows—leave these rooms all steamed
up with washing and the intimacy of talk, where she fears all the stories and gossip they've shared may have done nothing more than
hatch in Joe a desire to wander and roam.

But even before that future departure, that final severing, she fears
that he will break her heart by the sheer force of his attachments. He
feels too much, too deeply, too keenly, and it all shows up on his face—
slights, betrayals, humiliations, all manner of hurt and shame. Looking
at him, she feels her heart clench as she catches his expression, a pained,

bewildered look in his eyes that tells her something has recently happened to make him doubt himself. Something with his father, most likely, though Addie believes that despite all her husband's binges and threats, he doesn't mean any harm. Still, she knows what damage can be done by the slow erosion of faith, how confidence can be chipped at, picked at, until there is nothing left. So she does what she has always done, what mothers do: intervene.

"You've had words with your pa," she calls out to him, half a statement, half a question.

"No," the boy says, though he turns one last time to gaze up at the meadow, where his father stands, surrounded by the cows, all bending their mottled heads to the ground, great black and white shapes against green.

"Well, come in then and see what I've got," Addie encourages him, certain that she possesses the cure for whatever troubles or ails him.

It is true that the moment Joe walks through the door he forgets about his father. True too that his curiosity is piqued by what his mother has to show. She points out a stack of white handkerchiefs embroidered with the initials RK, a strange sort of robe that she thinks is Oriental, with long, slashed sleeves and a pattern of cranes painted on silk at the back. She shows him the pile of Turkish towels and the pillow shams embroidered with the words, "*I dreamt that life was beauty.*" And Joe admires it all, and her handiwork too, how astoundingly white she has gotten the linens, how crisply pressed the clothes. Yet he also feels unaccountably restless, strangely eager to be off, away from the steamy confines of the kitchen with its smells of scorched cotton and starch.

But before he can go, he must help his mother load the laundry into the wheelbarrow and listen to her final words of instruction about how careful he must be not to let any leaves or hayseed or burrs settle on top of the pile, and about how polite he should be to Mrs. Kipling, to say, "Yes, Ma'am," and "No, Ma'am." Then as if realizing she is fretting too much, telling him what he already knows, she stops and squeezes his shoulders.

"Go on then," she says, "and try not to dawdle. I'll have supper ready when you get home."

Joe heads down the drive, looking over his shoulder to give his mother one last nod. Then he turns on the road, following the old stone wall that borders the orchard while maneuvering the wheelbarrow between the ruts made by wagon wheels. By now the sun has climbed high in the sky. Light falls through the trees in bright dapples, glancing off the fruit in the trees and the wings of the monarchs that flutter and perch on the Queen Anne's lace by the roadside. It is high summer, though as Joe walks, he sees indications of autumn— the buds of bottled gentian by the base of the wall, the first petals of white wood aster—all the small, subtle signs he has taught himself to read from the classroom of the woods. Soon, he knows, the monarchs will leave, flying south to the tip of the continent. Soon the fruit will be picked, soon the windfall left to rot. Soon the flowers will lay tattered like real lace. Though Joe doesn't want to think of all that, lying in wait for the future, for the thought reminds him of his father, striding across the yard this morning as Joe counted the weeks left till frost—his father whom he knows hates the onset of winter as much as he hates anything. But before he can stop or censor himself, before he can latch onto something else, Joe pictures his father up in the high meadow, singing one of his railroading songs as he sits on a flatbed of rock. And the thought of him there, serenading the cows beyond Joe's earshot and vision, fills him with such a sense of privation, such a fear of what he might be missing, that he feels momentarily dizzy and woozy, his head swirling and reeling with loss.

So he grips the handles of the wheelbarrow tightly like the prongs of a witching rod, letting the front wheel divine the course over the packed dirt and bumps. He tries to pretend he is in a trance like the printer T. P. James, led by some strange, mysterious force instead of his own volition. And in that state what comes to his mind is the poem that his mother had shown him, the one that the two of them had tried to decipher as they sat in the kitchen together. Now it rises up like a vision before him that he gratefully embraces, letting the image of rice fields and temples displace the thoughts of his father. He tries to imagine this is not some country lane but a road in ancient Burma, where just around the corner he might see a flotilla anchored in a palm-lined bay that looks across to China and the distant spires and tiers of pagodas that form the golden skyline of Mandalay.

Of course when he does round the bend in the road he sees nothing beyond the usual: a split-rail fence, a grove of elms, a clearing overrun by goldenrod, and beyond that, the ramshackle hired man's cottage that he knows the Kiplings have rented while they wait for their home to be built. It is a house much like his own, with peeling white clapboards, a tar paper roof, a door, and four flush windows, all without the modifying grace of shutters or a veranda. But while he has passed this way often enough, Joe stares at it now as if he had never actually seen it before, noticing the lilac bush by the south wall, its leaves chalky white from mildew, the clump of day lilies near an old rusted pump, growing vigorously though neglected. Then he spies something else that catches his eye, the same shade as the lilies: a square of pale orange hanging from an eave, emblazoned with a kohl-rimmed eye, that Joe, for all his lore of the woods and hoard of odd facts and geography, doesn't know is a flag from a prayer wheel— though he rightly suspects that it comes from the part of the world conjured by the poem.

He is struck, as well, by what else he doesn't know—and not just about banners and prayers wheels. He's not sure, for instance, if there's a back door, and if so, should he use it or go to the front, stand beneath that strange flap and knock firmly on the door? And how should he introduce himself? With a handshake or a nod of his head? With an admission that he's read Kipling's poem and now can practically recite it? These questions leave him immobilized as he stands by the grove of elms, staring at the house and the laundry-laden barrow like pieces in a puzzle that don't fit. Then he hears a great whoop that makes him spin around just in time to see Rudyard Kipling, the very man himself, careen into view on a bicycle seat with his feet propped up on the makeshift footrests that have been attached to the frame.

"Heigh ho," he calls out as he sails past Joe and comes skidding to a halt near the house. Joe watches as he neatly swings his leg over the bar to dismount, then leads the bicycle right to the elms, propping it against a trunk, before he slaps at the dust on his tweeds and takes off his cycling gloves.

Then he turns to Joe and sees the laundry.

"Our savior's son," he says as he sets the palms of his hands together, his elbows pointing out, and bends at the waist, his legs locked at the knees, in a deep and grateful salaam.

"And what might your name be?" Kipling asks.

"Joe. Joe Connolly," he says.

"Ah, Joe," Kipling muses. "Joe, Joe, Joe, Joe," repeating the name so often it seems to lose all sense and meaning.

"I once had a horse by the name of Joe, a former charger with the Bengal lancers. Quite the sober one he was," he says with a snort, "though he could also be rude. He would throw me without a second thought if I tried to make him jump, then refuse to let me remount. I'd have to pretend that I didn't care if he let me up or not, till he'd come penitently trotting back over, dragging his reins in the dust.

"Now, I don't suppose you're rude," he says, peering at Joe over the rim of his glasses. "Though do I detect just a hint of soberness?" he adds, casting the question in the air.

Joe has no idea how he should respond, or what he should look at: the house, the clothes, the man before him, the bicycle there by the tree. He has seen machines like this before—in the pages of almanacs and mail-order catalogs, once or twice on the main street of town— but never this close, or on these roads, where the traffic consists of democrat wagons, the occasional carriage or cart, vehicles meant for transport or labor, not leisure or pleasure or thrill.

"Would you like to try it?" Kipling says, seeming to read his thoughts, though perhaps all he's done is follow the yearning trajectory of Joe's gaze.

Joe looks at him, then the bicycle again, eyes darting from man to machine. He has studied illustrations of cycles before in the Sears, Roebuck catalog and can identify the parts: the steel-tube frame and pneumatic tires, the saddle perched high atop springs, the geometry of chain sprockets and spokes that seems to him as confounding and simple as a double helix spiral. He takes it in, all the while feeling the specter of his father behind him. What would he call it? A newfangled contraption? A folly? Or something worse? Joe can practically hear his words in his head, see his lips curl up in a sneer. But he takes one more look at the wrought-iron trim, the brackets and lugs gleaming black, and he shakes the restraining phantom away and eagerly nods his head.

"The thing to remember," Kipling says, growing excited as well, "is to try and work up some speed. Slow and safe are not always the same. Build some momentum, that's what you'll need. And trust in centrifugal force."

Together they take the handlebars and lead the bicycle back to the road, positioning it at the crest of a slope that Joe will have to ride down.

"Come, I'll hold you until you get steady," Kipling says encouragingly, and Joe sets one foot on a pedal, as instructed, then swings his other leg up.

What a strange, precarious perch it seems, the seat as hard and unyielding as bone and everything wobbling beneath. He grips the ends of the handlebars and the front wheel jerks back and forth. His feet on the pedals shimmy this way and that, in stilted fits and starts, as if he were trying to ford a stream on the most unsecured stepping stones. And almost as strange is the hand on his own and the other at the small of his back, one set of fingers locked over his own atop the handlebar grip, the other applying a light but firm pressure that now makes the bicycle start.

"Now you need to push down on the uppermost pedal and let the other one rise. Then down with the latter and up with the first. That will start up the chain drive."

Joe does as he's told but with little conviction. Already he feels himself tilting. But Kipling swiftly compensates and pushes him back on track, and soon Joe manages a semblance of rhythm, his feet going round like the arms of a swimmer, his hands keeping the front wheel in check.

"Now I'm going to let go," Kipling says. "Keep pedaling and if you think you're going to fall, turn into it slightly then straighten."

Then Joe feels Kipling release his hands and he is on his own, sailing down the road he has traveled so often but that now looks astoundingly new. The leaves and trees and fields all blur so the sky seems streaked with green. The wind in his hair is a novel sensation, almost closer to water than air. He feels his legs bearing down on the pedals like the pistons of some great engine, his arms as taut as the molded steel tubes that form the diamond-shaped frame. In fact, he thinks he is a machine, a human locomotive, all surging power and imploding combustion, a part of the new Machine Age. But something is wrong: his foot slips from a pedal, and the pedals take off on their own, continuing their revolutions until one slams into his leg. Joe doubles over, contracting one arm while the other shoots out forward, which in turn makes the wheel swerve sharply to one side and skid on a patch of dirt. And before he knows quite what has happened, before he can stop or right himself, he is sprawled on the road by the bicycle, whose pedals still maniacally spin, his shin bruised, his pride smarting, his pants torn at the seat, while Rudyard Kipling comes running up toward him, whooping with laughter again.

"Good show," he says, first catching his breath then sitting down right next to Joe. "My first time I rode right into a henhouse. Feathers, straw, unimaginable squawking—you'd have thought I was a fox. Though there was some poetic justice to it," he says, his voice growing wistful. "You see, I was once terrorized and set squalling myself by a most bullying fowl. The Pater, my father, an honorable man, though not above an occasional bit of whimsy, memorialized it with a drawing and rhyme. Shall I tell it?" he asks, then starts right in before Joe can respond.

There was a small boy in Bombay
Who once from a hen ran away.
When they said: 'You're a baby,'
He replied: 'Well, I may be:
But I don't like these hens of Bombay.

"So, you see," he says, "as the Holy Ones say, all things do come around."

Rising up from the road, Kipling brushes off his hand then offers it to Joe. It's the cleanest hand Joe thinks he's ever seen, with short clipped nails and a fat signet ring inscribed with some curious lettering, though the bump on the side of his middle finger is stained blue-black from ink. Joe stares at the bump, like some foreign thing—a salver or a dance card—while his head spins like the bicycle wheel, around and around and around. His cheeks, his ears, his shins all burn, stoked by pricks of shame. He rubs his rump and feels the tear that his mother will have to sew, and a layer of guilt mixes in with the shame, forming a thick, choking mulch. But still the hand is there, extended. Still Mr. Kipling smiles, until finally Joe swallows a nugget of pride and lets the man pull him up.

"Come now," Kipling says sympathetically, giving Joe a pat on the back. "Perhaps you can help me with something I was working on this morning."

He lifts the bicycle up, as well, then starts back to the house, as Joe walks beside him trying to determine the size of the rip in his pants. And as they walk, Kipling tells him the story of a boy he says he's encountered.

"A feral child, raised by the wolves. No mother, no father to speak of. I found him sitting in a cave this morning, playing with some stones. And I thought, you being a boy yourself, you might be able to tell me what he could be doing with them. Or perhaps what else he has in there. You know, what things he plays with."

He looks at Joe expectantly, though Joe stares back at him blankly. And Kipling, oblivious or undeterred, continues with his prompting.

"I knew another boy once, by the name of Muhammad Din, who liked to build the most fabulous grottoes out of things he found. A polo ball, some marigolds, an old discarded soap dish. I could ask him, of course, but, alas, he died. Wrapped in a rag to be burned in the river with hardly a soul to mourn him." He pauses to shake his head grievously, then immediately brightens up. "And I thought to myself, why, I'll just ask you. Seeing how you've shown up too."

Again he stops and looks at Joe. Again Joe grows confused. A father penning limericks, a boy in tears over a hen, a grown man sitting in the middle of the road just as he would in a parlor. And now all this talk of wolves and caves, a dead child and a soap dish—Joe doesn't know what to make of it, and more than anything else is not sure that he's not, in fact, being mocked. There is something he can't account for in the voice, something sly and roguish and arch, the way it seems to move too fast from one thing to another. But when he steals a sidelong glance at Mr. Kipling's face, his eyes behind their spectacles seem so hopeful and guileless that he fears that by not saying anything Mr. Kipling will think he is rude.

"Sticks?" he says uncertainly then. "He could have sticks and stones."

"Quite so," Kipling answers, "undoubtedly sticks." Then he waits on Joe again.

"A porcupine's quill?" he offers next, even more hesitantly.

"Yes, that's good," Kipling says. "Just the thing," he adds, "though I fear that I've failed to mention that the cave of which we've been speaking is located in India. In the Seeonee Hills, to be precise. Of course, there they have only Old World porcupines, not quite the same as these here. They live in tunnels underground and have never been known to climb trees."

By now they've reached the starting point of Joe's ignoble journey. He sees the laundry still there by the trees, the house still awaiting its delivery, and he feels another pang of guilt at a duty unfulfilled, and a wave of fear akin to the one he just felt on the road that this whole elaborate detour, this distraction of joyrides and tales, has been constructed simply as a ruse to get him into trouble. Then he looks up at the trees by the roadside, at the uppermost reaches of branches, thinking it not inconceivable that he'd find a porcupine there, shaking down pine needles, elm leaves, seeds, making light of his mother's long labor.

But, of course, there is no animal there, no partner working in tandem, though when Joe does turn back to the house, he sees his fear of reproach incarnate in the figure of Caroline Kipling. She stands in the doorway, hands splayed on her hips, the swell of what Joe realizes is a baby, uncontained by any stays. And though he isn't absolutely sure, he thinks he sees a boot-clad foot beneath the hem of her skirts, tapping with what he is afraid is irritated impatience.

"Ah, the memsahib," Kipling says, throwing Joe a broad wink. "Would you be a good fellow and set the bicycle over there by the woodshed?"

Joe takes over at the handlebar helm and watches as Kipling crosses the yard to stand beside his wife. He slips one hand around her waist, lays the other atop her domed belly, then whispers something into her ear—a gesture that seems so intimate to Joe that he quickly casts his eyes to the ground and feels his own ears burn. Still, it's all he can do not to turn around and stare as he leads the bicycle away, just as he must struggle to keep his hands wrapped around the grips of the handles, thinking it better to walk straight and upright, even with a hole in his seat, than to falter and stumble as he surely would do if he tried single-handedly to manage the cycle while the other hand covered his rump.

Reaching the woodshed, he props the bicycle up against a tree stump then goes to reclaim the wheelbarrow, keeping his eyes still pinned to the ground, resisting the urge to look up. When he finally does raise his head, having pushed the wheelbarrow to the front door stoop, he sees that Kipling has gone. He has vanished into the depths of the house, where a bright woven carpet stretches back from the entry like a bed of primroses in the hall, leading to rooms that he cannot make out in part because Mrs. Kipling is still there, standing in the doorway, staring at him with eyes as piercing as the one on the eave's orange flap.

"You must be Addie Connolly's boy," she says, looking him up and down. And on her lips the words seem an accusation, a damning charge that Joe is tempted to deny.

COME ALONG, LITTLE BROTHER

The weeks slip by filled with haying and threshing and the endless chopping of wood, with the sound of Jack Connolly's ax ringing out over the hills like a bell. He has worked long and hard these past few weeks. Worked from sunrise to far beyond sunset, driven by an urgency he feels this time of year, as the days grow shorter and cooler and a sense of dread starts to steal over him, a feeling of apprehension that comes along with the dwindling light and the changing shade of the leaves. It is as inevitable to him as the seasons, this slow, creeping feeling of dread, and the only way he knows how to dull it, aside from eclipsing it with drink, is to make sure that the corncribs are full and the woodshed is stacked high with logs and the hayloft is crammed with so many bound bales they reach up to the rafters.

He has done that now—or almost has—and the fact fills him with a groundswell of relief. The hay is all in; enough wood has been split to last at least through December. Little more than the pumpkins, a few squash, and some beans remain on the garden vines, while most of the fruit in the orchard has been picked and already put up in cans, except for a final bushel or two that Jack is harvesting now, working his way from tree to tree with the help of his son.

They work methodically but slowly, taking turns climbing up the truss ladder they have hauled from the barn, filling the sacks they've slung over their shoulders with the last of the apples and pears. In fact, there is something almost leisurely about it, as if they were on a midsummer outing, not a race to beat the frost. They pause to watch a muskrat drag a stick to its lodge by the bog. They linger when they're up on the ladder, just to take in the sight of the trees, the yellow and gold and crimson leaves like the crackling flames of a bonfire. And when Jack Connolly spies a pheasant, pecking around the edge of the orchard, looking for black pippin seeds, he crouches down beside his son to show the bird to Joe.

"There," he whispers, as he points to the spot where the bird rummages through the windfall.

Joe nods his head as he stares at the pheasant. The ring around its neck like a slave's iron choker, the crown of its cockscomb and wattle. Then he whispers back, "Should I go get the shotgun?" and Jack Connolly shakes his head no. Let the bird be, he thinks rather grandly; he has had a good crop this year and needn't concern himself with a scrounger—albeit a savory one—who, unlike the partridges that come in the spring to eat the fruit buds off the trees, can do no real lasting damage.

Such magnanimity is unusual for him, as rare as this year's harvest. Usually he is here, wading through drifts of leaves to pump buckshot into plumage, to lay traps for the muskrats whose only true crime is to be a manner of vermin, and to ponder the mystery of maggots and blights that all too often have left his fruits shriveled and the leaves on his trees looking scorched. But the apples this year have been hard and crisp. The pears are fat and plentiful, and this, combined with the reassuring knowledge that the fall's work is mostly behind him, has produced a rare mood in him today. He stands and claps his son on the back, the sack at his hip full of fruit, and he feels light-hearted, almost redeemed, indulgent enough to spare the life of a bird and to grab two Northern Spies from the sack, burnishing them both, double-fisted on his shirtfront, before tossing one to his son.

Joe catches the apple and throws his father back a wide-toothed grin, and together they bite down through skin into pulp to taste the very essence of autumn. With the fruit, the washing, and the butter Addie churns and packs into crocks stamped with a design—an acorn or sheaf of wheat—to send on the train down to Boston, Jack Connolly thinks they can manage the mortgage payment due at the year's end, perhaps even have a little left over for something, the luxury of a small trifle. Of course, the fact that such solvency wouldn't be possible without his wife's laundering work is a bitter point for him, and his rare grand mood is not so ensconced that it cannot fly right away. All it takes, in fact, is the sight of a carriage barreling down the road: Caroline Kipling, who drives the rig at an almost breakneck speed, sitting upright, with a foot of space between her spine and the seat back, wearing a hat that, if he's not mistaken, is crowned with a stuffed puffin's head.

She has cinched and drawn up the check reins so tightly that the horse can't stretch his neck—a heartless way to treat an animal, though at least she knows how to drive, unlike her fool of a husband, whom Jakc had found stranded earlier that week in the buggy down the road. He had sat there hopelessly shaking the reins and pleading with his horse to go, so ignorant of the simple way to cramp the wheels and turn that Jack had to climb up and help him out, taking over the reins himself.

"I thank you for your kindness, sir," Kipling said, once Jack handed the reins back, "and Marcus Aurelius," he said, pointing to the horse, "extends his deepest gratitude as well."

Jack Connolly had been too flabbergasted by what he had deemed the man's lack of humility to utter a reply. And now watching the wife hurtling past him, oblivious to all that's around her, he finds himself speechless as well, though he's tempted to yell out some cutting remark when he sees his own wife in the yard. She has been hanging the wash to the line, pinning up the Kiplings' linens beside their own worn sheets, though she stops as Caroline rattles by to raise her arm and wave. But then, as Jack watches, she draws her arm down and holds it close to her chest, apparently realizing that such a neighborly gesture will be neither acknowledged nor returned. Then she turns back to the wash again and lifts a sheet from the hamper, seemingly resigned to what Jack is sure has been a purposeful snub. And seeing her there, wrestling with the sheet, holding a corner down with one hand while the other hunts for a clothes-peg, he feels something stir and start to roil in him, a gnawing akin to the one he felt on the first day they met.

He was working for the railway then, laying down tracks that would one day stretch from Boston to Montreal, provided the crews could blast their way through Vermont's mountains and piedmont hills. It was backbreaking work, full of risk and sweat and the thick camaraderie of men, Micks and Paddies like him who had traded one hardscrabble life for another. But it suited him, the railway life, moving from one makeshift camp to another, tramping over the countryside. He liked the exhaustion that would set in at night when his body was too spent and sore to do anything other than sleep, liked the feel of the sun on his back as he hammered, liked the hard bulge of muscle on his arms. He didn't even mind the gruffness of the foreman or the pittance of his pay, for being exploited made him feel somehow valued, just as being wronged made him feel righteous— besides which, such brusqueness and thanklessness was what he had come to expect.

But he did mind the blasting work. He hated the explosives. Hated the noise and the havoc they wrought and their unpredictable ways. But that's what he was forced to do on the day he met Addie. He'd been lowered that morning over a ledge in a woven basket more suited to carrying eggs than a man, to set plugs of powder into holes he had already drilled in the rock face. He wedged the plugs in and crimped the caps, tamping them down with his hand. Then he lit the fuse and tugged on the ropes to signal he was ready, and the basket had heaved and started to rise, the wicker groaning under his weight. But then something happened: a pulley jammed and the basket's slow ascent halted. The charge exploded and he watched the rock crumble, as if it were no more than ash, till he felt the first shower of hailing debris—bits of shale, whole hunks of limestone—and he crouched down, clutching his pick like a cross, and muttered a hasty Hail Mary.

When they finally managed to hoist him back up, they found him huddled, his arms over his head, covered with stone dust and dirt, so shaken he could barely stand let alone walk on his own. But someone pulled him up from the basket and took him off to the side, where he was left to sit by a tree to catch his breath and senses. And as he sat there, watching the men set back to work again, something in him snapped. He could still taste the grains of dirt in his mouth, still smell

the burning cordite, and the taste and the smell make him reckless
and brazen, filled with a cockiness borne of surviving and a gnawing
he did not know was rage.

So he got to his feet and walked from the tracks, following the
bank of the river all the way to Brattleboro. What he found when he
got there was a prosperous town, with staunch brick buildings and
sidewalk-lined streets laid out in an orderly grid, though the very
orderliness of it all seemed, to Jack, an incitement to riot. He'd
worked with others who'd felt this way, men who would leave the
camp on Sundays to rove about, marauding, raiding orchards and
potato fields, stealing eggs and chickens, stripping clotheslines just for
the thrill of running through a crowded street trailing a pair of
bloomers. But thrill was not what Jack Connolly desired, nor was it
amusement. What he wanted felt more necessary, more urgent and
defiant, a gesture to prove to himself and to others that he possessed
the same pent-up power as those cartridge clips of explosives.

So he walked through the town, filled with vandalist dreams,
thinking about what he could do. He passed the brook-side paper
mill and contemplated arson, walked by storefronts and shops with
their window displays and thought about heaving a rock. And he
wandered through the maze of backstreets where houses sat primly
behind picket fences and porch swings swayed in the breeze, where
the bright heads of tulips seemed to shout out for lobbing and ash
cans begged to be dumped, though none of this seemed as grand an
act as Jack Connolly needed. So he kept on walking through the outskirts of town till he found himself facing the entrance of the Brattleboro Water-Cure establishment. Beyond the filigree of black wrought
iron he could see the central building, where white, fluted columns
flanked a veranda studded with porch swings and rockers. A few

patients wandered about the lawn wrapped in woolen blankets and strips of linen sheets, on their way to various spring-fed bathhouses to undergo their treatments. There were cold baths, plunges, needle showers, sitz baths, jets and packs, medicated baths steeped in camphor and sulfur, douches, sponges, sweats. Jack Connolly had heard about the place and immediately despised it—the indulgence of it and the pampering, all the doting on flighty, imagined infirmities of organs, glands, and blood. And the grounds themselves with their manicured lawns and architectural follies—the whole place was a folly, Jack Connolly thought, solid proof, if anyone needed it, of the gullibility of the rich. But he saw soon enough the potential in the setting for his own cathartic needs, the way the grounds were like a grand stage waiting for some drama.

There was no gatekeeper at the gate so he easily slipped in, sneaking from one tree to the next, hiding behind the trunks. Adirondack chairs stood about the lawn, painted immaculate white, with matching side tables holding trays set with glasses and pitchers of melting ice water. For a moment he imagined toppling them over, upsetting the peaceful scene, so that when the patients finished their baths and returned to convalesce, they would find their awaited repose gone awry and a scene of chaos instead. But something egged him farther on, deeper into the compound. A glint of sun on a toolshed roof, like a conspirator's wink. A gust of wind that stirred up the pine trees. The gnawing, the burning, the dirt.

So he sidled in farther, behind the main building to where the outbuildings stood: the laundry, the icehouse, the carpenter's shop, the henhouse and smokehouse, the barn. Strangely enough there was no one about; the yard was eerily empty except for a handful of strutting bantams and some hens that pecked in the dust. Jack Connolly stood there and looked around, contemplating action. There were sacks of sawdust used to insulate ice that he could easily slash, several newly washed tea towels pinned to a line that seemed to cry out to be soiled. Then he heard a screen door open and slam and he hid behind a lilac, watching as a girl made her way across the yard, struggling with a hamper. She was young—sixteen, he would soon find out, as he'd find that her name was Addie—dressed that day in a cheap cotton print, with an apron and flounce of a cap, half heaving, half kicking the basket of laundry with the toe of a black-buttoned boot. When she reached the clothesline, she stopped and sighed and set her arms akimbo, and he watched through a scrim of pale, scented blossoms as she took a clothes-peg from her apron and gripped it in her teeth, holding it there as she opened the hamper and drew out the first sodden sheet. Then the wind picked up and a wisp of hair escaped from the hold of her topknot. The sheet billowed and snapped, an untameable thing; the cap blew off her head, skittering across the yard as light as the puff of a weed gone to seed. She looked around, flustered, buffeted by the wind, not sure if she should chase after the cap or secure the recalcitrant sheet. And he looked around too, following the wind-whipped course of the rascal cap, wondering if an act of gallantry was really what he needed, some chivalrous gesture that might blot out the taste of grit in his mouth.

But the wind died down and the moment passed. Addie returned to her work, first pinning the corner of the sheet to the line, then retrieving her cap. She wagged her finger at it as if scolding a naughty child then set it back primly on top of her head before she turned back to the hamper to tend to what was left. And watching her and the rhythm she established—hamper, clothes-peg, line—Jack Connolly found himself with the desire to be wrapped up in those sheets, to be bound and held, layer upon layer, by cotton and muslin and wool, until the dirt ran and sweat seeped from his pores and his skin was slick and clammy, ready to meet the shock of cold water, the heart-stopping, limb-numbing plunge, to be drained by submersion, purified, purged, of all fire, dank air, dark earth.

And now, as he stares at his wife in the yard, he feels that desire again, though he knows how hopeless and futile that is, how unlikely ever to happen. For whatever his wife saw in him that day as he stepped out from the lilac bush and offered to lend her a hand—whatever potential she thought he had, whatever promise or aura of power—seems to have permanently vanished. Now his timing is off, his luck nonexistent. He is saddled, compromised, drunk, forced to pull the teats of cows while his wife takes in other men's washing and his son looks down the road longingly, yearning to be the friend of a man who can't even drive his own trap.

And following the downward turn of his thoughts, his mood takes yet another slide, so that when he looks up at the fall-bedecked hills, he feels only the tidal, magnetic pull of his old friend, pessimism. It is like a blight, darkening his vision, reminding him not only of his own derelictions and ineffectiveness but also of the fact that the glory of autumn only leads to bleak winter days. He sees the trees stripped of their leafage, just skeletal shapes against sky, a landscape shorn of all life and color, reduced to stark white and dull gray. And the taste of the apple still in his mouth, the sweet fruit of his labor—instead of inspiring thoughts of rewards or the security bounty can bring, it takes him down to the dank root cellar, the cramped space dug under the house, where the apples winter over beside bins of rutabagas and the air is rank with their must, and quart jugs of cider sit on the dirt floor alongside other spirits, fermenting.

Then he thinks that nothing can save him from the dread that winter brings. No stockpile would be great enough, no cornucopia. Woodshed, larder, lock box, corncrib—even if all were full, they couldn't stave off the chill in his bones nor have the power to cut through the silence that envelops the house like thick snow. And as if to confirm these dire thoughts, make real his own premonitions, he sees a spearhead of Canada geese cutting across the sky, their wings seeming to beat a hasty farewell to a land they know can't sustain them.

The sight of the birds, with their necks craning south and their bellies a broad, easy target—plumped up most likely from kernels of corn they have pilfered from his own feed box—fills him with sudden fury, and he turns at once to Joe and barks, "I told you to go get that gun."

Joe snaps to attention and pitches his apple quickly to the ground, gulping down what he has in his mouth before he turns to run. He's been caught off guard; even Jack Connolly sees it and feels a pang of remorse.

"Never mind," he says, "they're too far gone now. No point in wasting the lead."

The boy stops in his tracks and turns back to Jack, looking up at him so confused and confounded that Jack's sense of compunction shifts back to irritation. It is not his fault that Joe is so thin-skinned, so easily shaken and flustered—even though he knows he said no such thing about him getting the gun. Still, the boy shouldn't look so nonplussed. If Joe has any chance of escaping this life, or at least making it succeed, he will have to inure himself to far more than his father's mercurial moods. It is what Jack Connolly most wishes for his son: that he handle the uncertainty, the capriciousness of things—of seasons, weather, a changing world, a new century soon to begin—all better than he has himself. Though looking at Joe, still standing by the

wagon, he fears such hopes may be futile. The boy has been so unfocused lately, idle, distant, dreamy. He does his work with only half his
mind then runs off to school, coming back to finish his chores and
wander in the woods, where he stays until it grows dark, returning
home hours later. Of course Jack Connolly is not so unfeeling that he
can't imagine the whiff of intrigue these woods might hold for a boy,
what with muskrats to track, woodchucks to flush out, black adders
to poke under rocks. Still, Joe is old enough, he thinks, to apply himself seriously, to prepare for the life that will one day be his with more
discipline and mettle. Besides, he thinks he is up to more than fash-
ioning slingshots and traps. He is up at the Kiplings', Jack would stake
his life on it, sniffing around like a dog.

Then without fully knowing why it's come to his mind, he finds
himself thinking of the tale of William Tell, a story he must have
heard as a child, as he sat by his mother's knee. Dimly he recalls it
being told as a political parable—the morality of insurgency when
enlisted in a just cause—with the apple being to the potato as the
marksman was to the Irish, each bravely trying to throw off the yoke
of their respective tyrants. Yet now it seems all too personal, and all
too close at hand: a father, a son, an old apple orchard nestled in a
mountainous land. And if Jack were challenged by an oppressor? If he
accepted the dare? If he stood with feet spread and bowstring taut,
with an arrow nocked and ready, his son before him, his arms pinned
at his side, the apple sitting in that slight indentation just beyond the
crest of his brow, that place he feared touching when Joe was a baby,
what was once the pulsing soft spot of his skull? Surely he couldn't let
that arrow fly, no matter what was at stake. His fingers tremble at the
prospect; his throat feels suddenly parched. And as if the cause were
somehow Joe, as if the fault were his, he yells again and tells him to go,

thinking it better to send him away, to dismiss him rather than fail him.

Addie too suspects that Joe has been searching out the Kiplings. Suspects and knows, because he has, indeed, told her of some of his forays. The day he returned with the first laundry money and the seat of his pants torn off he had told her of the bicycle and his wild, fateful ride, and she'd stopped what she was doing to repair the pants quickly before her husband returned, to sew on a patch as Joe tried to describe the sensation of flying on wheels.

He has been back since, with more washing to deliver and payments to collect, has entered the house and seen many things he's returned and told Addie about. She knows they have a gramophone and a parlor organ—five octaves and four sets of reeds with a row of circular stops, each labeled in high Gothic script with *Vox Humana*, *Violetta*, *Cornet*, and *Cornet Echo*, and the ones she likes to contemplate most: *Dulciana* and *Vox Jubilante*. She knows too of the several clockwork toys that adorn the mantelpiece. A monkey in a vest with brass cymbals. An elephant beating a drum. A cobra that rises up from a basket, charmed by a man with a flute. Mr. Kipling has let Joe wind them up, send them clanging and banging about. And he's let him view slides through the stereoscope—of the Klondike and the Nile—that was given to him personally by its inventor, Dr. Oliver Wendall Holmes.

"He's been kind to you then?" Addie has asked.

"Most of the time," Joe said.

"And the Missus?" she asked. "Is she kind as well?"

"I don't think she likes me," Joe said.

Addie had counseled her son to be patient, to think of Mrs. Kipling's condition. She remembers well enough her own dips in mood, all the myriad aches and pains that plagued her own days of confinement, and she tells him this, half hoping to prompt him to tell more of the famous pair. But while Joe for the most part has been more than forthcoming about the house itself, he has divulged little about the occupants. This is not, of course, that she thinks he must. He has the right to keep silent, though, like her husband, she has noted a certain strangeness in his behavior, a drift to detachment and privacy that she doesn't know how to explain and that seems to her different from the secretiveness he indulged in as a child. Then she had called him her changeling boy, claiming that he'd been switched at birth, stolen right from his cradle, her human son replaced by some elfin, enchanted, look-alike sprite. How else to account for his tendency to daydream or collect odd, useless things, like the porcupine quills she'd find under his pillow, the dried milkweed pods in his socks, the clump of red seeds from a staghorn sumac he had wrapped in a scrap of cloth from the rag bin, tying it up with a frayed piece of twine as if it were a rare present.

He seemed compelled by whim and instinct, like a crow who couldn't help but swoop down when he spied a bright bit of tin; though as he grew older, he used these things in the games he would play, acting out elaborate scenarios while she cooked or did the wash. Then the sumac seeds were wampum beads, the porcupine's quill a cutlass that he needed to use to save her from pirates or a rampaging, man-eating cougar—though they both knew as well as anyone in these parts that the last mountain lion in the whole of Vermont was shot the year Joe was born and now stands stuffed for all to see in the State House in Montpelier.

Of course, as he got older still these games were less frequent, what with his schoolwork and chores and the reticence that he seemed to grow into along with his trousers and molars. Yet never has she seen him as aloof and evasive as he's been these last few weeks, ever since the Kiplings arrived. Why, just the other day she found him in the barnyard, hunkering in the dirt with the chickens, almost eye to eye. And later at the pigsty, he hung on the gate, staring at the hogs with his eyes strained and squinting, the bridge of his nose pinched in furrows, as if he hoped to hypnotize or brand them with his glare—though the minute he saw her, he straightened up and scuffed off to the barn, thrusting his hands into his pockets, kicking loose stones with his boots.

What he was up to she didn't know and Joe didn't say, not even when she tried to ask him if something was wrong with the pigs. But she kept her eye on him for the rest of the day, as she keeps her eye on him now, peering out from behind the curtain of laundry to check on the doings in the orchard. Already she's seen Jack toss Joe an apple, seen him catch it and chomp down and smile. Seen him pitch it too, half eaten to the ground, seen him start to run then stop. And as she pins the last sheet to the line, she sees him walking back to the house with his shoulders slumped and hunched forward, pausing to turn, first once and then twice, to gaze back at his father.

What has caused all this she doesn't know—some falling out between them, she imagines, some parting of the ways. Nothing more unusual than that, though Addie can't quite bring herself to leave. She stands as if transfixed there, though she knows she should go back to the house, where she needs to clean the irons, wipe them down with kerosene, then rub them with coarse salt so there's no trace of starch or soot when the sheets are dry enough to be pressed.

But then she sees Joe emerging from the house to walk along the stone wall, so directly in the path of her sight that she cannot help but look. He has something in the palm of his hand—something knobby and brown, indistinct—and she watches as he sets it on the wall then pulls something out of his pocket, what she is sure is a strip of old calico she cut into rags yesterday. He takes the brown knobs up again and wraps them in the cloth, carefully tucking in the edges like a sheet of colored foil. Then he wedges the bundle between two loose stones, looks around once, and is gone, heading for the woods of birch trees and pine that stretch beyond the house.

Addie watches him go then turns around, convinced that she's done enough spying and snooping for one afternoon. She gathers up a few fallen clothes-pegs, hoists the hamper up to her hip, but just as quickly she sets it back down and wipes her hands on her apron. And without thinking more of what she is doing, without pondering what it might mean, she finds herself walking down to the wall, to the place where Joe has just been, almost running, in fact, with a brisk, eager trot and a quickening of her heartbeat, propelled by a mix of excitement and fear and a buzz in her head that drowns out the small voice that cautions respect and restraint.

Reaching the wall, she pulls out the cloth and sees that it is her old calico. A Sunday dress once, next demoted to housework and then cut into rags, with a few squares from the least threadbare part of the skirt saved for quilting and patchwork. She holds the scrap with its mysterious contents cupped between her hands and stops for a moment to reconsider, thinking that it is not too late to stuff it back in the wall, retrace her steps and go inside, to her own thoughts and business, not Joe's. But the fact that she'd identified the cloth—and that it was, at first, hers—seems to justify the trespass, confirm her right to pry, and she opens the folds of the calico quickly, hungry to see what she holds, only to find a pair of pinecones, nestled on a small bed of leaves.

Addie stares at the pinecones with incomprehension, as if she had never in all of her life seen such a curious thing. They are like the cones that lay by her feet, shed by a nearby hemlock, but more compact, more perfectly designed, like a rose that's been whittled out of wood. They seem to hold some message for her that she struggles to make out, a clue to the person that Joe is in the process of becoming. She stares at them, then looks at the woods where Joe has recently vanished, the border trees a brilliant blind she cannot see beyond. And she feels herself suddenly staggered by the vast otherness of her son's life, by the fact that it's so unequivocally *his*, to fashion or waste as he chooses, and the head she once held so close to her breast, to cradle and comfort and nurse, is now filled with thoughts she cannot imagine, let alone pretend to know.

She hastily folds the calico and sets it back where she found it, wiping her hands on the bib of her apron, casting her eyes to the ground. There she sees the scattering of hemlock cones strewn along the wall, some whole, some flattened by the hooves of cows or the general process of decay. And as if to prove they are really nothing— just seasonal flotsam, mere woodland debris, not some talisman or fetish—she steps on one with the heel of her boot and grinds it into the ground. Then she starts up the hill, looking over her shoulder, walking at first and then running, stung by the weight of her violation and an overwhelming regret.

*

Joe Connolly heads deep into the woods on a ridge above the farm, treading as lightly as he can through bracken and underbrush. There is no trail, only packed-down leaves he has trampled on before. A notch in a trunk he has carved with a penknife, a pyramid of small stones. He forces his eyes to attend to these markers, to focus on only what lies before him instead of what he's left behind. And with each step he takes, each marker he passes, he feels his mind emptying out, freed from his father's angry outbursts and his mother's querying eyes, from the chores that still need to be done in the barn and the questions that wait in the kitchen, until all that is left is the sound of the wind whispering in the branches, the rich scent of loam and pine pitch and rot, the panoply of bright autumn leaves.

If he thinks of his parents at all it is only of how he has managed to stump them. He knows they think he's been seeing the Kiplings, for he's heard them talking at night, his father saying that Joe shouldn't be allowed, his mother that she thinks it's all right. But although his parents' hunch is correct, they are wrong in the specifics. His route of choice is the woods, not the road, and he does not head for the cottage, preferring to see if he can find Kipling first by the building site of his new home. It's not because Joe doesn't love the house. The organ, the toys, the stereoscope, all the books and prints on the walls: it is like a marvelous treasure trove, filled with all sorts of riches. A pillbox stuffed with cardamom seeds. The tasseled hat of a Parsi. An engraving of a subaltern regiment, on camelback, in the Punjab. In fact, more than once he's slipped from his own house on the pretext of checking on the cows to hover outside Kipling's window at dusk, crouching beneath the ledge of the sill just to catch a glimpse of the organ and carpets and maybe even Kipling himself, like the time Joe saw him entertaining his wife by making shadow puppets on the wall, and the other time he spied him doing a cakewalk across the parlor floor.

And sometimes at the house he will give Joe things: a cardamom seed, a frail thread of saffron, once a pair of rose-shaped pinecones that he said came from a deodar tree, which the natives believe are godlike, *deo* being the word for God and *daru* the word for tree. And he'd shown him the whisker of a tiger that was singed by the hunter who had killed it, out of the belief that if the whiskers weren't singed, the tiger would come back to haunt him. He had let Joe hold it in his palm, let him touch the white bristle, the charred end; and while he hadn't said Joe could keep it, Joe had slipped it up his shirtsleeve, intending to return it as soon as he had a chance to inspect it more fully.

But at the house he must face Mrs. Kipling and her air of disapproval and contend, as well, with the constant lure of Mr. Kipling's desk, which can claim his attention and draw him away in the midst of a thought or a sentence. So, despite the obvious allures of the house, it's better to find him outside, where he is his most congenial, given to jokes and the telling of tales and the trading of information. In the weeks that have passed since their first encounter, this is what Joe has come to expect. He has learned to dismiss his initial suspicions and trust in Kipling's goodwill, to accept the sincerity of his apparent interest, even though such attentions still amaze him. With the exception of his mother—and, perhaps, the schoolmaster, though he asked only questions whose answers he already knew—Joe has never had anyone solicit his opinion with quite such eagerness, nor listen to what he has to say with such avidity. He seems so hungry for the very things that Joe has stored in his head, all the notions and omens and old Yankee saws that even Joe doesn't put stock in, though he's more than willing—he is flattered; he is honored—to share these scraps and bits. He's told Kipling, for instance, about the correlation between the first cricket and frost; how a cold, wet May means a barn full of hay, how rhubarb gone to seed portends death. He explained as well how some of the farmers still plant by the phase of the moon—the waning for crops like beets and potatoes that grow deep in the earth, the waxing for grains and beans and the like that bear their yield above ground—and Kipling wrote it all down in the small leather notebook he keeps in his waistcoat pocket, a remnant, he said, from his newspaper days when he learned a great lesson that he passed on to Joe in yet another rhyme about six honest serving men who taught him all he knew; their names were What and Why and When and How and Where and Who.

And when Joe described how a plucked buttercup could reveal buttery predilections when held beneath a chin, Kipling had countered with his own anecdote.

"My old Roman friend Pliny—the Elder, not the Younger," Kipling qualified as if Joe would be confused, "claimed that if a man were to eat a buttercup, he'd be stirred to fits of laughter.

"Do you think we should try it when the time comes? Do you think we'll become mad hysterics?"

Joe had seen the devilish gleam in his eyes as Kipling entertained the prospect, an arching of eyebrows and a smacking of lips that once Joe might have interpreted as a gullibility trap. Now he knows the man's penchant for mischief and fancy, hyperbole and jest, the way he can turn the simplest matters into fodder for tales or occasions. He's told Joe, for example, of the skunks in his cellar, those wily, incorrigible beasts, that are plotting—he has heard them, through the boards of the crawl space—his overthrow and demise. And he's testified to the erudite wisdom of his old horse, Marcus Aurelius, though the only evidence Joe has seen of the nag's philosophical leanings is the way he will stoically stand in the yard, hour after long hour, waiting for his master or mistress to come and unhitch him from his traces.

But best of all are the stories of boys he will sometimes tell to

Joe—of Muhammad Din and Little Toomai, who had the great fortune of seeing a herd of wild elephants dancing by moonlight. Kipling
told Joe that story just a few days ago and it filled his mind so completely that he found himself drawn outside that night, pulled by the
hoot of an owl that he thought was the call of an elephant trumpet.
He followed the sound to a grove of birch trees deep in the heart of
the forest, and there he stood, in the circle of trees, with the owl
hidden high in the branches, trying to imagine that the ghostly gleam
of the birches' white trunks was caused not by the light of the moon
shining on papery bark, but because the trees had been rubbed raw
and polished down to bare, ivory wood by the great heaving motions
and ponderous swayings of a grand pachyderm bacchanalia, a magnificent sight that he might witness too, if only he had the right luck.

His favorite of all, though, is the story of the boy he heard on that
first, fateful day—Mowgli, the boy Joe calls to mind now as he scrambles through the woods. Why this boy, in particular, compels him so
much, he doesn't fully know—though, perhaps, having been invited
to partake in his creation, Joe feels a proprietary interest, a personal
stake in what happens to him as the story unreels and unfolds. For the
past several weeks Joe has followed Kipling whenever he has let him,
trotting beside him as he surveys his land or takes what he calls his
constitutional, hoping Kipling will tell him more about that curious
child. Joe has even plied and barraged him with questions, if he
thinks that Kipling is listening, as over the weeks he has grown more
assured and comfortable in Kipling's presence.

"Could a boy really be raised by a wolf? Could he really grow up
in a cave?"

"Why, the papers in India are filled with such tales," Kipling told
him one day as they walked. "Babies suckled by bears or wild boars or

wolves. Children raised by whole families of apes. And let's not forget Romulus and Remus," he added, though Joe wasn't sure who they were.

"But what about his mother? His real mother, I mean. He had to have a mother, didn't he?"

"Well, yes, I suppose he did," Kipling answered, pausing a moment to ponder. "Certainly he had some human traits that marked him forever as different, like the capacity—or the curse, some might say—to cry when he was hurt. Of course, the first time a sob rose up from his chest, the poor boy thought he was dying, and Bagheera, the panther who had spent his early days living in a cage among men, had to inform him that the drops that spilled from his eyes were tears, such as men shed.

"But for all intents and purposes," he continued, "his wolf mother was his real mother, and I can assure you she was every bit as caring as a real mother could be. And if he ever felt an inkling of loss, of another life beckoning him, he had a whole passel of brothers he could play with—wrestle with, roughhouse with, romp. And the whole depth and breadth of the jungle to explore. Quite an Eden for a boy, I should fancy."

Joe felt all his doubts and questions give way for a brief but heady moment, as a vision of a wild, lushly green, primal place sprang up fully formed in his mind, with trees to climb and vines to swing from, deep pools to plunge into and float on, a veritable paradise made even more so by the lack of human adults.

"But could he do whatever he wanted?" he persisted on another occasion.

"Well, I wouldn't go quite that far," Kipling said. "There were things he had to learn."

"You mean he had to go to school?"

"Of a sort," Kipling responded, "though he didn't have to sit at a desk all day long and raise his arm to speak or learn to tell time by the hands of a clock or conjugate Latin verbs. No, the jungle itself was his school and his classroom, and his teacher was a bear named Baloo, who taught him practical, useful things, like how to tell a rotten branch from a sound one when you are climbing or how to warn the water snakes when you're planning to dive into their pool."

Then Kipling had told him about the Law, the set of rules and protocols that all the animals followed in order to live peaceably side by side, in relative good faith and order. He sang it, in fact, chanting a sample of right and wrong maxims in rhyme. And while Joe at first was tempted to laugh, as if it were merely a jingle, he found the urge to do so quelled by Kipling's seriousness and by something in the Law itself that seemed to speak to him—the way it so clearly, concisely spelled out both what was allowed and forbidden, laying out consequences in simple, blunt terms: "*And the beast that shall keep it may prosper / While the beast that shall break it must die.*"

Now winding his way through the brush and the trees, Joe tries to recall all that Kipling has told him about Mowgli's life in the jungle— how he must have feet that make no noise and eyes that can see in the dark—and about the other powers that belong to the man-cub alone. Only he, Kipling said, can wield the Red Flower, the animals' feared name for fire. Only he can command others with his eyes, staring down even the tiger, a feat that Joe himself has attempted on the animals in the barnyard. First standing, then squatting, he has tried looking fierce, honing his glare into a long, blade-sharp projection of power. But the cows only batted their long, doleful lashes. The pigs twitched their pink stopper snouts. And while the chickens did dart their eyes and nervously flutter about, it seemed no more than what they might do when faced with a field mouse or rabbit.

No, he thinks, they were all stupid beasts. Cud chewers, mud sloppers, fools, incapable of recognizing the true look of domination and supremacy when they saw it. But perhaps he will have better luck out here, where the animals are still wild and haven't yet had their instincts dulled by tethers and feedbags and pens. So he keeps his eyes open, his ears alert, slipping between protruding boughs to prevent the snapping of twigs, gingerly sidestepping piles of leaves to avoid any crackling crunch. And soon his stealth and care are rewarded: He hears a woodpecker still its knocking, respectfully, as he passes. A chipmunk chitters out an alarm, then makes a mad dash for its burrow. And there, downwind, in a sassafras thicket, he sees a white-tailed deer. A buck, in fact, with a great spread of antlers, pulling the last of the tender leaves from a branch with its delicate tongue.

Joe inches forward, then stops and stands still, bearing down on the deer with his eyes, and the animal, suddenly sensing his presence, raises its head and freezes. It is close enough that Joe can see the auricles of its ears quiver and a lone dusty patch of velvet on its antlers that it hasn't yet rubbed away. He sees the deer's eyes, deep pools of ink black, staring back at him, with a look of dare and prowess and threat equal to his own. Then the deer lifts up a cloven foot and stamps it to the ground, a thud that sunders the tension and stalemate of their four locked eyes. It leaps and turns half-circle in the air, then bounds away through the thicket, leaving only a ghost of its tail's underbelly hovering there like a sunspot, a dazzle of white that blinds Joe for a moment so that he's not exactly sure of what has just transpired, except that by holding his ground he thinks he may have achieved some triumph.

Then he sucks in his breath and takes off running, chasing the deer through the woods, mindless now of the noise he is making, the crackle of leaves, the snapped sticks. He runs as he's never run in his life, with all the speed he can muster, fast on the trail of some unfinished business, something crucial he must clarify. If only he can catch up to the deer and force it to stand still, square off a pace or two away, reenact their showdown. Surely something will be settled then, some status confirmed or conferred. But when the trees give way to a long and sloping, flower-strewn meadow, the deer is nowhere to be found. And Joe, out of breath, with the thump of his heart like a brass gong in his chest, must concede that he's lost the chase, if not the entire match, though looking around at the sweep of the pasture, he knows he has found something else.

This is not just a field but property. The Kiplings' property. A scant dozen acres sloping down to the road, bordered by a row of old cedars and studded with domes of gray rock. But where the last time Joe had seen wooden stakes connected by a length of string like the lines in a map of the stars, there is now a gaping rectangular hole, filled with clods of dirt, and a pair of oxen still yoked to a plow, idly chomping nearby.

Joe knows that Kipling must be close for he sees the peculiar straw hat he wears draped over the horn of an ox and he smells his tobacco—dark spice and ripe fruit—wafting in the air. Then he hears Kipling's voice calling out what's become his standard form of greeting. "Heigh ho, my friend," he cries, "up here," which prompts a complex reaction in Joe. There's the pleasure of being recognized, and the pride in being deemed "friend," though it's coupled with the nagging suspicion that Kipling's forgotten his name, despite the connection with his old, faithful horse, that veteran steed of the lancers.

Still Joe responds by scanning the ridgetop and energetically waving when he finally spots him, sitting cross-legged on a ledge of flat, protruding rock.

"Come see," Kipling says. "You must come see." And Joe scrambles up the hillside, settling down on a hillock of grass not quite at the author's feet.

"There," Kipling says, triumphantly pointing, and Joe trains his eyes down the man's straightened arm like the barrel of a shotgun, following the aim of his index finger across the river valley. There he sees the bulkhead wall of mountains that has boxed in his view his whole life, the staggered layers of piedmont hills like stage sets that can't be lifted. But what is he supposed to be looking at? What grand and noble sight? The tapestry of autumn leaves? The configuration of clouds? A great swath of shadow that slices the hills in two, as neat as a scythe?

Then Kipling drops his arm and slaps both of his hands on his knees:

Up! where the airy citadel
O'erlooks the surging landscape's swell!
'Happy,' I said, 'whose home is here!
Fair fortunes to the mountaineer.'

"That's Emerson, my boy, on the great Monadnock," he says, pointing eastward again, and Joe sets his sights this time on the uppermost hump of barren granite, the summit he knows as the most likely spot all around to be struck hard by lightning.

"An eyemark and the country's core / Inspirer, prophet, ever-more." I read those lines when I was just a lad, no older, I'd say, than you are. Down in the dungeon of the House of Desolation, an unspeakable, hateful place, where that name Monadnock seemed as bewitching to

me as Mesopotamia. Never did I think I'd actually stand in the shadow of the thing. And not just stand, but live, begads, for look here," he says, gesturing below, to the plowed-up hole. "That's where the house will rise and stand, atop a stone foundation. And here, exactly at this very height, we'll have a screened-in loggia, with all sorts of pulleys rigged up so the windows can open right up to the view."

He sweeps his arm across it all, the valley and the mountains, as if he has conjured them up in midair and now awaits applause. To Joe, though, this feat seems no more unlikely than the thought of Kipling driving the oxen and plow across the sloping field.

"Did you do it yourself? Just this afternoon?" Joe asks, his voice full of awe.

"Yes, and it dang nearly killed me. You mark my words, boy, and act as my witness: 'The Bulls of Bashan Were His Bane,' that's what I want writ on my gravestone, if I should die up here one day trying to plow the drive."

Joe looks at him. "But you're not going to die, are you?" he asks sheepishly.

"Never," Kipling says. "Or at least I hope not till I've finished the tale I just started."

"About Mowgli?" Joe asks.

"About Mowgli," he answers, with a sorrowful shake of his head. "It seems he's gotten himself mixed up with the Bandar-log, the Monkey People, a most shiftless lot, if ever there was one, in the jungle. They've promised him that he shall be their king, an idea that Mowgli rather fancies, though they have no leader, no rules, no laws; their promises don't mean a thing. And now they've gone off and kidnapped him, carrying him through the treetops. And poor Baloo, Bagheera, and Kaa, the great python whom the monkeys most fear, have gone to rescue him. I left them this morning running through the jungle as fast, I'd say, as the deer I just saw streaking through here a moment ago."

He looks at Joe then—knowingly, the boy thinks—and Joe averts his eyes, afraid that he's been caught, as well, presuming to have powers that aren't rightly his, fancying himself a king.

"But where did they take him? The monkeys, I mean."

"Yes, where did they take him?" Kipling says, drawing out from his pocket a collapsible knife, which he uses to stir up the wad of tobacco from the bowl of his pipe. "Shall we see if Monadnock can help us?"

Then he orders Joe to set his eyes right where the house will stand and he calls on Emerson again:

And think how Nature in these towers
Uplifted shall condense her powers
Rear eyes that frame cities where none be,
And hands that stablish what these see….

"Now, do you see anything yet?" he asks.

"No," Joe shakes his head. Just a sea of wavering, fawn-brown grass, dead leaves, the cedar trees. Here and there a bright burst of scarlet, the last display of joe-pye weed, along with a few dried stalks of mullein and the tall, brown husks of cattails.

"Well, let's see if I can make anything out," he says, producing a matchstick. Then he strikes the head of the match on a rock, lights the pipe, draws in, blows out. And as the smoke rises up in plumes toward the distant mountain, he tells Joe of a great ruined city, deep in the heart of the jungle, a place deserted by all but vegetation and conquered by snakes and ghosts.

"Can you see it, my boy? Right there?" he says, pointing at the construction site.

Joe lets Kipling's words worm into his head, as sinuous as jungle creepers, till it seems that he does, indeed, see it all just as Kipling's described. There are the courtyards, the spires, the domes, all overgrown with weeds. There are the crumbling battlements, covered with knotted vines. He sees the roots of banyan trees buckling stone walkways, great slabs of marble stained moss green, the fallen heads of idols. And he sees the palace, a vast, empty place, a mere ghost of its former splendor: the reflecting pools filled with dirty rainwater and nests of breeding cobras, the tracery walls all pockmarked with holes where once there had been gems—carbuncles, jasper, lapis lazuli—stones that Joe has never seen, though he senses their brilliance and color and worth right there in the words themselves.

"And that's where they're taking Mowgli?" he asks.

"Yes," Kipling gravely nods. "The Cold Lairs. A place no animal enters, except for the Bandar-log, those impudent monkeys who haven't a shred of decent respect or fear. And perhaps," he says with a wave of his hand that acknowledges the presence of the oxen, "a water buffalo who's wandered off or a pair of stray Brahmin bulls."

"But will the others go in to rescue him? Bagheera, Baloo, and Kaa?"

"I don't know, my boy," Kipling says slowly, drawing again on his pipe.

Joe thinks he has never heard in his life such an unabashed tone of uncertainty coming from a grown man, and it makes him feel strangely sad. And so they watch the smoke rise and drift up from Kipling's pipe as a lone black crow soars by on spread wings and lands on a newly plowed furrow.

"Do you think it's Chil the Kite with a message?'" Kipling asks, staring off in the distance.

"I hope so," Joe says, both wanting the story to continue and the sadness to disappear. But Joe hears a remoteness in Kipling's voice that makes that prospect doubtful, and a glance at the man just confirms it; for Joe sees the strange, abstracted look he's come to recognize, a look that means that the visit is over and it's time for Joe to go. No amount of prodding or pleading will change that. Joe has come to know that as well. So he slowly rises to his feet and begins the climb down the hillside, bracing against the steep pitch of the slope with the front of his legs and his knees, till he reaches the future site of the house, where he's struck with an idea.

"My pa knows how to set dynamite," he hollers up to Kipling. "Maybe he could help you with the drive. Help level out the grade."

"Does he?" Kipling says with a flicker of interest. "Well, perhaps you could ask him for me. I'd be ever so much obliged." Then he stares off again into the distance, absently puffing his pipe, as lost to Joe as that moldering city where a band of renegade monkeys jabber and poke at a captive boy.

THE COLD LAIRS

When the boy has gone, Kipling lingers, an Indian chief on his rock, sitting cross-legged with his hands on his knees, smoking his black briar pipe. He cocks his head and strains to hear something more than the shuddering breeze, stares off at the mountains searching for something beyond even the lordly Monadnock. His Daemon has been here, of that he is certain, leading and beckoning him. A flicker of candlelight, there, in the distance. A faint whisper guiding him through the dark.

Now, though, he fears his Daemon has gone and he is left alone, unable to summon that great, ruined city he'd envisioned just a moment ago. It's as if there is swaddling packed inside his head, thick cataracts clouding his eyes, and all he saw and heard before is now just a blur and a rumble, and the only thing he feels with any semblance of force or trace of true clarity is the nagging suspicion he can't seem to shake that the trees, the hills, the tall wavering grass, the wind that now whips up the leaves, are all conspiring to keep something from him. There are secrets being withheld.

This is, of course, the kind of thinking he is prone to late at night. But now, with the sky still holding blue and midnight still hours away, it is easy enough to remind himself of all the many felicitous things that come to those who can wait and of how very generous his Daemon can be as long as He is not forced. And he vows to himself that the next time he'll be ready with paper and a full inkpot, ready to pin down, with all the skill he can muster, whatever rare and precious gifts his Daemon sends his way.

Then he packs his spent pipe in his pocket, stretches his arms out and sighs. Behind him the sun dips below the ridgetop, throwing the field into shadow. And with its departure, the air instantly chills. The rock that he sits on grows cold. He could see this, of course, as another desertion. First muse, then sun, then warmth. But he loves the cold, the sharp bite in the air, the crisp edge to the leaves and the shadows, the knowledge that all that he sees will be covered soon by a thick blanket of snow, as it was the day he first arrived here, nearly six months ago. They had stopped to visit Caroline's family before heading off for Japan, arriving after midnight, in the thick of February, when the temperature was thirty below and each breath he took was as shocking and thrilling as a plunge into the North Sea. He had seen the snow-covered Himalayas from a distance ever since he was a child, but he'd never before experienced a winter landscape firsthand. The cold and snow were like a revelation, with a stark and unspoiled purity he'd never beheld before, and he knew right away that here was a place where he could concentrate and work, if only because it was so different from the India he'd known, where the seasons went from wet to dry and the dead never seemed to stay dead and the walls of gardens were set with old bones and vultures were as common as crows.

And now, as he gazes out at Monadnock, contemplating those differences again, he's besieged by a swarm of memories from his old Indian life. He remembers his mother's agitation and his own boyhood curiosity when a servant came to report to her that a hand, a child's hand, had been found in the garden, washed up by the rains among the lime trees and the marigolds. And he recalls with a shudder a ride he once took on old Joe through the outskirts of Lahore, when they crossed the site of an old Muslim graveyard where regiments staged parades. The rains that had pounded the city for weeks had broken just that morning, leaving the world looking fresh and renewed, purged of foulness and full of promise. Even Joe was frisky, clearly enlivened by the welcomed change in the weather, trotting across the sodden parade grounds at a brisk, rambunctious clip. But then the earth seemed to give way beneath them and he felt the animal panic as, looking down, he saw that Joe's hoof was caught in the prongs of a rib cage, the bleached bones, like the jaws of a single spring trap, what was left of a Mussulman's corpse.

Then he shakes his head as if he could literally swat all these memories away, preferring, for now, to take this landscape, this season, this brisk climate, the fields that surround him all russet and brown, the color of puddings and porridge. And when winter comes, he will take that as well: the sweep of snow like a clean white page, the pure, cold air, the silence. In that stillness, in those crystalline months when the snow lays over the roads and fields, holding the world in suspension, he will set himself down to the task of disentangling that whole tumultuous riot of muezzin cries and opium dens, of hawkers and lepers and filth. The jangle of bells and the brilliance of saris, the aroma of spice and the stench. Then whatever he chooses to bury will stay buried, deep in the frozen earth. Colors won't bleed and run into each other, sounds won't grow loud and commingle. And he can arrange and order what's left in whatever way that suits him.

But right now the rock beneath him is cold, too cold for him to sit on. So he stands and feels the stiff and sore ache of muscles unaccustomed to plowing as he sidesteps down the rocky slope to survey his recent work. The house, of course, is another dream, another thing envisioned, though one that today, by his own sweat and hands, is closer to realization. He looks at the foundation he's dug, long and narrow like a ship, and the pile of rocks he unearthed as he plowed and has saved for the local mason who is due to arrive by the end of next week to start on the house's base, a thick and solid wall of stone that he hopes will be impregnable to both nosy reporters and skunks.

In the spring a team of men will come to hammer the floor joists and rafters and the framework of studs that will hold sheets of lath to be plastered and wainscoted. How vividly he can see it all, as he steps down into the dirt, walking between the plowed-up furrows as if they were finished hallways. Here, at one end, will be his study, with an oriel window overlooking the hills that he plans to frame with a shisham screen he once salvaged from a Kashmiri houseboat. And above his study will be the nursery, where he imagines he will spend many hours, playing games and telling stories to his darling child. And here will be the parlor loggia, and above that, the home for his bath, the great boat of a tub they have already ordered, with brass claw-feet and fixtures, in which he plans to parboil himself nightly, for as long as the new well allows, having quite outgrown the spartan novelty of a basin set by the fire.

But what of those more intangible things: air, light, warmth? The spirit that fills the empty space between the floorboards and ceiling? He would like the house to feel like the Grange, that beloved home of his memory, where the entryway was a portal door that led to a realm of enchantments. But how did they manage to create that effect, Uncle Ned and Aunt Georgiana? There were the pictures everywhere by Uncle Ned and others: a gold-framed Europa and bull by Giorgione, reproductions of Mantagna, a hand-tinted print after Paolo Ucello, where horses reared up on massive hind legs all done in pale nursery colors. And, too, there were the games and stories, effortless and endless. There was Aunt Georgiana's cool, white hand opening up *The Arabian Nights.* There was Uncle Ned slipping the gift of a drawing beneath one's morning teacup—a piglet dressed as Little Bo Peep, a pug dog as a Bobby—or crawling under a hallway chair draped over with a sheet to provide the thunderous voice of the oracle in a game of pretend ancient Greeks.

It's as if it were all laid out for his pleasure, a banquet of delights. But now as he contemplates his own home and the wonders that it will hold, he finds his mind snagged on something else from those days at the Grange: the time when his Uncle Topsy, William Morris, paid a rare nursery visit; so rare, in fact, that he recalls no precedent, nor any recurrence. Morris said he had come to tell them a story—he and his cousin Margaret, who were huddled beneath a card table, feasting on brown bread and drippings—and finding no suitable place to sit, the chairs being child-size and wicker, he set his great bulk on a rocking horse, on the board that served as the saddle. Then he rocked back and forth, the poor wooden beast groaning under the weight of its rider, and told them about an old Icelandic village that had been subject to a series of strange and frightful visitations. It began one night when a shepherd noticed how the moon skipped about in his hut, its bedeviled light jumping from wall to wall, refusing to stay in one place. Then came a seal's head in a pile of dried fish, a cow's tail in a salt barrel that had the power to rip off men's flesh if anyone dared tried to pull it.

He remembers little else of the tale, no end, no resolution, though the names of the villagers have stuck in his mind: Thorolf Twist-Foot and Thorir Wood-Leg. But he can recall clearly Uncle Topsy on the horse, his head framed by a mane of wild hair and beard, his bright green melancholy eyes, and the small pool of moonlight in which the horse sat that was sliced by the rockers as he rocked back and forth, so that their moon seemed as restless and impish as the strange, possessed moon in the tale.

Now he thinks that Morris must have just found the story in the sagas he was then reading, and feeling a need to tell it himself, to hold the words in his own mouth, he had climbed up the stairs to the nursery, seeking out the young cousins. For who else, after all, could he have told it to? His wife who, probably at that moment, was draped across a lounge chair, lost in the folds of her Liberty gown and a thick haze of ennui and laudanum? Not Uncle Ned, seeking his own hazy grail, a sweet but fey courtly drama. Nor Aunt Georgiana, whom he suddenly realizes Morris must have loved and must, therefore, have not wanted to burden with all the gristly, messy thwackings of his own dark and icy obsessions.

No, it made sense that he'd come to the nursery looking for him and his cousin. Though, still, there is something troubling about it that he can't put his finger on, some unease he thinks he sensed even then when Morris abruptly rose up from the rocker and left them to finish their bread. It was as if, having discharged and dispensed with the tale—having satisfied his own teller's needs—he left the ghosts there, to run loose and rampant: the seal's head and cow's tail and pool of moonlight still quavering under the riderless horse that still eerily pitched back and forth. How different, he thinks, from Aunt Georgiana, who would rest her hands on a book's leather cover after solemnly saying, "The End," as if to press the words back to the page, secure them there, where they belonged, before she pulled the bedclothes up and swept the hair from his brow, turned down the gaslight and, closing the door, crept from the room.

Then for a brief moment his mind lights on Joe, sitting beside him so trusting and guileless, so eager to simply listen, before taking away the loose threads of a tale that have not yet been properly tied. He feels a pang then of remorse and misgiving at having put Joe to such use; though he does remind himself that the boy came to him of his own volition, wanting to hear whatever he offered, even if it wasn't finished, as much as he wanted to tell it himself, to test the tale out on a listener. Besides which, his own young, mistreated self is more compelling than a neighbor boy whom he hardly knows. So instead of Joe, he turns his thoughts once more to his childhood self, listening this time, not to Uncle Topsy, but to his Uncle Harry.

Uncle Harry was Auntie Rosa's husband and the father of her bullying son, another man who felt the need to tell stories again and again. Whenever Auntie Rosa was fuming over some wrong he'd committed—entertaining his sister with Indian tales he remembered from his ayah, assuming the tone of a little sahib, sprawling out on the sofa—Uncle Harry would offer to take him outside, for a stroll and a bit of a talk-to, saving him, thereby, from whatever reprisals Auntie Rosa might be planning to make.

And so they would walk, he and Uncle Harry, his scrawny legs scrambling to keep up with his uncle's, his small, sweaty hand in the older man's, which was wrinkled and dry and mottled with spots and scarred on one knuckle by a harpoon line he had gotten entangled with once. They walked through the streets of Southsea and Portsmouth, across the mudflats and the barren heath, to the dock-yards, the harbor, the sea. He tried to pretend it was really Bombay and he was with his ayah, out for an evening promenade or some morning marketing. But there were no palm trees, no makeshift stalls piled high with luscious fruit, no painted dhows bobbing out in the water, no Parsis performing their prayers. There was only the great rusting hulks of the ships and the mournful clang of the buoys and the breakwater wall that framed the small beach where at low tide fishmongers would spread out their catch and blue crabs would scuttle about.

But there were the stories Uncle Harry told, the same ones over again, about his stint at Navarino where he was wounded and left deaf in one ear, a fate that many of the midshipmen suffered from the thunderous roar of the guns. Uncle Harry would tell him about it as they walked, and at first he thrilled to hear it: A great sea battle against the Turks! Warships with cannons, three vessels deep across a Grecian bay! The enemy forces led by a pasha, allied with the land of the Pharaohs! But in Uncle Harry's telling it seemed as if the guns had blotted out more than the sound in the old man's ears, leaving the colors muted and drained, as gray as the hulls of the ironclads and the slabs of rotting cod on the beach. There were no stirring, soaring accounts, no tales of bravery, only an old man's bewilderment at the strange place he had found himself in and the role that he'd been asked to play.

Still, he was grateful for Uncle Harry, both then and, recalling him, now, for when he died, there was no one left to stand between

him and Auntie Rosa. Oh, Trix sometimes tried, but she was a child
in the same dependent position, and was mindful, even at her tender
age, of the need to stay in Auntie's good graces. No, he was completely,
emphatically, alone. Alone, just as he is now, and for a brief but terri-
fying instant it's as if he is there, in that basement again, with his eyesight fuzzy, his cheeks grimy from tears, his rump a hot coal from a
lashing, and a bristol-board placard tied around his neck, inscribed
with the damning word, LIAR. Then hell, the place Auntie Rosa assured
him he was ultimately destined for, was far more real and potent a
thought than his memories of Bombay, and Mount Monadnock were
just two words he had stumbled across in a book, something to dream
of and make a wish on, a faint star beyond all human reach.

But, of course, all that is balderdash. The plowing must have
addled his brain. For here he is, in the great mountain's shadow, on
his own plot of deeded land, where everything he has ever wanted is
within the grasp of his hands.

Still, he thinks it is time he should go, lest Carrie start to fret,
something she's been doing much of lately, worry seeming to stretch
out her belly as much as the child in her womb. So he steps from the
hole that will soon house his basement, vowing to himself that no
child of his will ever find its way down there except to play hide and
seek. Then he walks to the oxen. One is bent to the grass, picking over
the stiff, browning blades, while the other has discovered, to his
horror, the loose strands of straw from his hat.

"Cease and desist, or I'll give you a *put-put*," he shouts and tries
to look menacing. But the ox, ignorant or oblivious to Hindi, keeps
on grinding its jaw, stretching its slick, fat, pink bovine tongue out for
another loose straw. He holds his ground and snatches the hat, firmly
setting it back on his head, then uncouples the plow from the yoke's

curving crossbar and urges the pair down the hillside.

This is a task that requires all of his powers of persuasion. He prods them and pulls them and begs and implores, even offers back the newly won hat. And when he finally manages to get the two of them down to the road, he heaves a sigh of relief and laughs. Never let it be said that Kipling failed to take the bull by the horns, he says right out loud, to the trees and a jay that has watched the whole proceeding. Then he slaps the two beasts on the ridge of their rumps—the threatened *put-put* now delivered—and together they start ambling down the road, the oxen pulled by the nearness of home and the prospect of a stall with fresh hay, he by the thought of the newsman from Boston who had walked this same stretch last week, out hunting a story and interview, which Kipling had flatly refused. The man hoped Kipling would be receptive, having been a reporter once himself, but Kipling sent him packing back to town, without even a moment to rest, hurtling barbs and insults at him, calling him a yellow journalist. And the newsman repaid him for this churlish rudeness by writing a small but mean-spirited piece that claimed Kipling's neighbors all thought he was strange—that he wore shabby clothes, never carried any money, and was often heard saying "Begad."

What would he say, Kipling wonders, if that newsman saw him now: the world-famous author out for a stroll with a pair of ornery bullocks, his boots covered with mud and his waistcoat flung open, his neckerchief stained with his sweat, and with one of the beasts looking dashing and rakish with his straw hat draped over one eye?

As odd and improbable a threesome, he thinks, as that other trio: the panther, the python, the bear, whom his mind turns to for the first time since the boy has gone. He feels a great, sudden rush of fondness for this strange menagerie: the sleek and solemn, magisterial cat; the sinuous, sibilant snake; the humble, old, avuncular bear with his threats and affectionate cuffs, part buffoon, part jungle sadhu, keeper of the old jungle ways. He would like to be like the bear, himself, and he will, he imagines, when winter comes and he dons his buffalo robes: a dispenser of wisdom, a mentor of sorts, with his tales and tricks and shaggy coat—reporters, all be damned!—Uncle Ned, Uncle Topsy, Uncle Harry, and Baloo, all mixed up and rolled into one. Still, he feels troubled by Joe's final question: will the animals rescue their ward? Not the matter of if as much as of how: how will they manage to do it? For it suddenly seems that even Baloo, with his faithful fixation on the jungle code and his periodic antics, does not possess the strength or skill to offer more than a reprieve, just as even a small part of him must concede that the ursine role he imagines assuming—the jovial escort, the kind guardian—cannot satisfy all his needs.

But he lets his mind drift as he has learned to do, over the scene before him, the towering bear and the black slinking cat, the great python slithering forward. And he waits. He waits most patiently to see what he hasn't yet seen. And soon his patience is rewarded: Kaa, the snake, rises up in his mind like the bones in those long-ago gardens, washed up by a force as great as the rains, a churning, chimerical process. In his mind's eye, the snake rises up higher from the tight wrap of his coils, now swaying and weaving great mind-numbing loops, while the audience before him, the hoard of shrill monkeys, grows silent and still, enthralled.

The Dance of the Hunger of Kaa, he will call it. A mesmerizing performance, one that he hopes he can match with his own pyrotechnic display. For he feels a sudden voraciousness clawing deep inside him, a desire to stun and abash and astound all who have ever failed him or wronged him, to hold them all in his thrall. But deep as that desire is, he backs away from it quickly. He has so much already, he thinks. He must not ask for more, nor look beyond what's already been given: the benevolent presence of his guardian mountain, a vision of his new story's ending.

Acceptance, he thinks, that great lesson from the East. Acceptance and surrender. As good a creed as any he can think of, and one that conveniently manages to skirt any murkier, internal reaches.

But still some vestige of hunger remains. His stomach growls and rumbles, and he realizes that he's had nothing to eat since his tea and toast that morning. So he rummages around in the pockets of his greatcoat for the piece of fruit he remembers taking from the kitchen sideboard, and extracts a pear, only slightly bruised from its long confinement. He takes a whopping, greedy bite and pauses to savor the taste: the pale green skin, with a touch of resistance, like a strip of tender bark; the sweet, grainy flesh now dripping with juice that anoints his chin and fingers. And he thinks of something else Emerson wrote that he stumbled on years ago, that there are but ten minutes in the life of a pear when it is perfect to eat. Surely, he thinks, those minutes are these; surely this is perfection: the fresh, ripe pear and the rustle of leaves, the sky slowly bedding down to dusk, the satisfying ache in his muscles and joints from a day filled with honest, hard work. And again the poem that had been his companion through all those long, bleak years, when all that he loved had vanished from him and he found himself alone, rings in his mind like a prophesy that is finally being fulfilled: "*Take the bounty of thy birth / Taste the lordship of the earth.*"

But what of Joe, off in the woods, wending his way back home? Joe Connolly, whose birthright consists of little more than a tendency to be discontent and a vague inclination to yearn. Joe wanders back the way he came, past the sassafras thicket, the mound of small stones, the notch that he carved in a tree, barely visible now in the dying light that has turned the whole wood pearly gray. But he pays little notice to these signposts this time. His mind is somewhere else, in a tangle of creepers and coconut trees, wild beasts and ancient ruins, where a boy sits atop a crumbling throne, awaiting his promised investiture.

What will happen to him? Joe is burning to know, curiosity driving him forward, as if, just ahead, the tale might be unfolding. A clash of claws and fur and fangs, slick scales and deadly venom. Pursuit and deliverance, release and reunion. Scores settled and usurpers dethroned, all of which Joe imagines he might even partake in, if only he can catch up.

So he latches onto those handful of things that he can bend to this notion. A quick glimpse of river; the dull, plodding Connecticut transformed to the mighty Waingunga. A clump of ferns, like primordial fans, growing there, by the base of the hardwoods. The moon that suddenly appears straight ahead, fantastically orange and round. It is a harvest moon, that rare thing, child of the autumnal equinox and a northern latitude, seen at its best on a bracing night against a cloudless sky. But look how easily Joe turns it around and fits it to his own purpose: instead of the moon he has known all his life as a harbinger of frost, he sees a globe of tropical fruit, dangling in front of his eyes, so tempting and luscious it makes his mouth water, makes his arm automatically rise, as if he could somehow reach out and pluck it, pull it right down from the sky.

And once one arm is up, how easy it is to raise the other, to swim through the woods as if he were swinging through the branches of canopy trees and to hear the screech of the evening's first owl as the screech of a scurrilous monkey. He pretends he is flying from branch to branch, careening through the forest. And once that mind-bending feat is accomplished, once he's cast himself in the trees, how long does it take—one step, maybe two?—before he is not one of several pursuing but the one being pursued, the boy in the center, at the heart of the tale, not some minor player, let alone just a figure off at the margins, patiently, passively, listening?

He reaches out, his fingers splayed then closed tight in a fist, as if around a twist of rope he is holding onto for his life. Then the other arm swings. More air is grabbed, held fast and then released: a rhythm established, a gamboling dance, performed for an audience of trees. And he cries his trail just as old Baloo, the jungle's faithful warden, has instructed.

"I head toward the moon," he shouts, "to the place where it has risen. The vines are thick, the way is fast, my feet leave no mark in the dirt." And though he notes no animal presence, no signs of lurking beasts, he adds the call, "Good hunting all," as a last, deferential precaution.

Leaping and skipping, he bounds through the woods, a true child of the forest, till he comes to the spot where the trees open up onto a patch of new growth. There, beyond the line of scrub, Joe sees the slanting shape of a roof and a chimney spewing out smoke. It is his home, the worn clapboard house, the dilapidated barn, where his father right at that very moment is ushering in the cows, expecting his son to be waiting there for him, with pail and stool in hand.

What goes through his mind as he looks at the farm; what torn, conflicted thoughts? Does he think of his father and the certain annoyance that is bound to course through his blood when he sees that there are no lanterns lit, no bales of fresh hay in the stalls, and the cows, all accustomed to the speed of four hands, start to bellow at him with impatience? Or his mother? Does he think of her, there, by the stove that spawns the chimney smoke, pausing to smell the rich scent of apples she has set in the oven to bake, knowing, as well as her husband does, what the orchard harvest augurs—a change in their fortunes, an easement of worry, a small, long-awaited reward?

She has fixed the apples in celebration and has high expectations for them, one of which has already been met to her satisfaction. The peeling, the coring, the stuffing with cloves and cinnamon and sweet butter, have helped her to dismiss that moment earlier when a pair of pinecones made her feel that her son had slipped out of her reach, that he'd gone someplace where she couldn't follow, and where she didn't belong. The apples will bring him back, she thinks, draw him to the table where she hopes they will linger long after supper, basking in the warmth of the stove and the success of the harvest. Then she'll bring out a steaming pot of coffee and the mail-order catalogs she has stashed by the kindling box just for the occasion, in the hopes that they will gather 'round, united and bound together, to flip through the pages, assessing the gadgets and gewgaws they now might afford: harmonized sleigh bells for the horse's work collar, a new set of graniteware bowls, red woolen Jaegers for her husband and Joe, for herself a trim-finishing iron. They'll marvel, with none of the bitter envy they all have felt before, at those things—the Victrolas and zinc-lined iceboxes—that still lie past their reach. And they'll laugh together at the dubious claims of the balms and elixirs and tonics, believing that at last they may have found their own fount of prosperity and health.

Of course, though, what she doesn't know is that in the barn her husband's mood has already made these hopes moot, and that Joe, from his perch straddling the low ridge, has other plans in mind.

He stares at the spiraling plume of smoke, like a shard of a dream, half remembered. He watches as a lantern flares up in the house and another is lit in the barn. And he feels a sudden rush of confusion, a flash flood of discomfort and doubt that leaves him unsure of just what, exactly, it is he truly wants, as below him the lights sputter then flicker then steadily blaze and glow, and the woods behind him grow dark and remote. The wind keens through the trees, a low cackle.

He stands there, teetering, wavering, staring, waiting for something to happen. A waft of woodsmoke reaches his nostrils. A bat blunders out of the trees. He hears his stomach gurgle and churn, a hollow, most pitiful sound. Below, he knows, there is supper waiting, a warm fire, the comfort of bed; but also there are questions that will need to be answered, misdeeds to right and account for. While behind him is—what? Only indifferent trees and the company of nocturnal creatures? A place that can offer no more than the solace of darkness and the comfort of camouflage?

Then he stamps his foot as the deer had done and vehemently shakes his head no. No, he'll not be fooled by a trick of light or a screen of stovepipe smoke. He'll not be driven by hunger or fear or a simple desire for warmth. No, everything is different now. Everything has changed. Now he has no father with dark moods to decipher, no mother to disappoint, no silences thick with old grudges and resentments to muck about in and forge through. No, now there is only a strict code of ethics and laws he must obey: He must speak to each creature in its own tongue. He must hunt just for food, not for pleasure. He must not seek to plunder without cause or need. He must drink deep, but never too deeply. And if he follows these rules, he will prosper; a simple cause and effect. He will gain the favor of the jungle, garner respect, be revered, earn the right to cross whatever domains and lands he wants to explore.

So he turns and heads back into the woods, leaving the house behind. The wind bites his cheek, a whiplash of cold air. His ears start to sting, his hands tingle. But he feels himself warmed by the heat of his vision and the force of his resolve, by the lush, steamy place he holds in his mind and imposes again on the landscape, and by something else newly stoked inside him: a hot, fueling flame-lick of scorn.

Scorn. He feels scorn for all those who imagine they need things that he now vows to renounce: the insulation of papered walls and feathered ticks and pillows, the support of beams and upholstered chairs, banisters, bedposts, lintels. Such things are only trappings, he knows, made to bind and tie. Like apron strings, and guilt and duty, and the snarled, looping tangles of history. But he is free. He has cut himself loose from hearth, home, blood. He has cast himself off, a foundling child alone in the darkening woods, needing nothing more than a cave for shelter, a stream to quench his thirst, a tree or a bush bearing nuts or tart berries, his wits and his strength and his speed.

For what has he ever managed to gain by relying on anything else? What advantage has anyone reaped, he thinks as he comes to a burned-out clearing where the crumbling remains of a chimney stack stand, a testament, surely, to the fate of constructions built on misguided, misinformed faith.

Then he cuts across the clearing and ducks back into a bower of pines, keeping abreast of the river that winks every few yards or so through the trees. Nearby, he knows from his other life, the one he has now left behind, is the schoolhouse where he has sat at a desk, doing sums and recitations, storing lessons and numbers and facts in his head like rubble in an old attic. Now he feels only scorn for all that as well. For figuring, rhetoric, books. For his classmates who sit there as docile as cows—stoop-shouldered, dull-witted, dumb. He had tried to show them the pinecones and whisker he'd gotten from Kipling's house, tried to tell them how in India, certain trees were worshipped and dead tigers could come back as ghosts; but they'd all just looked at him skeptically, with barely any interest, till one of the boys had grabbed the whisker and claimed it was nothing but a bird's quill, snapping it in half to show how common and insignificant it was. Then one of the girls grabbed the pinecones as well and tossed them to the ground, so he had to scramble down on his knees as the children walked away, laughing, trying to gather the pinecones up and collect the halves of the whisker, which he knew with a sudden pang of guilt, he could never return to Kipling.

But from this moment on, he is done with all that, he thinks as he weaves through the trees. From this moment on he will teach himself whatever he needs to know, learning from experience—from his own, not from others'—what it is that should be done. And he'll have great adventures, grand, glorious ones, of which this is only the start, this trek through the forest, this moon-dappled quest for a ruinous, lost, fabled city.

And as if in reward for these plans and resolves, Joe sees a smattering of lights in the distance, shimmering between the near bank of the river and a spill of low-lying hills, pulsating like the bodies of glowworms deep in the jungle at night.

Such a thrill he feels, such a sense of attainment, seeing the lights all spread out below him, quite fabulous and quite real, that he forgets for a moment the jungle's injunction against hunting for pleasure or pride. And believing himself a free, unfettered agent with no ties to kin or past, he easily overlooks the fact that he's done nothing more than repeat the same journey his father made twelve years before.

For there is Brattleboro spread out before him, the town he knows so well, where horses stand at hitching posts while goods are sold and bartered and farmers gather at Brooks Hotel to discuss the price of grain while they chew on spicy nails of clove to mask the scent of whiskey on their breath. But it's also the site of other transactions, more mysterious and metamorphic, where a boy once pinned an ethereal sprite to earth in a hunk of hewn ice and a man's writing hand was possessed by another, his pen piloted by a ghost.

It's this view of town Joe chooses to see as he stares at the pulsing lights. Their strange, eerie glow seems to suggest that transformation is possible, that he might, indeed, be harboring within him the essence and spirit of Mowgli—though in the version he's already amended and is living out right now, he, the hero, the wily wolf-child, has not been tricked by flattery or abducted by quarrelsome apes, but is off on a quest of epic proportions, a discovery of treasures untold.

And might not those lights be the treasure he's after? Might it not be the Cold Lairs? For an instant Joe considers the thought only to discard it, not yet so bedazzled or immersed in this dream that he fails to see it can't bear the weight or intrusion of people and drays. So he keeps to the woods, to the shelter of trees that rim the far reaches of town, hunkering down through rows of corn stubble when the trees give way to fields. There are small farms here, set close together, with tidy, manicured yards. The occasional house built of brick, not of wood, iron fences instead of stone walls. Dimly he sees lanterns burning on sills and from stanchion hooks inside barns, small pools of light punctuating the darkness with a promise of comfort and warmth. But he turns his back on these beacons as well, without a second thought. He is after something stranger and rarer, a more unusual prize. And though he's uncertain as to what that might be, he is sure he'll know when he finds it. And he does, when he spies something glinting in the woods, a glimmer of moonlight on metal.

Joe pushes past the boughs of pines to see what he's discovered. The trees are thick here, casting dark shadows. The moon bright but only so strong. He spies his quarry, then loses it promptly as a bank of clouds drifts by. He catches its flicker, blinking teasingly again, sees it vanish and once more reappear. But by now he is actually close enough to discern what it is he's found. It's a section of some kind of flume, a conduit or channel, holding a trace of stagnant rainwater and decomposing leaves, raised up off the ground on a low wooden trestle that zigzags off through the trees.

Joe stares at his find and feels the word *aqueduct* rise up to his lips with amazement. "Aqueduct," he whispers and the word flies away, disbelievingly into the night.

Then he is off again, sweeping away branches, following the downhill course of this wondrous, most miraculous thing, an edifice, surely, from the civilization whose ruins he has sought and now found. It winds through the woods, twisting this way and that, its path littered with leaves and pine needles and obstructed in places by branches and trunks felled by lightning or snow or decay. Overhead the moon assists by burning a bright white aureole of light. The hill levels out. The trees open up, giving way to a small clearing. There he sees a circle of tall wooden huts, as strange as a druid's ring, each connected to the other by a spoke of branching pipe fitted at the end with a spigot, and set around a pool lined with dull, colored tiles that peek out through a mat of dead leaves.

Joe tries to peer into one of the huts only to be repelled by the dark and the noxious odor of mold. Then he hops down into the pool and starts to kick the leaves away. A centipede rushes out, looking for cover; a spider scurries away. Muddy scum from the leaves' underbellies streaks the tiles with smears of phlegmy green. Still, Joe sees a pattern emerging. A scalloped curve of blues and greens extends out from under his feet. There are specks of black rimmed around with white, like the dots in a Morse code message. He digs down into one of his back pockets and retrieves something from his old life. A thin scrap of calico, twin to the one he had earlier in the day, and which he now uses as was intended, as a rag to wipe dirt away.

Down on his knees, he scrubs and scrubs in a pool of moonlight, till the pattern emerges and he sees it quite clearly: a wreath of dolphins, bottlenose to forked fluke, leaping over a rickrack of waves, the arc of each back interrupted and echoed by the lesser arc of each dorsal fin.

Joe sits back on his heels and wipes his hands on the dirtied rag, feeling, as he does, something tug at his heart, the faint strain of a memory that begs to be heard but is drowned by his growing excitement. Rubbed cleaned and burnished, the tiles glimmer and gleam, the colors of tropical seas. The dolphins stare out with their tesserae eyes, a hint of a smile on their beaks. And here he is, at the center of things, at the fixed point of concentric circles: the bright ring of dolphins; the round lip of the pool; the circle of dark, wooden huts. But what lies beyond? What other strange treasures and sights might be orbiting around him? So eager is he to know and discover that he drops the rag to the floor of the pool and rushes back to the flume. He will follow it back to its source like a river, uncover its fountainhead, along with whatever secrets and riches he finds along the way. And with each step he takes, each log he leaps over, he plunges further into this dream, the darkness conspiring with his desire to black out all thoughts and memories that might destroy the spell and to make whatever he does see and hear a scaffold for his dreaming.

For look: there is Mang the Bat overhead. Listen well: there is Tabaqui the Jackal, yapping and snarling away in the distance, in all likelihood up to trouble. And here he is, navigating past boughs of what could be deodar trees. His feet make not even a whisper of noise. His eyes bore right through the dark. Though he cannot help but let out a gasp when he pushes past a last copse of trees and sees a great, deserted building, all locked and boarded up, encircled by a wide, pillared veranda and crowned by a cupola dome.

It is not the marble, moss-covered palace he'd envisioned hours ago, but seeing the clapboards glowing white in the moonlight and the tall shafts of columns, it will do. Slowly he approaches, climbing up a low knoll appropriately choked with weeds. Slowly he mounts the veranda steps, the boards creaking and groaning beneath him. There are chains that hang from hooks in the ceiling, like knotted, metal creepers. The door is nailed shut with thick, rotting planks. Shutters dangle, cockeyed, from their hinges. Joe dodges past the twists of chain and tries to peer in through the gaps in the boards that are nailed across the windows, but the glass beyond is so coated with grime he cannot see a thing. Then he reaches back for the rag in his pocket and feels once again that faint tug, a reminder, no doubt, that he foolishly left a still-useful provision behind.

Joe shrugs it off as nothing more than a minor inconvenience, though the feeling stays as he walks around the porch, growing more insistent, a nagging suspicion that he has forgotten more than a worn scrap of tattered cloth. But then he spies a sight that makes him forget the whole bothersome feeling. The boards of a window have been somehow pried open by another, earlier explorer, exposing a pane of shattered glass, still in place but veined with cracks. And on the floor sits a stub of tallow, milk-white with a charred black wick, its shaft slightly ridged and grooved by the hand that must have held it before.

Joe picks up the candle and sets his own fingers into the molded impression, pausing to consider what fear or compunction might have halted his predecessor. He envisions a threatening gun-toting groundskeeper, a teeth-bearing watchdog, a ghost, though nothing is quite so appealing to him as the thought that whoever jimmied the boards and tossed the candle there might have been doing no more than preparing and paving the way for him. For surely the candle has been left there for him. Surely he is meant to enter. But how will he manage to light it, he wonders. What would the real Mowgli do? Steal the live embers from a village bonfire? Wait for lightning to strike? Joe turns his gaze skyward, thinking it conceivable that the urgent depth of his kindling needs could, in fact, manufacture a storm. But the sky above him is a dark, blank slate, unsmudged by thunder clouds. The moon is ablaze but too far away to give off any igniting sparks. So he turns his attention to his pockets instead, pulling out a buckeye, an acorn, some lint, a tangle of horsehair and straw, and yes, at the bottom, a small chip of quartz, just the right size and shape for a flint.

Joe sets the bundle of horsehair and straw beside a fallen chain link, then strikes the flint against the chain, again and again and again, till he spies a tendril of smoke rising up and smells the harsh scent of singed hair. He plunges the candlewick into the pyre and draws out a teardrop of flame, feeling so clever and self-reliant, just like a true jungle boy—though he must, of course, sidestep the fact that a true jungle boy wouldn't know about flints, let alone possess candles or pockets. Then he takes the candle back to the window and presses his hand to the pane. Bits and shards of glass fall away, a brief and sudden shower, landing so softly, like wood chips or ash, that it takes him a moment—till he lifts up the candle and spies dots of blood on the tallow—to realize he's cut his hand. His palm is riddled with gashes.

Joe winces more at the sight than the feel and wishes he had a bandage. For the first time since he stood on the ridge, looking down at the farm, he pauses and wonders if he should continue. Perhaps he should simply content himself with what he's already found. Perhaps he should wait until daybreak and let the sun clarify things. But here is the opening. Here is the light. Here is his foot on the ledge, hoisting him up and over the sill, now rimmed with jagged glass, his injured hand curled and held fast to his chest, like a wounded, crippled paw.

Then he lands inside, the feat accomplished, another threshold crossed. And again he finds himself in the center, in a circle of candle-light. The flickering flame casts shadows above him, like refractions of light in a grotto. A reef of mouse droppings lies scattered by his feet, as black as the darkness that presses and crowds around the pool of light. Then he thrusts the candle out at arm's length to beat the dark-ness back. He takes a step farther into the room, sweeping the flame back and forth. He can make out the boundaries of the space now, see the peeling, stained wallpaper, and in the corners great lumpen shapes, like ogres crouched in caves—just boxes, really, in the process of collapsing from the weight of their loads and the damp, and a barrel or two whose staves have sprung loose from the rusting hold of their hoops.

Joe inches closer, holding the candle up to peer into a box. And what does he see, astoundingly enough, but the very thing he had wished for? A stack of linens, a bit yellowed and mildewed, but serviceable nonetheless, some already torn and hemmed into strips, just right for his injured hand. He sets the candle on the floor and starts to wrap up his hand, knotting the ends of the bandage by holding and pulling one length with his teeth. He marvels again at what surely must be the mysterious workings of providence, a benevolent force, like some storybook magic, that grants all he desires. But instead of feeling cheered and emboldened, safe in the hands of this power, he feels that troubling tug again, too persistent now to be ignored.

It follows him as he heads down the hallway that leads out from that first room. It accompanies him as he peers into doorways opening onto new chambers. In each room there are objects; broken, abandoned, some known to him, others quite foreign: an upside-down gurney, robbed of its casters; glass beakers; enameled chipped bowls. Lances, syringes, dusty vials filled with powder, bootjacks, a galvanic ring. There's a music stand guarding a room like a scarecrow, notched cribbage boards empty of pegs, a quiver of cue sticks and a stack of tin cups, all numbered, to play bagatelle. Joe stares at it all, at the scalpels and gameboards whose markings seem as arcane and strange as a book of spells covered with runes, trying hard to imagine these are the ancient remains he has been seeking. But by now he can't manage to shake that feeling, mushrooming like a regret, that there is another name for it all that he has forgotten, one that has nothing to do with royal ruins and cities lost in thick jungles.

Then the hallway ends, and he comes to the room that adjoins the nailed front door. The floorboards here have started to rot, leaving gaps and holes between planks. A chandelier hangs, a scaffold for cobwebs, from a fraying bit of cord. Joe carefully crosses the rickety floor to what seems like a table or desk. It sits beneath a shroud of gray sheet in whose folds he spies a small brass bell covered with a layer of dust. Joe sets the candle down again and lifts the bell up from its nest, his bandaged hand hovering over the striker, trembling in the air. He tries to imagine the sound of the ring, echoing down the hallways. He tries to imagine whom it might summon—a monkey, a panther, a bear? Instead what he hears is his mother's voice, telling him all her old stories. The young, crippled man in his carry-chair. The lame woman who miraculously walked. The registry book with its proud list of names, the signatures scored with a flourish.

For, of course, this is the old Water-Cure. He has known it all along. Known but forgotten, known but denied, known but refused to be bound by it. Now, though, he feels the weight of that knowledge shackled to him like a stone. He feels the whole artifice of the evening's adventure come toppling down around him. He feels oh so hobbled, so burdened and foolish, the last most strikingly of all. How foolish to imagine he was the pivot around which all things revolved. How foolish to think that he was heading forward, toward some triumphant conclusion, when in fact all he's done is wind his way back to another story's beginnings, one that leads only to dashed hopes and hardship, dull compromise and sharp regret.

Then he feels all the other debilitating things he has kept at bay until now: the gnawing of hunger; the chill in his bones; the bushwhacking sweep of fatigue; his poor, mangled hand, which, under its dressing, now starts to sting and throb. And he takes a step backward, grimly believing it is the only way he can go, though even here, as he promptly discovers, there is room for delusion and error. For his foot comes down on one of the planks that has succumbed to dry rot. The wood gives way, crumbling beneath him, nothing more than powdery pulp. His ankle twists, and he hears something snap. His whole leg collapses beneath him. Then he is down, that unforeseen direction, down and in pain on the floor, howling the wolf-cry he'd forgotten to make when he first saw the moon's glowing orb. And just before the pain grows too great and his thoughts are drowned out by his howls, his mind latches onto the bleak irony that of all the things he's imagined today and tried to call into being—all the landscapes and roles he has thrown himself into, all the dreams he had sought to give shape to—it is only the feeling of being bowled over and broken that has become real.

LAIR-RIGHT IS THE RIGHT OF THE MOTHER

Caroline Kipling sits at her desk, looking over the ledgers. The household accounts, the business accounts, her log of correspondence. There are bills to pay, to the milliner, the mason. There are checks to send off for deposit—from Heinemann's in London, and Mrs. Mary Mapes Dodge of *St. Nicholas Magazine*, New York—though first she dips her pen in the ink and records each one's amount, entering the figures in the long credit column of her book with a few sure strokes. Then she writes the date of receipt in her log of payments due and pending, ticking off each publisher's name with a check and a sigh of satisfaction.

How pleased she is with her husband's success, how proud and vindicated. Surely all those who questioned her marriage to a man whose income depended solely on the output of his pen—a man from nowhere, as James Barrie dubbed him, without property or private means, let alone an ancestral home—must now all concede her good judgment. And those who clucked and wagged their tongues when they returned from Japan, their honeymoon aborted when Rudyard's bank failed, leaving them, at least for a while, with little more than their unused steamship tickets—even they must be holding those very same tongues in envious, penitent silence.

Of course, they might not have been able to manage without the help of her family, particularly her grandmother who still lived in town and arranged for both the lease on the cottage and the down payment for their land. But by the time they returned to Vermont, their fortunes had begun to change. Rudyard's latest book of verse had gone into its third printing. His novel, *The Naulahka*, which he wrote with her brother, was doing surprisingly well—despite the fact that Wolcott had accidentally misspelled the word. And now look, she thinks, as she scans her ledger: the entries show a steady stream of royalty checks and payments. Her letter box is full of requests for reprints and serial rights. And here, right here, in a drawer of her desk, tied up with a slip of red ribbon, is a note from her husband's friend William Henley, expressing his sorrow at Tennyson's death and hinting that in certain high circles to which he has been privy her husband's name has been bandied about as Lord Alfred's laureate successor.

But for now they are still in this house, with its leaks and drafts and skunks, and with only one servant, a meek Swedish girl, newly landed, who barely speaks English. There she is in the vestibule, lugging a bucket of water to scrub down the grates, a task she has been told more than once not to do while Caroline's husband is working. Caroline taps her pen on the desk to get the girl's attention, then firmly mouths the words "Not now" when the girl looks up. "Sorry, ma'am," the girl mumbles, bobbing her head and making a small, nervous curtsy, which causes the water in the bucket to slosh and spill onto the floor. Then Caroline furrows her brow and glares. The girl drops to her knees and starts mopping, while Caroline's glare gives way to a sigh—most assuredly not of satisfaction—as she tallies up all the things she must do just to maintain some veneer of civility in these uncivilized woods.

At least, though, this new girl is more willing and able than the last one they had, a girl from town who flatly refused to wear a starched servant's cap and could never seem to get straight in her mind the difference between a butter knife and the one for deboning fish. After three weeks she vanished, without giving notice and leaving her trunk behind, claiming the silence and solitude were slowly driving her mad—a fact that Caroline's husband found amusing, those two things being the very features he loved most about the place.

As for the rest, the leaks and the drafts, he takes it on as child's play. He is like a boy building a treehouse, all enterprise and gumption, rigging up various improvisations without much thought to exigencies like ventilation or drainage. Just the other day, for instance, she found him outside piling spruce boughs he'd chopped down himself around the sills for insulation and nailing a notice to the cellar trapdoor, threatening the skunks with swift legal action if they did not cease to trespass. And he's gotten the notion stuck in his head that the baby should sleep in a trunk tray.

"After all, he's a Long Trail child," Rudyard said by way of explanation, referring to the fact that the child was conceived on their foreign travels and so his first bed should rightly reflect his roving, nomadic beginnings.

"After all," she concurred, with a smile of indulgence, willing to humor him, for she knows full well that in the new house there will be both a day and night nursery, a charming brass crib that she's already ordered, lace curtains with a pattern of ducks.

Caroline closes her ledger book and sets it back in the drawer, then she steals a glimpse of her husband at his desk and sees him absorbed in his work. At least he has not been disturbed, she thinks; at least she has managed that much. And despite her annoyance with the girl and the bucket, she smiles as she did with the trunk tray, as she watches Rudyard tap his finger on his desk to drum out the beat of a rhyme, then set his pen once more to the block to scribble another line. She knows that he dreams of the Long Trail himself, of leading a gypsy life—of sailing away to the South Seas like his great idol, Robert Louis Stevenson. But she also knows that he's never worked so well or productively before, grounded here on her home soil, in the sanctuary she's fashioned, where she shields him from curiosity seekers, inept servants, and neighbor boys. He's confided as much to her already—that he hasn't felt such vigor and strength, such firm belief in his own powers, since he first arrived in London, ready to conquer the world with a few brief letters of introduction and a stash of Indian tales. Not even when he wrote *The Naulahka* with Wolcott, a fact that made her willing to grant his desire to thus name their house, in memory of a collaboration in which she played no part.

Besides, this Naulakha will be different than that; she is quite certain of it. Her stamp will be there, throughout the house, in every nook and corner, from the hanging of the nursery drapes to the setting of tableware. Yet somehow that passing thought of her brother has given birth to a doubt, and she steals another quick glance at her husband, as if for reassurance. He has planted his elbow on the leather-rimmed blotter and now rests his chin in his hand, staring out past the window and the pile of spruce boughs to a land of his own invention. But seeing him there, so engrossed in that world, she only doubts herself more. And she finds herself drawn against her will to the time she first saw him that way, long before the prospect of marriage had occurred to either of them.

He was living on Villiers Street, off the Strand, just a block from Charing Cross Station. A third-floor walk-up above a banger shop and across from a music hall. She had planned to meet her brother there; they were due, all three, to have lunch, a celebratory meal to toast the men's new writing alliance. Yet as she climbed up the narrow stairs, she found herself disconcerted. The air was thick with smoke from the shop and the smell of greasy sausage, her thoughts drowned out by the rumble of trains and the flatulent blasts of a tuba that bellowed out from the music hall stage.

Then she came to the landing. On the door was a notice: "To Publishers: A classic while you wait!" What did it mean, exactly, she wondered. A facetious claim? An extravagant promise? The assertion of a braggart? Now she recognizes it for what it was—just play, a bit of fun, kin to the notice he nailed to their door, trying to intimidate skunks. But then it was one more jarring thing, like the smoke and the bawdy music, and she opened her bag and pulled out a card to check the address again, thinking that surely she'd made a mistake, she'd gotten the meeting place wrong.

But no, this was it. She knocked. No one answered, though the door gave way at her touch, and from somewhere within she could hear the swell of voices, men's voices, volleying back and forth.

"Hello," she called out, more a question than a greeting, and took a step inside. The room was as dim and dingy as the stairwell but cluttered with strange, foreign things. A poshteen rug thrown over a sofa, embroidered in frayed yellow silks. Carved cinnabar jars; great hammered brass trays; a fat, smiling soapstone Buddha. There were wads of paper everywhere, crumpled into balls, tobacco ash piled into conical mounds on tabletops and sideboards. It was a room in need of tending, of an orderly, managing hand, or so Caroline had thought to herself as she spied a lacquered umbrella stand full of fishing rods and polo mallets and a slatted wooden parasol, and a Japanese screen whose rice paper partitions had warped away from the frame. Then beyond the screen she saw her brother seated at a desk. His back was to her, as was his friend Rudyard's, clad in a long, loose tunic with matching loose, wide pants. He stood beside Wolcott, one hand on the desk, the other on her brother's knobbed shoulder, leaning over so far that the tassel of the fez perched atop his head ever so slightly brushed the rim of her brother's ear. And she heard him say, "Now this part here. That's brilliant. That's just what we're after."

Wolcott turned his head toward Rudyard and saw her there by the screen.

"Well, Caroline," he said, pushing off from the desk, the chair swiveling on its casters. "I'd say, 'Come in,' but you already have." And to Rudyard, whose hand had first dropped to his side and now fumbled with his pipe and a matchbox, he said, "Did you know that my sister was a dormouse? As quiet as one, though larger."

"But most welcome, nonetheless," Rudyard said in a moment, having finally succeeded in sparking a flame and stoking up his pipe.

"Yes, of course," Wolcott said. "Dear Carrie's always welcome." He rose and clasped her by the arm, dutifully pecking her cheek. Then they all three stood there. Rudyard puffed on his pipe. Wolcott shuffled some papers on the desk, while Caroline summoned what control she could muster so as not to reach up and touch the raw spot on her cheek that her brother had kissed.

Then Wolcott finished. "Right-o," he said, "Lunch?"

"Yes, to lunch," Rudyard answered with gusto.

She had met him before in Dean's Yard, at her brother's, where she had gone with the housekeeping books to discuss some domestic arrangement. It was what she had come to London to do, to assist her brother and take charge of his rooms, though he seemed to require little help. Already he had managed quite well on his own to wheedle and charm his way into the city's great literary heart, living a mere stone's throw from Westminster's Poets' Corner and landing, as his most recent coup, the newest and brightest star on the scene as his collaborative partner.

Caroline looked at her brother's new conquest. With his strange balloon pants and the odd, tasseled fez tilting precariously, his eyes magnified by his spectacle lenses behind a thick cloud of pipe smoke, he seemed more lost and out of place than her own expatriate brother, a figure quite at odds with the confident, boastful note on the door. But she watched as he traded in the odd fez for a neat straw boater trimmed with grosgrain and exchanged the monkey-skin slippers he wore for a pair of sturdy boots. Then he put on his jacket, Wolcott donned his plaid cape, and the three of them set off, the change of attire seeming to bring about a change in the air.

The two men took Caroline by the arm and escorted her down the stairs, making a great show of opening the door and bowing gallantly as she passed them. Then they strode down the Strand, arm in arm once again, and told her of their project. It would be a tale of East and West, with Wolcott providing the American bits and Rudyard supplying the East. A story of intrigue and espionage and the theft of a priceless jewel, beginning in an upstart pioneer town and ending on the ancient steppes of Asia.

She could feel their enthusiasm mount as they spoke, as they out-
lined all the twists of plot and the string of fabulous settings. Each
one slashed the air with his free hand, as if brandishing a saber,
plunging ahead with a neat fencing step to underscore a point. And
she felt it too. A great energy surged through the circuitry of their
looped arms. An excitement, a thrill that almost made her forget her
earlier sense of disquiet.

When they reached the restaurant, more fuss was made over the
door and her chair. A good claret was ordered and the menu perused.
Wine was poured, goblets raised for a toast. And perhaps it was
simply the wine, she now thinks, that made her lose track of their
story. There were too many characters, too many twists, all spinning
out around her. Ranchers, wranglers, railway barons, rug dealers,
snake charmers, thieves. Bribery, poisonings, a kidnapping scheme, a
child prince imprisoned in his own palace. Yet, of course, she
knows—as she knew even then—that the wine was not to blame.
Somewhere between the joints of beef and the currant pudding,
between the polishing off of the claret and the Madeira's uncorking,
the pretext of explaining their tale to her was all but forgotten. They
were talking to themselves again, each spurring the other one on,
their voices filled with that feverish rush she had overheard on the
landing. Even if she could gallop off too, across that verbal frontier,
she knew she could never join them. The access would be barred to
her, like the doors of the Savile Club, though not simply because of
her sex. For she knows as well that if she were to stand right now by
her husband's side and train her sights on the same distant point his
own eyes were fixed upon, all she'd see would be the ungainly line of
boughs, piled up haphazardly. Not some wondrous jungle or teeming

bazaar, seething and ripe with adventure. Just the eyesore of those tangled limbs and a yard in need of a rake.

Still, she thinks, it's this vision of hers that allows Rudyard to pursue his. She provides him with an uncluttered expanse, frees him from all household worries. And, of course, she's giving him something else that her brother could never have furnished, the child that now makes its small presence felt by shifting around in her womb.

Caroline sets her pen on the tray and places her hands on her belly, the swell of it seeming to match the swell of her pride and sense of triumph. For she is the one who has wound up here, by Rudyard Kipling's side. She is the one who is bearing his child, sharing his bed and his table. Yet she cannot enjoy this sweet victory without a pang of guilt, and in penance she forces herself to recall those days when her brother was dying, pumping herself up with deathbed scenes until she is full of contrition.

How horrid it was, how harrowing and strange: Wolcott lying on a regulation cot in a German fever ward, drifting in and out of delirium as she ran about, making arrangements and sending off telegrams. He had traveled to Dresden on a new business venture, hoping to start up a publishing firm for continental editions, though he got no further than a meeting or two before he was taken ill. Then Caroline was summoned. She rushed to his side, stunned to find the brother she'd left in London so dashing and able reduced to being hand-fed with a spoon and propped on the lip of a bedpan. She felt stunned as well by how ineffective all her usually deft ministrations seemed. She held his hand only to feel his grip grow weaker each day. She applied all manner of plasters and salves, and still his fever burned. And she tried to reach his dear friend Rudyard—his cherished, most valued friend—but as he was sailing around the world with only a vague plan of stops, she had little faith that the missives she sent would ever find their mark.

Still, her brother was grateful for her efforts. "What would I do without you, old girl," he whispered hoarsely into her ear during one of his last lucid moments.

These were, in fact, the very words she had longed to hear him say, though the shame of it was, by the time he pronounced them, she feared they weren't really deserved. For day after day as she sat by his bed, watching the typhoid consume him, she felt besieged by a sense of helplessness she prays never to feel again. And she found herself guiltily, eagerly, hungrily dreaming about escape. She would dab at the welts that bloomed on his chest, wring a cloth for his hot, fevered forehead, all the while counting the minutes until she could leave this afflicted place. She would try to attend to the doctor's pronouncements, clinging to the few words she did comprehend like a log in a swift, flowing river. But her mind kept drifting away, outside, beyond this room where the only sound was her brother's raspy breathing and the clatter of cups and syringes on trays as the nurses made their rounds. She felt the city beckoning her, the whole baroque foreignness of it. And she longed to stroll along the Bruehl Terrace, the balcony of Europe, where children ran, pushing hoops with sticks, and pigeons wheeled over gold statues. Or to sit at one of the coffeehouses that lined the Theaterplatz, where she'd order, say, a *kaffe mit schlag* and a thick slab of Dresdener stollen, or one of those platters of marzipan fruit, so deliciously artful and clever that she always had to pause to admire the confectioner's talent and skill—how he'd gotten the blush of a peach just right, caught the pocked, dimpled rind of an orange—before she popped them into her mouth, letting the illusion of fruit dissolve in the richness of thick almond paste.

But then came the day she found the nurse drawing a sheet over her brother's poor body, the chamber pot at the foot of his bed filled with a putrid, green soup.

"*Tot*," the nurse said, "*Er is tot, dein Bruder.*"

Caroline studied the nurse for a moment, trying to see if she had, indeed, detected an accusation in her blunt words. But the woman's face was as blank and coarse as the sheet draped over her brother, and she turned from the nurse to stare at the sheet and its worn, sweat-stained topography. It followed the contour of Wolcott's thin form, rising at the cant of hip bone and skull, dipping into his pelvis's crater. And seeing this landscape of sinkholes and peaks, the stark skeletal ridges and hollows, she felt revulsion at her own ample form—at her waist newly thickened with butter and cream, at her breasts straining at her laced stays—as if all her appetites had consumed his. He had shrunk while she had expanded, depleted by what seemed some cannibal act, not the slow, scalding ravages of typhoid.

"Yes, thank you," she said brusquely, turning back to the nurse. "I'll take over from here."

She gathered up his few belongings and filled out the necessary forms, vowing as she did to renounce all indulgence and not let her mind dally in daydreams any longer when there was work to be done. Then she set off at once to find a dressmaker who possessed at least the rudiments of English and a good hand with black bombazine and to hire a hearse and a mourning coach and pair, outfitted with plumes and a black velvet pall, two footmen with truncheons and staves. And she sat in that coach, bound in bolts of black cloth, on the day she'd arranged for the funeral, as the equipage made its stately way through the crowded, cobbled streets. She sat with her hands clasped tight in her lap and her eyes focused forward, not letting them stray even for a moment past the swags of crepe draped over the windows, past the straight, narrow line of the reins, as they passed the Altmarkt and the Theaterplatz, where in the life she had now forsworn, she had sat sipping coffee and licking whipped cream at what the *Herr Ober* had flatteringly called *Stammtisch*, her very own table.

Then they came to the cemetery. The footman helped her down, clicking his heels and murmuring "Fraulein" as he extended his hand. She walked to the grave where a few mourners stood, the English chaplain she'd engaged for the service and her family's old friend, Henry James. He'd responded to the cable she'd hastily sent by setting off from London at once, stopping only to collect a pot of hothouse flowers from the wife of a mutual friend. He handed them to her with his deepest condolence and she formally took them from him, feeling as she did the chill of the pot pass into her black kid-gloved hands. How they'd managed to survive a cold Channel crossing and a train across the Ardennes, she didn't really know. But there they were: a few sweet williams and a sheaf of Canterbury bells, some cottage pinks and love-in-a-mist, all drooping and wilted, in shock from the cold, but good English flowers nonetheless. When a faint fragrance rose up from the blooms, she knew just what she would do. She waited while the chaplain finished his prayers and uttered a final amen. Then she stepped to the grave, peered into the chasm and flung the lot of them in, not flinching as the pot hit the coffin's oak case with a fearsome, terminal thud, splintering, shattering into jagged clay shards, strewn petals, tangled clumps of bare root.

And here is where she would like to linger, here, at this mournful tableau, where she stands by the grave, bereaved but determined, in her new bombazine and hat covered with crepe, before the grave diggers she could see having lunch around the base of a near obelisk finished their pilsners and took up their spades to shovel back in the dark, German earth they had just that morning dug up. Yes, here, where she is the brave, steadfast sister, dabbing her eyes with her new handkerchief, embroidered with black and white teardrops; the one who, though having failed to thwart death, has managed to agent this last, final comfort, consigning her brother to his cold, foreign grave with a bit of the England he so loved.

But now here is that girl again, still bobbing her head as if in the throes of a palsy, drawing her away from the scene she's reconstructed, where the blossoms and shards are as sad and absolving as the sight of a broken Greek urn.

"What is it now," Caroline sighs, and the girl crumples up in a curtsy.

"I'm sorry, ma'am, but there's someone to see you. A Mrs. Connolly, she says."

"Please tell her I'm busy."

"I did, but she said it was urgent that she see you now."

"Very well, let her in," Caroline says, resigning herself to yet another round of domestic dispute, though this comes from an unlikely quarter. Of all the help they've been forced to depend on during this time of transition, Addie Connolly has always been reliable, her work of such consistent, high quality that Caroline has found little fault. Still, she thinks it must be something. Her hours, her wages, some perceived slight or wrong for which she wants compensation. So Caroline rises, quietly, swiftly, to close her husband's door, then settles herself back in her desk chair, assuming what she hopes is a look of firm and dignified resolve.

Then in comes Addie. A bird of a woman, Caroline Kipling thinks. All bones and knobs and jutting angles and swollen red-rimmed eyes. She stands by the hearth, wringing her hands in such obvious distress that Caroline feels her composure slip as she is taken by a sudden fear that something has been ruined, some cherished, valuable object scorched or bleached beyond repair.

But when Addie says, "It's Joe, my son," Caroline feels such a wave of relief at her own imagined loss now averted, that it takes her a moment before she can attend to what's being said, her concentration hampered further by the fact that Addie Connolly cannot seem to simply say what's on her mind.

"He's been missing since last night, you see. And since I know that he's fond of your husband—and, Mr. Kipling, why, he's been so kind to Joe. I do hope that he hasn't been a bother. Joe, of course, I mean, not your husband. I hope that Joe hasn't been a pest. But, you see, I thought, that since," she drifts off, her eyes darting to the floor. Then she looks up helplessly at Caroline Kipling, who takes this brief, anxious hesitation to recompose herself, straightening her back and lifting her chin to apprise the situation, letting a long, weighty minute pass before she finally speaks.

"Children amuse him and he amuses children. Your son has not been the only one. But I assure you, Mrs. Connolly, he doesn't bring them home and stash them away inside cupboards."

"Oh, no, ma'am," Addie stammers, "I didn't mean to suggest—"

"And beside, we'll be having our own soon enough," Caroline Kipling says, pausing to gaze at the knoll of her belly with such complete and tender absorption, it makes Addie Connolly blush.

"Yes, of course, ma'am. I know that. And very glad I am too. For your sake. I mean, yours and your husband's. I only thought that perhaps he might have seen Joe yesterday, maybe even talked with him some. And maybe Joe told him of some plan that he simply forgot to tell me about."

"I suppose that's possible," Caroline concedes. "But I can't possibly ask him now. He's working and he can't be disturbed. But if you like," she says, looking up brightly, "I'll ask him when he's finished, and if he has any pertinent information—which, you must understand, is doubtful—I'll send our girl, Anna, over to tell you sometime this afternoon."

"But—" Addie stammers.

"I'm afraid that's the most I can do for you, Mrs. Connolly. And now, as you see, I have work of my own, and you must excuse me."

Caroline stares at Addie until she lowers her eyes again, as if to sweep the floor with her lashes for any stray trace of her son. And when she finally shuffles out, Caroline rises and reopens the door that leads to her husband's small study. There he is, still toiling away, scratching out some new verse, though he raises his head when he hears her there and asks if there's anything the matter.

"No, no," she assures him. "It's nothing important. Nothing that I can't manage."

He turns back to his work again and she returns to her desk, dipping her pen into the ink, setting the pen to the paper, commencing once more the gratifying task of parsing the whole of the household into columns. Debits and credits, sweet balance.

Outside, Addie Connolly pulls her wool shawl tightly over her shoulders, clutching the ends near the base of her throat, her arms crossed over her chest. The wind has changed since yesterday, blowing in now from the north, bringing with it great banks of clouds that obscure all trace of blue. How yesterday's warmth and brilliance could give way to such a gray, sullen chill, she cannot fully fathom, just as she's unable to quite comprehend how it's happened that she's outside again, with no news of her son, and with only the barest shred of a prospect on which to now pin her hopes. Until what seems a mere minute ago she had truly believed she would find him inside, sitting on the floor with the clockwork toys marching all around him, so mesmerized by the mesh of their gears and their stuttering movements, that he'd simply forgotten the time. Or there he'd be, slouched by the door to Mr. Kipling's study, waiting for him to emerge, so fixed and intent on his fawning that when the day slipped into night and night slid into dawn, he'd simply decided to fall asleep there rather than give up his post.

She'd imagined, too, how she would scold him for all the trouble he'd caused. For making her nearly expire from worry, for sparking her husband's rage, for being a nuisance to their new neighbors, showing up at all hours of the day. She would make him sorry, that's what she'd do. She would chide him into shame, dragging him from the house by the hand and forbidding him to ever return. Yet now as she stands in the very spot in which she'd planned to upbraid him, she knows she would give away everything—all her rights to punish, forbid, or insist, to demand amends or repentance—just to have him back again, standing by her side.

She turns around then and looks back at the house, as if she might be mistaken. As if she hasn't already gone in and been so summarily dismissed. As if her son might still be inside, just waiting for her to fetch him. But there is the front door bolted against her, the prayer wheel flag shooing her away, the spruce boughs lined on the windowsills, impenetrable as barbed wire. And she knows in that moment that her hopes have been in vain, the product of a too-wishful mind that invests too much in fanciful thinking and always seeing a light, brighter side.

But if he's not there, where can he be? Addie racks and roots through her mind, unable to find any plausible answer, though she knows her husband has his theories. He thinks that this is all somehow Joe's doing—a deliberate act of truancy or some mindless straying, but not the work of a happenstance he couldn't forestall or control. He said as much when he came in last night, furious and fuming, so late that the supper she'd laid on the table had long ago grown cold, the apples she'd baked shriveled as prunes and stuck to the pan in a crust of burnt sugar she'd had to chip at with a knife.

"Your son," he began in a way that implied that whatever charges were to follow, she was to blame as much as Joe. "That fool boy of yours has gone off God-knows where. Hasn't done a damn thing around here. Got his head up his arse, that's what he has, when it's not somewhere up in the clouds."

He raised his arm and she thought he would strike her. She braced herself for the blow; though, with arm in midair, he changed directions and slammed his hand on the table, making her flinch and the cutlery jump, a small hop like the skip of a heartbeat. Then he stormed back out the way he had come, kicking over the bucket of slops she'd left by the door to take to the sty later on, and leaving her in the kitchen to clean up and wait for her son, whom she imagined would return any moment, grateful and happy to be home.

And there she waited, the whole night long, sitting at the table, rising only to perform a few small acts of faith, preparing for Joe's homecoming. He would be hungry, she imagined, hungry and tired and cold. So she set a pot of soup on the stove, fed the fire a few bits of wood, placed a brick on the rack to absorb the stove's warmth, wrapped the brick in a square of gray flannel. She climbed the stairs up to Joe's room and turned the covers down, set the brick between the thin, cold sheets, fluffed the feathers in his pillow. Then she went back down and stirred the soup. She sat and resumed her vigil, watching the hypnotic flame in her lantern oscillate back and forth, and the other across the dark chasm of yard, the twin flicker of light she could see in the barn where her husband sat and performed his own rites and devotions.

She drifted off sometime before dawn, her eyes glazed over from the light. And when she awoke it was with the idea that her son might be up the road. At the Kiplings', she thought shaking her head, the only wonder of it being that she hadn't considered it before. All she had to do then was to wait for a decent hour to call, and she passed the time with more preparations, kneading and setting some bread sponge to rise, spooning out fresh coffee grounds. Then grabbing her shawl, she set off up the road, so sure that she would find him there that even now, as she stares at the door and the barricade of spruce boughs, she can't quite reconcile the certainty she'd felt with the depths of her mounting despair.

And as if she has cried the question out loud—where, oh where, could he be?—the answer seems borne back to her on the wind: Gone, he is gone. It hardly matters where or how. He is gone, as she should have foreseen. Gone, just as he was fated to do from the day he slipped out of her womb.

Addie Connolly turns from the house and heads back down the road. All her life she has fought against bitterness, against sinking into despair, but as she makes her way back home, she cannot stop herself. Everything she sets her sights upon seems to speak of loss: the gnarled, bare limbs of the apple trees; the dry, silt-covered creek bed; the field where a rusting harrow sits beside an empty hayrack. Even the wind: it whips around her skirts, a menacing, heckling sprite, and she tugs at her shawl only to feel how poor a protection it is. Then her mind flashes back to Caroline Kipling sitting at her desk, so sure and complacent with her hands on her belly and that pleased, contented smile on her lips. She'd imagined as well, in what seems another life, that there might come a time when she'd enter that house under different circumstances. Arrive at the door on some more-cheerful errand, be received more cordially. She'd even imagined a friendship of sorts springing up between her and Mrs. Kipling, a warm though circumscribed intimacy based on a mutual sense of esteem and the fact that they were both mothers. Now, though, she knows that will never happen. *Never*, that implacable word. Yet if she envies Caroline Kipling for the future she holds in her lap, she takes a grim satisfaction in knowing it will be her lot, as well, to feel this wretchedness, that she'll have at best a few sweet years before hitting this same wall of worry.

Then spying something, there, in the road, Addie feels her bleak envy turn to panic. It is a dead frog, thin and flat as a leaf, the front hands splayed like the slats of a fan, the hind legs bent in a plié, as if in preparation to spring and leap away from the crush of a cart horse or carriage. Of course, Addie knows this is a common sight. Frogs often stray from the ditches by the road to find themselves marooned, their blood grown sluggish from the chill of fall or brought to a midsummer's boil. But seeing it there, with its once-bulging eyes looking as if they'd erupted and splattered like a bubble of griddle cake batter, she feels her own blood chill. She cannot look at the lifeless form without thinking of her son, imagining him stranded some place far from here, mangled or crushed on the ground. It is almost more than her heart can bear, and she turns away from it quickly, letting her eyes rest instead on the wall of stone that borders the orchard. Yet this sight is no more reassuring to her than the sight of the frog's brittle carcass, for she's near the place she came yesterday to spy on her son. And recalling that now, she's gripped by a new fear: What if she's being punished for yesterday's transgression? What if her own breach of boundaries somehow forced her son to cross boundaries as well?

Then Addie closes her eyes and tries to will herself to stop. She must not do this to herself, torture and flog herself endlessly when her thoughts should be focused on Joe. Besides, she reasons, if this day has taught her anything, it's the danger of leaping to unfounded conclusions, of investing too much in slim hopes, and relying on omens and her own intuition, which has proved a faulty faculty at best. She opens her eyes and takes a deep breath, as if air could offer her insight. And, miraculously, it seems to work. Her mind fills up with a new notion, as her lungs fill up with air, until she finds herself ready to leap once again, to stake her life on a hunch. For surely, it isn't her husband, she thinks, nor the Kiplings; not even the frog that can point to the fate of her son. Surely, it's whatever she might—or might not—find tucked in that gap in the wall. And she's pulled by a twisty line of logic that seems as persuasive, as irrefutable to her as a mathematical sum: If yesterday's bundle is still where she left it, she'll know that Joe hasn't gone. But if it is missing, if it has disappeared, she'll know that her son has as well.

Why this should be so, Addie can't truly say, though she feels the rightness, the certainty of it deep in the marrow of her bones. Joe simply would not leave the pinecones there if he was planning to go. And if his disappearance wasn't intended? Addie tries not to think about that, as she scrambles up the roadside embankment and quickly climbs over the wall, landing at the edge of the orchard, not quite in sight of the house. Now all she must do is find the spot, an easy enough task, she supposes. Though here, from this angle, in the flat gray light, the wall doesn't look quite the same, as if all the stones had scrambled themselves into some new configuration. But she scans each rock, peering into every crevice. She runs in a strange, gooselike crouch, the ends of her shawl slipping out of their knot, the hem of her skirt in the mud. Then she sees it, not far from the house, obscured by a runnel of ivy, the pattern of flowers as faded and gray as the stones from too many washings. Such an innocent, ordinary thing it seems, too limp to bear so much meaning, though Addie tugs at it anxiously, pulling it out so fast that the pinecones come tumbling down to the ground. She holds it to her breast and feels her heart fill with thanksgiving, as if it were her son, himself, that she held in her arms. And she turns to the house, half expecting to see him standing there on the doorstep, waving to her as though she were the one returning home from a long voyage.

Yet the sight that greets her when she raises her eyes cancels out the relief she just felt. A black basket phaeton stands in their yard, hitched to a pair of black geldings. The town doctor's carriage, it dawns on her, though it looks for a moment like an apparition of a fearsome, death-bearing rig sprung right from the pages of the Apocalypse. And there is her husband, standing by the blinkered pair, patting the neck of one of the horses in a rare display of warmth, cupping its muzzle in the palm of his hand as he offers it a bright, ruby apple.

What boggles her more? The sight of the carriage or her husband's hand on the horse, his calloused palm following the nap of the hair as it ripples over sinew and muscle? What does it all mean? She cannot imagine, though again she is seized by fear. And bursting with questions, Addie runs up the hill, the calico still in her hand, though reaching her husband who steps backs from the horse at her near-breathless approach, the only word she seems able to utter is a plaintive, half-whispered, "Joe?"

"He's here," says Jack, thrusting his chin up and back toward the house. "Broke his damn leg snooping round the Water-Cure. Some poacher found him late last night. Saw a light in the building and this on the grounds," he says as he draws a rag from his pocket that matches the one in her hand. "The doctor's here now, setting his leg. Not a bad break, he says, but bad enough. It'll take eight weeks or so to heal, and he won't be worth much until then."

He stares hard at Addie, and she takes in his face as her panic slowly leeches away. His eyes peer out of dark, swollen pouches. A crust of dried spit rims his lips, and the outcrop of stubble sprouting over his jaw seems to her more grizzled and gray than she has ever recalled. And she has an urge to say something to him, a few words that will both acknowledge and lighten the worry she's sure they've both felt. But before she can speak, he tosses the scrap of cloth to the ground, like a gauntlet.

"There goes the orchard money," he says, before walking away to the barn.

THE LAIR OF THE WOLF IS HIS REFUGE

From his perch on his bed Joe stares out the window, waiting for the first snow to fall. The sky is bloated, the color of pewter, with near-to-bursting clouds. The wind whistling through the thin beaverboard walls carries the sharp scent of damp. Joe has lain here now for nearly four weeks, his leg, strapped to a long, narrow board, propped on a pile of pillows—four achingly slow and tiresome weeks in which it seems he has done little more than watch the shafts of sunlight on the floor recede as the days grow shorter, and chart the length of time he is able to stifle the urge to scratch both his leg and the poor, chafed cheeks of his buttocks, which constantly prickle and itch.

He has hoisted himself up a few times to hobble to the pine commode, where he's splashed his face with cold water from the jug and stared into the depths of the mirror nailed to a stud in the wall. There he's seen the face of a strange, hardened boy, hollow-eyed and ashen. A boy stripped of illusions, he might even say if he knew how to frame such a thought. At the very least a boy who is too old to play with the things that his mother's brought up. These offerings sit at the foot of his bed, just beyond his reach. A basket of clothes-pegs she'd said he could use as a corps of cavalry men. Some yarn for cat's cradle. A tin spinning top. His school *Eclectic Reader*, with its mildly informative, instructional tales and poems about skylarks and dewdrops. He knows she has brought these diversions to him in the hopes that they'll amuse him, that the bouncy rhythms and sprightly rhymes will cheer him up a bit. But although he has thumbed through a few random pages and made a Jacob's ladder with the yarn, he cannot seem to focus. He reads the words but their meaning escapes him. He stares at the etched illustrations only to feel his eyes glance off the page and return again to the window.

Nothing else compels him much. Nothing sparks his interest, not even the imminent prospect of snow, which drums in him only a muted response, a dull, muffled sense of foreboding. He stares at the sky and notes how the gray seems tinged with a queer shade of green. He smells something burning, along with the damp, like the faint but harsh scent of singed wool. And he listens to the sounds that rise up from downstairs—the clatter of cookware and the scrubbing of pots, the whisk of the broom on the floorboards—each noise that pierces the late-autumn silence seeming to reverberate, as if the clouds bearing down on the house had formed a sealed echo chamber.

He keeps listening, too, for his parents' voices drifting up to him, disembodied, the ebb and flow of their talk like a tide on which he floats and bobs. How strange their voices seem to him, familiar but somehow discordant, with the meaning and tone of their words ever so slightly at odds. Take his mother, for instance: He can hear her now, singing snatches of hymns as she drags the hall rug out to the yard to beat it, a task Joe knows she normally does with a certain grim, silent forbearance. Yet now her voice soars up to him: "*When morning gilds the skies,*" he hears, "*My heart awaking cries,*" the honeyed melody so at odds with the day and her steady, resolute whacking. And she'll call up to him from the bottom of the stairs, delivering daily dispatches. "There was riming on the pumpkins this morning," she announced last week with fanfare. "The ice on the trough is as thick as my thumb." "There's a fox scrounging round in the elderberries." "I hope it doesn't snatch one of the hens," she added as an afterthought, though the chortling way she had said this made Joe think that, far from being alarmed, she found the idea rather amusing.

And then there's his father, a conundrum as well. Many a night Joe has heard him complain about all the endless work he must do now that they're short a hand. And he's heard him yell and harp at his mother, accusing her of coddling him, of treating Joe like a spoiled, pampered child, saying his muscles and limbs will go limp and slack if he doesn't get out of that bed. But although the first week he fashioned a crutch out of a forked hickory branch, auguring holes on each side of the fork for the dowel that his mother had covered with batting and wrapped with some strips of old linen, his father hasn't prodded him much. He walks down the hall, past his door in the morning, with only a grunt and a nod. He returns in the evening, a lone and bent figure, hunched by the weight of Joe's usual hauls and his own load of worries. And once when Joe heard him climbing the stairs, he rolled over and tried feigning sleep, only to open his eyes a crack and peer past the fringe of his lashes to see his father standing in his doorway, holding a lantern aloft and staring at him with such an awkward look of concern that it made Joe wish he would simply holler, drag him up, force him back on his feet.

It makes him wish, too, that his mind would go blank, or that he would fall asleep, that he'd sink his head into the pillow and drift off to some dreamless place he wouldn't have to leave till his leg was mended and the household was back as it was. Or better still, he would sail back in time to before the accident happened, erasing with his slumbers all that fatuous play that now makes him queasy with shame. But he cannot seem to will himself there no matter how hard he tries. He can't seem to pull his eyes from the window, where, any moment now, he thinks, those distended clouds might finally release their first, small, negligible flake. And he can't stop straining his ears to listen and catch every stray word and sound.

What he hears now is his mother—or more precisely the silence that comes when her singing and beating both stop. He hears the crunch of footsteps and wheels coming up the drive, some squawking and clucking as the chickens dash away, the feet and wheels coming to a halt. Then he hears an exchange of pleasantries, a brief volley of banter he makes out from the tone more than the actual words, since whomever his mother is talking to stands a ways from the house. But then clearly he hears her exclaim, "Oh, my," the words swollen and stretched with amazement. "Oh, my, look at that one. And this one," he hears before her voice drops to a murmur. Then the footsteps retreat and he hears his mother ferry back and forth, in and out of the house, each transit marked by the creak of the door as it swings on its rusty hinges and by the change in the sound of her tread as she moves from packed dirt to planked floor-boards. He hears a firm thud as the door is set back into the hold of its jambs, a moment of silence, then his mother's light step as she hurriedly bounds up the stairs.

Then there she is standing in the doorway, flush with some new bit of news, wiping her hands on the bib of her apron and tucking a loose strand of hair.

"Did you hear, Joe?" she says coming into his room, sitting down at the edge of his bed. "That was Anna, you know, the girl from the Kiplings. She brought over the wash and a pile of baby things she says that Mrs. Kipling just got from her grandmother this very morning. Oh, you should see them, Joe, you should. There's a little cashmere cloak and some white lawn caps with the sweetest silk floss and ruche. And some flannelette sacques and some slips and bibs all trimmed with braid and lace. And a christening gown! Oh, I'll bring that one up just so you can have a look-see. Real Valenciennes lace, Anna said, though I said I didn't know anything about that. 'Nor do I,' she said, but Mrs. Kipling assured her it's quite the very finest lace there is. Of course, there's a stain or two to get out, and the lace needs a bit of attention … but, oh," his mother says, rummaging through her pockets. "I almost forgot. Look at this: we've got letters. One for you and one for me. Shall I read yours out loud? No?" she says doubtfully when Joe fails to respond. "Well, perhaps I'll read you mine then."

She sets the envelope marked JOE on the bed by the top and the basket of clothes-pegs, and she opens the one that's addressed to her, untucking the flap to draw out a slip of paper all inky with writing.

"Dear Mrs. Connolly," Addie reads out loud.

"I know that I haven't even properly arrived yet, but look how many fine things I have! Papa says there's no use in fixing them up, since I'm bound to just soil them anyway. But Mama says they must be quite perfect, and since Papa always listens to Mama, do you think you could try?

"Of course, Mama listens to Papa, as well. He's taught her how you sing Humpty-Dumpty in the East, and, see, I've learned it too."

Then Addie pauses, her bottom lip puckering out from the pull of a frown.

"Do you think you could read this?" she says to Joe. "I can't make out what it says."

She passes the letter across to her son who stares at it uneasily, as if it were a trap, before he tries to twist his tongue around words that seem to slam against the roof of his mouth.

Hamti-Damti chargya chhutt!
Hamti-Damti girgya phut!
Rajah ki-pulton Ranee ki-ghoree
Hamti-Damti kubbee nahin joree!

Finished, he hands the letter back, without looking up, without comment. He had tried to read without inflection, keeping his voice low and flat. But the rhyme seemed to have a life of its own, a gait that couldn't be stopped, and despite all his efforts to remain impassive, he summoned the character up: the fop of an egg he once saw at school in an illustrated book of rhymes, with a silk cravat and black and white spats and a pair of pantaloons. But this time instead of him sitting on a wall overlooking a small village garden, Joe pictured him high on the wall of a fort, an escarpment built of red sandstone, perched so incongruously, so precariously there that, of course, he is bound to fall.

Then his mother takes over and reads to the end:

"Don't you think I'm frightfully clever!
Very truly yours,
Kipling Batcha"

"Well," she says slowly after a moment in which the words of the rhyme still hover, jangling and quixotic. "Well," she repeats, seemingly unable to call forth any other words. "Imagine writing a letter for a child who hasn't even been born yet. Do you think it's unlucky?" she asks her son, and Joe gives a halfhearted shrug before he turns to the window again and stares once more at the clouds.

The sky is still, as gray as a dishrag, as if the day is holding its breath. Nothing stirs or shifts or sounds, except for a crow who flies past the dormer, cries out a lone caw, then is gone. And he senses his mother still sitting on his bed, her patient, quiet presence. She traces the lines of stitching on the quilt, following the squares of the Irish chain pattern with her index finger, till her nail nudges up against the other envelope that lies on the bed, still unopened.

"Aren't you going to read yours?" she asks, her voice so soft that it seems, to Joe, to come from a great, weathered distance.

"Maybe later," Joe says. "I'm feeling tired now. I think I'd just like to sleep."

"Very well," says his mother, though she makes no move to go other than to draw her finger back along the stitched path it had come.

She folds up her letter, slips it back in her pocket, and rearranges the things on the bed, scooting up the top, the basket, the book, so that they're all in Joe's reach. Then she stands up and heads to the door, where she pauses at the threshold.

"Well, you get some sleep then. I'll check on you later. And I'll bring up some biscuits for supper. And, remember, just call if you need anything. Anything," she repeats with a fierce, emphatic firmness, as if all that he could possibly want was hers to grant and give.

Downstairs in the kitchen, Addie Connolly sighs and sets her hands on her hips. What is she to do about Joe? And what's she to do with this washing, the whole jumble of bedding and clothing and towels she has piled on the table and chairs? She, too, after all, has had more work to do these days with Joe infirmed. Feeding the chickens, stacking the wood, scrubbing the dairy cans, the baking, the churning, the dusting, the mending, the old, endless litany of chores. Still, Addie knows that the wash won't get done by wishing it away, let alone by just standing there, staring dumbfounded, allowing the mere thought of tackling it to swamp and engulf and defeat her. Besides, it's a simpler matter to solve than the mystery that is her son. So she takes a seat and starts to sort, by color and fabric and bulk, the heavyweight linens that can stand a good boil separated from more delicate ones and the lace that she'll have to dab at by hand with a cotton ball dipped in benzene with the velvets that she'll need to rub with some bran or a stale piece of bread. And as she works, turning the tangled heap into neat, orderly piles, she starts to hum with efficiency and a humble gratitude. This is what work can do: take you out of yourself then bring you back again, renewed and redeemed by a task undertaken and brought round to completion, by gestures repeated again and again until they accrue a burnished grace.

She has always known this, though she feels it more now, with her son sequestered upstairs. She is grateful for what keeps her busy these days, for what stops her mind from looping back to that tormenting night last month when she sat here, at this very table, clutching a thin thread of hope, while Joe lay pinned at the Water-Cure, alone and in pain through those endless, dark hours she shudders to think of. And sometimes when she's intent on her work, her hands busy with the scrub board or a needle and thread or the paring knife's quick, shaving flicks, she is able to perform that high-wire feat that Joe cannot execute, where she skips right over the recent past and lands in an earlier time, leaving all that's grown troublesome far behind. She thinks of those years when her son was small, when she'd hoist him up on the shelf of her hip and carry him around the farm, pointing out the apples, the pigs, the cows grazing lazily under the elms. He would look at each thing, then turn back to her, his face filled with amazement, as if she had summoned them into being, conjured them out of the air, given them life as she uttered their names, like God on the day of creation. Yet if she rendered that miracle for him, he gave her one in return, for in his eyes she saw those same things as she never had before—or perhaps had once, when she was a child, in a time she'd long since forgotten—not as something to harvest or butcher or milk, but as marvels simply in and of themselves. Then she saw the apples dangling from branches, as festive and bright as glass balls. She saw the pig, the sheer wonder of it, with its saucy snout and corkscrew tail, the improbable shade of a peony. And the cows, bending to their alchemical work, turning the blades of meadow grass into the stuff of cream: with her son in her arms, she saw them transfigured into more than they had been before, into something essential, resplendent, astonishing, a source of delight and joy.

She feels a glimmer of that old feeling now as she sorts through the linens and clothes, with a good fire crackling in the kitchen stove and the whole house smelling of yeast. It all fills her with a sense of well-being that she attributes, again, to her son, as if his very presence upstairs, beneath the pitched peak of the roof, radiated a kind of benediction on everything below.

And she finds herself thinking of those days long ago before Joe was even born, when it was just her and Jack on the farm and the sheep they believed would one day lead them to another, more prosperous future. How young they were then! How staggeringly young! Little more than children playing at house, chasing and catching the sheep like a game of tag or snap the whip. It was Addie's job to hold the sheep down while Jack attempted to shear them, since neither possessed the skill or the strength to pin them and clip them at once. She would dig her hands deep into their coats until her fingers smelled of lanolin, try to coax them to stillness by singing lullabies or offering bribes of sorrel, while the sheep attempted to wriggle away, tucking their great wooly heads in to butt her, protesting with kicks and shrill bleats. Then "Quick," she'd beg as she got one down and Jack started in with the shears, wielding the blades inexpertly, trying hard not to tear at the fleece. There'd be a testy moment between them, with each wanting more from the other: Jack needing Addie to keep the beast still, Addie desperate for Jack to hurry. Though the moment would pass when Jack stood up straight with the wrested fleece in his hands and Addie released her own pressing grip so that the sheep bounded up to its feet, looking so dazed and affronted, with its newly shorn trunk as pale as a tuber yanked up from the earth, that they'd both burst out laughing, clutching their sides to stop from doubling over, till the sheep went off to pout and graze, and they repeated the whole process again.

They named the sheep after the towns on the railway that had helped to finance their purchase in a moment of intimate whimsy and hope she can barely believe existed. But she thinks of them now—Boston and Concord, Sherbrook and Montreal—the memory as distant as those namesake cities and brought on, perhaps, by what she'd imagined as Joe read that nursery rhyme: the vision she can't seem to shake from her head of Caroline Kipling enthroned at her desk, with her husband kneeling down at her feet, broadcasting those strange, nonsense words to her belly, as if through a megaphone's funnel.

Addie feels her cheeks heat up at the thought of that intimate scene down the road, and of she and Jack too, bestowing those outlandish names on a flock of dumb sheep. But when did all that foolishness stop, all that laughable larking and romping? When the wool market dropped and the sheep took ill and could fetch only cottywool prices? When even the lambs had blisters in their mouths and along the tender slit of skin that divided their small, cloven hooves? Certainly by the time Joe was born their old comradeship was over. Addie had the washing and the housework to do. Jack had the orchards and fields and the handful of cows he had managed to save from the poor, fatal plight of the sheep. Neither intruded much on the other, except when necessary: at the table, when platters of food needed passing; in the bed, where her husband still sought her. And once Joe was old enough to help out and shoulder his own load of chores, it seemed as though a further line was stretched and drawn between them, a boundary between their two domains that only the boy was able to cross with any mite of ease.

Now, though, with Joe holed up in his room, Addie has had to cross that line and venture into Jack's territory. She has had to claim the milk from the barn that she needs for the cheese and the churning, to haul scuttles full of kindling from the woodshed after her husband has split it. And she's had to scale the ladder to the hayloft, looking for the nesting spots of the biddies who've eschewed the crowds at the henhouse, preferring to lay their eggs alone in some dark and hard-to-reach place—between the sprongs of the cultivator, beneath the eave of the scaffold.

She's even had to help with the pig, not just with the boiling and salting and mincing, but with the actual slaughter, first tying the rope around the front and back trotters, then looping it through the pulley, so that Jack could heave it, still pitifully squealing, over the barn's stanchion hook. Then she set a bucket beneath it to catch the blood as Jack sliced through its neck, the two of them working, solemnly, quickly, not speaking but matched, task to task. Once it was drained, they hoisted it into the kettle she'd set in the yard, the deadweight even harder to haul than the bulk of the live, squirming beast. Next they scalded it in boiling water until all its color had leeched and hauled it again to the butchering board that Jack had set on a pair of sawhorses positioned in the middle of the yard. Then they parted, each going their own separate ways: Jack to the toolshed to retrieve the knives he'd need to scrap off the pig's bristles, Addie to the kitchen to pour brine into crocks to start in on the process of pickling.

Yet for all that she hated the squeals and the blood and the smears of entrails on her apron, she found herself wandering outside a bit later, just to see how her husband was doing. And he came to the kitchen more times than was needed to deliver the shoulders and ribs, standing by the table as she rubbed the pig's tongue and heart with a good coat of salt. Likewise, she'd tarry in the hayloft sometimes after collecting the eggs, just to watch the dust motes and loose chaffs of straw swim in the stream of sunlight that poured through the gaping hole in the roof, as her husband worked, pitching the hay or currying the horse. And he'd amble to the back door in the late afternoons, ostensibly to fetch things—a canteen of tea, a pint of molasses to mix in with the cow's feed, a spare quilt to spread over the last of the vines when he thought the night threatened a frost—staying not really to say anything much, just to linger and rest for a spell.

Of course, once Joe is up and back on his feet, she imagines things will change. He will gather the eggs, bring his father his tea, once more shuttle and weave between them. And Addie? Will she miss those idle encounters, the feel of her and Jack working side by side, the peace of the barn that she seemed to have forgotten, the worn wood insulated with straw? Perhaps—though now, as she looks out the window and notes the darkening day, she has no time to dwell or mull over some future, intangible loss. She must ready the tea that Jack will want to take with him to herd in the cows, then start in on supper, peel the squash, bake the biscuits she has promised Joe. So she sorts through the rest of the clothes hastily, then fans the cookstove fire, primes the pump in the sink till the water springs forth, fills the kettle, sets it back on the stove. And all the while she thinks of Joe, her increasingly mysterious son. How brooding and gloomy he seems to her, so much—too much—like his father. If only he would rouse himself more, take an interest, turn his thoughts inside out, at the very least say what's troubling him and not keep it all bundled inside him.

She's still thinking of Joe when her husband arrives looking for his tea. He stands in the doorway with his hands in his pockets and the collar of his oilcloth turned up, a scrap of a scarf tied tight around his neck, as withdrawn and laconic as Joe. Two peas in a pod, she thinks to herself, each one sealed as tight as a clam. Though as she pulls the tea canister down and packs the tin steeper with leaves, she has an idea for prying them open, a scheme she knows is perhaps a bit conniving, but one that might do them both some good.

"You know, I've been thinking of Joe," she says. "He seems so sad and glum. Do you think you could talk to him, maybe draw him out some? Say something—I don't know quite what. But I'm sure he'll listen to whatever you say more than he listens to me. I seem to just vex him lately, no matter what I do. And even the letter he just got from Mr. Kipling hasn't seemed to cheer him up a bit."

She watches as this last bit of news sinks in and he screws up his face to absorb it.

"Well," Jack replies. "There's the cows to get now. It's going to be dark in a while."

"Oh, I didn't mean now. Whenever would suit you," she says as she fixes the tea.

She waits a minute, two minutes, three, the silence thick between them, as the leaves steep in the boiling water till the brew turns a dark mahogany. Then she pours it into an old tin canteen, screws the stopper, and hands it to Jack.

"All right then?" she says.

"All right then," he answers before he turns and heads out to gather the cows, leaving the matter settled enough that as Addie rolls out the biscuit dough and cuts out full moons with a cup, she picks up the thread of the hymn she'd left dangling hours ago. "*O hark to what it sings,*" she resumes, "*As joyously it rings ....*"

Through the course of the day the cows have wandered from the heart of the meadow where Jack Connolly left them to the very edge of the woodlot. He spies them there, all huddled together, butted close against the hemlocks, as near the trees as they can be without actually entering the woods. He imagines they sense a storm as well, feel that strange, electric charge in the air, smell that damp, slightly sulphurous smell, though as he comes closer, he can see no hint of fear or distress in their faces, nothing that's disturbed their round, lolling eyes or their jaws' steady grinding and chewing.

He approaches them across a field that was covered this morning with hoarfrost. Here and there, he sees traces of it, in the hollows and shadows and the frozen creek bed, where it sprouts in depressions made by boot heels and hooves like tufts of icy mold. By tomorrow, though, it should be buried by at least a few inches of snow, making the whole venture of pasturing the cows little more than a foolhardy thought. But even if the snows hold off for a while, Jack Connolly knows that the time has come to stop all this traipsing through meadows. He should just leave the cows on their own in the barn, to feed on the hay he slaved to grow and cut all season long, letting them out, if they even need it, in the paddock that's adjacent to the barn.

He should, he knows, though the prospect makes him shudder even more than the frost and the cold. Four months, maybe five, cooped up in the house, with no place or reason to go, except to dig the trough and the woodpile out from drifts of snow. For this is the truth behind all his grumbling about the work he's been shouldering: there simply is not much left to be done, with the hay all in and stacked in the loft and the pig already slaughtered and the cows content to stay in the barn and forgo this cold trek to the meadow.

No, he's the only one not willing to waive this daily outing, the one who balks at accepting confinement as the price to be paid for warmth. And this knowledge makes his mouth go dry and his throat ache for something to swallow. So he opens the canteen slung over his shoulder, puts his lips to its mouth, and drinks. The tea is hot, just a tad short of scalding, and steeped to a sharp, bitter strength—just the way he prefers to take it these days since his son first broke his leg, as if the point were not to slake thirst, but to somehow burn it away. He takes a gulp and feels the liquid barrel down to his gut. Not the best substitute for the drink he really craves but one that, for now, will do.

He screws the canteen closed again and starts to round up the cows, slapping them on their haunches and rumps when they seem reluctant to leave this provisional shelter of hemlocks for home. He will take them back the long way, he thinks, cross the hayfields then down the road, a route that might manage to preserve the illusion that he has some freedom of movement and, if nothing else, give him time to think about what he might say to Joe. For the other truth he has come to acknowledge, despite all his griping and grousing, is that he wishes the boy had gone, packed a bag and left this place without ever once looking back. It is what he found himself hoping that first night when the boy had gone missing, when he drank himself into a stupor from which he remembers little except for the visions he had of his son: Joe straddling the ties of a train's coupling, with his head lifted up to the wind. Joe walking along a broad, sloping road toward a horizon that glowed.

Of course, why he should think the boy would fare better than he has, he doesn't know. For every time he has set off, no matter how intrepid, he has never once managed to meet up with an ounce of serendipitous luck. Take the boat that delivered him to these supposedly promised, golden shores: a sailing packet, one of the last to ply the North Atlantic, less than half the price of the new steamer ships, though the voyage took three times as long. He remembers the thrill of seeing the sails run up for the very first time—the double topgallants, the royals, and the spankers all billowing in the wind, the great web of rigging that seemed to command him to fashion a foothold and climb—though that vision was soon replaced by others of a far less inspiring sort.

He spent most of the trip in the pit of the hold, with his mother and his sister, the sea so rough that it made them ill and dashed all his mast-scaling hopes. There they lay, crammed together in a single, small berth, whose bedding was prone to soaking when water came sluicing down through the hatch. There they retched and moaned as their poor insides sloshed and pitched back and forth like the waves, and the air grew thick and foul around them and the privy buckets all overflowed. And when the sea finally calmed enough to calm their heaving stomachs, they lay there still, then gripped by a chill that was followed, in turn, by a fever. How long that lasted Jack Connolly wasn't sure, though he knows that when his own fever broke, he found his mother and sister beside him, pale and stony and cold, with their heads tipped back and their mouths gaping open, as if frozen around a soundless wail, and the weight of their bodies bearing down on him like millstones he had to frantically shove and push off just so he could breathe.

He remembers, too, how they were brought to the deck wrapped in the soiled sheets they'd lain on, their boots wedged back on their stiffened feet as weights to help them sink. The deckhands who hauled them wore long leather mitts and neckerchiefs tied around their faces, so that they looked like pirates or bandits, hauling away bags of loot. They laid the bodies on the deck as Jack followed through the opened hatchway, crouching beside a dog's kennel crate once he was outside—the home to a pair of rail-thin, edgy greyhounds that had more room and fresh air to breath than the passengers in steerage. One of the men took a needle and thread usually used to mend sails and sewed up the ends of the sheets with a row of hastily basted stitches, as the chaplain recited the words of a psalm:

"Save me, O God; for the waters are come in unto my very soul." Then they lifted the first sack, swung it once, then twice, then three times before releasing. And Jack watched the bundle that had once been his mother sail up into the air then hover there, poised between rise and descent, for a single, hesitant moment—just long enough for Jack to think it might not be impossible for the thread to unravel and the sheets to come undone, unrolling like a scroll or a carpet, and his mother to emerge as if from a cocoon on linens transformed into wings, to fly away high up into the heavens, his safekeeper and guardian still.

Of course, though, she plunged down into the sea, followed by his sister. He watched each one go, heard the slap of their bodies as they hit the dark, roiling surface, saw the water displaced then knit back together, as each sack disappeared.

Then, finally, came Boston. "The Flourishing City of Boston," as the ship's flyers had put it, though the only ones who appeared to flourish were the runners who clogged the wharfs each day, looking for new immigrants to fleece, and the child-saving matrons who marched through the streets with their Bibles and Transcendentalist tracts, looking for waifs to pray for and deliver to the Home for Little Wanderers or the Children's Friends Society—places he knew well enough to avoid despite their congenial names.

Still, he stayed near the docks those first few weeks, sleeping in makeshift shelters, vying for scraps with the rats and the thin, feral cats that crept out at night. He stayed there, reluctant to leave the water's edge, as if, even then, he still believed that what happened might yet come undone and his family might still be returned to him, washed up in the dregs of the tide. Though finally, urged on by the need for food, he entered the heart of the city. And there he did find a few hints and glimpses of that advertised flourish: cobbled streets lined with gas lamps, a few elegant hansoms, market stalls filled with great heaps of oranges, and at Haymarket Square, a whole bevy of trains, gleaming and belching out smoke. He watched them pull into the terminal station, brakes hissing, piston rods shooting sparks. And he watched them depart, a parade of sleek cars all curtained with dark velvet, pulled by the firebox he glimpsed flashing by where nuggets of coal glowed bright red as rubies and the great boiler shuddered and spat and the men, too, with their shovels and stained skivvy shirts, seemed to emanate heat and light.

What was it about that sight that so moved him, that made him keep returning, risking the billy club blows of patrolmen whose job it was to rid the place of guttersnipes like him? Some glamour or intrigue hinted at by those drawn-shut velvet drapes? That sense of barely containable power that seemed to infuse not only the firebox coals but also those laboring men? Whatever it was, he made up his mind as he watched those trains heave forth. He would join the ranks of those railway men as soon as he was able, hitch his future to iron and the promise of steam, mount the ties like the rungs of a ladder. Of course, this plan, which he did pull off, almost blew up in his face. And recalling that whole sorry chain of events, all those missteps and miscalculations, he thinks of the story he heard as a child about a poor man who stumbled one day on a robber's full purse only to fritter it away. He traded the purse for a milking cow, the cow for a set of pipes, the pipes for a cap, the cap for a walking stick that he thought he must have. Each object seemed so desirable to him, desirable and necessary, the very thing he had to possess to make his way in the world. But then a bird perched in a nearby tree mockingly twittered at him, and he threw the stick up in a fit of pique to stop its taunting song, only to find the stick stuck in the tree and his own hands once again empty and the bird, unperturbed by his bungled assault, twittering again, scornfully.

"Foolish, foolish man," the bird said, just as he's said to himself. He's a fool to have come here, a fool to have stayed, a fool to think either made a difference. Certainly a fool for bringing the cows out here on a day like this, when the ground beneath him is hard and ungiving and the wind cuts his cheek like a knife. He cups his hands around his puckered mouth and blows out a gust of warm air, thawing his fingers enough that they're able to unscrew the canteen lid. Then he takes a long, slow, guzzling draft that he hopes will drown out his thoughts, only to find that the tea has grown cold and lost all its purgative bite.

"Christ," he mutters, spitting the tea out. Another disappointment, though that seems too mild and tame a word for the sentiment he's feeling.

He kicks at the cow that's closest to him, his boot flying up to its fetlock, as if it were the one responsible for all that foils and thwarts him. The cow protests by insipidly mooing and stumbling down in a ditch. Then it clambers up toward the roadbed that the rest of the herd has just reached and where Jack Connolly finds himself face to face with yet one more irritant. For although he feels little comfort in solitude, company seems far worse. And now here is his neighbor, the Brit from up the road, apparently out for a stroll, looking absurd in a long coat of pelts with another fur wrapped around his head.

For a moment Jack Connolly thinks of retreating and ducking back into the woods. But by now he's been spotted and some thin shred of pride makes him stay there and keep to his course.

"Good day to you, sir," Kipling calls out, tipping his head in greeting. "How's that boy of yours doing? Better, I hope."

"As well as can be expected."

"Good, that's good. In fact, what could be better than an expectation that's been met? And you, sir, do you expect it to snow?"

"I expect that it will or it won't."

"Ah, now that's good too, quite wise, in fact. For as someone once said—Mr. Pope, I believe—'Blessed is the man who expects nothing,' or in your case, expects all contingencies, 'for he shall never be disappointed.'"

He laughs then, his body convulsing with mirth, then turns suddenly serious and grave as he falls in step beside Jack Connolly and the slow parade of cows.

"I've been meaning to talk with you, Mr. Connolly. I hope that this moment's convenient, for while it seems premature to speak of the spring when winter's not yet fully upon us, I need to find someone to help level the drive to the house when the ground has thawed, and your son thought you'd be just the right man, what with your experience with explosives and such. He said—"

"That was a long time ago," Jack Connolly interrupts him.

"Of course. But you know how. Am I right in that assumption? Your son hasn't misinformed me? If not, I do hope you'll consider it. Your boy, I dare say, would relish the chance to see a bit of his father's old fireworks. And it would be a great convenience for me, for which, of course, I'd offer compensation."

Then he turns to Jack Connolly, fixing him with his eyes, and Jack Connolly fixes him back. For here's the man's impertinence again, all his staggering presumptions, thinking Jack will jump at his offer like a dog leaping after a bone or a stick, sprinkling his talk with that patronizing "sir," and speaking behind Jack's back. With his son, of all people, whom he's writing letters to, saying God-only-knows what.

It's enough to try a man's patience, he thinks, or warrant a harsh telling-off, though more than anything else, Jack simply wants the man to go. So he says only, "I'll think about it," wagering that the concession's enough to send him on his way.

"Good. That's finished then," Kipling says, just as Jack Connolly hopes, though Kipling keeps walking along by his side, matching his pace, step to step.

"Now tell me about these cows of yours. Holsteins, I'd say by the look of them. Good milkers?" he asks.

Jack Connolly shrugs.

"Yes, I see, they are and they aren't. Now you must excuse me, sir," he goes on, "if I seem too bold. But I fear I know nothing about cows such as these, and living here it seems that I ought. Of course, elephant cows, that's a whole other matter. I know a fair bit about those." And to Jack Connolly's growing astonishment, he launches into a long, involved story about an old elephant—a grand dowager, he calls her—whom he says he had the honor once to know.

"Her name was Garuda and she'd acquired throughout the years quite a taste for arrowroot biscuits; though unfortunately, like some of her human counterparts, she lived under a grave delusion concerning the size of her waist and would often try to squeeze past doorways through which she couldn't possibly fit in search of those sought-after treats. I had to deal with her once when she tried to gain entry into my bungalow, and I can tell you, sir, it is no small thing to face down a four-ton behemoth intent on your biscuit tin. But I did what I'd been told to do. I hit her on the foot with a tent peg—the foot, not the tent peg, being the key here; the tent peg was simply what was handy. And sure enough she stopped in her tracks, all penitence and meekness, and raised her foot to be beaten again, before she backed out onto the veranda, swinging her great head in shame."

He pauses then to shake his own head at this sorrowful recollection, though, as Jack Connolly fears, he is not yet done. There is more he still wishes to say.

"The foot—that's the thing to remember about elephants. Hit the foot and they're gentle as lambs. Not that I think these cows of yours can be subdued in the same way, though there's something in their eyes, I think, that reminds me of old Garuda. A look of long-suffering forbearance, I'd say, with a hint of ancient wisdom. I'm sure they could tell us many a tale if they had a mind to."

He stops again and looks at Jack as if for corroboration, though Jack Connolly has nothing to add. Never in his life has he credited a cow with wisdom of any sort. And he has only the dimmest, vague picture of an elephant in his head. A barrel-shaped thing, he imagines it, like a giant, gray, wrinkled pig whose snout's been stretched out like a long rubber tube and whose ears sometimes flap like the wings of a goose preparing to land on a pond.

But here, at last, is the cutoff to the farm where surely Kipling will leave him—turn back or keep walking, Jack Connolly doesn't care, as long as he doesn't have to listen to him rattling on about tent pegs and biscuits. And as if that's his plan, Kipling stops at the gate and watches the cows proceed. He bows at the waist, sweeping his arm to etch a loose corkscrew in the air, a gesture Jack hopes signals farewell, though again he is doomed to disappointment. For, blast: if the man doesn't stick with him still, up the drive to the front of the barn, pausing as Jack undoes the latch and swings the great door open, bowing deferentially and graciously again, as if he, and not Jack, were the host stepping back to permit his guests to pass.

Then he follows Jack right into the barn, as cheeky and presumptuous a thing as Jack Connolly can imagine. He follows and waits as Jack ushers in the cows, perusing the tools by the harness room door: the lister, the bucksaw, the scythe. But still Jack says nothing. He just lets the man enter without a word of protest, once again stunned into silent submission by the sheer force of Kipling's audacity. But he'll not give him more, he vows to himself. He'll answer no more of his questions, nor pay any heed to the muttering stream Kipling's embarked on again. And when this long imposition is over—as eventually he knows it must be—he'll wash the whole burdensome weight of it away with a long, intemperate drink.

To hasten that moment's arrival, he ties the cows up in their stalls, lights the lanterns that hang from the hooks in the tie beams, takes his stool and his milking pail. Sitting down squarely with his back to Kipling, who leans against the stall, talking now about water buffalo—how they like to submerge themselves in mud wallows when they're let out to graze, settling down so completely in the mud that they look like mere bumps of floating log—Jack grabs the cow's teats, squeezing them fiercely until the animal bellows. He clenches, releases, clenches, releases, pumping up his fist till the muscles and veins in his wrist start to throb and the first drop of milk hits the bottom of the pail, echoing against the empty tin sides as loud as a blast of buckshot. Then down comes the milk, in spatters and spurts. Like a stream of piss, he thinks, the first trickling bit even tinged a pale yellow, with a faint but stale, excremental smell that leaves him, as always, feeling sick.

Still he milks the cow dry then moves on to the next. Milks that one and moves on again, stopping only to pour the milk through the strainer when his pail is full. And Kipling keeps following, moving along with him from stall to stall, setting his elbows atop the top rail, smacking his hands eagerly. He asks Jack questions—about each cow's yield, its temperament, feed, and care—questions Jack tosses off with a shrug, too busy and bothered to answer, until finally Kipling abandons his grilling and just stands there, quietly staring. Jack feels the man's eyes on him, watching him, goading him, taking in his every move, as if he were some curious specimen trapped in a jar or a cage. But at least Kipling's stopped talking; there's that to be glad of. At least that onslaught's over, though the silence that now descends upon them seems another form of oppression that Jack tries to lift by sounds of annoyance, planting his stool by the last of the cows with an extra show of force, clanging his pail against the storage can as he pours the last bucketful in. He hastily drags the rake through the stalls, scraping the prongs across the dirt floor like a fingernail on a chalkboard, and he rummages loudly through the loose bedding hay, looking for the jug of hardened cider he stashed there just the other day. Finding it, he walks to the door and slings the jug over his shoulder, standing there, with his feet spread apart, in an attitude of defiance. But his grumblings and grunts all seem lost on Kipling, who stands for a moment in the center of the barn with his hands clasped behind his back, looking up at the hayloft, the rafters, the beams, all stippled with swallow droppings. He pivots his head slowly to take in the whole view, then sighs and turns around, walking to join Jack Connolly near the door with a strange and rueful smile.

"You know, Mr. Connolly, I confess, I envy you. Now that you've finished your work, you can go right inside, wash up, and sit down to your supper, while I have to wrestle with a bow tie and cufflinks before I'm deemed fit to dine."

"I wouldn't know about that," Jack Connolly says, pushing open the barn door again.

"My point precisely," Kipling says, with his finger raised in the air. And as if this is what he has wanted all along—this point of concurrence, this solidarity—he says that he should be heading off now. He's stayed long enough for one day.

"But do give my best to your wife and your boy," he says as he heads down the drive. "And perhaps when next we meet, we'll have snow," he adds, looking up at the sky.

Jack Connolly looks at the sky as well, where only a grain of light is left and the clouds still refuse to let go. Then he watches his neighbor trundle off to the road, his figure so swaddled, so obscured by fur that, if he didn't know any better, he might think the man was a bear.

"A damn fool bear," he says to himself, though his words lack the hard edge of ire.

Then he feels his anger seeping away as Kipling's figure recedes— all that indignant, put-upon, self-righteous fury he's been grooming and feeding all day. And for just a brief moment, as he turns to the house, he's not sure that he wants it to go. He longs for the crooked satisfaction of anger, the justification it brings, the way it can make him feel fully alive as little else but the jolt of drink does. So he tries to stoke it up again, recalling how intrusive and absurd the man was, with his condescending airs, trespassing to make those insidious inroads on his land and his mind and his son. But he's just as unable to rekindle his anger as he is to hold onto it firmly, and he enters the house, not slamming the door as he imagined he would, not setting the jug by his place at the table with a loud, confrontational thud.

And there is the table: the patterned oilcloth, the tin plates, and enameled tin cups. The basket of biscuits covered up with a towel, the steaming chipped bowl of mashed squash. And there is his wife, standing there by the stove, frying up patties of pork, and the pump at the sink where he washes his hands, scrubbing them clean of the smell of cold cow, warm dung, and sour milk.

"Was that Mr. Kipling out there?" Addie asks.

"That was him," Jack Connolly answers.

"Did he want something?"

"Yes, to talk about elephants."

"Elephants?" Addie says, turning to peer at him quizzically.

"Yes, he followed me all the way out to the barn just to say that should I ever run into an elephant, I should hit it on the foot with a tent peg."

"He told you that, did he?"

"Yes, he did," Jack says, leaving Addie once again to distill her bewilderment down to one small, meager word.

"Well," she says heavily, turning back to the stove as Jack dries his hands, watching as his wife neatly flips the patties over, then pats them in the sizzling grease. She holds the frying pan handle in one hand and a slotted wood spoon in the other so that when a strand of hair falls in her eyes, she must brush it away with the back of her hand, pushing it up from her forehead. The rest of her hair is coiled in a knot just above her shirtwaist's collar. And there, between the frayed edge of the collar and her swept-up hair, he spies a bit of ivory skin: the shaft of her neck rising up like the spout of a jug from the curve of her shoulders. Would it be cool or warm to the touch? Jack Connolly cannot say, though he longs to lay his hands there, rest his palms at the base of her neck, let his fingers comb through the whorls of her hair, securing those renegade strands.

Instead he sits down at the table and lifts the towel from the biscuits. He takes one and digs his thumb in to split it, letting a small cloud of steam escape. Then he takes up his knife and a fat hunk of butter from the crock and slathers it on, helps himself to some squash and a few of the patties that Addie's now set on a platter. She takes her seat, a mere arm's length away, clasps her hands and says a quick grace. And although he feels the urge again—to touch her, to cover her hands with his own, to absorb her calm coolness or warmth—he does not reach out for his wife. Though nor does he reach for the earthenware jug that still sits on the table beside him.

Joe wakes to the sound of his parents' voices, murmuring below him—wakes, though he has no clear recollection of having fallen asleep, no memory of laying his head on the pillow, closing his eyes, growing drowsy. He does, though, remember longing for sleep, for the sweet oblivion of it. Yet now, waking up, he feels only flustered, wary and suspicious, as if sleep were a prank that had been played on him, a blindfold tied over his eyes, and now that the blindfold's been removed, he looks around, dazed and distrustful, afraid that while he lay asleep another trick might have been played. Some bait and switch or sly amusement wherein his belongings were stolen or hidden or rearranged just to confuse him.

So he lights the candle on the bedside table and takes a quick inventory. There is the commode in its usual corner. There is the jug and basin. The rush seat chair, the hickory crutch, all accounted for and present. He acknowledges the mirror still nailed to the wall and the dormer window, where to his relief he sees that he hasn't yet missed the start of the snow. Then he turns to the bed, sees the basket of clothes-pegs just where his mother had left it, the top with its rusting red and white stripes, the book, the yarn, Kipling's letter. Even that is here, though just for a moment he finds himself wishing that an imp had, indeed, snuck into his room and plucked it. But there it is, with his own name written across the envelope, the *J* like a fish hook crowned with a plume, the *o* and the *e* looped together.

Had he still needed proof that Kipling knew his name, here it is, attested to in print; though staring at the envelope now, Joe feels only a dim, abstract connection between the name dashingly scripted there and his own undashing self, as if the letter weren't meant for him, the *real* him who's crippled and common. Yet despite this, Joe picks the envelope up and holds it in his hand, feeling its weight, as light as a leaf, in the flat of his opened palm. How easy it would be to crumple it up, to ball it in his fist, to set it alight with the flame of the candle, reduce it to nothing but ashes. Instead he runs his hand over the edges, pressing the pad of this thumb on a corner till it feels like the prick of a pin, as he listens once more to the sounds from downstairs—the murmur sporadic but not yet punctuated by the stacking or scrubbing of plates, from which he assumes that his mother and father must be occupied at the table. Then he slips his finger beneath the flap and unfixes the sealing wax, drawing the letter out furtively, holding it up to his eyes.

"My dear boy," he reads with his heart strangely racing and his blood pounding in his inner ear.

"You'll be pleased to hear that our mutual friend has managed to escape from those miscreants with only a few scrapes and bruises, the worst of which, I confess, he incurred at the hands of Bagheera. The old panther, I fear, has knocked him about some, cuffed him and boxed his ears in—all out of love for the boy, I daresay, though Mowgli might beg to differ. When last I saw him, he was licking his wounds, curled up in the great coils of Kaa, who, out of his own affection for the boy, is allowing himself to be used as a chaise for a short, recuperative spell.

"Here's wishing that you are resting as well and will soon be back on your feet. I'm quite certain that Mowgli's adventures aren't yet over and I may need your help once again.

Your friend,

Rudyard Kipling"

Joe reads the letter once, then twice, then sets it down on the bed. He is not quite sure what he expected to find—some edifying call to buck up, he supposes, or some cheery command to get well—but not this, not a note quite so personal and private, like a secret whispered into his ear. And now, having read it, Joe feels confused, unsure of what to think. Since the night he spent at the Water-Cure, he hasn't thought much about Mowgli. He hasn't wanted to, unable to rid himself of the thought that Mowgli had led him astray—deceived him, betrayed him, lured him to that place where all his heroic and idyllic dreams had shattered just like his leg. But looking out the window, at the black expanse of sky, he pictures the scene: the tall columns of palm trees with their fanning, serrated fronds. Bright flowers like trumpets, leaves big as dinner plates, the ground dappled with brilliant light. And there is the python, basking in the hot sun, the scales of its coils patterned like a Roman mosaic, cradling a boy who winces and scowls as he touches a flaming red bruise.

And hasn't that boy been injured, as Joe has? His pride and his body wounded and hurt, after receiving a good, stern comeuppance for a similar act of conceit? Perhaps, Joe thinks, as he stares out the window at the vision he has conjured, feeling, as he does, something stirring inside him, a twisted knot loosening up. He feels the jungle beckoning him as it did the other night, urging him on to that lush, profuse place where the days are meant for lounging and loafing and the nights are spent tracking prey, where punishments are meted out swiftly and surely and then just as surely forgotten.

Joe lets himself sink down in his bed like Mowgli in his nest of coils, trying to imagine the cool feel of snakeskin under his neck and his shoulders. He sinks and he drifts, released for a moment from the earthbound board strapped to his leg and the strange weight of shame he's felt bearing down on him ever since he was brought back home. But in that same moment, as he drifts and relaxes and starts to daydream again, he fails to attend to the sounds from below him—to the talk that has ended, to the plates being cleared, to the creak of the rusting pump handle—until he hears footsteps approaching on the stairs. His father, he surmises from the slow, heavy gait and the ponderous weight of each footfall.

Quickly Joe scrambles to find Kipling's letter and stuff it back into its envelope. He shoves the whole thing under his covers, where he prays it won't be seen, smooths out the sheet, sets his hands on the quilt and his eyes on the open doorway with a look that he hopes perhaps will seem bored but, to his father, guileless.

"So you're up," says his father as he enters the room, carrying in a supper tray. "Your ma said you were sleeping," he adds as he sets the tray by the bed. Then he stands there with his arms laced over his chest, staring down at the covers where, to Joe's chagrin, he sees a wedge of paper peeking out from under the sheets.

"You know, I talked with your Mr. Kipling today," his father says, staring at the letter. "He said that you told him I'd help him with his drive. Help him blast half the whole hillside out."

"I didn't say that you would. I said that you could," Joe answers, his voice low and bitter.

"Well, I might," his father says, "I just might," as he slowly draws in his bottom lip and scrapes it with his teeth. "Well, there's your supper," he says, nodding at the tray. "You should eat it before it gets cold. And you might think about getting out of that bed. It'll give you nothing but sores."

"Yes, sir," Joe says, though he makes no move to get up or to eat.

"Suit yourself then," his father says, before he turns and walks from the room, leaving Joe there, staring down at his hands, now balled up into fists.

Joe listens as his father retraces his steps and says something to his mother—words that he wouldn't want to make out even if he could. Then he hears the back door swing open and shut. His father most likely, since he thinks he hears his mother still tidying downstairs. Then he looks at the plate on his bedside table. Two patties sit in a small pool of grease that's started to congeal. The biscuits lay by a mound of squash, their bottoms stained orange and soggy. He picks up a fork and moves the squash, making as wide a lane as he can between the mound and the biscuits, then lays the fork down to survey his work before pushing the whole tray away. Then his eyes glance down at the wedge of envelope still poking out under the bedclothes, a small triangle that seems startlingly white against the dullness of the sheets.

Joe pulls it out slowly and once again stares at his name boldly scripted there, following the curving course of each letter as if it might lead him somewhere. Then he sets it before him, on top of the quilt, propped up by the basket of clothes-pegs. And for a while all he does is sit there, staring at the paper. Then finally he turns to the window again, half expecting to be greeted by the vision of Mowgli nestled in the coils of Kaa. But beyond the glass is just the night sky, still clotted with dark clouds, the expanse broken only by the limbs of bare trees and the black monolith of the barn. He stares at this too, until his mind seems as blank and empty as the sky, willing himself back into a state of detached indifference.

But then there, right there, he sees a small light, zigzagging a few feet off the ground, erratically flitting like some luminous insect that has strayed from some warmer climate. Joe watches it, mesmerized, as it darts back and forth, unable to stop himself from thinking that it could be some emissary from that faraway tropic, bearing a message just for him to discover, decipher, and follow.

He sees the spark of light reach the barn, vanish, then reappear, not skittering now, skipping from side to side, but just stationary and dim. And he knows what he should have known all along: it was only the light of the lantern his father must have swung as he walked to the barn and now has hung on a tie-beam hook while he beds down the cows for the night.

Dismayed and disgusted by the workings of his mind, Joe turns from the window and stares once again at the envelope, there on the bed, glaring as though his eyes had the power to set the whole thing aflame. Then he lifts his legs up under the covers, first his good one, then the one with the splint, starting slowly, then faster and faster, till the bed seems the site of some massive upheaval—an eruption, an earthquake, a tempest—and the things lying there start to jiggle and topple, slide off and crash down to the floor.

Once they've all tumbled off, Joe looks at the damage, peering over the side of the bed. The clothes-pegs are scattered all over the floor; the top spins, on its side, on the rug. The letter lies trapped beneath his old primer, which has landed propped up, like a tent. Such a gratifying sight it seems, though the pleasure is only short-lived. Joe sits back up, feeling the sense of accomplishment drain away, for now he doesn't know what to do. He has no appetite for dinner, no need, any longer, for sleep, nor any desire to read or play with the clothes-pegs, the yarn, or the top. So his eyes gravitate again to the window, as they have done all day, where still there is no trace of snow, and still the speck of light beckons.

Why he does what he does then, Joe cannot say, except that the light seems to be pulling him, like a poor moth to a flame, and his father's words keep ringing in his ears, scolding him for just lying there. So he swings his splinted leg over the bed and hobbles to the corner, clutching the knob at the top of the bedpost then hopping to the chair. He takes up the crutch that leans against the wall and fits the dowel under his armpit. Then he limps to the door, his good foot, the crutch, making a slow, fitful progress, bypassing the mess he just made on the floor with only the briefest of thoughts.

Then comes the hallway, the landing, the stairs, which are almost impossible to manage. Joe plants his crutch on the step below him, grabs the banister with his free hand, and takes what seems like a wild, flying leap—though the riser is only a foot. He lands, his good leg on the same tread as the tip of the crutch, the muscles of his outer thigh aching and tense from absorbing the shock of his landing. He pauses, then casts himself off again, repeating the whole awkward process—the crutch set firmly on the next step, his knuckles gripped tight around the banister, his eyes focused steadily, willfully forward to avoid being sideswept by vertigo—till after another step or two he must sit down and rest, exhausted by his strenuous efforts and taken aback by the view of the kitchen that now opens up before him.

He has not seen the room for over four weeks, having not been downstairs once, and now it appears both strange and familiar, like a room that exists in a dream. He stares at the table with the oilcloth streaked by the still-damp wipes of a rag, at a bowl full of apples, a towel set out to dry, the black iron beast of the stove. Each object seems to stand out and quiver, as if lit by an otherworldly light. The mason jars filled with dried beans and buckwheat. The meat grinder clamped to the cutting board. The ladderback chairs set along the far wall, all stacked with piles of laundry. But then he sees his mother by the window, sitting with her back to the stairs, with a shawl around her shoulders, the mending basket at her feet, a skein of thread falling from her lap. He instantly freezes and stiffens right up, sucking in and holding his breath, as all that vertiginous, light-headed dreaminess promptly evaporates.

Joe hadn't thought of his mother at all when he started down the stairs, and he has no idea of what he will say if she turns around now and asks questions. But the slump of her shoulders and the way her hand dangles, not quite grasping the unspooled thread, makes him quite sure that she's fallen asleep, right there, by the hearth in the kitchen. All he must do, though it's no simple feat, is to proceed quietly, down the rest of the stairs, to the landing, the door—and then what? Just what was he thinking? Going out for a stroll in his long johns and stocking feet when it's cold enough to snow?

Then he's smacked by the fear that this whole enterprise is as ill-conceived as that other recent doomed trek and all he's accomplished is the folly of making the same mistake twice. Yet didn't his father urge him to get up? Isn't he simply complying, being a good, obedient son, doing more than what had been asked? He bats the question around in his head, settling, finally, on the latter view when he spies one of his father's old sweaters hanging on a coat hook, and his muckraking boots, like a pair of worn sentries standing by the door.

Joe shuffles slowly, haltingly, to them, stealing glimpses of his mother with each step. But she doesn't stir and he doesn't stumble. Full of stealth, he reaches the landing. Though still, with the stairs now solidly behind him, there are other hurdles to cross. To put the boot on his good foot, for one, he must place some weight on his bad leg, which he does to the accompaniment of a sharp pain that shoots up the shaft of his shin. But the pain is not really all that bad, and his father's boots not too big, nor is the sweater once he rolls the sleeves up to the thin, bony knobs of his wrists.

Then he slips outside. The clouds still hover, a low, uniform ceiling of gray, except for a small and round, pale, hazy patch where it seems that the clouds have sopped up the moon, absorbed all its light like a sponge. Joe feels the punch of the cold hit his chest and almost doubles over. His eyes start to tear as the rush of cold air he breathes in seems to ice up his lungs. He thinks of his bed, of the warm, mussed-up sheets and the soft, downy depths of his pillow, though that thought is offset by the compulsion he still can feel spurring him on. Besides which, he reckons, the barn can't be harder to reach than the top of the stairs. So he juts his lower lip out and exhales, sending up a cloud of warm breath. He breathes in his own self-generated heat until he feels steadier, warmer. Then he starts in again, making his hesitant way across the yard, careful to avoid the few patches of ice and the water trough, exerting himself enough with his hopping that before he's even halfway there, he actually starts to sweat.

Then he comes to the barn, lifts the latch of the door, and leans into the wood, pushing with his forearm and shoulder and hip until the door groans and gives way. He steps inside, shuts the door behind

him, and takes a deep, fortifying breath, looking around him, at the
scaffold and stalls, all bathed in the light of the lantern his father has
hung from a tie-beam hook.

Of course, it is not really warm in the barn, though it gives off an
aura of warmth. The aisles and the stalls are all strewn with straw.
Bales of hay sit stacked by the wall. Steam rises up from the animals'
muzzles. In the loft, the hens rustle their feathers. Joe watches the
cows stirring around him as he starts to limp down the aisle. One
flicks its tail and shifts its dull weight from one foot to another.
Another slowly turns its black-and-white head to appraise him with
its blank eye. He sees a barn cat, a calico blur, slink along the wall, the
humped woolly backs of the lone pair of sheep his parents still keep,
in the shadows. And he listens to the sounds that accompany his passage. The low nicker of the horse as it paws the ground, the snuffling
grunts of the pigs. All the soft murmurs of the roosting birds, the
cows quietly, patiently chewing.

Compared with all this, Joe's own staggered movements seem too
loud and clumsy. His crutch tolls each step with a faltering cadence.
His good foot lands with a thud as he reaches the end of the aisle with
the stalls and comes to the barn's back transverse. But apparently he
is quiet enough not to have disturbed his father, who Joe now sees off
in a corner, bent over the rim of a grindstone, sharpening a tool. He
sits on a chair he must have fashioned from two bales of hay, and as
he works, tapping his foot on the lever and moving his hands to keep
the blade centered against the spinning stone, he hums to himself an
old railroading song whose melody Joe recognizes.

Well, at least he seems to be sober, Joe thinks with a shudder of
relief. For now that he's come all this way just to find him, he is overwhelmed by the thought of his father's possible wrath, the anger he

could rain down on Joe if he feels interrupted.

But his father looks up then, his eyes drawn by the sparks from the stone or some sense of Joe's presence. He utters Joe's name, his voice startled, not harsh as Joe had feared it might be.

"Joe, is that you," he says as he squints and peers down the length of the aisle.

"What for the love of God ...," he begins as Joe steels himself for a rebuke. But his father stops and lets his words drift, seemingly staring right through him, so stymied and transfixed by something he sees that Joe tries to turn around too. He pivots awkwardly on one foot and anxiously scans the barn, eyeing the stalls to see what's the matter, looking for something askew. Then finally he sees what his father has seen, what has caught his eye and left him speechless. A whorl of white floats down in a column through the unrepaired hole in the roof. A maelstrom of flakes, fat spangles of snow, all silently, soundlessly, falling.

THE WORD OF THE HEAD WOLF IS LAW

Snow falls off and on for most of the month, sometimes drifting and floating as light as goose down, sometimes pounding the earth like a fusillade. Kipling watches it fall from the desk in his study, reveling in winter's elements. He loves the grand theatrics of the storms: the winds that pound and howl and roar, the deep groundswell of drifts by the door, the pall of night skies stitched and studded with flakes, and those blessed, storm-cleansed dawns when the sun finally breaks, as it has this morning, through a thick mantle of clouds to shine down on a pristine world, all dazzlingly sparkling and white.

He loves, too, the way the snow seems to obscure all trace of human presence. Fence posts, boot prints, till lines, furrows—all have been blurred or erased. Even the road seems to have vanished beneath the mounting snow, leaving an expanse stretching out from his door as white and blank as the block of writing paper before him on his desk.

Of course, while he prefers his landscape unmarred, he would not mind some marks on the paper. But although he has sat here most every morning, just as he sits here today, with a blank sheet before him, his pen poised in his hand, his mind receptive and ready, he hasn't gotten much work done. There's the weather, for one, which he finds so compelling that often when he does set pen to paper it's to write a letter to family or friends describing the season's high drama. And, too, there's the havoc the weather has wrought—frozen pipes, wind-ripped shingles, fallen branches—which has forced him on more than one occasion to exchange the tools of his trade for a hammer, an ax, once even a blowtorch that he had to hold beneath their lead pipe in the hopes that the damn thing would thaw.

And then there is Carrie, confined now upstairs until the baby arrives. Though the doctor's advised her to stay in her bed and save up her strength for her labor, he can often hear her pacing above him, worrying a trail across the planked boards of the floor right over his head. He hears her, too, frequently holler at Anna, who seems to grow meeker each day, hugging the wall of the stairs as she carries a tea tray up to her mistress, bowing and cowering as Carrie complains that the beef tea has not been properly strained, that the soup spoon shows traces of tarnish, that her step is too loud, or when not loud, too soft, that she cannot go creeping or sneaking about in a way that gives people a fright.

With all of this he has tried to be patient, for it clearly is a difficult time, what with the limitations imposed by the doctor, the harsh weather, Carrie's burgeoning shape. He has watched her grow these last few weeks even larger than he'd thought possible, has seen how she has to press down her knuckles into the mattress just to leverage her weight. One night as she thrashed about in bed, tossing this way and that, seeking comfort, he caught a not-quite welcomed glimpse of her belly. The skin was pulled as taut as a drum and flushed a bright shade of scarlet except where it was riddled by blue spidery veins and that ominous line heading south, down from the starting point of her navel, which he saw had popped out like a cork.

It made him toss and turn as well, with a kindred restlessness, disturbed by the sight of that swollen protuberance and the thought of the child all knotted up in there and soon to be expelled. In fact, he was so unable to sleep that he rose and went to his desk, a true sanctuary in the dead of the night though not always in the daytime, when he is often so distracted by his wife's anxious pacing that he sometimes finds it easier to take up the tea tray himself.

He did this, in fact, just yesterday: carted the tray up, set it down on the bed, and tried his best to look patient, as Carrie worriedly clutched his hand and launched into her list of fears about how the house was falling into ruin while she lay there, sentenced to rest, and how nothing, she was certain, would be done right for the baby if she wasn't there herself to supervise.

"Now you're getting all hot and bothered," he'd scolded. "Shall I tell you a story instead?"

"If you like," she had replied, sinking her head with a sigh into the pillow as he'd dragged the maple chair to her bedside and poured them each some tea.

Then he told her one of the tales he'd concocted from their own life together, the saga of The Englishman and His Bride, as he's honorifically dubbed them, this one about their poor, ill-fated stab at a honeymoon.

"Now, there once was an Englishman who took His Bride away halfway round the world, wanting to show her those parts of the East that had been his stomping ground as a youth. It was an ambitious undertaking, quite admirable, though some might say unwise, since The Englishman had little to recommend him to His Bride but two thousand pounds in fixed bank deposits and his word about the prospects of his pen. Besides which, he didn't have much of a head for things like timetables and budgets, though he'd already discovered that His Bride was adept at those very skills he sorely lacked."

He had paused there a moment to look up at Carrie, who archly rolled her eyes back, protesting with a pursed-lip frown that he thought belied her amusement.

"Still, The Englishman," he continued, "didn't want His Bride to have to engage in such matters, since this was, after all, their honeymoon, and he was to be their guide, and since, most delightfully, she had recently told him that she was carrying their child." And here he was certain he saw a small smile and a hint of a faint blush emerge.

"So he bade His Bride stay in their rooms one beautiful spring morning as he set off to make arrangements, stopping at Cook's and the P&O office and the Yokohama branch of his bank. At that last he struggled to fill out a form requesting a modest withdrawal—incorrectly, he assumed, since upon its presentation the bank manager came to the floor.

"'Are you sure, sir,' asked the manager, 'that you wouldn't like more?'

"'No, no,' replied The Englishman, most relieved to discover that he hadn't really bungled the form and most anxious to show His Bride just how prudent and financially responsible he could be.

"'But truly, sir, it's as easy to withdraw a large sum as it is a small.'

"'No, no,' said The Englishman, beginning to feel miffed. 'I am quite sure that this is all we'll need.'

"'As you wish, sir,' said the manager regretfully, with an air of doomed resignation that, in hindsight, The Englishman wished he had paid a bit more attention to."

"But couldn't, of course, hindsight being hindsight," Carrie had interjected helpfully.

"Perhaps," he had said, "though I think we shouldn't try to offer him any excuses. Let's suffice it to say he was simply too pleased with all these completed transactions to pay the man any heed. Why, he almost skipped along the Bund to meet His Bride at their hotel, where he hired a rickshaw just outside the lobby to take them around that afternoon.

"And what a lovely day they had, The Englishman and His Bride, perched atop their rickshaw seats, riding through the town! They poked their heads in old curio shops, emerging with a pair of black lacquer boxes and an ivory-handled Samurai sword, and stumbled upon a charming teahouse set in a raked-stone garden where they drank green tea from crackled cups beneath a weeping plum tree and watched tangerine carp dart about in a pond encircled with red paper lanterns.

"But between their trinkets and the cups of tea and the coins they threw in the pond..."

"...and the rickshaw driver and the bean paste sweets that you bought for some urchins," Carrie added.

"...The Englishman found that he had little left at the end of the day and so was obliged to return to his bank just before its closing hour.

"He went sheepishly, afraid that the manager, with some knowing and withering look, would say, 'I told you so.' Yet arriving at the bank he found the entrance closed and a notice nailed to the door. He read the sign, or attempted to—it was filled with legal jargon—and while much of the content was lost upon him, he was able to gather that his deposits, which he had thought of as fixed, were not quite so fixed after all. In fact, at this point, they amounted to nothing. He had virtually nothing left, except for the handful of coins in his pocket and a pair of Cook's travel vouchers, until, that is, they got back to New York, where a royalty check awaited.

"So back to the hotel he was forced to go, even more shamefaced than he had been when he set off to the bank the second time. For now he had to confess to His Bride that not only had he failed to provide for a full day's worth of spending money, they were stranded in a foreign land with barely a cent to their names and with all his vainglorious promises and plans revealed as no more than hot air.

"And how did His Bride take this desolate news? She was simply superb," he'd said, though Carrie here demurred again, brushing off his praise with a shake of her head as if shooing away a fly.

"Right then and there she proposed that they form a Committee of Ways and Means and convened on the spot an emergency meeting, wherein they went over their few, meager options and agreed on a plan of retrenchment, deciding to return posthaste to Vermont if Cook's could be persuaded to exchange their forward vouchers for a pair of confirmed return tickets. Then just before the meeting adjourned, The Englishman vowed that he'd never again fail to live up to His Bride's faith in him. He would build her a mansion, a palace, he promised. And hasn't he kept his word?" And coming to the end of the tale, he had swept his arm across the room, commanding her to behold it, as if this cramped, ramshackle place were proof of his pledge's fulfillment.

Then Carrie had actually laughed right out loud, a skeptical but good-natured guffaw that acknowledged the absurdity of their current situation, however temporary. Though when the laugh faded, she had sighed again and once more clutched at his hand.

"Oh, Ruddy, how are we ever to manage?"

"Chin up. We're almost there. The baby will be here any day now and the house is nearly finished. Or will be when the snow lets up," he amended with a glance out the window. Then he pulled his hand out from under hers and gave her arm a brief pat.

"Yes, of course you're right. Of course, we'll manage," she had said with enough conviction that he left her there and returned to his study, where he actually managed to knock out a first draft of a new barracks-room verse.

But no such diversions are needed today. All is quiet upstairs. There's no fretful pacing or creaking bed, no summonses or histrionics. The only sound comes from the kitchen, where the girl is preparing Carrie's tea, and when he hears her mount the stairs, he turns to watch her ascend, staying there, with his head cocked and craned, until he sees her return, seemingly unperturbed, flicking a feather duster lightly along the banister. Then he turns back to the paper before him. He dips his pen in the ink, encouraged to see it hasn't frozen again as it did just a few days ago. Perhaps today he'll gain a foothold on a new jungle story. Perhaps he'll receive a vision of Mowgli, off on another adventure, and feel himself embarked as well on some new torrent of words.

He stares out the window as a dollop of snow falls from the bough of a pine tree. A camp robber flits from one branch to another looking for something to scavenge. A small bead of water, warmed by the sun, slides down the ridge of an icicle only to freeze at the shaft's pointed tip, caught right in the process of dropping. But although the signs all seem auspicious—with no household repairs demanding his attention and his ink thin and warm enough to flow—nothing seems to happen. His mind can't manage to find that place where icicles turn into vines. He's unable to conjure a kite from the jay, can't leap from one world to another. And the snow, that broad, white, untainted canvas, remains just simple, white snow, a substance too cold, too deep, and too barren for anything much to emerge.

Kipling sets his pen back down and lifts up his inkpot instead, holding it contemplatively in the palm of one hand. It is a large, pewter tub of a pot that he bought on Villiers Street, on whose surface he's taken to gouging the names of various stories he's written. He scans the titles he's carved there with a knife until he finds the ones he's after—MOWGLI'S BROTHERS, TIGER! TIGER! and last of all, KAA'S HUNTING. He runs his thumb across the words, fingering the letters, like a gypsy stroking the lines of a palm in the hopes of foretelling the future. Yet if his touch doesn't summon the future, it does bring back the past: the morning several months ago when he'd awoken with a vision of Mowgli and rushed down to the desk in his study where his Daemon ignited his pen. The tale seemed to spill fully formed from him then in a single, headlong rush: the boy; the wolves; and Shere Khan, the dreaded tiger who has a score to settle with the child, a vendetta the wolves so fear being embroiled in that they banish the boy from the pack. And the next, where the boy went to live among men and exact his revenge on the tiger, only to find himself ousted again, cast out from the village as a demon: this one virtually wrote itself too, as did, at least in retrospect, the last, the story of Mowgli's adventures with the monkeys in the ruined Cold Lairs. That was a good bit of scribing, he thinks, even if he says so himself. Though now, with his hands still cupping the inkpot and the weight of it heavy in his palms, he senses that that story was no more than a detour from the book's true course, and if he is to meet Mowgli again, he must return to the troublesome matter of those dual expulsions.

So he stares out the window again and tries to turn his mind to Mowgli, walking past the village gate with the tiger's skinned hide on his head, nimbly evading the hurled stones and jeers of the villagers. He tries to will himself to see him, heading off to the jungle alone, turning his back on both the closed-off worlds of wolves and men. But instead what suddenly springs to his mind is an image from a dream he'd forgotten: Mowgli standing out in the snow, shivering from the cold, his eyes trying to peer through Kipling's own study window, his nose pressed to the cold, frosted glass.

It's a vision that makes him shiver as well, the sight of that poor, misbegotten, wild child hovering, half-naked in the snow. It jars and unnerves him with a wave of guilt, as if he were the one who'd abandoned the boy, not the village or the council of wolves; and the smug disdain he'd imagined Mowgli feeling as he walked through the angry crowd with the hide like a crown on his head was just a thin façade that hid a vast longing he can't bear to see, coming too close, as it does, to his own buried needs to belong and be admired.

Shaking, he sets the inkpot down and pushes it away. So much for trying to force his Daemon, he thinks, feeling humbled and chastened. He should never have attempted to push; he should have just drifted and waited, accepting nothing if nothing was all his Daemon had to give. Then, penitent, he sets his elbows on the desk and perches his chin on his knuckles, prepared to wait for however long he must, without complaint or impatience. And after a while what does drift into his mind is the thought that if Mowgli is outside in the snow, perhaps he should go outside, too. At least clear his head with the brisk, tonic air, if not manage a rendezvous.

So he heads to the hallway where his fur coat hangs, and his hat and his gloves and his snowshoes, which look like a pair of sawed-off beaver tails fashioned from birch bark and leather. He dons his gear and opens the door, taking an invigorating breath. The air is as dry and heady and bracing as a glass of the finest champagne. The weave of his snowshoes sinks into fresh powder as light as the wisps of a cloud. And in the shadows, he sees a strange light, blue-green and indigo, glinting off the snowdrift, spectral and tantalizing.

It makes him think this is where he should be—out here where the trees are frosted with white and the deer tracks are filled with new powder, where the air and exertion will undoubtedly manage to reconcile him to his work. He wanders a bit, checks the tracks and the bird feeder he has filled with seed and millet and the tin cans he's set about the yard as putting holes for snow golf. These are filled to the brim with snow as well, almost buried beneath his white links, and he trudges through the snow from can to can, emptying the contents of each, then traipses over to the figure he built when the last blizzard broke. He had meant to construct not a mere, simple snowman, but a mighty and lordly Ganesh, like the fat-bellied god with the elephant head that once sat by his dear ayah's bedside; though now, with its features obscured by new snow, it looks more like a nondescript heap. He brushes it free of its most recent dusting, then pats down the belly and trunk, uncovering, as he does, the golf balls he had used in lieu of bricks of coal for the eyes and the god's bulging navel. He has painted these balls a bright vermilion—all the better to find them amid the white snow after a long iron drive, and better as well for the eyes of a god, more preternatural and fiery. And now with the balls pocketed in his coat, he goes off in search of his clubs, only to spy another diversion that catches his fancy instead: the coaster he uses to sled down the slope that rises behind the house.

It sticks straight out of a mound of snow like a wooden gravestone—and has, in fact, seemed an agent of death on more than one occasion, sending him flying into a drift when it hit a patch of rocks once, almost crashing into boulders, fence posts, tree stumps, until he learned to steer. But seeing it now, he can't quite resist the prospect of a ride, and so he pulls it out from the snowbank and hauls it up the hillside, pausing when he reaches the crest of the slope to look back at the house. There he sees Carrie at the bedroom window, watching him pant and trudge. She lifts her hand and waves at him and he makes a great show of waving back, rocking his arm from side to side like the pendulum of a clock. Then he sets the coaster on the snow with its curved prow facing downward, and he climbs aboard, holding onto the towrope like a set of reins, even shaking them once to mime giddyup before pushing off with his hand.

Then he is sailing down the hill, the sled gliding over the snow, the sound of its swooshing filling his ears like the sound of pounding surf. Bits of kicked-up snow fly into his face, each a tingling pinprick of cold, clinging to the near-frozen tips of his mustache and numbing the cleft of his chin. His eyes start to tear and he feels the tears freeze as they're whipped back along his eyes' creases. The hairs in his nose are encrusted with ice and his ears are so cold they burn. But he lets out a walloping cry of joy, a great, echoing hoot of amusement, as the coaster skims the final bit and comes to a stop, sliding into the drift of snow that extends from the back of the house. Standing, he claps his hands on his arms in self-congratulation, sending down a shower of snow that had lodged itself in his furs. And he grabs the rope and heads back up the slope to do the whole thing all over, pausing again at the top of the hill to give a salute to Carrie, who still stands guard by their bedroom window, watching his comings and goings.

Then down again, and again once more, each time the coaster gaining more speed as it forms a track of packed snow, grooving a trail down the hillside. Each time the speed propels him a bit closer to the back of the house, where, instead of coasting and gliding, he plows into the drift with some force, coming to a stop a mere arm's length away from the buttress of the wall. But despite all this mounting speed and risk, he feels some momentum in him fade, and after a final halfhearted ride, he heaves the coaster out of the snow, unsure of what to do next. Perhaps he could take the sled to the schoolhouse, as he has done before, enticing the children away from their desks, much to the schoolmaster's displeasure. Or he could take it down the road to the Connollys' and try to tempt young Joe, who he knows has finally had his leg freed from the constraints of his splints.

But the last time he ventured down the road, he found himself oddly discouraged. The boy's mother, for one, was so startled to see him that she actually gasped and went pale. And the boy, when he finally came down from his room, stood there, uncomfortably still, blinking like an animal caught in the flickering light of a torch glare. Of course, he listened politely enough as Kipling told him things— how the skunks have miraculously decamped for the winter, how he must come and see his Ganesh. But when he paused between anecdotes, Joe said he had to go. He had to help his father, he explained, nodding toward the window, through which Kipling, turning, could make out Jack Connolly standing in the yard, hacking away at the crust of ice on the trough with a pick and a hatchet.

"Yes, of course you must," he sympathized, backing up so Joe could pass. He watched as the boy edged warily by him and headed to the door, one hand clamped to the side of the leg that he seemed to have to hitch up with each step so as not to drag it on the floor.

And now with that memory still strangely smarting, he turns to the house and looks up at the window where Carrie stood watching only to find that she's left her post, apparently not in need of more of his antics or tale-telling company either. And he finds himself wondering: Where would they be at this very moment if his bank hadn't failed? India? Burma? Ceylon? Samoa, where he had hoped they might visit Louis Stevenson and his own American bride? Through mutual friends—Henry James, Rider Haggard—he's heard how Stevenson's been restoring a house in a clearing hacked out of the jungle, riding a horse bareback through the trees, wielding a machete. By all accounts he's gone somewhat native, having shed his shoes and formalities to eat all his meals on the floor, sharing his house with flame-tufted cockatoos, chirping tree frogs, hoards of murderous bugs.

How keenly he would like to see that, Kipling thinks as he stands in the snow. To sit beneath the frangipani and swap tales with his idol, scooping out fish paste from coconut shells and feasting on sweet papaya. Why, he almost can hear the sigh of the trade winds, feel the hot sun on his back—though he can't for the life of him imagine Carrie walking barefoot through garden rows, chasing wild pigs and runaway hens as he's heard Fanny Stevenson does, or being forgiving and tolerant of servants so ignorant and unaware of the ways of the civilized world that, rumor has it, they'd taken guests' dress boots set out overnight to be blackened and washed them with a garden hose, both inside and out.

And then there's the fact that he did have the chance to visit once before, an opportunity he failed to act on for reasons far less obvious and extrinsic than a bank closing. That was when he'd set off round the world after finishing *The Naulahka*, a trip he hoped would be both recuperative and regenerating. He had hoped, as well, that Wolcott would join him and together they'd make a great pilgrimage, journey all the way to Stevenson's doorstep, two gypsying acolytes. But Wolcott declined the invitation and he himself never reached Samoa, making it as far as the dockside in Auckland before he aborted the plan.

To those who have asked, he's said that he did so because the arrangements were intolerable. He would have to have taken an old, tottery cutter, whose decks smelled rancid from coconut oil and were slick from loads of guano, that was captained by a man who reeked of fish and sweat and drink. He has even told himself this was so, has almost convinced himself of it, that he would have gone had he found a good ship with a sober, reliable skipper. Yet a small bit of him that he hasn't yet managed to bury knows this isn't quite so. For, of course, he had faced such discomforts before, had even turned them to advantage, gaining a nice bit of profit and fame by setting them down with his pen. He had, in good measure, embarked on this journey precisely to have such adventures, to replenish his store of eccentrics and mavericks, stock up on local color and grit. But he could not bring himself to step aboard that brig's warped gangplank, couldn't even have done it had the ship been outfitted with deck chairs and a good cellar. Having knocked about Capetown, Hobart, Melbourne, all the empire's far, dusty outposts, just to reach this launch point, he couldn't go any farther. He stood on the dock and watched the ship slowly slip away from its mooring, saw it hoist its sails as it reached the outer harbor, then head toward the horizon, where it became just a speck, a brief comma, between the sea and the sky. Then it disappeared into the Pacific, lost to all that blue. And he was left alone on the dock with his Gladstone bag at his feet, and with Stevenson, the island, the half-finished house, still vivid in his mind, unmarred by any unpleasantness he might have actually encountered—no insect bites or thorns or nettles, no soddened, ruined boots, nor late-night exchanges with the great master that might leave him wishing for more—and with all the allure of a thing long desired but forever untested, preserved.

And, too, he now thinks with the wisdom of hindsight, had he actually boarded that most sinkable vessel, he might not be here now. No, he might be lounging stuporously beneath a breadfruit tree or lying bloated, beside Davey Jones's locker, at the bottom of the sea. Though hindsight being hindsight, as Carrie has said, he can't quite take credit for that, unless, of course, he does what he does now: revises, rewrites the whole scene, turning hindsight into foresight with a mental sleight of hand that he pulls off so quickly and nimbly it seems it must always have been so.

Then he sees himself on that dock again as the ship sets out to sea, not dumbstruck by his own needs and failings or immobilized by fear, but harkening to some other behest he thinks he must have heard then: the hum of cable wires bearing summonses and news that would draw him back to Lahore first, then London, then finally land him here. Here, where he stands in a bowl of white hills, framed by a brilliant blue sky, on the trail of a character of his own ripe creation, and on the blessed, eager brink of fatherhood. In that moment, it seems he made a choice, a conscious, moral decision. He obeyed the pressing call of duty over a mere siren song, let himself be pulled by the thought of his friend and his soon-to-be-grieving sister instead of some shimmering, beachcombing fantasy that could yield up at best fleeting pleasures. This thought seems to bolster and steady him so that he thrusts the coaster back into the snow and heads into the house. He will work on the verse he began yesterday, if Mowgli still eludes him. He will hammer it into meaning and shape, burnish it until it shines, erect out of a few random letters and words an immutable, durable thing.

Caroline Kipling turns from the window as her husband sails down the hillside, not as amused by his gallantries and stunts as she thinks she ought to be. But then little amuses her these days, little makes her smile. Not the verses Rudyard triumphantly brings her, storming the staircase two steps at a time with his scribbled pages clutched in his hands. Not the homespun tales he invents to divert her or the nursery rhymes chanted in Hindi. Nor the steamer trunk he's set between their two beds and fashioned into a crib—an impossible arrangement she should never have agreed to, though she can't seem to veto it now.

Looking at the trunk, she feels herself shudder, not just at the sight of the poor cradle flannels spread over the hat box and tray, each checkered with peeling, faded labels for Rangoon, Colombo, Calcutta. She also can't seem to shake the feeling that events are spinning beyond her control, just as they did back in Dresden, leaving her as unable to outlaw the trunk tray as she is to stop her ankles from swelling—though at least with her ankles she is spared the sight of them by the solid blockade of her belly.

And just as in Dresden, she longs to be somewhere, almost any- where, other than this room. She cannot stand its four bare walls and low slanting ceiling, the way the window is sealed shut with frost, and the pitiful fire, which only offers a whisper of warmth because once again Anna has not set it right, laying the logs too far out on the hearth where the flames can't draw in a good draft.

Of course, though, she knows there is nowhere to go. Even if she could manage the stairs without losing her breath or her balance, stretch her coat across the great mound of her front without having the buttons fly off, she'd be met at the door by a mountain of drifts she couldn't possibly scale. So she stands there, considering calling the girl back up to fix the fire, though the thought of her skittishly skulking around, her head bowed and arms all a-twitter, is almost as loathsome to Caroline as the prospect of being cold. She cannot stand having the girl underfoot, with her stuttering and her excuses and, more and more as the birth draws near, the apprehensive looks she keeps casting Caroline's way. She seems as anxious about Caroline's state as Caroline is herself and has even undertaken certain superstitious measures, despite Caroline's remonstrations, that she thinks will ensure a safe birth. More than once, for instance, Caroline has caught her unfastening the ties of the drapery pulls and undoing the cupboard door latches—all out of the senseless, foolish belief that Caroline's labor can be hastened and eased if things in the house are left loose. And she's taken to steeping Caroline's tea in water she's boiled two eggs in, another of the nostrums the girl foolishly believes will make the birth run smoothly, though all it has managed to do so far is spoil Caroline's taste for tea.

Yet what else is there for her to do but to have a cup of tea? Press her fingers and palms to the curve of the cup and just hope that the brew warms her up? So she walks to the dresser where the girl has set the tray and suspiciously looks about. There is tarnish on the sugar tongs, a faint dusting of crumbs on the plate, a spoon for the tea and the marmalade pot, but no small knife for spreading in sight. Caroline shakes her head in dismay at the poorly set tray, though what dismays her most is the glimpse she now has of her own tired face staring back at her from the mirror that rises up from the dresser top, framed in carved scrolls of dark wood.

She stares at the face in the wavering glass: the thin, pinched lips, the pale, watery eyes blinking out of their shadowy sockets, the wide plain of her forehead pulled tight at the temples where she's twisted her hair in a knot. It is not a lovely face, she knows; her features are too broad and blunt, so unlike her brother's, with his elfin nose and his neat, decisive chin. But never has she looked so worn and so haggard, so simply and visibly plain, and she lets her gaze slide from her face to her belly, her eyes full of misery and blame.

How huge and ungainly her belly seems, like a growth that's gone monstrously awry. Even Rudyard, she's noticed, averts his eyes as if it ought not to be seen, though earlier, she knows, he had looked upon her with such unabashed adoration she had actually felt herself blush. She, too, can recall the shy pride she first felt when the mirror reflected back to her the winsome silhouette of a woman newly showing she was with child. She had pulled her dress back then to gauge the swell better, had stood there, astonished, delighted, amazed at the miracles her own body housed, its ripe curves and dark, life-giving chambers.

She'd imagined then that her happiness would grow just like the child in her womb. Threefold, fourfold, her joy multiplying until it overflowed. Now, though, she feels so removed from the bliss she then thought would be hers, the sight that confronts her such a cruel mockery of that first sweet, tender mound. And the child itself: such a part of her it seemed in those early carefree days, curled up deep and contentedly in her, so attuned to the beat of her heart! Just the thought of it there had warmed her and thrilled her, much like the locket Rudyard had given her early in their courtship and that she had worn beneath her chemise, out of sight, pressed against her bare skin. Yet now the child seems like a foreign invader, assailing her, holding her captive. It has ransacked her body, drained her of strength, robbed her of much-needed sleep. And if she does finally manage to doze, it worms its way into her dreams, which are filled these days with misplaced keepsakes and baking she's burnt to a crisp, with pipes that spring leaks, jelly molds that won't set, cook fires that flare up, unattended, and which leave her on waking more tense and exhausted than if she had never slept at all.

Of course, she knows this siege soon will be over, though she finds little comfort in the thought. Every time her mind edges to the moment of birth, she fills up with panic and fear. She's afraid that the doctor won't arrive before the baby does, that he'll be stopped by an ice storm or blizzard that will make the roads impassable, and instead of his calm, reassuring words and his steady, practiced hands—and his sturdy black bag filled with tinctures of ergot, iron forceps, vials of sweet twilight sleep—she'll have to rely on Rudyard and Anna, whom she fears, between the two of them, couldn't manage to scramble an egg.

She's afraid of the pain, of how it will grip her, possess her like a wronged spirit, making her do things she normally wouldn't: whimper, thrash about, scream. And what if the child cannot make its way out? What if it's stuck or entangled, its feet somehow lodged where its head ought to be, its arms blocking the passageway out? Like every woman, Caroline knows how easily birthing can veer to the grave. Too much blood can be spilt, too much strain can be placed on an already weighted-down heart. Yet even if the child is delivered from her safely, healthy, without incident, with her own life and modesty in tact, she is not without her fears. Turning her sights from her haggard reflection, she opens the uppermost drawer of the dresser and looks at the things Addie Connolly has cleaned and Anna has arranged there—all the white crocheted sacques with their rows of pearl buttons, each as small as the head of a pin, all the lawn caps and bonnets with their thin slips of ribbons to be tied in bows under a chin. They all seem too fragile, too impossibly small, for Caroline ever to manage. And the neat stack of diapers and swaddling flannels to be folded and tucked and pinned—so daunting do those tasks seem to her, she forgets for a moment the plain, simple fact that she has, indeed, wanted this child. She must force herself, through a sheer act of will, to remember that original longing, that desire to give her husband the child he has always wished for and awaits now with an eagerness that, compared with her own muddled feelings and fears, seems uncomplicated and pure.

Caroline cringes with something like shame as she thinks of the difference between them. While her days are filled with worry and waiting, his are brimming with projects. He is making a set of drawings and rhymes, one for each alphabet letter, to hang in the new nursery and is gathering logs for a wigwam-shaped playhouse he has said he will build in the spring. He's even arranged for his parents to send him his old childhood skin hobbyhorse, the one he had ridden as a child in Bombay up and down the crushed-shell paths of the garden. But thinking of all he is planning and has done, she is set upon by a new fear. She pictures the pair of them, her husband and child—a boy, she envisions, convinced as she is that she's destined to bear Rudyard sons—galloping off on the hobbyhorse to the wigwam set in the woods. There they'll sit cross-legged, feet tucked under knees, and pass a peace pipe back and forth, pressing the pads of their thumbs fast together after pricking them each with a pin, so that their blood flows and mingles together in a bond of brotherhood—while she is where? Nowhere to be found. Expendable and excluded.

But that, as her husband is wont to say, is another story, one that she pushes away from her mind as firmly and decisively as she pushes the dresser drawer closed. She pours herself a cup of tea and carries it to her bedside, careful to avoid another encounter with the worn face in the mirror, and careful, as well, to hold onto the cup, clutching the rim of the saucer so tightly that her knuckles almost turn white. This is a hold she feels she must take, a necessary precaution, since among the many indignities she has suffered in her pregnant state—all the swollen joints and the bulging veins that rope down the backs of her legs—her grip has grown unreliable, unsteady, her hands losing their knack to hold onto a thing in direct proportion to her inability to bend down and pick anything up.

But she makes it safely to her bed without a drop or spill. She sets the cup on her bedside table, sets herself heavily on the bed. And there she stays for the rest of the day and most of the day after that, listening as the household settles around her, going about its own business. She hears Rudyard the following morning as he stomps once again in and out, clapping his snowshoes together like cymbals to dislodge the last clumps of snow, and later as he pauses from the work at his desk and calls out for help with a rhyme. And she hears an odd shuffling and scuffling below her—what she hopes is not Anna on her hands and her knees crawling across the dining room floor to untie the fringe knots on the carpets. Then there is nothing. A great yawning silence descends on the house until dusk, when the circle of sky she can see through the peephole of glass that has yet to frost over turns all pearly and opalescent, like the mantle of an oyster shell, and fills her with a deep melancholy that the darkness, when it finally descends, does nothing to dispel.

She braces herself for another night of troubling dreams and unrest. The child twists inside her, the heel of its foot traversing her belly's circumference. Anna knocks on the door and she sends her away, too consumed by her spectrum of woes to think much about having supper. And when Rudyard finally returns to their room, planting a kiss on her strained, furrowed brow before he climbs into bed, she accepts his lips meekly, with a slight moan, as if she were simply too burdened and weak to respond in a more tender manner.

Later, when the house is dark and the only sounds are the sputter of logs collapsing into embers, Caroline is dragged from the shoals of her sleep by a fierce, insistent pain. It is not an ache or pang or twinge, an annoyance or discomfort, not a stitch or a twitch or a spasm or prick, such as have ailed her before. No, what she feels now is a blast of pure pain, so keen and raw and unleavened that it makes all her other previous complaints seem instantly inconsequential. It starts with a punch at the small of her back and radiates from there, shooting out tendrils of terrible pain that twine across her belly. Yet instead of reducing her to a puddle of whimpering and tears, the pain acts like a clarion call, stirring her to action, burning off all the dullness and lethargy she's felt as a blazing sun burns off fog, and leaving her when it wanes and then ebbs as resolute, clearheaded, and steady as she has felt in weeks.

She swings her legs over the side of her bed, setting the soles of her bare, icy feet on the equally bare and cold floorboards. She sits there a moment as another blast comes, gripping the bedpost as tight and as hard as the pain clutches her belly. When it finally releases her, she lights the candle that sits on her nightstand and staggers across the room, where, at the edge of her husband's bed, she nudges Rudyard, who wakes with a start and blinks at her, anxious and puzzled.

"It's time," she whispers, feeling strangely comforted by hearing those age-old, declarative words come forth from her very own lips.

"Shall I go fetch the doctor?" Rudyard asks as he sits up and fumbles for his glasses.

No, Caroline shakes her head but then stops as another contraction begins. She stands stock still and breathes in deeply, flaring her nostrils out, as though, if only she could draw in enough, she could simply displace pain with air. She holds her breath as the pain hits its peak and she squeezes her eyes shut to block it, embarking again on her list of instructions as soon as the moment has passed.

"No, you must wake up Anna and send her up here, then run down the road to the Connollys'. Have the husband get the doctor and come back here with Addie. She'll know what to do more than Anna."

She watches as her husband nods, accepting his assignment, all the while trying to hook his eyeglasses around the curve of his ears. Then he stuffs his nightshirt into his trousers and hoists up his suspenders, while another swell of pain washes over Caroline. Raising her arm, she extends her hand, palm up, as if to stop it. A futile gesture, though one she makes involuntarily. Yet this time, in the pain's jagged wake, she feels a counter swell and surge of tenderness and pity. For this poor, dim room that seems so ill-suited a setting for the drama to come. For her husband, who stands there, bleary-eyed and befuddled, with his hair all rumpled and rifled and his eyeglasses askew, offering to take her up by the arm and lead her back to her bed.

"Now, don't you worry. I'll be back before you know it," he stammers unconvincingly. But Caroline nods and gives Rudyard her arm, letting him steer her across the room, with his hand on the tiller of her elbow.

And then he is gone and she's back in her bed, thinking in those bright moments of clarity that stretch between contractions of all she must have Anna do. There's the fires to stoke, pots of water to boil— or snow if the pipe's frozen again. Towels and linens to fetch, extra candles, bars of soap, iodine, paregoric, scissors. She runs through the list, arranging the tasks in order of importance, letting the details ground her and calm her, so that when the pain descends again and takes her in its grip, it seems to her simply another item on her list, one more thing that she must attend to.

But where is Anna, she begins to wonder, now that her thoughts are clear again and the girl still hasn't appeared. How long can it take her to grab a shawl and hurry up the staircase? With the question knocking about in her head, Caroline feels the first stir of agitation, a quickening of her blood and nerves that in turn gives way to the needling doubt that Rudyard will succeed in his mission, that he'll manage to hitch the horse to the sleigh and then get the sleigh down the road, let alone rouse the Connollys from their bed and convince them to do as he bids them. The odds of it all going quickly and smoothly seem almost insurmountable. Though not impossible, she thinks with relief as Anna finally appears in the doorway, panting and catching her breath from what must have been her dash up the stairs. But slipping across the threshold, she slinks into the room, pressing her back and her palms to the wall and staring at Caroline with a look of such fear that whatever hope Caroline has held onto immediately starts to unravel.

"There are things that must be done," she says, trying to regain control. But before she can reel off her list, another contraction begins, constricting the vocal cords in her throat as tightly as the muscles in her womb, so that all that manages to come out of her mouth is a strangled, muffled groan.

Anna lunges toward the bed, and Caroline raises her hand again, shaking it hastily to stop her approach then shooing her away. She will not have the girl fussing around her, with her misguided gestures of help—though nor, it appears, will she get very far with her commands and instructions. Anna, for one, has retreated to the corner where she has started to weep, wounded by the harshness of Caroline's dismissal or simply distraught to find herself in such a precarious position: alone and snowbound, in the cold dead of night, with a woman now in advanced labor. And Caroline can no longer be concerned with the girl's fragile feelings. Those moments of clarity when she might have been able to muster some patience have left her, with the time between contractions too short to do much else but recover from one and prepare herself for the next.

She does this in the only way she knows how, by marshalling all the reserves of her body and recruiting the force of her will. She grits her teeth, balls her hands into fists, digs her elbows into the mattress, clenching her jaw so tightly the tendons in her neck start to bulge and throb, and squeezing her eyes shut with such force that starbursts seem to shoot up and explode across the insides of her eyelids. But the pain defeats her every effort, bowls her over, sideswipes her each time. And she wonders: Should she have listened to Anna, let her do what she wanted to do? Fling open the windows, unlock all the doors, untether the horse and the oxen? Would the child then just slide out of her, float like a leaf down a brook, unimpeded by any obstructions or barriers, freed from all restraints?

Surely such measures could be no more ineffective at warding off pain than her own. In retrospect, she finds herself thinking that it might have been worth a try, no more foolish and useless an act than a prayer or the hedging of a bet. As it is, though, the child seems stuck fast inside her, unable, or unwilling, to budge. And the only one unbound is Caroline. More and more the pain seems to sever her from the world around her, dragging her off to some nether place where comfort, time, the damp rumpled sheets, Anna weeping in the corner, don't exist. It is like a vortex, pulling her down, sucking the very life out of her, obliterating the landmarks and anchors of bedpost, mantelpiece, windowsill, moon. And when the pain is done with her, it tosses her back, so spent and drained that her vision is all unfocused and hazy, her thoughts disjointed and blurred.

She sees Anna at the foot of her bed, gnawing on her knuckles, though when she looks that way again, the girl has disappeared. Then there she is, gliding wraithlike through the room, carrying a stack of linens. A vision of mercy, Caroline thinks, for despite the fact that the girl's chest and shoulders still heave and shudder with sobs, she appears to have enough wits left about her to fetch a few vital items. And later still, the girl reappears with no transition or warning, cupping her trembling hand around a flame to light the candles that Caroline cannot remember her setting about, her fingertips circled by a nimbus of light that catches the gleam of a tear as it slowly slides down the ridge of her cheekbone.

And when Caroline next resurfaces, the room is all ablaze. Candles flicker around her, on the nightstands and dressers, so that the bed seems lit like a shrine or some ancient votive site. And there is Addie Connolly as well, hovering beside her, the candlelight carving the planes of her face into pockets of shadow and light. For a moment Caroline cannot imagine what the woman is doing here, upstairs in her room, in the middle of the night, plucking at the bedclothes all twisted around her to lay a cold hand on her belly. But then another pain starts to claim her and it all comes rushing back. She reaches out for Addie's arm as the pain lifts her from the bed, dimly recalling before she's dragged off how timid and frail the woman had seemed when she stood by her desk all those weeks ago, asking about her son. The arm she grasps now is sturdy, unflinching, even when she digs in with her nails. And when she looks into Addie's eyes, certain she'll see reflected there some confirmation of the fear that's newly taken hold—that the laws of physics must surely preclude a mass as huge as the child in her womb from squeezing through such a tight tunnel, so that if it's ever to finally emerge, it will have to scrabble and claw its way through her, through membrane and tendon and bone, leaving her insides torn and ripped open, all shredded and bloodied and bared— what she finds instead are two calm pools, offering reassurance.

"There, there," Addie says. "It won't be long now. You're almost through the worst of it."

She whispers something to Anna then, and Anna rushes off, returning in a moment with a basin of water that Addie uses to dampen the cloth she then lays on Caroline's forehead—though Caroline's senses are so addled and dazed she can't tell if the washcloth is warm or cool. She can feel Addie, though, brushing away the strands of damp hair that her sweat has plastered there, hear her steadily, quietly crooning, "There, there," as she wipes the cloth over her forehead. And after the first shock of touch has passed, Caroline thinks she might almost melt with gratitude and relief. So welcome is the woman's presence, so soothing the sound of her voice. Yet as if part of her is truly dissolving under Addie's ministering hand, she feels something suddenly spill out of her, a swift gush tapering to a trickle that leaves her thighs and her buttocks all wet and her heart stricken with shame.

"That's just your water breaking," Addie says. "If it didn't happen, the child might drown, and we wouldn't want that to happen, would we?"

No, Caroline meekly shakes her head, still mortified, but grateful. Then the next round of pain begins its assault and the swing of her nod starts to widen and quicken until her head is jerking back and forth, thrashing on the pillow. Her back arches up, her spine as bowed as the stave of a barrel, twisted into such a contorted position that she thinks she will break. Then the pain lets go and she falls to the bed, shuddering, limp, exhausted, her ears ringing with the echo of bestial cries she can't quite believe she emitted. Yet she's not so dazed that she fails to note that Addie has somehow managed to spirit the wet bed-sheet away, replacing it with a set of dry towels that are warm from a spell by the fire. And Addie sits at the bedside, staring at Caroline, seeking out her eyes, as if that gaze could pin her there, keep her from slipping away, or at least be the harbor to which she returns when she's summoned and dragged off again.

And so it goes, for minutes, whole hours, both the pain and the night seeming endless. Caroline clutches Addie's hand as she clenches then cries out and writhes. Addie sits by her side, her handclasp as constant as her unwavering eyes. And when the first hint of dawn appears, flushing the sky with a faint grainy light devoid of any inkling of warmth, Addie leans toward Caroline, her lips poised near her ear.

"Do you think you'd like to push now?" she asks. "Do you think you could try, just a little?"

Such a reasonable, soft-spoken question it seems, that Caroline, in her weak, grateful state, feels obliged to at least make an effort, though she's not at all sure what's expected of her, let alone if she's up to the task. Still, she nods yes, and the moment she does so Addie leaps into action. Wedging her hands under Caroline's arms, she hoists her up in the bed, propping her up with a wide bank of pillows that she quickly arranges around her. Then she calls Anna over to the side of the bed and motions her to sit there. Reluctantly the girl does as she's asked, though it's only the pressure of Addie's hand bearing down on her shoulder that stops her from flinching then bolting from the room as Addie takes one of Caroline's legs and lifts it by the ankle, setting the heel of her foot in the hollow just below the girl's collarbone and the curved rim of her shoulder.

"For the pushing," Addie explains to them both before she takes up a similar position on the other side of the bed, so that Caroline's legs are straddled between them, her feet buttressed and braced by their shoulders.

Then she looks at Caroline encouragingly and Caroline draws her knees up a bit and gives a small, feeble kick.

"No, from inside," Addie prods her gently. "From in here," she says, pointing to her belly.

Caroline stares at her, uncomprehending. Whatever reserves of strength she once had have long since been depleted. Her lungs can barely draw in enough breath to carry her through a contraction. Her heart feels so jostled, so battered and rammed, she's amazed it continues to pump. And her muscles have become flaccid and slack, strained beyond their usefulness from trying to counter the pain. She is barely able to flex one at will, let alone muster enough of the force needed to actually push. But still there is Addie looking at her, nodding with encouragement, urging her on toward what seems an impossible, futile task. So Caroline closes her eyes and tries to burrow deep inside her, taking advantage of the pause between pains to grope for some last bit of strength. And what she finds, to her own surprise, lying dormant within her, is a strong, pliant muscle that, far from diminished, is ready and waiting to push.

So she gathers the muscle from the bowels of her belly, draws it back like the strap of a slingshot. And when the pain comes again she releases, sending the pain barreling down to the portal between her legs, not ejecting it fully but moving it closer to the longed-for point of expulsion. She lets out a shout, as much as in shock and amazement as in agony. That the means to harness and channel the pain were inside of her all along seems nothing less than astonishing, another of the mysterious facets and wonders hidden inside her own body. Despite the bone-numbing crush of exhaustion, she feels exhilarated. After all those senseless hours of pain she couldn't fend off or deflect—when she felt herself buffeted, powerless, lashed—there is something now that she can do. And as the sun reclaims the sky, rising up from the icy horizon, Caroline feels as if more than light is being restored to the world. Now there's a remedy; now there is recourse, where none had existed before. Now she can push, and she pushes with every last shred of energy she has, not only to rid herself of the pain but to bring her child into the world.

For this has been restored to her too: the reason she is here, on this bed, straining and suffering. A reason that she kept losing sight of as the night wore on and the pain became less like a means to an end than a horrible end in itself, an ordeal invented to test and torment her, a punishing purgatory. Now, though, she thinks of the child still within her, not as an opponent or nemesis but as a poor, lost, blind, flailing thing in need of her care and assistance. So she plants her elbows firmly on the bed, pressing her feet against Addie's steady shoulder and Anna's more tremulous one, as she gathers and coils the muscles within her, squeezing her eyes shut, clenching her temples, tensing her shoulder blades, until she feels the pain start to rise up and crest and she launches another great push.

Then she pushes again and again and again, so intent on the effort she is barely aware that the doctor has finally arrived, registering only the words Addie utters in response to his probes and queries. "Fine," she hears. "Mrs. Kipling's doing fine. And the baby: it's almost here now."

The doctor stands by the dressing table, fastidiously preparing. He removes his cufflinks, sets them on a small tray beside Caroline's hairbrush and comb. He rolls up his sleeves, turning and folding each one by the width of a cuff, as over his shoulder he asks Addie questions about the course of the labor—questions that Addie answers as calmly and methodically as they were posed. But then Addie lets out a gasp of her own and takes in a sharp, sudden breath. There, at the junction of Caroline's legs, she sees the crown of a mottled head. A slick spike of dark hair, the pink whorl of an ear, as intricate as a seashell.

"One more push," Addie urges, her voice rising with excitement.

One more push and the child is there. First the head, then the shoulders, the curved keel of its spine, the slippery, tight-fisted buttocks, the drawn-up knees and the small wrinkled feet, the toes curled like the fronds of a fern. One more push and Caroline feels the child burst forth and slide beyond her, connected now only by the thick, pulsing cord that lies draped over the child's sunken chest like a bloodied sash of honor. Then Caroline collapses onto the bed, suddenly so overwhelmed by fatigue she can't even hold her head up, and so oblivious of the activity around her that when, minutes later, Addie brings the child to her, all washed up and dressed in a white crocheted sacque and wrapped in a swaddling flannel, she stares back at it in confusion.

"A boy?" she asks.

"No, a girl," Addie beams. "A beautiful baby girl."

What a jumble of mixed feelings Caroline feels—triumph and failure, jubilation and grief, the twinned poles of relief and regret—all so tangled and knotted together that she barely even knows what to think. But she takes the swaddled child in her arms and looks searchingly into its face. Its eyes are open, a deep midnight blue, like a remnant of the long night. Its lips pucker and purse as if forming a question to a problem it can't quite yet phrase. Caroline sees a small hand emerge from the wrap of the swaddling, the half-moons of nail-like thin chips of mica that reflect all the colors of the world. The fingers reach out, stretching and groping, then close back into fists. The child shuts its eyes, its lids fringed by thick lashes, shudders then lies calm and still. And Caroline feels all her conflicts resolve into a simple pure feeling, the solid weight of the child in her arms seeming to cancel out all that is tentative, questioning, doubting, fearful.

She looks up at Addie and sees her still beaming triumphantly back at her. Even Anna is smiling, a great simpering grin stretched across her tear-stained face. The doctor too: he stands there nodding, so clearly pleased and approving, it makes Caroline feel almost giddy. And she thinks it only fitting and right that birth should be this hard, that it should require this arduous effort, be such a gargantuan task, as if anything less would somehow diminish the miracle she holds in her arms. A reward commensurate with its long labor. The most precious and dearest of gifts.

But then Addie flinches and shakes her head as if coming out of trance.

"Mr. Kipling," she says. "We've forgotten Mr. Kipling! Shall I go get him now?" she asks.

Before Caroline can compose a reply, Addie is off, bounding down the stairs in search of Caroline's husband, whom Caroline, indeed, has not thought of for what seems like years, not mere hours, not since she imagined him trying to coax the horse out into the snow, grappling with the bridle and harness, attempting to master the reins.

Such a grievous lapse of attention it seems, to have thoroughly forgotten about him! Usually he is there, in the front of her mind, with all of his likes and dislikes and desires arrayed and spread out before her, ready to be accommodated, indulged, at the very least acknowledged. Now, though, he is so removed from her thoughts, she must scramble to bring him back into focus. As she hears his step on the stairs, she casts her eyes to the ground, afraid he'll guess how he slipped from her mind and will gaze at her, if she dares meet his eyes, with the injured look of one abandoned.

But entering the now-sunlit room, Kipling is hesitant, almost sheepish. He stands for a moment at the foot of the bed, his head bowed and hands dangling at his side until Addie takes one in her own and leads him closer to Caroline.

"You're all right then," he asks her.

"Yes, I'm fine. And you?"

"Oh, yes, fine," he says, dismissing her concern, though when Caroline finally looks up at him it is clear that he's exhausted, his face lined and pitted with vestiges of worry that must have slid into something like terror as the night wore on and he sat alone in the cold, darkened parlor, listening to her screams.

"Oh, Ruddy," she murmurs. "How ever did you manage?" she

asks, and Kipling shrugs.

Then Caroline feels the baby squirm in the nest she has made of her arm.

"Look," she says, her voice instantly brightening.

Carefully she draws the swaddling clothes back and tilts up the crook of her arm so that Kipling can see the child nestled there, her eyes again opened and unblinking, staring calmly at the strange new world she has suddenly found herself in. Caroline tries to lift her arm higher, to pass the child to her husband, but a sharp stab of pain clutches her side and, wincing, she beckons Addie Connolly to come over quickly and help her.

Addie takes the child from her and smoothly transfers the baby from mother to father as Caroline sinks back into the bed, her hand pressed to her side. She feels so tired and fragile again, so raw and trampled and bruised. And with the child no longer beside her, she feels again uncertain. Looking at Rudyard, she worries that he will be disappointed, that she'll see some shadow of regret or misgiving pass across his face as he takes in the now-irreversible fact that she's borne him a daughter, not a son. But on his face she sees only wonder. Wonder and delight. He nuzzles the crown of the baby's head, brushing the dark patch of fuzz on her scalp lightly with his mustache. He unwraps the swaddling, inspects fingers and toes, plants a kiss on the pad of each foot. And he says that surely nothing is more perfect than a baby's toe—unless, of course, it's a baby's lips, or its eyebrows, or its earlobes.

"She will be my best beloved," he declares. "*Our* best beloved," he amends, as unlocking his eyes from the child's probing pupils, he looks back at Caroline.

And as if to second the pronouncement—or protest the fact that her father's attention has momentarily strayed—the child scrunches up her small, delicate features and lets out a bloodcurdling wail, stunning the adults into a pool of silence and making all eyes return at once to her pinched, persimmon-red face.

LETTING IN THE JUNGLE

*A*nd then comes the long, slow progression of months. January, February, March. Each one as cold and bleak as the last, each one a cause for despair. Or so Jack Connolly has always thought, winter being for him little more than a test of sanity and endurance, one that he's tried—and most often failed—to pass with the aid of a jug. Yet strangely, this winter seems different to him. Bearable, if not quite welcome, a fact that he thinks has as much to do with Joe as with the weather. Ever since the night of the first snowfall when Joe had doggedly limped to the barn in order to seek him out, Jack Connolly hasn't wanted to disappoint the boy. Even more than that, he has felt a desire to win his son's approval, to be the one the boy looks up to with admiration and pride.

So, for Joe, he has tried to accept the season's inevitable hardships, not to bristle or chafe when he feels diminished like the buntings he occasionally spies in the barn, poking their beaks in the piles of manure to feed on excreted seeds, or the deer that stumble out of the woods on half-frozen, spindly legs, hoping to strip a bit of fresh bark from the unseasoned logs in the woodpile. And he's undertaken certain precautions to avoid the lure of temptation: sending Joe down to the cellar, instead of volunteering himself when Addie needs someone to fetch her a turnip or to weed through the half-dozen barrels of apples that sit by those fiendish jugs, picking out the fruit with soft or brown spots to stem the spread of rot. He has even tried to shrug off the panic that flutters and thumps in his chest as the snow proceeds to bury the fence posts, the stone wall, the turnstile, the gate, all the landmarks that usually form the compass points of his own bearings. And with that panic at least somewhat stilled, he's been able to see, as he never has before, the benefits of isolation, the best of which is he's spared the spectacle of Kipling riding by in his liveried carriage and the happenstance meetings that are bound to occur when the road they share isn't closed. In fact, other than the night Kipling arrived on their doorstep, ludicrously dressed in his nightshirt, Jack Connolly hasn't seen much of him—a fact he's especially grateful for since he fears that as Kipling gave him the reins and sent him to town for the doctor, he managed to extract a promise from Jack about helping out in the spring.

But while he is spared the strain of these encounters, Jack still occasionally hears him, the sounds of his comings and goings ricocheting off the bare white hills. A whoop will cut through the winter silence. The woods will echo with hammering. And once, while Jack was out checking the traps he had set at the edge of the meadow, he was certain he heard Kipling yell the number four—that single word launched over the fields, isolated and unconnected, though it was followed by what sounded like the smack of a pinecone hitting the ground.

Jack tried to ignore it and get back to his work, resetting the traps that had been sprung by an accident or some animal's ingenuity; yet he found himself drawn to the place where he thought he had heard the smacking sound. And investigating, he found a ball about the size of a crabapple. It was waxy and hard, neither rubber nor wood, but made from some substance in between, dimpled like the fruit of a bramble and colored a queer shade of red, as if a pumpkin had been crossed with a currant. Scooping the ball up, Jack dusted it off then held it in his palm, twirling it around with his thickly gloved fingers, considering what he should do. He could toss it back, send it over the field along with a muttered "good riddance"; leave it there where he found it for some animal to maul or more snow to fall and obscure it. But instead he slipped the ball into his pocket, where it bulged, a hard knob at his hip, and made him feel oddly satisfied, accomplished, as if he'd recouped a long-standing loss or settled some age-old dispute. He even showed it to Joe later that evening as they sat at the table after supper, the ball between them, sitting on the oilcloth after Addie cleared the dishes.

"What is it?" Joe asked.

"Don't know," Jack responded. "It belongs to your friend Mr. Kipling."

"He's not my friend, not really," Joe said with a halfhearted shrug.

Jack leaned back in his chair to give Joe a long, hard look that slowly dissolved into a nod of approval and acceptance. Then he plucked the ball from the tabletop and slipped it back into his pocket, where it seemed to take on the heft of a talisman or fetish. In fact, he even developed the notion that as long as he had the ball in his pocket, he could keep Kipling at bay, away from his house and his barn and his land and the heart and the soul of his son. Though, of course, Jack knows this is wishful thinking of the sort that's never worked for him before.

And so, with mixed feelings, Jack waits for the spring. He notes how the ice starts to soften in March, turning to slush in the trough, how the snow is often heavier and wetter, sometimes turning to sleet, even rain. And soon he hears the patter of dripping at all hours of the day and night as the snowmelt sluices down from the roof and the water in the creek starts to trickle and the sap in the maples drops down from the taps he and Joe have bored in the trunk to fall in the buckets they girdled with rope around the maples' trunks.

These are the sounds he has heard every year since he first came to Vermont, sounds that he usually embraces as harbingers of spring. But this year they're accompanied by other sounds that are not so usual or welcome, sounds he remembers from his railroad days when he was laying track. At first he hears them only in the distance, though they grow louder each day. The thud of wood, the creak of winches, the ringing of hammers and axes. And while he tries to ignore it at first, believing it isn't any of his business, the noise soon comes so close to the house that he feels compelled to look.

He puts on a pair of hip-high boots and grabs a walking stick, knowing that at this point in the year both the drive and the road will be little more than two sludgy rivers of mud. And he tromps down the road, mud sucking his boots so they squelch with every step, until he comes to a team of bedraggled-looking men that are setting logs in the roadbed, laying four thick, undressed lengths of timber crosswide in the mud, where they form humps like corduroy wales that have been repeated end to end.

Jack looks down the road to where the logs stretch as far as his eye can see.

"What the bloody hell," he says to no one in particular, though one of the men who is straddling two logs in order to lash them together pauses and wipes the mud from his hands, smearing it on his trousers.

"For the wagons," he says, nodding up the road to where Jack knows the Kiplings are building. "Seems there's deliveries to be made just past here. A regular convoy, I've been told."

Jack shakes his head and scratches his cheek, dumbfounded again by what he can't help but see as another of Kipling's encroachments. First his son, then his land, now the road he depends on and will soon need to cross with his cows: everywhere he turns there is Kipling, interfering with his life—though he'll be damned if he's expected to idly stand there, waiting at the edge of the road with a herd of hungry cows, so a detail of wagons can take its sweet time to pass and deliver its load.

Still, he thinks, there might be something to be gained by the road being more passable, some advantage that he can't yet see because he feels too galled. And he takes some comfort as well in the thought that winter may not yet be over, that there could be more setbacks and hurdles to cross before the season's through. Why just last week he noticed the cows rubbing against the posts in their stalls to shed their thick winter coats, only to spy them the following morning looking as shaggy as yaks, their flanks frosted and ghostly with rime and their jaws seemingly clamped in place by a vise of icicles. And while the other day he was pleased to see the first furry knobs on the catkins, he was not surprised to find them soon after strewn across the yard, a scattering of pitiful, shriveled gray pellets all felled by the chestnut-size balls of hail that lay beside them, melting.

So he trudges back up the road to the farm, dragging his boots through the mud, feeling a grim, perverse pleasure in knowing that there still could be a blizzard to thwart his neighbor's plans, as the hail had thwarted the catkins.

But then something happens. All the changes speed up. The ground thaws, shoots poke through the mud. In the woods there are clusters of bloodroot and trillium alongside dirty patches of snow. The sky fills with the calls of songbirds returning. The apple trees burst into blossom. Addie greets these events by flinging the doors and window casements open, hoisting the mattresses off the beds and heaving them out the windows, so they hang there, sunning and airing, like banners of blue-and-white ticking. She is bursting with industry, energy, zeal, scurrying through the rooms with a mop as she sings an old Easter-week hymn, darting like the finches that swoop across the fields holding tufts of thistledown in their beaks. Yet as much as Jack resents the winter and is glad to be free of its hold, he can't quite stop himself from wishing he could slow down the movement of time, dig his heels into the Earth's surface and still the planet's spinning. For he knows it's only a matter of time before the wagons arrive, clogging the road and filling the air with splattered mud and dust. And only a while until Kipling himself decides to make an appearance.

And sure enough, before too long, the wagons start to file by. For a week they judder over the logs, pitching from side to side, laboring up the hill with their loads, then quickening as they head down. Jack tries to ignore the commotion and attend to the work of the farm, but the racket accompanies him everywhere, to the barn and the orchard, the high meadow and the fields. When he milks the cows, when he prunes the fruit trees, when he sits at the table for supper, he hears the drumming of hooves on logs, the rasp of wheels against axles, the knocking of crates as they skid across flatbeds and hit the wagons' sides. And then there is Joe to add to his troubles. Whenever Jack needs him to lend a hand with the milking or planting or plowing, he must holler and fetch him from the end of the drive, where Joe has taken to lingering whenever he thinks he can, standing next to the ditch by the road to watch the wagons pass.

It's as close a thing to a parade as the boy has ever seen, and even Jack Connolly has to concede how compelling such a sight can be. He remembers, as a child, watching tinkers' caravans heading up the road to the manor, bedecked with clanging cookware and ribbons and sometimes swags of bells. He'd chase after them, hoping to beg some food or scraps of ribbon, though his mother strictly forbade him, saying that the tinkers were not to be trusted any more than the folk at the manor. Compared to those, these wagons are drab, just the usual buckboard and dray, carting nothing more exciting than planks and beams, drums of paint and barrels of nails. But the way they advance, as majestic and solemn as a church processional, makes them seem unusual—though the whole spectacle strikes Jack as far too high-flown and showy.

Still, sometimes he too will stand by the road, watching the wagons with Joe, hovering next to the boy as if to keep his excitement in check. He will fiddle with a piece of straw or chew on a wad of tobacco, letting himself fill up with disdain as his mouth fills up with chaw juice at Kipling's extravagance. And when he spits, he feels a kind of pride that he's not driving one of the wagons, not holding the reins and prodding the horses when they balk at the weight—though he recognizes some of the men who do, from encounters and sightings in town. They are men who live on small farms as he does, carving out a living from a few rocky fields and a herd of dairy cows, occasionally taking on the odd job as Addie takes in laundry. Most keep their eyes set forward as they pass, with a grim set to their lips, as if they were hauling something distasteful instead of timber and bricks; though a few offer Jack a nod of acknowledgment, a single bob of the head that seems, to Jack, also to acknowledge the compromise of their position.

And one day he sees his neighbor Frank Waites, who lives down the road on the far side of Kipling's rented cottage, driving the buckboard he's hitched to the mule that has plowed his fields for years.

"So he's got you roped into this too?" Jack says with a nod up the road.

"For a price," Waites replies, "and a good one at that," he adds with a wink and a chortle, as if Kipling were the one who had been roped into some dubious arrangement.

Jack chuckles as well and nudges Joe's arm, hoping he'll join in the humor, but the boy is too busy looking at what Waites has in the wagon. It's a bathtub as big as some of the skiffs and punts that ply the river, with brass claw-feet and porcelain sides, so gleaming and dazzling and blindingly white that Jack can barely look at it without shading his eyes. Yet Joe stares at the tub with such obvious longing that Jack feels smacked by defeat. He cannot bear the idea of his son becoming Kipling's stooge again, can't stomach the thought of Joe following him, envying his house and his plumbing, begging for scraps of stories.

But what can Jack offer the boy instead, other than his indignation, the self-righteous contempt that he often feels is his only true possession? How can he possibly attempt to compete with a man who has orchestrated *this*, summoning more wagons in a single week than usually pass by in a year? Jack feels the futility of even trying, though he doesn't want to lose Joe, not after the winter when the boy seemed so willing to be his helpmate and companion. And so when Kipling finally appears, poking his head in the barn one day to discuss Jack's excavation work, Jack finds himself agreeing to come, despite his reservations.

And now, inevitably, the day has arrived, a morning that dawns with a mackerel sky and the clamorous cawing of crows. Jack Connolly wakes up reluctantly, dragging himself from the depths of a dream whose specific details evaporate the minute he opens his eyes, though he's left with the vague and troubling sense that the world cannot be trusted, that the ground beneath him could give way at any moment, crumbling right under his feet. He lies there, thinking about rolling over and trying to fall back to sleep, but he isn't sure he wants to return to the world of his dreams. Besides which, he sees that Addie is up, and Joe is up as well, appearing suddenly in the doorway, already washed and dressed, asking if he should harness the horse to the buckboard or the flycart.

"Might as well take the buckboard," Jack Connolly says, and Joe spins around and dashes downstairs, heading out to the barn, leaving Jack with what seems little choice but to rise and join the day. So he kicks his legs free of the quilt and sits on the edge of the mattress, giving his head a few swift shakes as if knocking water from his ears. Then he shuffles to the washstand, pours water in the bowl, and wraps a towel round his neck, pausing for a moment before splashing his face to peer at the bloodshot eyes that stare back at him from the washstand mirror and to draw his flattened hand across the stubbled plain of his jaw. He has no idea what the day will hold, and little desire to know, as already he feels almost sick with misgivings at what he's agreed to do. But he soaps his face with the lathering brush, hones his razor against the strop. And setting the sharpened blade to his throat, in the gully alongside his voice box, he slowly scrapes up against the grain of the growth, not noticing until he nicks his chin that his hands are trembling.

He blots the bright blossom of blood with the towel then finishes shaving and dresses, lacing his boots and testing the strength of the knots before he heads out. Then he strides across the yard to the barn, trying to reclaim his composure, and attending as he walks to certain aspects of the weather in a way that he hasn't for years. He registers, for instance, the current of the breeze and makes a mental note of its direction. He spies the gossamer of dew on the meadow and feels a sharp breath of relief, recalling how a fuse is like a snake in the grass, how it travels, a quick slither of flame, shedding sparks instead of skin that could ignite a whole field or forest if the ground were drier.

It is a small comfort to remember this, a brace of knowledge to cling to; though he now may have to dig a trench in order to lay the fuse down—a messy, time-consuming job that under other circumstances he would certainly resent. Today, though, it's not an unwelcome prospect, deferring as it does, for a little bit longer, the moment he has to face Kipling. And the cows, as well: he is grateful for the diversion they'll offer and the calm they'll provide, the slow pace of the milking he can find so annoying now seeming like a respite. But reaching the barn he finds that his son has already milked the cows and led them to pasture. Joe has even cleaned out and raked up their stalls so that the barn seems as quiet and tidy as Jack thinks he's ever seen it.

He shoots a questioning glance at the boy, who is busy harnessing the horse, trying to fathom what prompted this sudden burst of enterprise—though, of course, Jack knows. The boy is excited, flushed with anticipation and the prospect of feeling proud, eager to show Kipling what his father can do and eager to see it himself. But while Jack would like to tell his son to temper his expectations, he doesn't know what to say. And as if Joe doesn't want to hear that either, he averts his eyes from Jack, concentrating instead on quieting the horse as he buckles the hames to the traces. Then Joe cinches up the belly band and checks on the fit of the breeching, leaving Jack Connolly with little choice but to look for his drilling gear.

He had saved the equipment in case of some need that had never materialized. A beaver dam he couldn't break up without blasting. A rock too large to heave. Yet the further he got from his railroading days, the less he could imagine himself going through those movements again. Boring a hole into a substance that was meant to be inviolable. Wedging a charge in then tamping it down, crimping the cap with his teeth. Laying out a line of cordite, as carefully as a trip wire. Striking a match and setting the flame to the fraying end of cord before running for cover as he desperately prayed that he'd given himself enough time.

Yet even then, when he was expected to set charges regularly, he could never do so with the dispassion and ease of something routine, for he was afraid, simply afraid. Afraid that this pitiful life of his could be dashed or blown away. Afraid that it was, in fact, fated to be, given how much else had already been taken or lost. And with that fear came a sense of shame that this life, which he saw as so meager and worthless, could mean so much to him, that it could be so cherished, so precious, so dear, he would do anything not to lose it.

He felt it each time he lifted a charge and packed it into a rock, felt it the instant the rock splintered and heaved, sending up geysers of shards. He felt it too when he backed from a charge and let the line of the fuse out, imagining that his fear was coating the cordite as he ran the rope through his hands, that it seeped from his pores or was being secreted like the thin, gummy trail of a snail that twined with the path of the fuse so that another element was added to the already-volatile mixture, making each step of the whole chain reaction even more unstable.

He felt it most keenly that day on the railroad when the charge had exploded on him and he huddled in that useless basket, cradling his head in his knees, crouching and rocking as panic shot up through him, loosening his bowels and tear ducts. And as the shards showered down on him, he began to whimper and babble, calling on a God he hadn't believed in since that day on the packet, two weeks out from Tralee, when his mother was wrapped in soiled sheets and sailcloth and tossed from the stern of the ship, and he sat on the deck through the comfortless night, with nothing to hold or to eat, waiting, just waiting, for her to rise up from the black, choppy water and claim him.

He was willing to make whatever bargains he could then as the basket swung back and forth—willing to barter, to deal, and to plead—agreeing to anything that unjust God wanted as long as he survived. And he wonders now, as he heads to the barn, if this is his moment of reckoning, the time when he must pay back that debt, securing the life that had been saved once by risking it again for his son. For here he is now, retrieving the tools of that loathsome trade, pushing aside cans of rusty nails and a bale of poultry netting, rifling through the rakes and pitchforks that hang from the toolshed wall. He searches the shed then moves to the tack room, combing through the tangle of bridles and straps, carriage reins and collars, though still he can't find what he's after. And he thinks that perhaps it's not too late to call the whole business off, to exempt himself without losing face because he can't find his gear. But just as he's recalled the effects of wind and moisture on a fuse line, he finds himself remembering how he stashed his gear in the cellar over twelve years ago, banishing it there, under the house, far from the light of day.

Immediately he wishes that he hadn't had the thought, that he could just go and talk to Joe, sympathetic but resigned. He even imagines lying to him, saying that he's done his best and tried. But pausing by the door of the barn, he sees his son sitting up on the buckboard, straddling the front seat, waiting for him, so trusting and guileless that Jack knows he can't deceive him.

So he walks across the yard to the cellar, feeling Joe's eyes follow him. And when Joe sees where Jack is going, he scrambles down from the buckboard.

"Pa?" he calls out hesitantly.

"I'm still looking for my gear."

"I'll go. I'll find it. You don't have to bother."

"No bother," Jack Connolly says.

He reaches the cellar and swings back the door, letting a shaft of sunlight angle down the wooden stairs. Then, grabbing the handrail, he ducks his head and carefully starts to descend, his hunched body blocking out enough light so that when he reaches what appears to be the bottom, he must tentatively tap the floor with his foot to make sure that there's no further step. He gropes for the lantern that hangs from the newel post, strikes a match, sets the flame to the wick. And holding the lantern up so his knuckles scrape the packed earth of the ceiling, he peers into the room.

The bins and the barrels are near empty now, depleted by the long needs of winter, though here and there a few vegetables remain. A handful of onions shedding papery skin. The pale, scored globe of a turnip. Some potatoes dotted and pockmarked with eyes and the shriveled spears of a few carrots that in the darkness have sprouted new roots, as coarse and wiry as whiskers. On a shelf sit mason jars of preserves—damson plums, pickled watermelon rind—all connected by the filament bridgework of cobwebs and covered with a fine film of dust. For a moment Jack stares at the jars of fruit, which glow in the lamplight like jewels. Then he thrusts the light into a dark corner, probing the dank, moldy reaches where, just as he had remembered, he finds his old packing crate.

Like the mason jars, the crate's covered with dust and the wispy threads of old cobwebs, making Jack reluctant to touch it. So he lifts his foot to the rusty lock and nudges the hasp with his foot, half hoping that it will be rusted shut and beyond his ability to open. But the lock gives easily at his touch and the lid swings back on its hinges, releasing an old musty odor of cedar, tar pitch, and decay. Jack sets his lantern down on the ground then sits back on his haunches, planting his hands, palms flat, on his knees, scraping his lip with his teeth. Before him he sees his old railroad pick and his various tamping rods, a stone sledge, an auger, a pocket-size awl, all lying on a blanket like the surgery tools used for eviscerations. Jack stares at them, still not sure that he wants to touch them. But then he hears Joe calling down from outside—"Pa, are you all right?"—and pushing aside his hesitation and disregarding his fear, he quickly gathers everything up, slipping the awl into his pocket, grabbing the rods, the auger, and sledge, whose weight tugs at his arm, pulling at his shoulder socket.

Then he shuts the crate and takes up the lantern, turns and heads for the stairs; though, turning, he sees what he hadn't before: the barrels of now mostly rotting apples that sit by a scant dozen jugs, which seem to have sprouted from the base of the barrels like a ring of hoary toadstools in the woods.

Pausing, Jack Connolly stares at the jugs then looks quickly over his shoulder to the top of the stairs where a square of blue sky is framed by the jambs of the door. Then his eyes return again to the jugs, his gaze intemperately drawn there. How easy it would be to pull up a stopper, yank it free with one tug of his teeth, slip his forefinger through the ring of a handle, wrap his thumb round the squat neck and lift. As easy as striking a match on a rock. As easy and just as conflagrative, for he knows and he fears what might be set off with a single, imprudent touch, another chain of imploding events that could not be easily stopped.

He stares at the jugs, reminding himself that all winter long he successfully managed to avoid this very encounter, mustering enough strength and resolve to bypass such temptations. But along with the fear, he now feels desire. A desire that takes shape as thirst, so pressing and urgent he thinks he'll explode if it can't be quenched right away. So he drops the gear he holds in his arms and reaches out for a jug, brushing away a dried patch of lichen that clings to the base like a barnacle. And, yes, it's as simple as he had imagined. The spout fits snugly in the crook of his thumb. The cork yields, unresisting, to his teeth, and the drink rushes forth from the spout to his mouth then down the rapids chute of his throat with the inevitability and ease of a stream flowing down to the sea. And when it reaches the estuary of his tight, hungering gut, he feels the familiar burn and flush, the old magic easing of tension, so immensely satisfying that he lifts the jug to his lips once again and takes another long swig.

Then he wipes his mouth with the back of his hand and hears his son calling, "Pa," that lone word burning a path inside him just like the liquor, like a fuse.

"Coming," he yells back, as he sets the jug down and gathers the lantern and gear, half expecting the load to feel lighter now and somehow less encumbered. But while the drink seems to have thinned out his fear, something else has replaced it, a feeling as ornery and sharp as a thorn, a prickling goad of annoyance.

He feels it as, after extinguishing the lantern and throwing the room into darkness, he bumps his head on the half-timbered joist that frames the staircase landing and, again, as he climbs the stairs and is blinded by the dazzle of sunlight outside. Blinking, his gaze finally settles on a shape silhouetted before him—what he sees as his eyes adjust to the light is the slouched, waiting figure of his son. Joe stands there with his mouth slightly open and his arms hanging limply at his side, and this sight fills Jack with annoyance as well, as does the way Joe looks at him sideways once they climb onto the buck-board, furtively stealing worried glances as Jack takes up the reins.

Jack flicks the whip and urges the horse down the drive to the corduroy road, following the route that the other wagons took a few weeks ago. They pass the lower meadow where the cows now graze, pass the bog where pale lady's slippers grow, until they come to the first of the cedars that mark the Kiplings' land. Through the trees, at the base of the hill, Jack sees what looks like an encampment, with canvas tents and fire pits, ringed with rocks and filled with ashes, and piles of what must be building supplies covered with tarpaulins. Joe sees it too, and almost twitches with excitement, pointing to the tents and the tarps, as he tells his father what he heard from Kipling, that he'd purchased a whole crate of dynamite and had it delivered from town, with the sticks frozen first so they'd be stable if they were jostled on the ride.

Jack listens to him but doesn't reply, feeling his blood go cold, and Joe, sensing that he has said something wrong, goes quiet and still as well. But then the buckboard sways to one side as they hit some uneven logs, causing the auger and the rods to roll and Joe to slide in his seat, listing until his arm inadvertently knocks against his father's.

"Sorry," he mutters, as he rights himself and scoots back to his seat.

Jack nods to acknowledge his son's apology, though the word does nothing but grate: for Joe has no idea, he thinks with resentment, just how sorry he should be, making Jack deal with a man he despises, on an errand that fills him with fear. And while Jack knows that Joe really hasn't forced him, that he's taken on the challenge himself, he feels a need to blame brewing in him, an urge to strike out and accuse.

He imagines Joe feels this brewing as well, for when Jack steals his own sidelong glance, Joe seems to be conscientiously trying to stay out of his way, keeping his arms pinned tight to his side and his eyes trained down on his feet. And while he thinks that Joe is right to look sheepish, having gotten him into this mess, the sight of Joe there, trying so hard to contain himself for Jack's sake, moves him and makes him relent enough so that as they reach the point where Kipling's new house can be seen, Jack lets the reins go slack.

"Like a man with his nose stuck up in the air," Jack says, gesturing to the site, where a fortresslike structure of squared posts and beams sits high up on the hillside.

Following his gaze, Joe vigorously nods, as if he's grateful to be offered this chance to demonstrate his allegiance. And they sit there for a moment as the horse bends to graze, Jack feeling bolstered by his son's solidarity, Joe feeling redeemed and relieved. But then the horse raises its head from the grass and restlessly paws the ground, and Joe leans forward in his seat, impatient to be off as well. And as Jack takes up the reins again and signals the horse to move forward, he feels suddenly struck and overwhelmed by all that he can't control. The march of the seasons. The designs of his neighbor. The interaction of powder with rock. The pitch of the sea and the health of his loved ones. His fears, his desires, his son. Feeling that, his hands grow clammy, his palms start to itch and sweat. And he runs his tongue over the front of his teeth, along the ridge of his gums, hoping to find a stray trace of whiskey, one last little drop that might somehow lessen what he now recognizes is dread.

Rudyard Kipling waits for Jack Connolly at the end of the row of cedars, along with his wife, the English nursemaid they've hired, and the baby, whom they've christened Josephine. They've come along to try out the new trotters that Kipling has given Caroline to celebrate both the return of the spring and her return to full health. For much of the winter Caroline remained behind the closed door of her room, unable to shrug off the weight of fatigue that had clung to her since giving birth. But this morning not only has she ventured outside, she's insisted on driving herself, assuming the reins in a new riding jacket and a topper neatly trimmed with pheasant feathers.

She sits in the carriage with the nursemaid and child while Kipling paces about, not anxious exactly, just too eager and full of the day and himself to sit still. He is pleased, inordinately pleased, with everything around him. With the house that rises up from the hillside, commanding and majestic. With the hillside itself, ablaze with wildflowers. With Monadnock in the distance. He is pleased with his wife, with her fine horsemanship and her generous, competent figure; pleased with the horses, whom he's dubbed Nip and Tuck; even pleased with the names themselves—so much so that as he walks by the pair, pausing to stroke their strong necks, he says them out loud, with amusement and relish, nipping the vowels and tucking the consonants under his tongue as he does so.

He is pleased as well with the child who now lies asleep in the arms of her nursemaid. With the spit-curl lock of flaxen hair that has slipped from the hold of her bonnet. With the thick fringe of lashes that rests on her cheeks, which Kipling has declared to family and friends are as fat as a Burmese idol's and the source of inspiration for her new moniker—the Joss, his sweet bundle of luck. He is even pleased when she fusses and squawks, as she sometimes does, with her chin, which he fears she's inherited from him, quivering and crimson. And when he bounces her on his knee, to ride a cockhorse to Banbury Cross or hear pussycat visit the queen, he is equally pleased when she squeals with delight or eyes him with suspicion, her skepticism seeming to him like a sign of her good sense and judgment.

But most of all he is pleased with his work and the turn that it's recently taken. Finally he is moving forward again, after the limbo of winter when his thoughts too often were scattershot, his concentration short-lived, accessible only in snatches and bits, like his sleep on those nights he was woken up hourly by the hungry cries of the Joss. Oh, he'd managed to eke out some ballads and verse, nearly a bookful, in fact. But he couldn't wrap his mind around Mowgli, no matter how hard he tried. He couldn't bring him into focus, couldn't summon or ferret him out, let alone solve the problem he'd created when he sent Mowgli off to the jungle alone, spurned by both men and wolves.

Perhaps Mowgli simply was hibernating, biding his time, lying dormant. Or perhaps Kipling's Daemon was. For as the snows began to recede, revealing the dark ground beneath, he felt an image begin to take hold as he sat at his desk each day. He saw Mowgli squatting in an empty lair, littered with sticks and old bones, holding in his hand the knife he had used to skin Shere Khan, the tiger. Some days he pictured Mowgli running the blade across the pad of his thumb. Other days he envisioned him casting it down so its tip dug into the cave floor, tossing it over and over again until it gouged a deep hole in the ground. And sometimes he saw him just sitting on his haunches, letting the sunlight that spilled through the cave mouth catch and bounce off the blade so that flecks of light danced on the walls like the sparks that shoot up from a forge.

For a good many days he applied himself to just letting the image fill him. He concentrated on Mowgli and the knife: how he bore down on his thumb with the blade, building up his threshold of pain; how he tested ways of angling it to increase the sunlight's deflection. And he contemplated what he thought was the fury Mowgli harnessed and then disciplined, the wild rage he reined in and brought under control each time he threw the knife to the ground and hit the eye of his target. Until slowly he thought he understood what lay at the heart of the image: Mowgli was plotting an act of revenge, a stunning, vindictive reprisal that would leave him triumphant and avenged, transformed from a small, helpless ward of the jungle to its mighty, rightful lord.

Of course, what that act was Kipling couldn't yet say, though he waited for it to reveal itself with patience and obeisance, trusting that if he waited long enough the answer would eventually come. And while he waited, he stared out the window, his mind drifting over the landscape—the fields now bare and strewn with dead stalks crushed by the weight of the snow; mats of ragged leaves, like old, tattered bedding; clods of earth; the scattered rubble of stones—until the lifeless, snow-flattened landscape merged with the images he'd culled, and he saw a scene of willful destruction, almost terrible to behold, a whole village razed by a vengeful stampede, commandeered and commanded by Mowgli.

He began to write then, slowly at first, then more steadily, laying out scenes and dialogue with a few sure strokes of his pen. He described how Mowgli first summoned Bagheera and told him of his plan and how the panther had shuddered and cowered, awed by the magnitude of such an undertaking and more than a little daunted by the rage that inspired it. And he wrote about how Mowgli called upon Hathi, the most ancient of the elephants, and commanded him to call forth his sons and all the hoofed beasts of the jungle in order to trample the men's village and fields, leaving no structure in place.

And as he wrote, he felt his own strength and mastery swell inside him. All the power of language was at his disposal to wield and direct and display, just as the force of the jungle was there to heed and to serve Mowgli's will. But he needed a reader or someone to listen, to gauge the effects of the tale. And now, as he sees Jack Connolly approach, he is pleased to see that he's brought his son just as Kipling had hoped—though the few times he's tried to talk with Joe since his laundry-shuttle duties resumed, he's found the boy to be distant, distracted, with a wariness hooding his eyes, as if something more than his leg had been broken those many months ago.

Still, he knows that the boy's not completely immune to the pull of a good, rousing yarn. He's shared with him some of the verse he hacked out over the winter, telling him about Danny Deever, hanging in the gallows, and of Gunga Din who proved himself worthier than a mere waterboy. In fact, he recited that whole poem to Joe in his very best Cockney accent, clutching his heart when he came to the part where a stray bullet struck the poem's narrator and plunging to his knees, his hands clasped in a prayer, as he told how one hit Gunga

Din. But while the boy seemed captivated as he groaned and staggered then mourned, his voice choking out the last line of lament,
"You're a better man than I am, Gunga Din," when he finished, Joe
had just one question.

"Were you really shot in the chest?" he asked.

"Well, no," Kipling readily admitted.

"So it isn't real. It didn't really happen. You just made the whole
thing up."

He had tried to explain the difference then between fact and
artistic truth, though by then the boy had already started to load up
the laundry. But Mowgli, he thinks, surely Mowgli will draw him,
make him set all such questions aside—provided he can manage to
get the boy away from the hold of his father.

Jack Connolly is one of those men Kipling has dubbed "aborig-
ines" in his letters to England: men who brandish their ignorance like
a hard-earned badge of honor and who've let whatever virtues they
once might have had fester and warp in the harsh Vermont climate
like an inflamed ingrown nail. He has seen such men on almost every
farm he's had the chance to visit, has even been forced to hire them
when he needs extra labor. They are bitter and stunted, worn down
and defeated by years of hard, profitless work—intriguing to study as
character types, but not always easy to deal with. Or so Kipling's
reminded as he watches Jack Connolly pull the buckboard off the
road and size up the carriage, his eyes taking in the presence of Caroline, the nurse, and the still-sleeping Joss, before his face settles into
a tight grimace and his hands pull back hard on the reins.

But watching him, Kipling's also reminded of what he's more
publicly stated: that he's a man who prefers to believe the best of all
he meets—if only because it saves so much trouble, trust being a

more expedient foundation than doubt for most sorts of exchanges and dealings. And he chooses now to operate from this more lenient principle, ignoring Jack Connolly's disgruntled stare to march straight forward and greet him.

"Welcome, welcome, welcome," he says. "Welcome to Naulakha."

He sweeps his arm through the air like a showman then clicks his heels and bows—a not unaffected performance, he thinks, though he's able to catch Joe's eye as he rises and toss him a self-knowing wink.

"My wife will be off in a moment or two. She's just come to try out the new horses. Whom you absolutely must meet," he says now directly to Joe, as striding to his side of the buckboard he offers the boy his hand.

Joe stares at Kipling, his face flush with discomfort, then looks back at his father, waiting until Jack gives a nod of assent before he clambers down.

"This is Nip and Tuck. Nip and Tuck," Kipling says with his arm wrapped around the boy's shoulder.

Reaching the horses, he runs his hand through Tuck's coarse mane and forelock, drawing out two snow-white cubes of sugar he claims to have discovered behind the horse's ear. He sets the cubes in his open palm and again holds his hand out to Joe, who cautiously looks back at his father still sitting on the buckboard, waiting until Jack gives another terse nod before he extends his own hand.

"And your fine steed," Kipling asks him, encouraged. "May I ask what name he goes by?"

"Morgan," Joe replies under his breath, offering up the sugar.

"That's his breed, not his name," Jack Connolly says, as he too climbs down from the buckboard. "We don't have the time to be giving fancy names to animals like some do."

"Yes, of course, I see," Kipling says, readjusting. "Then perhaps we'll keep introductions short and move on to the business at hand."

Directing them to the far side of the carriage, he shows Jack where the dynamite sits, warming in the sun in a tub of creek water, and the spool of cordite, pointing out where he wants the gate to stand to herald the start of the drive. Then as Jack begins to unload his gear, Kipling spins on his heels toward Caroline and gives her a farewell salute. He hoists himself up on the carriage step to tweak the fat cheeks of the Joss, who wakes up hollering, her pitiful cries only subdued when Caroline finally flicks the reins and, with a snort, the horses head off.

Then, "Gentlemen," Kipling says, bowing again and ushering them up the hillside.

He heads up a wide sloping path bordered by the stumps of the trees that have been felled for the drive. Overhead a blackpoll warbler trills, the first Kipling has heard from this season. In the woods something stirs—the slither of a milk snake or a chipmunk's nervous scurry, he can't tell. But he sees the wildflowers he has come to know, their names and shapes lodged in his memory. Starflowers, foam-flowers, Solomon's seal. Snakeberry and Dutchman's-breeches, which to his delight look like tiny pantaloons hanging from a green wash-line stem. As he breathes in the sweet, pine-scented air and ticks off the names of the flowers, he feels that sense of pleasure return, so boundless and rich that it feels a true shame not to share it with anyone else. He could, of course, point out the flowers to Joe and see if he knows their names, too, or plunge right into the story of Mowgli, which still smolders in him, burning to be told. But when he turns to talk to the boy, he sees that Joe has fallen behind. He lags a yard or two behind his father, whom Kipling fears would be just as dismissive of the whimsical name for a flower as he was with the name for a horse, and equally disdainful of a tale about a child who'd been raised by a pack of wolves.

So he keeps on walking until the path abruptly ends at the base of a scraggly scree that, in turn, gives way to a steep, rocky slope no carriage could possibly mount.

"This is where we need your help, sir," says Kipling, turning to Jack Connolly, "unless we're to haul our visitors up with ropes and weights and pulleys the way I once read your pioneers did when they pulled their Conestoga wagons up over the Continental Divide."

Jack Connolly scales the scree with his eyes then fixes his sights on the snaggletoothed rocks that crown the crest of the scarp, his hand, Kipling notices, drumming his leg to some hesitant, jittery beat.

"You want the road to go straight up here?" he says with unveiled disbelief.

"Oh no, not straight. Never straight," Kipling says, as if he were shocked by the thought. "It should weave and wind, weave and wind," he says, "through the trees then over the meadow. Meander, so that the house isn't visible until the final bend, since after all," he adds turning to Joe, who has finally reached them, "the journey should always be as important as the destination."

"Well, I don't know about meandering, but I'll do what I can to soften the grade so the road can bank up and around."

Jack Connolly thrusts his chin up to indicate where he thinks the road could go, and Joe, misinterpreting the gesture as a signal to go, begins to scramble up, clutching an exposed loop of root as a handhold, digging his boot in the dirt. He hoists himself up, pushing off with his toe, then loses his footing and skids, which triggers a small, sudden landslide. A cascade of stones rolls down the scree then rumbles right down the hillside, a few not coming to a full stop until they reach the flat of the roadbed. Joe pauses to crane his head over his shoulder and see the commotion behind him, unaware of his role in the disturbance until he hears his father.

"What the hell do you think you're doing?" Jack barks, his words slicing the air like a razor and startling both Kipling and Joe even more than the tumbling stones.

Joe freezes in place, hands splayed against the scarp, like a thief who's about to be frisked; while Kipling tenses, unnerved as well, as a memory rears up inside him, filling what seems like the rent in the sky created by Jack Connolly's words. For there is Auntie Rosa, towering above him, at the top of the basement stairs, one hand gripping the cellar door, the other wrapped tight round a cane, her nostrils flaring like the hood of a cobra that's preparing to draw back and strike. He sees her there just as surely and clearly as he sees Jack Connolly before him. Her old crone's jaw and her pinched, scolding lips, her knuckles bony and bloodless. But he also sees opportunity here, a way to successfully deal with Jack Connolly and squire Joe away by himself. And sweeping the vision away from his mind, he turns to Jack Connolly, deciding once more to proceed on his best-of-man theory.

"Now, why don't I take the boy off of your hands so that you can get down to work. Give him a tour of the property. Keep him out of your way."

Jack Connolly closes his eyes for a moment, takes a deep, steadying breath.

"All right then," he says. "You two can go off. But I don't want any 'meandering' near here," he says, still glaring at Joe, who lowers his own eyes and nods his head yes, avoiding his father's stern gaze.

Jack heads down the hill then to collect his equipment. Joe watches him as he goes, while Kipling, in turn, watches the boy, waiting until his father disappears around a bend before he suggests they head off.

"Shall we?" he says, as Joe slowly rises and dusts the dirt from his pants.

They circle around the scree to a point where the slope, while still steep, is less riddled with stones. Kipling slows down to accommodate the boy, who stops periodically to look over his shoulder, trying to locate his father, whom Kipling can see through the column of trees nearing the clearing where the buckboard stands hitched and the tub of explosives awaits. He offers his hand when the footing gets tricky, calls out warnings and words of advice. But each time he slows, the boy slows down further, as if determined to keep a set distance, a wide buffer of space between them, so that Kipling sees it may be a challenge to gain the boy's attention. He will have to woo him, as he'd woo a reader, by choosing the right tone and details. Create an air of complicity. Stake a claim, reestablish connections. But he must not rush, lest Joe shy away further. He must proceed carefully, making sure the boy doesn't feel put upon or cornered, so that when he finally turns to Mowgli plotting his revenge, it might seem to Joe that he's arrived there himself, drawn by his own fascination, the tale fueled as much by the interest of the listener as by the storyteller's intent.

But where to begin? That is always the question. Where to launch the conversation, so that while it may seem to digress and diverge, it will lead them back to the Seeonee Hills and that cave hidden deep in the jungle?

Kipling starts by abandoning his solicitous comments and his helpful hand, letting the boy choose his own route instead; while he, once he's reached the top of the slope, strolls across the broad, flower-strewn meadow that stretches right up to the house. He feigns non-chalance, clasping his hands at the small of his back, his head raised to absorb the sun's warmth. Spotting a bright clump of buttercups growing out of a marshy depression, he hunkers down and plucks a flower, then waits on his haunches, patiently as a cat, for Joe to wander closer.

"Do you remember that walk we took in the fall," he says when the boy's within earshot. "I told you how Pliny the Elder once wrote that these flowers, if eaten, could induce wild hysterics, and we thought about putting his claim to the test when springtime came around."

Kipling tosses the boy a sly, devious grin, the flower now raised to his mustache's edge, held there, by his lips, like a dare. He's prepared, if need be, to pop it into his mouth and mash it up with his molars, prepared even to roll around on the grass as if in the grip of a lunatic fit of unstoppable, spasmodic laughter. But the boy looks at him with such skepticism and such stolid reserve, he decides then and there to abandon the course, backpedaling to find a different tack.

"Of course, Pliny wasn't always a reliable source," Kipling says as he rises to his feet. "He believed in the existence of a certain kind of snake that he said could propel itself into the air to catch small birds in flight. And he thought that the African basilisk was more than a creature of myth. According to him, it was a real serpent whose venom was so transmittable and deadly that once, when a horseman speared one with his sword, the poison rose up through the blade and the hilt and killed both the man and the horse."

Where this rush of lore comes from, he isn't sure. Some musty reach of his brain, he supposes, where he stores odd facts and stories, the remnants of a lifetime spent reading. But while he is pleased to have dug it up now, he also fears that he's prattling, blathering on about something that has no relevance or import. Yet between the accounts of the airborne snake and the basilisk's murderous venom, he senses a change in the boy. He is listening now. Kipling feels his attention, like a galvanic charge in the air. His head is tilted, one ear cocked forward; his shoulders and limbs relax, as if his guardedness has finally given way to admit a modicum of interest. He has even moved a step or two closer, though he still stands beyond Kipling's reach. So Kipling continues, summoning up whatever stray facts he possesses: how the basilisk withers and burns all it touches, how it bursts apart rock with its breath.

"Why, if only we had a basilisk here, we could let it handle the drive!"

He is tempted to laugh at this bit of cleverness, this melding of necessity and myth, but the moment the words slip out of his mouth, he knows he has made a mistake. Joe instantly turns, scanning the hillside, once more anxious to locate his father, as if, should he wander away from Joe's sight, he might abscond or vanish. Kipling looks too, his eyes sweeping back and forth like the beam of a lighthouse, feeling strangely, unaccountably apprehensive as well when he fails to spot Jack Connolly. But then there he is, with a pickax in hand, rising up from a crouch just beyond a large boulder that must have blocked him from their view when he bent over to dig. He wipes his forehead with the back of his hand then swings the pick over his shoulder, disappearing momentarily behind the boulder again as he resumes his work.

"He'll be a while yet," Kipling says to Joe, trying to sound kind, though he can't fully mask the disappointment he feels now that the boy's eyes are fixed back on his father and the glint of light that flashes off the pickax when he swings it over his head.

So Kipling turns his own sights to the half-finished house, staring at the second floor, where the nursery will be. He tries to envision the room completed: the walls painted or papered, windows valanced and hung with curtains of voile or white lace. In summer, French doors will open onto a terrace overlooking a path lined with holly-hocks. In winter, a fire will crackle and blaze, warming islands of braided throw rugs. And in that room the Joss will grow, sprouting and thriving in the fresh Vermont air, basking in front of the fire, until she's ready to sit on her dear Papa's lap with a fat book of tales spread before them. Then surely his Best Beloved will be spellbound by her father's words. Surely she will beg and clamor for tales at all hours of the day and the evening. And when he sits by her bedside at night, spinning out the threads of a story, her face will be transfixed in the lamplight, her breath stilled lest she miss a single word, until he comes to the end and she lets out a sigh of contentment and satisfaction, closing her eyes on a world made right and shot through with wonder by her father.

Of course, though, that moment is years away. For now he has only Joe and the flower he realizes he still holds in his hand, the stem nearly mauled by the pinch of his fingers, the petals starting to droop. He lifts it up and stares with bemusement, twirling it again against his thumb, and as he does, another fact comes to mind that he thinks he could put to some use.

"You know Pliny was the one who named the buttercup. *Ranunculus,* he called it, which comes from the Latin for 'a little frog,' and refers, I believe, to the fact that it shares a liking with frogs for damp places. Certainly it doesn't look like a frog—at least not to my addled eyes. Though it does make me think of our own Little Frog, who, rumor has it, has been hatching a plan that could have grave effects on the jungle."

"You mean Mowgli?" Joe says, slowly turning to Kipling.

"Yes, Mowgli. Would you like to hear about him?"

It is risky, Kipling knows, to pose this as a question, for the boy could simply say no. And for a moment Kipling fears that he will. Joe has pivoted again, turning back to his father who, having now traded his pick for the auger, walks along the base of the scree, absorbed in his own calculations. Joe watches him as he paces back and forth, halting occasionally to investigate the scarp, looking for possible fissures, running his hands along the thin veins of rocks and down the runnels etched by snowmelt in the hard-packed dirt. But after a while Joe turns back to Kipling.

"I suppose so," he says with a shrug.

They head off then, climbing higher up the hillside, heading for the ledge of rock they had sat on when Kipling described the Cold Lairs. Joe casts a last glance over his shoulder and immediately trips on a hummock, unable to keep from stumbling until he turns his head around once more and aligns his eyes with his feet. Then they reach the rock. Kipling takes a seat, facing Mount Monadnock. Joe sits before him, with his back to the road, unable from this vantage to see his father, who has now set the bit of his auger to the scarp and painstakingly started to bore.

Kipling leans forward. "Well now," he says, his voice thick with anticipation.

He tells Joe what he's sketched in so far. How Mowgli has spent many weeks by himself, nursing his wounds and his outrage. How he's lit on a plan, an ingenious plan, to address all the wrongs he's suffered. He tells him how Mowgli called upon Hathi, the Silent One, head of the elephants, and asked him about the Sack of Bhurtpore, when the elephants descended upon a small village that harbored a man who'd harmed Hathi and trampled it into the ground. They stomped through the fields and the grazing grounds, crushing the crops and the grasses. They ripped thatch from roofs, yanked up posts from mud huts with their trunks as if they were saplings. And they pierced the village granaries and cisterns with their tusks so that seed corn and barley and water spilled and seeped out of those ivory-bored holes to mix with the mud and the billows of dust churned up by the elephants' feet.

"And then they departed, letting the jungle reclaim whatever was left. Vines crept in and pulled down what few walls still stood. Grass swallowed up doorsteps and alleys, choking the roots of the handful of crops that survived the elephants' rampage. And finally even the trees returned, the teak and the banyan and sal. They rose from the ashes of fire pits and sent roots down the holes of old wells, shrouding the site with a canopy of leaves that now seamlessly stretched across what once was cleared, to knit the whole jungle back together."

"And that's what Mowgli wants to do?"

"Yes. To let the jungle in."

"And Hathi. Will he help him?"

"Not just Hathi," Kipling says, solemnly shaking his head.

Then he paints for Joe the scene he's imagined and has started to pin down on paper: an assembly of animals summoned by a boy whom their own kind has snubbed and dismissed, but who now stands before them, with the blade of a knife tucked into the band of his loincloth. There are sambar deer, the color of cashews, wild pigs with their sickle-shaped tusks. Large blue-bull nilgai with their short, stubby horns and the black tufts of hair that sprout from their chins and hang, curled like a mandarin's beard. There are gaur, great bison. Chinkara, gazelles. Barking deer that yelp out like dogs. Chital with their coats all peppered with spots, wild buffalo with horns wide as yoke bars. And beyond them hover the elephants, waving their trunks like semaphores, nodding their ancient domed heads, directing their wise, rueful eyes to the rock where Mowgli stands with his hands on his hips, his legs splayed and his chest bared and gleaming, no longer the child who would bumble and fall as he tried to keep up with the pack.

He describes how the animals quiver and flinch as a current of fear runs through them while they huddle there, awaiting Mowgli's words. Tails flick, hides twitch. Legs tremble and tense. Eyes widen, hooves paw on the ground—except for the elephants, who just nod and sway, impassive, colossal, inscrutable. As Kipling speaks, he notes how Joe's eyes have widened and quickened as well, as if he is imagining the scene with all of the drama and meaning that Kipling had hoped to convey. His face seems wiped clean of all but concentration. He leans forward, straining to listen, as he tries to take in this turn of events and Mowgli's new incarnation. And as Kipling watches the boy absorb the audacity of Mowgli's plan, he feels himself swell with audacity too. He is daring and fearless and bold, and so utterly smitten with the tale he is telling that he actually rises and stands on the ledge, assuming the same imposing stance he has just described Mowgli striking, and shedding the dispassionate role of the narrator to directly broadcast Mowgli's words.

"Let in the jungle, Hathi," he cries. "Let the jungle in."

He casts the words like a net across the meadow, aiming to snare every living thing, every listening ear, in his reach, and the cry is rejoined, like an echo's retort, by a distant, thudding boom. It is the first of the charges Jack Connolly has finally set off, though for a clouded moment or two, Kipling thinks it's the words themselves, thundering and roaring like the hooves of wild beasts whipped up into a frenzy. And when the ground shudders and quakes at his feet, it seems no more than what might occur as the herds all rise together, bewildered and panicked by what they must do, but unable to resist Mowgli's words.

Then he looks at Joe who has risen too, seemingly stirred and swept up by the scene Kipling has called into being, his eyes filled with such awe that Kipling feels another surge of power bolt through him. But instead of submitting to the pull of the tale, as the herds yield themselves up to Mowgli, the boy leaps forward and lunges for him, so swiftly Kipling has no time to prepare himself for the blow. In fact, he's barely able to register the sight of the boy's body hurtling toward him before he's knocked right off his feet and tackled to the ground, where he finds his legs pinned to the grass by Joe's knees, his arms trapped by the bars of his elbows, and his face so completely smothered by Joe's chest that he can hardly breathe. He pushes and squirms beneath the boy's weight, trying to cast him off, until Joe loosens his hold and Kipling gasps for air, feeling as he does something pelting his face, a blur of brown that he can't quite make out because his glasses have fallen.

He finds them lying on the grass beside him once the boy rolls off him. The frames are bent, one lens is shattered, riven into a web of cracks that radiate out from a hatpin-sized hole, the impact point of a pebble. Still Kipling manages to put them on, looping the crooked arm over his ear, setting the bridge on his nose, and he looks at Joe who sits nearby, with his head bowed and buried in his knees.

With his vision restored, though a bit distorted by the spidery lines of the cracks, Kipling sees that Joe's shoulders and the crown of his head are covered by a fine film of silt, a dusting of dirt that coats the grass as well, and the outcrop of rock, his own boots. And for another brief, confused minute, it seems not completely inconceivable to him that his words have created this havoc, that they spawned such a fully imagined stampede they actually churned up real sediment, sending shock waves and tremors across the Earth's crust, potent enough for upheavals. But then his eyes take in the meadow and the path heading down to the road. Where the scarp had been there is now a great gash of raw, exposed, naked earth. The ground is pale, the color of skin kept from light by the wrap of a bandage, and strewn here and there with upturned tufts of grass, shards of rock, twists of gnarled, severed root, which makes it look like the site of a scourge, a place desecrated and scarred.

And there is Jack Connolly rising up from behind the rock that he must have used for cover. He wipes his forehead with the back of his wrist then reaches out for the boulder, laying both hands on the rock as his knees give way and buckle. He hangs his head between his arms and shakes it mournfully—with repentance or sorrow, exhaustion or shame, Kipling cannot rightly say. But as he watches him teetering there, trying to gather enough strength and resolve to climb back up the hillside and drill another plug hole, another line from Pliny comes to his mind, rising up to the surface like ether. *We neglect those things which are under our very eyes and pursue those which are afar off.* A crime he is certainly guilty of, a selfish, inopportune lapse, for which he imagines there will be repercussions, consequences he will have to endure.

GO FORTH AND GET FOOD OF YOUR OWN

*B*y the time they head home, the clouds have converged and knitted themselves back together, dulling the light and turning the sky the color of old, weathered mortar. Joe sits by himself at the back of the buckboard, his legs dangling over the rim, while his father drives, retracing their route back down the road to the farm. No words have been spoken between father and son. No apologies, no explanations. Though something is wrong, Joe feels that for certain. Something's gone terribly wrong. There's the set of his father's shoulders, for one, the way that he sits there, sullen and slumped, with an aura of surliness rising from him like steam spouting up from a kettle. There's the day itself, which now threatens rain. There's the texture and edge of the silence. And without any clear cause or reason to point to, with no defined rationale, Joe does what he's done for most of his life: he assumes the fault must be his.

Surely, there was something he might have said or done that

would have led to a far different outcome, with his father and him heading amiably home, buoyed up with success from their outing. And so he rakes over the events of the day as he'd pick at a scab or a hangnail, worrying the crust or the dead blade of skin until he's rubbed a whole patch raw. If only he wasn't so eager, he thinks. If only he'd gone to the cellar. If only he hadn't gone wandering off and allowed his attention to stray.

If only, if only, the words drum in his head with a pounding and punishing cadence until, with a jolt, the thought barrels through him that he's doing the same thing again: he has let his mind wander, gotten sidetracked by rue, when he should be staying alert. Then he tries to clamp down on his errant thoughts. He tries to still his body, stopping his legs from swinging back and forth. He resists the urge to raise his eyes as they pass by the gap in the cedars where they first spied Kipling's house and where now, he imagines, if he did look up, he might see a skyline punctuated by the spindles of antlers and horns, a hill crowned by a figure whose head, arms, and legs formed the shape of a five-pointed star.

Instead he keeps his eyes on his lap, his legs hanging plumb to the ground, ignoring the badgering voice in his head to attend to the sounds that surround him. He listens to the crunch of the buckboard's wheels, the steady, plodding clomp of the horse, the occasional grunt that comes from his father, the chirrup of nesting birds. And he mentally gathers up all that he's felt—all the agitation and the self-reproach, all the eagerness he thinks has betrayed him—wadding it into a tight-fisted ball that he crams away, deep down in his gut, where he hopes it will stay, irretrievable.

So he makes his way home with his back ramrod straight and his mind wiped clean as possible, until the buckboard turns up the drive to the house and he sees his mother waiting for them, standing by the back door. He can tell right away that she, too, recognizes that something is not right. Her face takes in the configuration—Jack up front and Joe behind, their backs confronting each other—and she frowns and casts a questioning look that Joe declines to acknowledge. Instead he hops down from the buckboard and circles around to the horse where, hoping to win back his father's esteem, he offers to help with the harness.

"I'll do it," his father says, shooing him away, his voice dismissive and gruff.

Joe takes a step back then but doesn't leave. He just stands there, watching his father as first he unfastens the lazy strap then uncinches the belly band, pulling the leather up through the billets so he can loosen the rump safe. But when he tries to unbuckle the traces his fingers appear to seize up. They fumble and slip, unable to work the prong through the hole of the grommet, though when Joe steps forward, again offering help, his father pushes him away, shoving his shoulders with the flat of his hand as he utters a half-mumbled curse.

"I told you I'd do it myself," he says, as Joe flinches and falters another step back before he turns away.

He walks to the house then, scuffling his boots, head bent, chin tucked to his neck, though out of the corner of one eye he sees his mother, still there by the doorway, poised as if ready to sprint. He knows she is tempted to run to him now, to place her hands on his poor, maligned shoulders, wrap him up in the web of her arms. Weld him to her side as she used to do when he was just a child. He can feel concern pouring out from her, part sympathy and part worry, and while for a moment he contemplates yielding to her protection, the prospect of rescue feels complicated, desirable but shameful. And to her credit—or perhaps her fear—Addie doesn't leave the doorstep, stepping aside only to let her son pass, according him the courtesy of space.

He edges past her into the kitchen, where the table is set for supper. A hunk of bread on a cutting board, a crock of stewed beans mixed with salt pork, a bowl of canned peaches covered by a towel to keep the flies away. Joe pulls a chair out and turns it around, sitting so he straddles the seatback as his mother closes the door behind her and comes into the room. She wipes the blade of the bread knife on her apron before setting it by the loaf, mops up two rings of water on the oilcloth left by a pair of tumblers. Then she brings a pitcher of tea to the table. She straightens the cutlery, moving from one place setting to the next, aligning the knives and the forks. And as she fusses and flutters about, careful not to disturb him, Joe feels her concern pooling around him again, all her unasked and unanswered questions, her curiosity eddying against her restraint until she simply must speak.

"So your father managed to get the job done?"

"Yes," Joe nods his head.

"And Mr. Kipling was there?"

"Yes," Joe says again.

"And Mrs. Kipling?"

"For a little while," Joe answers.

Addie pauses then while she debates whether to press on or not, adopting a breezy, offhanded tone when she decides to continue.

"And you were a help to your pa?" she asks.

"Yes," Joe starts to say, though the word seems to stick to the roof of his mouth, wedged there like a wad of old chaw.

"Actually," he confesses, "I talked with Mr. Kipling."

"Did you?" his mother says.

"Yes, he told me a story."

"A story?" she says.

"Yes, a story. About a boy."

And now it is Joe's turn to debate just how much he wants to reveal and how much he wants to keep hidden. For months the story has dwelled inside him, a secret, invisible friend, waning and waxing in influence, but always, reliably, *there*, offering him companionship, solace, or simply diversion. Now he fears that by speaking, some of that might be lost. The tale could lose its power, like some magical charm unearthed from a tomb, that will turn to dust and then disappear if exposed to the bright light of day. But he also feels the urge to tell, an urge to unburden himself, coupled with something he can't quite explain, a feeling he has that by telling the tale with his own voice and in his own words he might somehow come to possess it more fully, inhabit it in a new way.

Biting his lip, Joe pulls off a flap of chapped, dead skin with his teeth.

"His name is Mowgli," he says.

The words tumble out before he has a chance to reconsider, and immediately he wishes that he could retrieve them, stuff them back into his mouth. But already his mother has stopped what she's doing to pull out a chair beside him, sitting down with her elbow propped on the table, her chin cupped in her hand.

"He was raised by a pack of wolves," he says. "In India," he adds, and his mother nods as if such a thing were an everyday occurrence, needing no explanation.

But now that he's started, Joe feels a need to explain welling up inside him. He wants to get the story right, to tell it to her as it's been told to him, though doing that is difficult, and not just due to gaps in his memory. The story seems so large and unwieldy. He doesn't know where to begin, nor how to weed out what is essential from what is just incidental, how to steer a straight course without getting lost in too many superfluous details. But while he tries to be selective—describing how Mowgli toddled into a wolf lair, chased by a man-hunting tiger, how the wolves raised him as one of their own, how the tiger said the child should be his—he finds himself pausing again and again to inform her of other matters that he thinks she doesn't know. The color of a panther, for instance. The devious nature of jackals. How a kite is a bird, not a flying contraption. How tigers set traps with their purr.

With all of this stopping and starting, he fears that his mother will grow confused, though each time he detours she nods her head as if to reassure him that she understands what he is saying and is happy to hear more. And she stares at him with such an encouraging, serious, and rapt expression that he feels compelled to keep talking, making things up when his memory fails him, filling in what at first he'd left blank, building the jungle up word by word, from the spiked grass right to the treetops.

He tries to describe the Seeonee Hills and the muddy Waingunga River and Council Rock where the wolf pack meets to plan and settle disputes. He tells her about the village of men—the mud huts, the buffalo, the cattle—and lists all the animals that come to the banks of the river at dawn and at dusk: the panther, the jackal, the deer and the bear, the chattering monkeys, the tiger.

"And elephants too?"

"Yes, elephants too," Joe says, looking curiously at her and wondering if he has underestimated her knowledge all along.

Then he tells her about the Jungle Law, all those precepts the animals live by that Kipling claimed he transcribed from Baloo, the bear, in rhyming quatrains. There are laws that cover the drinking hole, laws that govern the kill of the hunt, laws that spell out how to gain jungle favor, laws that regulate dealings with men.

"A wolf cub," Joe says by way of example, "has the right to gorge on the prey that's been killed once the hunter has finished eating. And a mother wolf can claim one haunch of each kill for her litter without any question."

"It's very," Addie pauses, "very elaborate," she says, slowly drawing out the word.

"Yes, and all the animals follow it, sort of like a pact. And every law has a reason behind it. Every law tries to be fair."

And while he hadn't planned on chanting—hadn't even thought he knew all the words—he launches into a recitation, drumming the back of the chair with his hands to match the marching rhythm, winding through the lines he remembers until he comes to the end:

Now these are the Laws of the Jungle
And many and mighty are they;
But the head and the hoof of the Law
And the haunch and the hump is—Obey!

Joe finishes by drumming a quick two-beat coda then immediately is silent, afraid that he may have spoken too much, that his mother will laugh or dismiss him. But Addie just sits there looking at him, her face awash with wonder at this strange, foreign world he has conjured up and set down here in the kitchen, so that the room almost shimmers and pulses with the heat of jungle life. As though there were animals crouching in the corners, by the washtub and under the stove, staring at them with unblinking eyes the color of amber and jade.

Joe can see in her face that she feels it too: how the room itself seems to be teeming, all crowded and steamy and dense, while at the same time, the exact same moment, it feels more expansive, more capacious and vast than it has before. And seeing her reaction, he would like to tell her the rest of what Kipling's told him. How Mowgli outwitted Shere Khan, the tiger, who had vowed to hunt and destroy him. How he let himself be tricked by the monkeys and carted off to the Cold Lairs. How he grew in strength and wits and skill till none in the jungle dared presume to trap or trick him anymore. Joe imagines they could sit there straight through till evening, the room and sky darkening around them, while they huddle around the spark of the story, immune to the pull of real time. He imagines as well how light he will feel, how light and unencumbered, with the tale no longer twisted and tangled and balled up tightly inside him, but out in the open, rangy and free, disseminating its many beguilements like pollen, while still staying, irrevocably, his. But while he begins to plot out in his mind just how to present each adventure, he sees his mother's eyes dart to the doorway, her jaw clench, her shoulders stiffen, and he knows she has heard what he should have listened for: the arrival of his father.

There is just enough time for Addie and Joe to exchange a quick, worried glance before Addie springs up from the table and Joe leaps up from his chair. Then Jack Connolly is there at the threshold of the doorway, with an earthenware jug slung over his shoulder that he holds by the crook of his thumb. His body blocks out what little light has managed to slip through the clouds, casting a shadow over the floorboards and the kitchen table. Even without his occluding presence, the room appears to have darkened. It has contracted, closed up like a flower that has reached the end of its bloom; the very air seems to have turned thick and caustic like a substance that's hazardous to breathe.

And as if the air were truly toxic, Joe holds his breath as he studies his father, trying to gauge his condition. Jack grips the doorknob for a moment, trying to steady himself, though he bears down on it with so much pressure that the knob swivels under his hand, making him briefly lose his balance. He takes a step forward, staggering slightly, just enough for Joe to notice, before he walks to the head of the table, where he swings the jug back over his shoulder and slams it down on the oil-cloth, glowering at Joe as if daring the boy to question or defy him.

"Where's the goddamn plates?" he says, the words all jammed together as he pulls out his chair and takes a seat, bracing his arms on the table.

Addie casts a furtive look over her shoulder, trying to catch Joe's eye, though Joe is too anxious to risk meeting it and just sits down at the table. He has been here before, navigated his way through meals rigged and planted like minefields, where every act carries the risk of incitement, a spark that could cause an eruption. His father will likely bristle and pounce at any perceived offense. If Joe scrapes the tines of his fork on his plate. If he chews or swallows too loudly. If he slouches his shoulders and slumps in his seat or, conversely, if his posture's too rigid. His father will be there, snarling and ranting about how inconsiderate he is, how unfit for a civilized table, where a man should be able to sit down to supper without the screeching of silverware or the rudeness of chomping, surrounded by those who know how to sit in a simple goddamn chair.

And so Joe sits and watches and waits as his mother brings the plates. He clasps his hands and bows his head when she suggests they say a quick grace. When the prayer is finished, he passes the crock with the salt pork and beans to his father, then takes it back once his father is done, careful to not let their hands touch. And he saws off two slices of bread from the loaf, leaving one on the board for his father, though Joe knows there is danger in this route as well. He is almost as likely to incur his father's wrath if he seems too inoffensive, with his father suspecting he is trying too hard to be ingratiating.

No, the only way of avoiding his father is to be as inconspicuous as possible—though, thinking that, Joe feels another stab of discomfort and shame. Mowgli, after all, didn't try to hide when Shere Khan, the tiger, sought him out. He stood his ground and faced him squarely, calling the tiger a dog before he singed his fur with a branch he had kindled into flame. And when the villagers cast him out, he took bold action again, calling up that militia of beasts instead of just meekly retreating.

But what could Joe possibly say or do to change the course of the evening, to stop his father's drinking and ranting, without simply provoking him further? Joe can no more imagine an answer to that than picture himself growing old. So he does what he usually does at these times: he adopts his vigilant stance, sneaking a hasty glance at his father when he raises the jug to his lips, looking back at his plate when he finishes drinking and glares around the table, challenging Joe and Addie to voice any word of objection or complaint. But once his father sets the jug down and turns back to his own plate, Joe looks up again to see the jug sitting at the corner of the table, where his father has set it down perched close to the edge. And this is what Joe thinks he could do: nudge the jug back a bit. Not a gesture to stop his father from drinking or sinking into more virulence, though it would stop his temper from flaring up as Joe is convinced it would do if the jug tipped over and fell.

So he slips his hand beneath the table, fingers creeping like spider legs, moving an inch, then two, then another, before his hand comes to a stop. What if he's caught, he suddenly wonders. What if his father sees him? Surely he'll unleash a storm of invectives, perhaps even raise his fist. Surely his temper will spark and blaze, its heat all directed at Joe. And fearing this, Joe draws his hand back into the fold of his lap, while at the same time chastising himself for being so passive and timid. But then his father pushes his chair back, signaling that supper is over, and Joe feels such a sense of relief that it almost makes him swoon. Even though he contributed little to get through the meal without mishap, it seems a not-inconsiderable feat to have reached this point, with supper behind them and few harsh words exchanged. It makes Joe feel like he's been pardoned, or given a reprieve, though he knows there may be other pitfalls to skirt before the evening is through. There are still the dishes to clear and wash up, still the floor to sweep and mop. Still time before his father takes to his rocker and Joe can slip upstairs. And even then there is no guarantee that his father won't pursue him, storm up the stairs and march into Joe's room to deliver some slurry indictment or a catalog of Joe's flaws. But the odds are he'll retreat to the rocker, cradling the jug in his arms, that he'll rock and drink and rock and drink, becoming more withdrawn and morose, until finally the liquor will extinguish the fire that it helped to stoke and his father will rise up from the rocker and stumble off to the barn or, if he is too far gone for that, slump down into the rocking chair and drift off into sleep.

His mother, Joe thinks, must feel grateful, too, to have avoided an outburst, for when Joe's father pushes his chair back, his mother gets up as well, eager to clear the plates and the food and release them all from the table. She stacks Joe's father's plate on her own, then comes around to collect Joe's, relieved enough to meet Joe's eyes and offer him a smile. Then she adds Joe's plate to the stack in her hands and heads toward the sink, though turning, her elbow grazes the jug, which needs no more than this light and brief touch to come toppling down to the floor.

For a moment no one moves or speaks. All three just watch the liquid spill and puddle on the floor, the jug not breaking, just rolling back and forth like an empty swing tipping in the wind. But then his father is on his feet, kicking the jug with his foot and shoving his chair back so that it too falls over, while his mother retreats to the far end of the table, still clutching the plates at her waist.

"You bloody fool," he says to her. "You goddamn bloody fool."

Joe, too, has stood up to see the jug spin, twirling like a top across the floor, though at his father's words he freezes, paralyzed again. For he knows that he, not his mother, is the fool, the one who should have acted and moved the jug before, but who was too scared and cowardly, too concerned with his own preservation. And now look what has happened: his mother cowers at one end of the table, while his father looms, bloated with rage, all because of Joe's inability to take decisive action. But still he doesn't know what to do, except to keep on watching, his eyes darting between his mother and father, as if his gaze were the static force that might keep them apart, pin them at either end of the table, out of each other's reach. But as his eyes flick back and forth, they are caught by something on the table, the knife that lies on the cutting board along with the last of the bread. It is long and serrated, discolored by rust and flecked with specks of crumbs, and as he looks at it, Joe's mind floods with thoughts. He pictures Mowgli with his hunting knife, his father with his pickax, his own hand sitting limp in his lap, too feeble to hold onto anything. And thinking this, he feels his hand itch. His palms start to sweat, his nerves tingle. He reaches out then pulls his hand back, extends and withdraws it again, sawing the air with indecision, hesitation, and his old friend, fear, until he sees his father stagger forward and lurch toward his mother.

Then with no further thought, Joe grabs the knife, wrapping his hand around the long wooden handle, fitting his fingers in the grooves. He lifts it, clutching it in his fist, holding it up like a flag. But once in the air, Joe is unsure what to do with this new appendage, this eight-inch length of serrated steel on which a few bread crumbs still cling. He stares at it, and his father stares too, adjusting to the knife's presence, the blade between them as the table had been between his father and mother. But then his father sets his arms wide and low, his shoulders hunched and pitched forward, as if he's prepared to wrestle with Joe and snatch the knife away.

"So you want to play," he says, his voice dripping with derision. "Well, why don't we just play then."

Shifting his weight from foot to foot, his father stretches his arms then retracts them, flapping his fingers tauntingly, daring Joe to come closer. He shoots out a hand that grazes Joe's own, moving with more agility and speed than Joe thought he'd be able to muster and surprising himself as well, Joe thinks, as he watches his father's lips curl up in a smug, self-satisfied smile. Then his father shoots out his other hand, delivering a tentative blow to Joe's arm that prompts him to tighten his grip on the knife and swing it through the air, swiping and swatting as if his father's fingers were a swarm of flies, and carving the space between them with slash marks that, if they could be transposed onto paper, would look like the scribble of a child.

Joe feels the knife make contact with something more substantial, more resistant than air. He feels it meet his father's arm, feels his wild, frantic swinging held in check, as his father attempts to push the knife back, countering Joe's thrust with his own. So Joe leans forward too, applying more force, keeping his father in check, until the skin on his father's arm gives way and the blade cuts a neat slash through flesh. Then instinct deserts Joe, as do whatever notions of heroics he had held in his head. He stares at the gash on his father's arm, and his father stares at it too, as bright beads of blood slowly rise to the surface, as deep and lustrous as garnets. Joe stares at it with fascination, then incomprehension, then horror, as the beads pool together to form a rivulet that runs down the length of his father's arm then forks above his wrist bone, where it breaks up into beads again that fall, drop by drop, to the floor. Joe looks at the knife, sees it rimmed with blood, a broad smear that has started to darken, and instead of Mowgli wielding his knife before the quieted herds, instead of his father digging his pickax into the Earth's crust, what comes to his mind is the basilisk, that deadly, incinerating beast, and the fate of the horseman whose bloodletting sword became the means of his own ruin as the basilisk's venom seeped up through the blade to poison and taint his own blood.

Joe drops the knife then, releasing his hold as if the handle were on fire, flinging it as far away as he can before he turns and runs. He bolts out the door, terrified and shocked at what he has just done, as behind him the knife clatters to the floor and he hears his father moan. It is a sound too horrible to bear, thick with anger and pain, and Joe wants only to distance himself from it as much as he possibly can. So he dashes across the browning yard, his feet slipping and scrambling beneath him, not slowing down till he hears his mother plaintively calling his name. Pausing, he peers over his shoulder to see her standing at the kitchen door, palms pressed flat against the fly screen, her face obscured by the mesh. And a sob catches in his throat like a bone. Her voice wraps around him like fetters, tugging at his ankles and wrists, pulling at his heart. But then his father pushes her aside and storms across the doorstep, shouting at Joe so threateningly that Joe spins around and runs full throttle toward the dark shelter of trees, sprinting across the rest of the yard, past the barn and the cows' winter paddock.

Reaching the woods, he crooks one arm to shield his eyes and forehead, then crashes through the front line of trees and stumbles into dense bracken, careening with such noise and force that he startles two woodcocks, who fly from their cover in a flurry of brown, beating wings. Equally startled, Joe watches the birds, overcome with envy of their ability to simply fly away. But then he hears his father bellow, shooting off another harsh round of curses, and he tosses aside all thoughts of the birds to quickly scan the forest, searching for anything resembling a path, any opening wide enough for his passage.

Beyond the bracken, the trees are thick, mostly hemlock and spruce, a few birch. Joe looks around, feeling panicked and trapped, his blood prickling with fright, until he spies a gap and hurls himself toward it, barreling through the underbrush, pushing through the trees. Then he runs. He runs as he did once before when he tried to catch up with a deer, running as though something huge were at stake. His pride, his very survival. He runs and runs as fast as he can, leaping over fallen logs, beating back brambles and branches, pushing aside a chokecherry shoot that springs back like a horsewhip to lash him. He runs, heading deeper into the woods, without ever once looking back, running until all he can hear are the urgent sounds of his body. The thud of his feet as they hit the hard ground, the hammering of his own heart. He runs till he feels that his lungs may well burst, till his breath comes in shuddering wheezes. He runs till he's sure he's beyond any danger, till his father's not anywhere near. Still he keeps running, driven by more than fear or the need to escape. Now he runs fueled by anger, by a bludgeoning rage that courses through his body, surging through the circuitry of arteries and veins and the clenched, chambered fist of his heart, as if his blood has indeed been infected by his father's fury, transfused the moment the bread knife cut through the surface of skin.

Joe can feel the anger tunneling through him, down the twisting coils of his gut, burning a path to that place deep within him where all that he's stifled, suppressed, and submerged starts to rumble and churn up until it all comes bowling back in one swift, sickening rush: all the times that he has held himself back, reined his thoughts in, censored his movements; all the times he's contorted himself just to please, accepting the blame for whatever transgressions his father charges him with, even blaming himself in advance of his father, all too willing to assume the burden of failure and fault without a question. Now he sees how wronged, how used he has been, how misunderstood and mistreated; and this only rankles him more, making his mind simmer and seethe with visions of retribution, grand scenes of revenge cataclysmic enough to match the depth of his fury.

He thinks of all he will say to his father, all the scathing and withering speeches. He thinks of how he will smite him, trounce him, crush him right into the ground. And he thinks of Mowgli, imagining that he too could recruit the force of the forest, press all the animals into his service, enlist all the streams and the trees. And the very idea of this spurs him on, makes him run with more speed and purpose. He will order the pines to uproot themselves and will hurl them like javelins. He'll instruct stags to charge, form battalions of badgers, troops of woodchucks and muskrat and voles. Then he'll order the creeks and the rivers to flood, command lightning to strike from the sky. He will make boulders topple, bedrock crumble and heave, call forth gravel and stone to rain down. And when the floodwaters have covered the fields and the lightning has charred the hills black, when the stags have all struck and the woodchucks and badgers have scarred the ground with their claws, he will call back his legions, disperse the clouds, make the rivers return to their banks. And then with his rage and his energy expended and the earth all around him in ruin, he will wait for some new, finer world to emerge and rise up from the mud and the ashes, a world where everyone's place is secure and everyone shares equal power.

These scenes flicker before him, egging him on, until he bursts through a stand of stunted pines that gives way to a meadow, where he sees in the distance the shell of Naulakha, rising from its foundation. It looks like the hull of a once-mighty ship, now beached on the bank of the hillside, a structure that could be in the midst of collapse instead of the midst of construction. Joe slows to take account of the sight and to catch his breath. He had not known that he was heading here, having lost all sense of direction, and now he feels both confused and exposed, out here beyond the concealment of trees, in the open sweep of the meadow. But with the rage still pummeling through him, Joe starts to run again, heading toward the half-finished house as if it were the very thing he'd been aiming for all along, and Kipling were the source of his anger, the target for all of his rage: Mr. Kipling, with his fancy talk and his poems and niceties. With his basilisks and his buttercups and his blinkered pair of horses. He has used him too, Joe realizes, used him for his own purpose, filling his head with impossible tales and grand claims of affinity and kinship, only to leave him, as he left him today, once that purpose has been met, heading back down the road to his wife and child and that home where Joe never can join him.

So he races across the meadow, heedless now of the flowers he's trampling, the grass being flattened by his feet. There are no branches to catch his sleeves here, no roots on which to trip, and without these obstructions to slow him down, he reaches the house in no time at all, propelled by a need to take some kind of action, to ravage or pillage just as Mowgli has done. He looks around, circling the site like a predator circling his prey, noting the scalable height of porch walls and the unglazed frames of windows, the space between the studs and posts, some wide enough to slip through. He peers through the gaps, sees the flooring nailed down and swept free of all but sawdust, one empty room leading off another with nothing to ransack or loot. Then he turns and sees where the carpenters and roofers have left their building supplies, and he feels himself instantly drawn to the spot, pulled there as if by a magnet.

On a flat stretch of ground just beyond the front door a pile of hand-split shingles sits, stacked into columns, beside boards and planks of various sizes and slats for lathwork and sheathing. Some of the wood leans against the slab of granite that will serve as the carriage mounting step, as do several large, thick sheets of plate glass for the windows in the loggia and some smaller panes that are destined for mullions and the dormers in the attic. Joe races toward the stacks of shingles, shortening his stride as he nears and prepares to kick. He draws his leg back then lets it sail forward, right into the nearest column, sending shingles into the air, like a shower of wooden confetti. Then he kicks the rest of the columns like duckpins, so the shingles fly again and land all scattered across the site like the detritus of a great blast.

Next he takes up one of the wooden slats and swings it at the glass, holding it in both fists like a bat, driving with the force of both arms. He hits the panes again and again, aiming right for the center, and when the glass refuses to break, he unleashes his wrath on the slats instead, jumping and stomping on the pieces of wood until they splinter and snap like twigs or sticks of kindling. Then he turns his foot on the glass as well, kicking it with all his might, his toe jammed into the front of his boot, his face knotted in fury. He kicks and kicks until the glass finally gives and fractures into shards that, rather than bursting in the air like a squib and raining down in a fountain, simply collapse and fall to the ground, like a box caving in upon itself.

With the glass shattered, Joe feels something break and give way in him as well. He grinds his heel into the shards in one last act of desecration, grabs a scrap of wood, and tosses it away, throwing it into the meadow. Then he slumps to the ground, crumpling against the granite mounting block, as he stares at the wreckage around him. The splinters of wood and bits of glass, the broken backs of shingles. Boards flung askew or cleft in half, the sundered ends sharp and jagged.

Without knowing the word, Joe had thought such a scene would offer a kind of catharsis, the satisfaction of a problem resolved, of a wish brought to its fulfillment. But looking around him, Joe only feels pain, emptiness, and sorrow, as though his insides have been scooped out and hollowed, leaving his body a shell. His foot smarts in his boot; a cramp seizes his side. His legs feel too wobbly to hold him.

And while, before, his head had hummed with the thrill of unleashed fury, it now just throbs and aches, making him want to do nothing more than close his eyes and lie still.

Then he feels a wave of exhaustion sweep through him and the shuddering heave of a sob. Tears well up then slide down his cheekbone to the cliff edge of his jaw, and as Joe brushes them away with his hand, he thinks about Mowgli again and how the first time Mowgli had cried he thought that he was dying, having never once seen a rain of tears pour from an animal's eyes. He'd learned then that tears marked him as human, not a beast and not a god, and while the fact was meant to console him, to assure him that nothing was wrong, the knowledge had filled him with such anguish and sorrow that he cried and cried and cried.

And now Joe cries too, with a kindred sense of despair and isolation, and a hopelessness as deep and vast as his rage had been before. He lets the sobs rise up and rack through him, crying until his lashes are plastered together and his nose drips and snivels with mucus and his vision becomes so blurred that, when he finally raises his head and looks toward the ridge, the meadow seems to blend into the sky, the trees are no more than a smudge. And the sight triggers off a fresh swell of grief, the way the landscape looks as bereft as his own forlorn heart, not the sanctuary he had hoped it would be, but a cold and unknowable place. And just as his sobs start to ratchet up again, Joe thinks he sees something move in the trees, right there, where the field turns to forest, a rustling, a shift, that he is sure is caused by more than his bleary, watery eyes.

Joe straightens his back and tenses up, afraid it's his father who's come to find him or Kipling out for a stroll. Either way, he will surely be called to account, be given a thrashing or a reprimand, sent home in the most shameful manner. So he tries to catch his hiccuping breath and quiet his sniveling, drying his eyes with the heel of his palm while keeping them trained on the spot in the woods where again he sees something move. It is just beyond the ledge of rock where he and Kipling sat earlier that day, in the stretch of woods that curves around Naulakha. He scans the trees, looking back and forth, ready to leap to his feet and run if he sees his father or Kipling. He strains his ears, listening for movement, imagining he heard something before. But now there is nothing. So still are the woods that he thinks he must have been dreaming. His ears pick out nothing but the whisper of wind rustling through the branches; his eyes see nothing but the green of leaves and grass, the blue of sky. But just as he starts to let out his breath and relax his shoulders, he sees it again, a flicker of gray moving through the forest.

Joe squints and scrutinizes the spot, still anxious but now also eager; for while he still can't tell what he sees, he senses that it's not human. It is an animal, he feels certain of it, watching him through the trees. Stalking him, though strangely enough, Joe doesn't feel any fear. Instead, what he feels is a rush of desire, a longing that shoots through him, filling up his emptiness so forcefully and fully it seems to seep out his pores, where it turns into the conviction that there is a wolf hunkered there in the trees. A wolf that has come to claim him, and take him from this troubled spot to that lair he still desperately wants to believe in, where his true patrimony awaits him.

Joe stares at the trees with mounting excitement, waiting for the wolf to emerge. The broad, canine snout and the thick ruff of fur, the gray crescent tail tipped with black. He can almost see it standing there, proud and exacting but kind. Ready to guide and instruct and advise, but also to stand back and pass on its power in a time-honored, law-decreed way, imparting to Joe all its knowledge and skill until Joe surpasses its stature.

And so he waits, preparing himself to receive this longed-for gift, to be worthy of it by showing he is ready to listen and follow and learn. He holds his shoulders and head erect, wipes the last of the tears from his cheek. But then he sees a catbird take flight from the branch of a hemlock. He sees the bough stir, bounce once, and then settle. He hears the faint clapping of wings. And he knows with a certainty that pierces his heart that there is no wolf waiting to lead him away, no pack of kindred brothers, no secret lair ruled by a canon of laws that are orderly, equitable, fair. There is only this welter of pain and confusion, this seesaw of longing and loss. There is only his own faulty mind and torn heart, his poor, aching, fallible body. And stripped clean now of his dreams and illusions, left alone with his stark, naked needs, Joe tips his head back on the mounting step and lets out a deep, mournful howl.

THE LAW RUNNETH
BACKWARDS AND FORWARDS

It has been unseasonably warm this summer. Hot and clear and dry. Good weather for haying, though not for the crops that rely on the moisture of rain. The corn, for instance, is only waist-high, though it's nearly the middle of August. The tassels droop. The small, stunted ears are as thin as the forearm of a child. Addie looks at the stalks as she walks past the cornfield, heading to the house, recalling how she dug up the rows and sowed the seed by hand after coating the kernels with pine tar and flour so they wouldn't be snatched up by crows. That such effort and care produced nothing more than this dwarfed and meager crop could easily make her lose heart, though Addie refuses to despair, not on this particular day when in the hollow of her apron pocket she carries a letter from Joe, the second one that she's received since he ran off in the spring.

She claimed it just a while ago, at a neighbor's farm down the road that Mr. Kipling, through persistence and clout, has had turned into a post office. He was tired of making the daily trek to town to collect his mail. Three miles down and three miles back, two hours at least if the road was good and there were no other diversions. Now he has only to make a small detour while out on his regular stroll, sometimes pushing a barrow if he expects a weighty or cumbersome shipment, sometimes using a sheaf of letters as a fan to cool himself in the heat.

It was he who delivered the first letter from Joe about a month ago, a thin envelope that was forwarded from town where it had sat for a while. He brought it to Addie, compliments, he said, of the newly established *dâk*, and Addie had been so flustered to see her son's familiar hand on the envelope that she hadn't even asked what he meant. Ever since Joe had gone, she'd been praying for a sign that might reveal his whereabouts or condition. Some configuration of leaf or cloud, a spattering of feathers, a shaft of sunlight angling into a room that would telegraph a message to her that her son was all right. But although she had spied a bluebird nesting beneath the eave of Joe's window and a clump of petunias that had somehow managed to reseed itself back to life, she didn't feel any true sense of certainty, in her heart, in the marrow of her bones—until, that is, Mr. Kipling arrived, wagging the letter in his hand.

She took it from him and sat by the table with the envelope resting in her lap, staring at the letters that formed her own name, tracing the line of Joe's script. It seemed enough to know he was alive, able to procure some paper, a pen, the few coins required for postage. To ask for more—to be granted more—was almost beyond her imagining. But Kipling nodded and gently said, "I think they're meant to be read." So she took the envelope in her hands, slid her thumbnail under the flap, and pulled out a slip of cream-colored foolscap, creased and folded in quarters.

There were only a few lines scratched on the paper, just a handful of words to hold onto. An apology for making her worry. Reassurance that he was fine, with a job, in fact, helping the cook at a fishing lodge way up north, where the Connecticut was just a small stream that meandered among lakes and bogs. How he got there, how he managed to wangle his way by boat or train or carriage, how he talked the lodgekeeper into employment, how he passed his days and nights—all of that was left unsaid, so that Addie was forced to picture it all: Joe stowing away on an upriver ferry or stealing a ride in a boxcar, huddled and hungry in a bed of old straw behind a stack of crates. She read the letter again and again, scouring every line, looking for some intimation that he might return. But she found nothing. No suggestion, no clue, on which to pin her hopes; though beneath the closing, "Your Loving Son, Joe," there were two additional lines—"Anglers' Haven, Lake Willoughby, Vermont"—which Addie took as an invitation to further correspondence, a door that Joe had left open a crack.

So she wrote a letter back to Joe, carefully composing it so as not to seem to probe or pry or demand too many explanations. She tried to adopt a casual tone, describing to him the new post office—the American flag above the farm door, Grover Cleveland overseeing the kitchen where Mr. Waites kept a locked tinderbox in his wife's cutlery drawer, filled with postage stamps printed with engravings of Columbus landing with his armada. She told him about the lack of rain, how the nights were as hot as the days, though she tried to avoid any mention of hardship, not wanting to stir up pity or guilt, any feeling that might cause him to shy. Nor did she say much about Joe's father, not the storm of anger he unleashed upon her nor the sullen repentance that followed as both he and Addie began to realize that Joe was not coming back. Instead she used a communal "we" to allude to her husband—"We were glad to get your letter. We hope that you are well. We send you our very best wishes"—though, in fact, she had not consulted her husband other than to say that she'd had word from Joe and was planning on writing him back. Instead, she relied on Kipling.

He accompanied her down the road to the farm once she had finished her letter to personally introduce her to the various procedures—the weighing of the mail on the small brass scale, the proper affixing of postage—inquiring on her behalf about the means and the route of delivery. He showed her the map that was tacked to the wall of the Green Mountain State of Vermont, pointing out the Connecticut River and its headwaters far up in Canada, and there, in the upper-right corner, the thumbnail shape that denoted Lake Willoughby, colored a deep Prussian blue. He encouraged her, too, to return periodically to see if there'd been a reply. And while at first she had found it awkward, poking her head through the Waites's back door, repeating the same eager question, she came to look forward to these exchanges—the trading of pleasantries that gave way to business, the air of official transactions, the way it all made her feel more a part of, more connected to, the world at large.

And now here she is, with her persistence rewarded and a new letter from Joe. A fat one at that, nearly three pages long with small print and tight, narrow margins, filled with anecdotes and facts about his new life. She read it the moment she left the post office, right there, in the Waites's front yard, and now, reaching the orchard, she pulls it from her pocket and draws the sheets out from the envelope, taking a seat on the old stone wall to read it once again.

"Dearest Mother," she begins and immediately pauses, wanting to savor the salutation, the superlative in the address.

"Dearest Mother, I hope that you are well and not too troubled by the heat. It is hot here too, and so dry that the lake's waterline has dropped by two feet."

Addie skims across these first few lines, noting her son's considerate manner, his tone of respectful concern, though what she wants is not his well wishes nor his report on the weather but the stuff of his days. She wants the observances and incidentals that will give her a glimpse of his life, and so is thrilled and pleased when he tells her how he spied a moose by the lake one evening as he walked along the shore: a fantastic creature with legs like stilts and a rack as wide as he's tall. He tells her how, climbing some cliffs another day, he found a peregrine's eyrie, a ledge of rock littered with vole bones and feathers, a few of which he stuffed into his pocket to use for fishing flies, tying the barbs around the end of a hook so it looked like a midge or mud dauber. He describes how he's learned to tie these flies after studying the water, paying attention to which insects are out at various times of the day in order to fool the fish into biting a lure made of hackle and thread. He even includes a brief note to Mr. Kipling about something called a *monadnock* that he asks her please to pass on to him if they should happen to meet. Then he ends the letter with the same closing line he used in his first correspondence: "Your Loving Son, Joe," which she now reads again, lingering over the words, letting the claim of connection and possession move her and fill her and ground her.

When she's finished, she folds the letter up and sets it down in her lap, not wanting to consign it to her pocket quite yet, nor stir herself to go. She rubs the paper between her fingers, runs her thumb along the folds' creases, closing her eyes as she draws in her breath and holds it still for a moment. She's aware she's near the very spot she had come to that morning last fall when she'd frantically searched the orchard's stone wall, looking for signs of her son. She remembers the panic that swept through her then and her desperate need for assurance; but while the very thing she feared most then has happened, she feels reconciled now to the fact that Joe's gone, his disappearance somehow forging the way toward what she sees might actually be a stronger and deeper attachment.

She opens her eyes, takes another slow breath and fills her lungs with resolve. She will start a letter to Joe this evening, after Jack has gone to the barn, share the dross of her life as her son's done with her, in a way that will give it shape and meaning. In fact, she'll begin with this very moment, how she sat on the wall reading his letter as the bees buzzed all around her. How the air was thick with the rich scent of apples, how the sunlight fell through the trees. And in order to pin the moment down, to grant it the full justice it deserves, she attends to the sights and sounds around her, noting the chattering clack of cicadas under the drone of the bees, watching a damselfly flit past her shoulder, picking out the song of a wren. In fact, she's so absorbed in her surroundings that she fails to notice Rudyard Kipling until he is almost upon her, heading down the road to the Waites's to post and collect his own mail.

"Greetings, Mrs. Connolly," he calls out as he nears.

"Mr. Kipling," she says, clearly startled.

"I'm afraid I've given you a fright," he says, "or intruded, perchance, on a private moment," he adds with a nod that acknowledges the letter still sitting in her lap.

"Oh no, not at all," Addie rushes to assure him, though her words belie her fluster. "It's just that I've heard from Joe again," she says as she hastily runs her hand through her hair and tidies the bun at the back.

"As I told you you would," Kipling mockingly scolds, shaking his forefinger at her.

"Yes, you were right. I should have trusted him more. I should have had more faith. For look: he's even written to you," she says, growing eager to fulfill the one request Joe has made of her.

She flips through the pages, scanning the lines until she finds the ones that she seeks. Then she holds the page up, at arm's length, like a broadsheet, snaps it once and clears her throat.

"'Tell Mr. Kipling that I've learned that a monadnock is any peak that stands alone and rises up from the plains. They're considered young as mountains go, though they've been here since nearly the Ice Age.'"

Addie reads the passage carefully, trying to enunciate each word, her brow furrowing as she stumbles at "monadnock," her eyes narrowed down to a squint. When she's done she looks up at Kipling, who stands there broadly smiling.

"He's a good lad," he says, "and resourceful, too. He'll go far if he's given half the chance. In fact," he says, pausing to cup his chin in the crook of his thumb, "in fact, I've been pondering this very matter and I have a proposition to make. I've heard that the old Water-Cure has been sold and is being turned into a school. A military academy for boys, to be precise, just like my alma mater, Westward-Ho. I think it could be just the ticket for Joe, as my old school was for me. Discipline, rigor, high expectations, the very things the boy could use. And if you'd allow it, I'd consider it an honor if you let me handle the arrangements. Finance his way, if you see what I mean, as a token of my appreciation for all that your family's done for mine."

He clasps his hands behind his back and rocks back and forth on his heels, looking at Addie expectantly, clearly pleased with himself.

"Oh, Mr. Kipling, I hardly know what to say. It's a very generous offer. But—" Addie stammers, unable to sort through all her hesitations. There's her husband, for one, who's bound to object, and vehemently at that, not wanting to be beholden to Kipling on any matter or score. She can barely imagine raising the question of schooling with him in the first place, let alone contemplate what she is sure will be his fierce opposition. And then there is Joe himself to consider, up in the far northern woods. Would he even want to return to a place he so longed to escape? Could he manage to retrace his steps without feeling the weight of defeat? Addie tries to picture him back in the house, studying at the kitchen table, scribbling notes in the margins of a primer as she works beside him, folding the laundry or scrubbing a cast-iron pot. Or living in town, in a dormitory room, weaving through streets clogged with wagons and drays to join the ranks of uniformed boys lined up in a designated row to practice the synchronized steps of a march or be drilled in the flicks of salutes. But try as she might, all that comes to her mind is a vision of Joe on the shores of a lake, skimming stones over the surface, as the setting sun bleeds into the dark water and a moose wades through the tall reeds and a peregrine falcon flies overhead, soaring in a spiral of widening circles like the rippling rings in the lake.

"But I don't think Joe will come back," she finally says. "I think that he's happy where is."

"Yes, I see," Kipling says, musing again. "And, I suppose, rightly so. I myself traveled up north last month when my father was here for a visit. Magnificent country. Very vast, very wild. And almost primordially untouched. We both were hard-pressed to leave the place—though I fear that my wife would never have forgiven me had I not returned to lend a hand in the move up to the new house."

At first Addie fears that she's given offense by turning her back on a chance she's sure that others would deem her a fool to reject. But once Kipling mentions the house, she's relieved and grateful for what seems like the opportunity to leave talk of Joe's future behind.

"So you're settled in, are you?"

"For the most part," Kipling says, "though we're still knee-deep in boxes. But enough so that both Mrs. Kipling and I have had time to embrace other projects. My wife, for instance, has become obsessed with growing lace-cap hydrangeas. She wants a particular shade of blue she once saw on the Isle of Wight and to that end she's been making me plant the shrubs in different mixtures of soil, adding eggshells to some, coffee grounds to some others, orange peels, sulphur, peat moss.

"I, on the other hand, have been researching wells. Artesian wells, to be exact. And beavers. Fascinating creatures, beavers. The last time I was in Washington, your president Cleveland arranged for me to visit the beaver enclosure at the zoo there. I was actually able to accompany the keeper right up to the side of their lodge—a remarkable structure, reminiscent of a teepee, with a handful of entrances under the water for access and speedy escapes. I've half a mind to flood my lower mowing and set up a colony there. Watch them build their lodges and dams, catch them felling trees with their teeth. I've a hunch there's a tale there waiting to be told and I just might be the very man to do it, provided that I could study them, of course, take notes on their comings and goings.

"But," he leans forward and lowers his voice so that Addie finds herself holding her breath, unsure of what might come next. "I have to confess to you, Mrs. Connolly, that despite all the glories and rewards of the house, I seem to have a case of go-fever."

"Go-fever?" Addie asks.

"Yes, go-fever," Kipling says. "What other men call wanderlust. That gnawing urge to be off and about, heading down the Long Trail, with little more than a rucksack hitched to your back and the unknown on the horizon. I suppose, of course, it could just be the heat that's made me feel nostalgic, but I've had quite a hankering to see Lahore again, to set sail for London, Suez, Bombay, take the train across the plains—though Allah only knows that if it's this hot here, in Lahore it will be an inferno."

Then Kipling tries to describe the full shock and blast of the heat in Lahore, where rooftops sizzle like frying pans and trees grow dry as tinder and men sleep at night in the courtyards of temples, lying still and silent as corpses, while their children and wives toss in cramped, fetid rooms, thick with the dark smoke of oil lamps. He tells her how once, while riding one day, the sun heated the frames of his spectacles up till they seared the bridge of his nose, and how night after night lightning crackled the sky without bringing the relief of rain. He tells her, too, how when the heat finally broke long enough to draw an unstifled breath, he arranged for a party of friends to picnic in the Shalimar Gardens at midnight, where they sat among the pools and pavilions and the marble colonnades bathed in moonlight, drinking in the rich scent of roses and jasmine along with their sherry and Pimms.

"'...and the splash and stir / Of fountains,'" he says, "'spouted up and showered down / And all about us pealed the nightingale / Rapt in her moonlit song....'

"Tennyson, not my own words," Kipling confesses. "I fear that I can't do it justice."

"Oh, but you have. I feel like I can see it. I feel as if I've been there myself."

"Well, perhaps you'll visit one day," he says. "Perhaps you'll go see it firsthand."

"Oh, no, I think not," Addie demurs, unable to actually picture herself anywhere other than here, traveling no farther than the Waites's farm or to town three or four times a year. And this difference between them, in each one's perception of what life might yield and offer, hovers in the air for a moment, like a cloud or a dense patch of fog, leaving them both with little to say and little to form a connection, until they're released from their awkward silence by the sound of a carriage on the road.

"If I'm not mistaken, I'd say that's my wife," Kipling says with an air of disbelief, as Addie too peers up the road to see Caroline Kipling sitting in a trap, driven by their new groom, Howard, who holds the reins in his white-gloved hands and wears a cockaded hat.

"You've forgotten the parcels that were meant to be mailed," she says as Howard pulls up the trap, drawing the horses to a full halt with the slightest squeeze of his hand. Caroline pats the seat beside her, urging her husband to get in, as with her other hand she points to the packages, all wrapped up in paper and twine. And then, only then, does she acknowledge Addie Connolly with a brusque, clipped nod.

"Mrs. Connolly," she says.

"Mrs. Kipling," Addie replies with a similar bob of her head.

It is, perhaps, the fourth or fifth time that Addie has encountered Caroline Kipling since the night of Josephine's birth, and each time she has found herself replaying the events of that night in her head. She remembers Kipling knocking at their door and how, at first, she had tried to absorb the sound into her dreams, only to be pulled from the depths of her sleep by his steady, urgent pounding. She remembers, too, how she groped for her shawl and a match to light the candle, how her fingers trembled as she struck the match head then carried the flame to the wick, certain that nothing good could come from a knock at the door in the dark, dead of night in the barren wasteland of winter; and how even awake, there remained something dreamlike—something heightened, allusive, unreal—as she rushed down the stairs and opened the door to find Rudyard Kipling standing on their doorstep, half-frozen, half-speechless, half-dressed, unable to wrap his tongue around any words but *Caroline, baby,* and *come.*

Then came the ride through the still, frozen night, the snow all glittering and sparkling around them, the moon a fat jewel in the sky. The wind whooshed through the boughs of the pines, whipping up skeins of loose, swirling flakes that skittered across the hills and the fields like a host of ghostly sprites, while the stars seemed to pulse in the sky overhead to the tinkling sound of the sleigh bells. Addie sat in the back of the sleigh by herself, wrapped in a buffalo robe, with a tiger skin drawn and tucked over her lap, her hands in a borrowed fur muff. Her husband had refused to join her there, or to sit with Kipling up front, insisting on standing on a runner instead, where the snow kicked up by the horses' hooves found its way into his boots. She could feel him behind her, sense his obstinate refusal to do any more than he had to, though she gave herself over to the journey completely, closing her eyes to more fully hear the jingling of the sleigh bells and drawing her hand from the depths of the muff to run her fingers lightly across the nap of the tiger's stripes as she tried to imagine how it might look in daylight, the skin the shade of an apricot, the stripes as black as pitch.

She would have been happy to sit there for hours, traveling

through this magical landscape transformed by the snow and the moon, though soon enough they arrived at the Kiplings' cottage, which, like everything else she remembers from that night, seemed to be under a spell. The fire in the parlor had burned down to ashes, leaving the room dark and cold, while upstairs the bedroom was too stuffy and hot, lit by what seemed like hundreds of candles all in the process of smoldering down to puddles of milky tallow and filling the room with such thick, choking smoke she could barely see Anna huddled in the corner, clutching her knees to her chest, and Caroline Kipling, adrift on her bed, her eyes wide and wild, glazed with terror.

Never had Addie come across a woman who seemed to know less about childbirth. She was like a mare caught in a fire, all paralyzing instinct and fear, with only the vaguest awareness of the basic facts of delivery. She was willing, however, to let Addie guide her, to give herself to her care; though on each subsequent occasion when they've met, she's returned to her usual demeanor, dismissing the intimacy that developed between them with such a curt nod that Addie can't help but question her memory. She wonders whether it all really happened quite the way that she recalls—with that summoning knock and that magical ride, the room full of candles and smoke, and the woman who now sits in the carriage before her stripped bare of all haughtiness and pride.

For a moment Addie searches Caroline's face, looking for some small trace or remnant of what they shared that night, though all she finds is the same snubbing countenance she's known before and since. But this time she refuses to doubt herself or let her mood be spoiled, turning instead to Rudyard Kipling as if for reassurance. She would like to return to the talk they were having, learn more about Lahore, but Kipling only gives her a halfhearted smile and a feckless shrug before he grabs onto the carriage railing and lifts his foot to the step.

"As you see, I'm but a cork bobbing blindly on the sea without the help of my wife," he says as he hoists himself into the trap and side-steps over the packages.

Addie watches as he settles in, placing his arm around Caroline's shoulder, muttering at his forgetfulness, while Caroline proprietarily sets her gloved hand on his knee. And again Addie feels the distance between them—in mobility, privilege, and wealth—stretching and spreading and widening out until it seems she's a continent away. Yet now it is Addie who attempts to reach out and bridge that great expanse, calling out just as Caroline Kipling gives Howard the signal to go.

"Mr. Kipling," she says, and Kipling turns, stilling Howard's arm as he prepares to crack the whip.

"Joe told me about the stories you've been writing. About the boy in the jungle."

"Did he?" Kipling says. "Well, I shouldn't wonder. He proved an enormous help to me when I hit a few sticky spots and he gave me his ear when I needed it most, so I'm glad that he found them so amusing."

Addie nods, both pleased and proud to hear Kipling praising her son, though she finds herself balking at the mention of amusement. It is not the word she would have chosen, nor one that she thinks Joe would use. For a moment it seems important to find a more suitable expression, a term or a phrase that might capture and convey something more transforming, more profound. But no alternative comes to her mind, just a feeling she can't pin down. And so she finally, simply, says, "Thank you. Thank you, Mr. Kipling."

"Believe me, Mrs. Connolly, the pleasure was all mine," Kipling says with a tip of his hat.

Caroline motions to Howard again and Howard snaps the whip. The horses stir and break into a trot. The carriage groans and rumbles. And as it starts to head down the road, churning up billows of dust, Kipling pivots, looking over his shoulder to offer a final farewell: *Wood and Water, Wind and Tree / Jungle-Favor go with thee!*

He waves his arm and Addie waves too, her hand held high above her head as her arm sways back and forth, until with a lurch, Kipling turns in his seat and the trap rounds a bend in the road, vanishing in a cloud of dust that lingers in the air for a moment. When the dust settles, Addie turns too and resumes her walk back home as well as the letter to Joe she had started composing in her mind. She will tell him how she met Rudyard Kipling and passed on his facts about monadnocks, how he spoke of beavers, hydrangeas, wells, a moonlit picnic in a rose-scented garden, a temple that looked like a morgue. She will tell him, too, about Caroline's rudeness and her condescending manner, perhaps even relay how Kipling himself seemed to be cowed in her presence. And she'll tell him how proud she is of the help Kipling claimed Joe had given to him.

But in what she knows is an act of censorship, she decides that she won't pass along Kipling's offer to underwrite Joe's schooling. This isn't because she wants to spare Joe the awkwardness of refusal, nor simply because she's so surely convinced that he wouldn't want to go. No, as she reaches the cutoff to the barn where she sees her husband bringing the cows in from their late-afternoon grazing, girding himself to deal with the milking by slapping each beast on the rump, she understands it is really because *she* doesn't want him to. She prefers to think of Joe living up north, on his own, in that aptly named haven, carving out a life of his choosing instead of one that's been foisted upon him. In fact, she thinks, she needs him there, just as once she needed him here, his decision to stake out and claim his own future validating the difficult choices that she herself has made.

Of course, though, eventually she'll have to mention it to Jack, just in case Kipling ever brings the matter up when and if the two men meet. And she'll probably need to tell Joe one day, too, so as not to feel guilty of the sin of omission. But not now, not yet, not when she feels a kind of strangeness, like the lingering cast of a dream, attending to all her movements and thoughts, coloring all that she sees. Now everything looks different to her—more expressive and suggestive—as if her eyes were noticing more than they ever had before, seeing the possibilities in things, what could be, not just what was.

Now, for example, as she walks up the drive, she sees a clump of cornflowers growing wild in the dirt, and she pauses to wonder if this is the shade of blue that Caroline Kipling is after, or is it more like the blue of the flax or the cow vetch that grows in the meadow. She sees the pump by the barnyard trough and thinks of the word *artesian*—not one that she'd like to be asked to define, though she feels fairly certain it doesn't refer to an old, hand-dug well like their own, which in this drought, has been dry for days, forcing her to lug buckets of water from the creek just to deal with the cooking and wash. And when she finally comes to the kitchen, the room seems somehow altered, as it did that day she sat at the table and listened to Joe talk about Mowgli, though she cannot now, for the life of her, manage to pinpoint the change. The pie she baked that morning still sits cooling off on the sill. The churn stands in the corner by the basket of linens she planned to iron that evening, while the scraps of ham she saved for supper still sit on the table, along with a bowlful of peas she intended to shell and boil with green onions.

No, everything is just as it was when she left to go to the Waites's except for the light that streams through the window and falls in a pool on the floor. It is a softer, mellower light than the one that burned this morning, a light that casts deeper, more languorous shadows and fills her with restlessness and longing. Perhaps it's this light that accounts for the change and induces her own case of go-fever. Or perhaps it is Addie herself, for as she looks around the room, with the letter from Joe still tucked in her pocket and visions of moonlit picnics in her head, she is brimming with a sense of possibility she hasn't felt for years and a swirl of ideas that only this morning she would have seen as preposterous or foolish.

So she takes one last look at the hills out the window, bathed in that beckoning light, then turns to the corner where she grabs the laundry basket and dumps its contents on the floor, except for a sheet that she hastily folds and stuffs back into the basket, along with the pie and the leftover ham and a posy of small green onions. She takes the last of the bread from the breadbox, gathers two forks and two plates, fills a mason jar with strong, sweetened tea, wraps two cups in a towel lest they break. She lays these in the basket as well and tucks everything in with a towel. Then she hauls the basket out the back door and carries it across the yard, not stopping to think what her husband will say until she comes to the barn.

There she sets the basket down in the doorway and peers down the aisle of the stalls, past the swishing lariat tails of the cows, past the horse with its head in a feedbag, until she finds her husband, in the back by the trough, pouring a pail of milk through the strainer into one of the tin storage cans. For a moment she watches him unobserved as he stands with his shoulder hunched over the strainer, one foot propped on the base of the trough, resigned to a task that she knows he finds demeaning in a way that floods her with pity and reminds her of what she had heard from Anna a few days after Joe left: how her husband stormed down the road with a shotgun, intent on seeing Kipling, only to be met by Caroline instead, who stood in the doorway, barring his entrance, refusing to listen or budge, and told him in no uncertain terms to put the gun down and go home.

She had felt her heart go out to him then as she pictured him trying to hold his ground in front of Caroline Kipling—though she shuddered to think what he'd have done with the gun had he managed to get past the door. But now he turns and sees her there and his face twists into a scowl, and all the compassion and possibility that had blossomed so brightly in the kitchen begin to wither and shrivel and curl into a tight knot of dread. For surely, she thinks, he will be disinclined to hike back up the hillside, to sit down to a meal without the benefit of chairs or the solid support of a table, particularly if she chooses to tell him where she first got the idea. And while she knows how hard he has recently tried to quiet his temper and rein in his pride and not leap, without thought, to contention, she also knows from their history together how disinclination can turn to resentment and resentment can lead to strife, and how a gesture borne of goodwill can unwittingly goad and provoke.

Addie cups the back of her neck and tugs at the tight cord of muscle, thinking that perhaps she should simply pretend that the basket is filled with washing she intends to hang on the line. But then she slips her hand in her pocket and feels Joe's letter there, and the thought of him somehow emboldens her, makes her want to keep to her course, so that when her husband comes shambling up, warily eyeing the basket, she blurts out, "I've fixed us a picnic. For supper," before he can quiz her or protest.

"A picnic?" he says.

"Yes, a picnic," Addie says, "Mr. Kipling put the notion in my head."

"Kipling?" Jack repeats, his voice thick with suspicion.

"Yes, Mr. Kipling," she says. "I met him on the road, you see, and somehow we got to talking. He told me about a picnic he'd gone to on a hot night, just like this. And I thought," Addie falters, "I thought it sounded pleasant," she continues, looking squarely at Jack.

"Well, I don't know what's pleasant about eating outside with all these bloody flies," he says as he raises his hand to his face to bat a swarm of them away.

But Addie catches his hand in her own and holds it firmly there, not loosening her grip when she feels him pull back in a brief, scuffling show of resistance. Then his hand goes slack; he yields to her pressure, letting her guide him to the basket where she sets his hand on one of the handles then takes up the other herself. Then she shoots him a look like she used to do, long ago, in their sheep-shearing days when she'd signal her readiness to pin down a sheep and he'd snap the blades of the shears, and at that glance they both lift up and carry the basket from the barn, taking no more than a handful of paces before their steps fall in line.

Outside, the air is still freighted with heat. The sun still burns in the sky, a wafer of blinding white light that hovers over the ridgetop and hills. Addie waits while Jack pauses to wipe the sweat from the back of his neck with a rag, catching the skeptical look he throws her as he stuffs the rag back in his pocket. He could turn, she knows, and go back to the house, without so much as a word, retreat into his own sulking thoughts, leaving her there, on her own. Yet when she tugs on the basket again, he lifts it and continues, helping her hoist it across the stone wall and the bramble of blackberry canes, following her as she leads the way up the path that climbs to the high meadow.

The sun is directly behind them now, beating down at the small of their backs. The ground is alive, crackling with crickets, like the fur of a flea-ridden cat. They walk without speaking, eyes cast to the ground, careful to avoid the loose stones and fresh cow pats that dot the path and the hillside, and careful as well not to let the basket knock against their legs. But as they climb higher, walking through a field of milkweed and parched goldenrod, Addie lifts her head, convinced she feels the faintest wisp of a breeze that carries with it the scent of the river and a current of fresh, cooler air.

Reaching the crest of the hill, they stop, arrested as much by what's spread out before them as the need to catch their breath. Below them the river cuts through the valley, a ribbon of molten gunmetal, hemmed on one side by the rails of the train tracks that wink up from the wide valley floor; while across stretch the foothills of southern New Hampshire, receding into the distance, each summit more hazy and pale than the last, until finally they blend and merge with the sky, which stretches and vaults overhead.

"Shall we stop?" Addie says, and Jack nods his head, setting the basket down on the ground to stand with his hands on his hips.

Addie takes the sheet from the basket, snaps it open, and spreads it out between a bald outcrop of rock and a patch of thistle. Jack carts the basket over to her and she kneels on the sheet beside it to extract the pie, the ham, the bread, the tea and the cups, and the onions, all of which she arranges in the center of the sheet, in a circle of chipped china dishes. Then she fixes up a plate for her husband and pours him a small cup of tea, handing each to him where he's chosen to sit, on the flat crown of the rock. And she fixes a plate for herself as well, pours out another cupful of tea, though after taking a bite of the ham, she finds that she's not very hungry, more absorbed in the view and her thoughts than in the food.

So she sets down her plate and looks around at the bowl of the valley with its patchwork of fields and the serpentine twists of the river. Behind her the sun slips below the ridge, turning the stack of hills in the distance a deep shade of indigo. A ghost of a moon appears overhead, as slim as the blade of a sickle. She watches a flight of swallows dip and dive, flitting in the crosscurrents. A freight train steams north toward Bellows Falls, trailing a dark plume of smoke. And as she watches the train speed away, rushing past the range of her vision, she slips her hand back into her pocket and once more fingers Joe's letter, pressing her palm to the envelope flap, touching the scalloped rim of the stamp.

Then she turns to her husband.

"I heard from Joe again," she says, her voice pitched to a whisper.

"You did?" Jack asks, holding his fork aloft with a piece of speared ham.

"Yes, just today. There was a letter waiting down at the Waites's farm. I picked it up this afternoon, just before I ran into Mr. Kipling."

"I see," Jack says, though his voice is uncertain, as if he sees nothing at all. "So what does he have to say for himself?" he says, less a question than a challenge. And for a moment Addie wishes that she hadn't even mentioned the letter as if, by so doing, she's betrayed her son's trust, exposed him to ridicule and scorn.

But instead she continues, "Shall I read it to you?"

"If you like," Jack replies, noncommittally.

For the fourth time that day, Addie pulls the sheaf of paper out from the den of its envelope, unfolds the sheets and smooths out the creases, then lifts the pages up to her eyes. Then she reads. She reads the whole letter again, speaking the words out loud, not as theatrically as she did with Mr. Kipling, her voice inflated and arch, but quietly, steadily, giving each word its own weight and worth until it has the effect that she'd hoped it would have and she feels herself transported again to the shores of that northern lake, where she stands by her son as he spies a lone moose raising its head from the reeds and hovers beside him as he scales a rockface to uncover a peregrine's eyrie.

Reaching the end, she folds the letter up and sets it down beside her. She looks at her husband, studying his face in order to read his expression, just as Joe has described his attempts as an angler to read the shifting surface of the lake. She notes how he scratches the back of his head and scrapes his lips with his teeth, seemingly mulling over some matter that continues to elude or confound him. Then he looks up at Addie.

"He's a good boy," he says, with a nod of his head. And Addie is so surprised by his words that she can't help herself from exclaiming, "Why, that's just what Mr. Kipling said."

"Kipling," Jack mutters, spitting the word out as if the very name were distasteful. Then he takes a long, deep swig of the tea, wincing as he swallows, before he sets the empty cup down and stares out at the hills.

"Well, I guess that's the one thing we agree upon then," he concedes after a brief silence. And Addie again is caught by surprise at her husband's conciliatory words and the way that his voice no longer seems choked with resentment and anger.

But then he stands up and stretches his arms, effectively drawing the conversation to a close. Addie watches as he shakes one leg then the other to work the stiffness out then lumbers to the edge of the bluff where he pulls a dried stem of sedge from the ground to twirl between his teeth. Then slowly she begins to pack up the basket, throwing the dregs of the tea on the thistle, scraping the plates with a fork. She gathers up the cups and the pie plate, sweeps the bread-crumbs from the sheet with her hand, until all that remains, aside from the sheet and the basket, is Joe's letter. She tucks that in her pocket and rises, laying her hands on the curve of her hips, arching her shoulder blades back.

They will need to leave soon no matter what, she thinks, lest they find themselves stumbling in the dark. Already the valley is bedded in twilight. The swallows are heading back to their nests, while the under-bellies of the clouds overhead have turned the pink shade of a rosehip. Yet despite the signs of nightfall approaching, Addie feels reluctant to go. Her husband, she knows, will say nothing more, at least not about Kipling or Joe; still she feels restless and unsettled again, longing for something she can't quite name, a word or a gesture that might act as a coda to this summer day, which in its own small, circumscribed way now seems to her rather remarkable.

And as if she might find what she's seeking overhead, Addie tips her chin and looks up at the sky where, beyond the darkening streaks of the clouds, she spots the faint glimmer of the evening's first star, a dim twinkle of light to the north. She doesn't possess enough knowl-edge of the heavens to know its name or constellation, but she does know enough to feel fairly certain that if by some twist of chance or fate her son were looking up too, he would see this very same pinprick of light shining above him as well. The thought both thrills and com-forts her, making her feel that they are connected in some grand, geo-metric design, two vertices joined by the baseline of the river and the apex of the star. And she finds herself suddenly thinking as well of the words Kipling uttered when they parted, a simple rhyme that now rises up in her with the force of a godsend or blessing. If, indeed, Joe is looking up, standing alone on the porch of the bunkhouse or the pebble-strewn shore of the lake, composing the petition of a wish in his head or seeking navigational guidance, Addie casts those words up in a whisper through the clouds and the darkening dome of the firmament, hoping they'll ricochet off that far star and hurtle back down to her son: *Wood and Water, Wind and Tree / Jungle-Favor go with thee!*

BURWASH, SUSSEX

MARCH 1935

AND REMEMBER THE DAY IS FOR SLEEP

There is no moon outside the study window. At least none that Rudyard Kipling can see. Not on an overcast night in mid-March from a house nestled in the Sussex Weald. In fact, beyond the thick panes of the glass and the fretwork of transoms and mullions, there is little to see but the blackness of night—not the stretch of lawn leading down to the river, not the roof of the dovecot or oasthouse, nor the row of pleached limes and the border of yews that frame his view in the day—even though he was mindful to slip on his glasses before he headed downstairs, hooking the arms around the curve of his ears as he padded down the hallway, adjusting the frame on the bridge of his nose before he descended the stairs.

Still he stares out the window, knuckles pressed to the desktop to give him a bit of support, straining to see something more than his own reflection in the glass. He does not know the hour precisely, nor can he hear it being tolled, for out of a habit of thriftiness that's grown niggardly over the years, his wife has arranged for the clocks in the house not to chime between midnight and dawn. She claims to have done this so that neither his sleep nor hers will be disturbed. The night won't be hacked into chunks of quarter hours, each announced by the tolling of a bell. Yet given the fact that he's regularly awoken by far less than the sound of a clock, he suspects that she really just wants the house quiet so as to hear him when he stirs. Lying in bed, she monitors his movements in the night as she does in the day when she sits at her own desk just outside his study, keeping track of all those who enter and logging in each signature he happens to write on documents and letters to curtail the traffic in pirated autographs that has sprouted up over the years.

Yet even without the aid of a clock or the light of the moon, he has a sense of the time. Based on his long acquaintance with the night and his intimate knowledge of darkness, he ventures to guess that it's somewhere between the hours of four and five. And when he lifts his hand from the desk to pull on the chain of his desk lamp, he sees that he is right. The hands of the watch that he leaves out each night expressly for this purpose show the time as 4:27, almost midway between the two poles. He feels a brief flush of satisfaction knowing that his hunch was right, but the feeling does little to mitigate the pains that have woken him up and followed him here to the sanctum of his study, where he now sinks deep into his desk chair and clutches his side with a shudder.

His doctors say that he has gastritis, an inflammation brought on by nerves, though he has little faith in their diagnostic judgments and even less in their advocated cures. Over the years he's submitted to various recommended treatments—agreeing to have all his teeth pulled out, acquiescing to a regimen of purges—only to find his pain and discomfort grow worse and worse each year. And this makes him believe what he's always suspected and what he's always feared: that there is a cancer growing inside him that has been there ever since he was born, a malignancy that's as much a part of him as his pitiful eyesight, the bald dome of his head, the deep furrowed cleft of his chin.

He can almost feel it growing, in fact, he thinks as he settles in his chair. The manic cells proliferating in a frenzy of division, the tumor invading and staking its claim on the commonwealth of his gut. And the fact that his instincts and predictions have been right on so many other occasions makes him all the more certain now that his layman's take is correct. He foresaw, for instance, the age of the wireless and a world crisscrossed by flight paths, as evidenced by the great globe on his desk on which he invited an airman to paint the flight routes he had envisioned twenty years before they appeared. And he placed his money on the automobile even though some thought him a fool, like the seller of his dear house, Bateman's, the Jacobean manor that has been his abode for the past thirty-odd years. When they first came to see it, the owner had asked how he and Carrie thought they would manage in such an isolated place. Four miles from the station, up a long, steep hill that would tire the most fit team of horses. He replied that he planned to use a motorcar, like his newly purchased Locomobile, though this only prompted the seller to laugh. "Oh, those things haven't come to stay," he guffawed, betraying not a whit of prescience.

As for politics, he's been right there as well, all his fears and warnings proven justified. He predicted the whole sorry debacle in Ulster and the war against the Boers, warned those he knew in power of the dangers of the Kaiser in the years before the Great War. And now he feels trouble brewing again, fears the world is careening toward disaster. He can practically smell the carnage in the air, hear the telegraphic beat of distant shells, as he actually did during the Battle of Passchendaele when the scent and the sounds and the smoke drifted up from the battlefields of Flanders, crossing the channel to settle here, in the hollows of these old Sussex hills. Yet despite all the editorials he's written, all the poems and the speeches he's made, no one seems to be listening to him. No one is paying attention, though he feels this new threat keenly enough that he's ordered his publisher to remove the swastikas that have adorned his books for years from all new, subsequent editions, convinced that that old Hindu symbol of luck is now tainted beyond repair.

And what of his own luck, the great good fortune he attested to in his new book, the autobiography he's been working on these past few months? He began the book by thanking Allah, the Dispenser of All Events, for dealing him a hand of cards that naturally led to winning. Yet what, he wonders now, has he really won? A degree of notoriety that opened the door to constant assaults on his privacy? A resilient constitution that has beached him here, on the sad, ugly shores of old age, where despite all his claims of foresight and knowledge, he feels himself out of step with a world that is spinning too recklessly and fast and that seems to have forgotten the values he has lived by: discipline, sacrifice, honor?

He clenches his side again as another torque of pain twists through him, making him grab the edge of his desk, his thumbs pressed down on the wood. It is always worse this time of year, when his pain and discomfort are aggravated by the damp of a dank English winter. But while he would like to travel somewhere—to the South of France, the Algerian coast, an island like Cyprus or Sicily—Carrie refuses to leave the house for a warmer clime. She has her own battery of ailments and pains that makes travel difficult at best. The constant throbbing of rheumatism, the swollen ache of gout. And just readying the house for departure and packing is almost more than she can handle, particularly since her frugal nature demands she make certain economies—turning off the house's electricity when they leave for more than a week, doling out candles and matches to the staff after logging them into her ledger with the expectation that what isn't used will be returned when they get back.

Still he feels bound to her, united by losses that span nearly half a century, their marriage a seawall set up and maintained to hold back a tide of grief. There was Wolcott, of course, whose untimely death first threw them so precipitously together. They were wedded, in fact, in mourning clothes, their marriage vows exchanged against a backdrop of bereavement. Then, too, there was Josephine, his Best Beloved. His cherished, most radiant Joss. She died at age seven, in New York City, in a nondescript hotel room, having contracted pneumonia, just as he had, on a winter voyage back from Liverpool. Caroline nursed them both, despite her own bouts of fever and croup, spending her nights at alternate bedsides, shuttling between their two rooms. The doctors thought that he might, indeed, die, so congested were both of his lungs. For days he lay there, gasping for breath, trapped in the throes of a fitful delirium that had him believing he was on a submarine bound for Stevenson's house in Samoa, all the while unaware of the drama down the hallway, where his daughter, too, was fighting for her life. And when she finally lost the battle, Carrie kept the news to herself, not informing him of his dear child's death until she thought he'd recovered enough to handle the hideous blow, and forcing the reporters who had camped in the hallway to pledge themselves to silence.

Such a valiant act it seemed to him, to bear the weight of that grief on her own, ignoring the depths of her own profound heartbreak for the sake of his tenuous health, that he thought, perhaps, they'd be exempt from experiencing such anguish again. But then came John, his only son, blown to bits in the Battle of Loos. Though they searched, his body was never recovered. No remains were found, so that after those terrible years of uncertainty during which John was listed as missing, they had neither the comfort nor closure of burial. No flag-draped coffin or churchyard grave where their son might rest in peace, no headstone or marker to which they could turn to pray or place a wreath, except for a name, one among twenty thousand, carved on a marble plinth in France that he himself had fought to erect through his work on the War Graves Commission.

And then there were those other losses that he bore alone. His father, his mother, Uncle Ned, Aunt Georgiana, all dead, all buried, all gone. He felt each death, each absence, as keenly as he'd felt the first, though, strangely, the one he returned to the most was the loss of his friend Louis Stevenson. Even now he can recall how the news reached him of Stevenson's death in Samoa, the telegram arriving at the door of Naulakha on a bitterly cold Vermont day. He took it to his study where he sat at his desk and stared at Mount Monadnock, on the cusp of a grief so deep and so vast that he couldn't work for weeks. It was as if some door within him had closed, some flame been irrevocably doused—though, in fact, between the failure of his bank on one hand and the failure of his nerve on the other, the two men never actually met, maintaining a friendship through a correspondence that spanned the girth of the globe. And when he set pen to paper again, he returned once more to the jungle. He slipped into that world as he'd slip into a bath, finding solace and warmth, channeling his grief down the shaft of his pen where it mixed and dissolved in the ink. Yet the tale that emerged, to his own surprise, was ultimately far from consoling, as it ended with Mowgli leaving the jungle, convinced his trail no longer lay there, though the animals pleaded and begged him to stay since they'd come to think of Mowgli as their Master.

"And this is the last of the Mowgli stories," he wrote when he came to the end. Then he set down his pen and rose from his desk and opened the door to the hallway, where he found his wife, seated at her own desk right across from the door to his study, waiting for him with some checks to endorse and a tray full of mail to peruse.

And then the jungle was lost to him too, and Baloo and Bagheera and Kaa, though, of course, they remain in the pages of his books for any who might care to find them. But that feeling he had of losing something dear even while it ostensibly remains is one that he has repeatedly felt, even more so now in his old age. Take Elsie, his one surviving child, who, after years of living abroad, now resides with her husband in Hampstead: she comes to visit every now and then, bearing cakes and pamphlets and news and an air of matronly satisfaction borne of being the wife of a highly regarded and successful captain in the Irish Guards. Yet the child she once was, that fey little girl who would scamper and skip down the slope of Pook's Hill, wearing a pair of pink gauzy wings, pretending to be Titania, is now so completely, so thoroughly gone, that it's as if she never existed. And his sister, Trix, who was once the belle of the viceroy's hill station balls: She is now no more than a ghost of herself, spending her days in the questionable company of theosophists and clairvoyants, and wandering about the Regent's Park Zoo, where she's been spotted on several occasions embroiled in what appears to be heated conversations with the chimpanzees and the elephants.

Even his Daemon seems to have left him. At least His visits these past few years have grown more brief and sporadic, that whiff of

inspiration that would herald His approach fading as he lifted his
pen. With this last book, this account of his life, he has felt a sense of
futility hovering whenever he sits down to work. There is no excitement, no kindling spark that lights up one word then another, nor the
pure, sheer delight that he used to feel when he stumbled on a deft
turn of phrase. No, now his writing sounds brittle and thin, even to
his own ears, attenuated by the burdensome weight of all he doesn't
wish to reveal, and trimmed of its vigor by the effort required to
maintain a spry, chipper veneer.

It seems that every sentence he writes is like a rickety bridge
erected over a chasm of grief that he only manages to safely cross
through an act of perseverance. And even then he cannot always
make it. He will stop midsentence, sideswiped by a vision that
threatens his whole composure, seized by a memory that seems so
real he forgets where he actually is. His doctors have said these are
optical delusions of the sort he has suffered from for years, ever since
his aunt found him a lifetime ago batting at the branches of that mulberry tree, convinced it was really an ogre. But they come now with a
frequency that feels alarming, sneaking up on him when he's least
prepared—when he looks out the window at the yew-lined path, say,
at some rustling that's caught his eye, and he thinks with confusion
that it is Josephine, pushing her doll pram as she did at Naulakha,
though she's been dead for more than thirty years. Or he'll take off his
glasses to rub his eyes when they've grown weary and strained, and
before he puts them on again, he'll mistake the blurred shape of an
armchair or sofa for the figure of his son, crouching next to their old
bulldog, Jumbo, to pick out the currants caught in the dog's teeth
from the buns John fed him under the table during his afternoon tea.

And how often does he find himself swept away by some memory from his own childhood, the details of which he recalls with a clarity and force that seems startling? He can be seated at his desk, staring at the gray Sussex clouds, though what he'll see is the stuffed leopard head that hung in his nursery in Bombay, and what he'll feel, in lieu of the damp and the dull, throbbing ache in his joints, is exactly the mixture of comfort and menace he would feel as he lay in his bed, hopelessly trying to drift off to sleep beneath the beast's watchful presence, while the moonlight that spilled through the jalousie's slats caught and flickered in the leopard's glass eyes and the snores of his ayah lying beside him twined with the whirring of the ceiling fan and the chatter of the palm fronds outside to form a refrain that seemed simultaneously soothing and disconcerting.

He can summon up, too, that despised basement room in the House of Desolation—can see it, can smell it, can feel its cold damp as if he were there yesterday, sitting again on that three-legged stool with his hands red and itchy from chilblains and the twine from the placard that condemned him a liar digging into the back of his neck. In fact, it seems that he cannot forget, no matter how hard he tries, how he sat there nursing the hurt and the outrage that has stayed with him all these years, as he looked out the window that was level with the ground, at the mean little yard with its bank of Saint-John's-wort and its wall of soot-blackened brick, and felt his heart turn to stone.

"Give me the first six years of a child's life and you can have the rest," he wrote at the start of his memoirs, plucking the quote from the Jesuits as proof of those early years' impact. And now as he sits alone at his desk, in the dim forgotten hours of the night, he recalls something else from those long-ago days: the book that his father had sent Auntie Rosa when he was learning to read that he stashed inside the basement's cupboard so he would have something soothing to look at during his frequent internments. It was an illustrated volume of tales by an author whose name he's forgotten, though he recalls with a poignancy that makes his heart ache, the sense of thrill and wonder he felt as he snuck to the cupboard, then crept back to the stool with the book tucked under his arm, then sat with it there, hunched over the pages to read about a little "darling" who would sweep the stars from the sky or a boy who fell in with some wicked baboons, which, in turn, were in league with some cannibals.

All his troubles seemed to fade away then as he slowly turned the pages. Auntie Rosa with her thrashing cane, Harry spreading his false accusations, even the betrayal and desertion of his parents, which lay just below the rim of his days like a roiling underground river: the pain of those years simply slipped away as he lost himself in the tales. In fact, he thinks, if only he could look at that book once again—feel the satisfying weight of its pages in his lap, run his hands down the table of contents—all would be right in the world. But that, too, is lost, as is the leopard's head, the nursery, even Bombay, which he hasn't seen now for forty-five years, not since he received that telegram from Caroline announcing her dear brother's death and he straightaway boarded a ship bound for London, not knowing as he stood on the deck as the ship steamed out from the harbor that the view he had of the coconut palms swaying behind Chowpatty beach would be the very last glimpse he ever had of the land that had formed and sustained him.

Then it seems that the only thing left to him is the solid support of his desk—the desk he is still clinging to even though his pain has subsided. He loosens his grip and runs his hand along the edge of the desktop, following the grain of the wood with his finger and the rings of a knot still visible beneath the layers of varnish and wax. It is not, of course, the exact same desk that he worked at over the years. Not the desk that he shared with his fellow reporters at the *Gazette* in Lahore. Not the one he had squeezed into the flat he had rented on Villiers Street. Nor is it the desk he used at Naulakha, that great barge of polished ash, on which, one restless night long ago, he carved a line from a Longfellow poem—*Oft was I weary when I toiled at thee*—not having an inkling, at age twenty-six, what the true weight of weariness was.

That desk was left behind in Vermont along with the rest of their furniture when he could not bear to set foot in the house after their daughter had died. But he did arrange for his books and some trinkets to be packed up and shipped off to England, where most of the latter now sit on his desk, here, within his arm's reach. There's the sandalwood alms bowl, for instance, that through the years has held pen nibs and stylos and now cradles pink rubber bands; the old pewter inkpot, now empty of ink and home to a quiver of pencils. There's the leather crocodile that has been his paperweight, guarding his manuscripts for years, and its companion, the weighted fur-seal he bought a hundred years ago in Canada. And, last, there's the bellpull that once hung at the Grange, a double-helix twist of iron attached to a brass bell that he begged to be given when his uncle and aunt left the Grange for a smaller home.

Now he moves his hand across the desk and touches each of these objects, rubbing his fingers over their surface as if they were oil lamps holding jinn. He feels the smooth, sanded curve of the alms bowl and the ridge of stitched seams on the crocodile, runs his thumb across the sweep of the pewter, looking for traces of the words he once gouged there that have been all but polished away. Then he wraps his hand around the braid of the bellpull and gives it a light, gentle tug, recalling as he does how he'd stand on the doorstep, sprung free from

Auntie Rosa's house for an all-too-brief stay at the Grange, so eager, so happy to find himself there, at the entrance to that cherished domain.

And as if there is some magic left in those old, forged twists of iron, some enchantment aroused and called forth by the tinkling of that long-silent bell, he thinks he sees something at the edge of his vision, some movement at the far end of the lawn just before it slants down to the river. It could, of course, be a trick of his mind, one of those optical delusions, a conspiracy of starlight and shadow that suggests a ghostlike form. But he thinks, he hopes, that instead it's his Daemon, presenting him with the gift of a vision that he will want to see, leading him to a place where he'll find inspiration, maybe insight, perhaps even brilliance.

And so he waits, trying to drift as his Daemon has taught him to do, not latching onto the threads of stray thoughts that might pull him away. He waits and he watches, turning off the desk lamp to better see what's out there. And as the first hint of dawn appears, a faint grainy light that mottles the darkness into differing shades of gray, what he thinks he sees are children. Dozens of children flitting over the lawn like a flurry of gypsy moths. Children twirling, prancing, swaying, weaving in and out through the trees in a loose and rambling parade. And with a gasp he can barely contain, he sees that these aren't just anonymous children, like the cutouts of a paper doll chain. No, these are children he knows. There is Elsie in her gossamer wings holding a star-tipped wand, John draped in a bedsheet tied like a toga, a scampish Puck to his sister's Titania. There is Josephine, too, pushing her pram hurriedly over the grass, and his sister, Trix, at the age of five, when they lived in the House of Desolation and would call Auntie Rosa a *Kuch-Nay*, using the Hindi for

"Nothing-at-all" as the password to their own secret club. He sees his cousins, Philip and Margaret, as they were when they were young, when they'd lounge on the sofas of the Grange's sitting room with scarves wrapped around their heads like turbans, calling each other "O True Believer" as they did in *The Arabian Nights*. And he sees other children whose names he can't remember but whose presence he dimly recalls. The band of waifs that would follow him as he wandered through the alleys of Lahore, the boy who would chase him through the dark Vermont woods, begging for stories of Mowgli. He sees the children who would huddle around him as he sat cross-legged on the deck of a ship steaming south toward the Cape of Good Hope, leaning forward to hear how the leopard got its spots or the stubborn, lazy camel got its hump, as an escort of flying fish leaped alongside them and the Southern Cross rose in the sky. And he sees the sons of the Kaffir tribesmen who would wander in from the veldt to stand at the edge of Cecil Rhodes's garden, where his family wintered for years in hopes that he might tell them again of their very own Limpopo River all set with fever trees and the Elephant Child whose "curtiosity" eventually got him his trunk.

And there at the head of this swirling parade he actually sees himself, wearing the papier-mâché donkey's head he had bought in order to join John and Elsie in their Shakespeare games. It is festooned with the wreath of daisies his daughter made for him, the flowers circling the base of the ears, which point up, straight, like a rabbit's. And he is prancing and dancing as well, kicking his legs without any trace of self-consciousness or stiffness, holding in his hands a pair of lighted faggots that illuminate the way with a shower of sparks that fly through the air like shooting stars. He spins and turns, etching arcs of light and spirals in the air with the faggots, as the children follow, fanning out from his coattails, eager to go wherever he leads them, clamoring for just one more tale.

And at his desk he feels how profoundly he would like to do just that: gather a group of children around him, form a circle like a charmed fairy ring, in which he'll perform a great conjuring act, create a phantasmagorical world out of a handful of words. He imagines how they might fidget at first, then slowly grow still and quiet as he runs his glance around the rim, making sure to catch every child's eye. And then he will draw in his breath and begin. He will launch straight into a story, knowing that the words that spill from his mouth will never be attended to more closely or more keenly and he will never be so free, so accepted, so purely himself, as the moment he casts the tale into the circle and then reels the children's wonder back in.

But as if he's committed some violation by letting his longing interfere with his Daemon's injunction to just wait and drift, the vision starts to vanish. Where he saw that winding stream of children there is now just a thick strand of mist. What he thought were the ears of his donkey-head mask is revealed as the fork of a branch. And as the landscape comes into focus—the roof of the oasthouse separating itself from the expanse of the sky, the border of yews becoming distinct and emerging from the general shadows—he is seized by another fit of grief that he doesn't think he can bear. But he reaches out to his desk again to collect and steady himself. He closes his eyes and clenches his jaw, willing away the pain and all the distress and heartache it harbors. And after a moment the spasm passes. He feels in control of himself, enough to realize that it's time he should go. Soon the clocks will start tolling again. The maids will be up and about, wanting to dust the desk and the bookshelves and light the logs in the grate so that when he returns after breakfast to work, some of the chill and the damp of the day might already be burned away.

He straightens the treasured objects on his desk, aligning his watch with his papers so he can once more find it tomorrow when he imagines he'll be stranded again, marooned by the whims of the night. Then he rises up, feels his knees lock in place with a creak like a rusty old hinge, takes a look out the window at the mist-covered lawn, blinks at the view once, and turns. Then he makes his way across the hall and slowly mounts the staircase, heading for the room that he shares with his wife, for the sometimes shaky mooring of his bed, where, with any bit of good fortune, with one last lucky card in his hand, he might slip undisturbed between the cold sheets and be blessed with the amnesty of sleep.

ACKNOWLEDGMENTS

This book would not have been possible without the support of certain individuals and organizations. Of the many authors and books I consulted, several were critical to my understanding of Rudyard Kipling and life in late-nineteenth-century Vermont. In particular, I would like to acknowledge the work of six Kipling biographers: C. E. Carrington, Lord Birkenhead, Angus Wilson, and Martin Seymour-Smith, as well as Thomas Pinney, who edited and annotated Kipling's letters in four indispensable volumes. Haydn S. Pearson's *The New England Year* provided a delightful and intimate glimpse of turn-of-the-century farm life, as did Ralph Nading Hill's *Contrary Country: A Chronicle of Vermont.* Additionally Christina Walkey and Vanda Foster's *Crinolines and Crimping Irons* offered invaluable information on nineteenth-century laundry practices, while Harry B. Weiss and Howard B. Kemble's *The Great American Water-Cure Craze* thoroughly explained Vermont's hydrotherapy culture.

I am also indebted to several organizations and institutions, foremost among them the New York Foundation for the Arts, which awarded me an Artist Fellowship in Fiction in 2004; the Landmark Trust, which owns and maintains Kipling's house, Naulakha; and the Brattleboro Historical Society.

Special thanks also goes to family and friends who at key points offered critical feedback and a supportive ear. These include, but are not limited to, Helen Adler, Dorothy Barnhouse, Debbie Bechtel, Mona Behan, Robin Cohen, Mary Ehrenworth, Lois Ellison, Jill Entis, Andrea Lowenkopf, Nan O'Shea, Bettina Schrewe, Debora St. Claire, Thomas Vinton, David Wagner, John Weir, and Deborah White. And finally, more thanks than I can express to my agent, Maria Massie, who stuck with me through the birth of children and several professional moves; and to the wonderful people at MacAdam/Cage, especially my editor, Anika Streitfeld, who again and again proved to be the most careful, insightful, and supportive reader possible.